Strange Neighbors

Ashlyn Chase

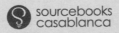

sourcebooks
casablanca

Copyright © 2010 by Ashlyn Chase
Cover and internal design © 2010 by Sourcebooks, Inc.
Cover design by Kathleen Lynch
Cover illustration © Monika Roe

Sourcebooks and the colophon are registered trademarks of Sourcebooks, Inc.

All rights reserved. No part of this book may be reproduced in any form or by any electronic or mechanical means including information storage and retrieval systems—except in the case of brief quotations embodied in critical articles or reviews—without permission in writing from its publisher, Sourcebooks, Inc.

The characters and events portrayed in this book are fictitious or are used fictitiously. Any similarity to real persons, living or dead, is purely coincidental and not intended by the author.

Published by Sourcebooks Casablanca, an imprint of Sourcebooks, Inc.
P.O. Box 4410, Naperville, Illinois 60567-4410
(630) 961-3900
FAX: (630) 961-2168
www.sourcebooks.com

Printed and bound in Canada.
WC 10 9 8 7 6 5 4 3 2 1

To my husband for being the kind of guy I write about.
Yup, these great heroes are real, folks—and I'm so
lucky I found one!

Author's Note

I apologize in advance if Chad the ghost is a smartass. He feels he can get away with it, since no one can do much about him—it's not as if he can be evicted, or slapped in the face. Hey, if it had been up to me, I'd have chosen a polite nineteenth-century nanny to haunt the building instead of a sarcastic journalist from the sixties, but what can I say? Who would want to murder a sweet nanny?

Prologue

"WHEN YOU'VE HAUNTED A BUILDING SINCE THE BEATLES MET *Ed Sullivan, you see a lot of changes,"* Chad said to Harold, who haunted the building across the street.

The two ghosts floated between their buildings, high enough that the air currents from traffic below didn't affect them. Still, they swayed occasionally in the autumn breeze and had to compensate to remain face to face.

Harold contemplated the elegant old brownstone sadly. *"I don't like to complain, mind you, but when your new owner ripped off the roof, did he have to replace it with a God-awful glass and steel penthouse? It's an eyesore here in historic Back Bay!"*

"I miss the old owner. He was a crotchety, grumpy, eccentric recluse, but he didn't change anything."

"Change comes hard for most of us, Chad—living or dead—yet change is the nature of the world. You'd think we'd get used to it after all this time. I've been going with the flow... but enough is enough."

"I know what you mean, Harold. Change can kiss my ass."

Chapter 1

A HAND REACHED OUT TO HER. "WOULD YOU LIKE TO DANCE?"
She followed the line of a crisp white sleeve and looked
up into the sparkling eyes of her mystery man. He had to
be a GQ model to possess a face and body like that.

"Merry? What on earth are you doing?"

Poof

And just like that, Merry MacKenzie's daydream
evaporated.

"Dad, I'm exhausted. I have to rest."

Merry collapsed on the worn leather sofa sitting in
the middle of the sidewalk in front of a beautiful an-
tique townhouse. She yanked an inhaler from her denim
jacket, shook it vigorously, and squirted the mist into
her mouth. Inhaling a deep breath, her constricted lungs
eased. *Ah, relief.*

"We're almost done. But while you're resting, let me
say this again—if you ever need or want to move back
to Rhode Island, you can."

She rolled her eyes. "Fine. But right now, I'm still
moving into my apartment. How about letting me unpack before you make me feel guilty for leaving you?"
She reclined on the sofa so she could expand her dia-
phragm and rest.

"Come on, Merry," her father said as he loomed over
her. "One last push."

"No. I'm tapped… Gonna die now."

"I know you're tired. We've been moving your stuff into your new apartment all afternoon. Or, I should say, new to you, old by any other American's standards."

"Well, I happen to love it. Jeez, did you look around? Did you notice that thick, solid mahogany banister? I don't know how you could miss it. It practically blinds you, gleaming in the light of the crystal chandelier," she said. "Everything is in really good shape. Apparently the landlord lives in the building and made sure it was all replastered, but kept the period details like the wide crown moldings. And while you're noticing, check out the marble stairs. The elevator is all mahogany and brass inside."

"Why do you care about the elevator? You live on the first floor—thank God. I can't imagine carrying all this crap up to the second or third floor."

"And moving *in* is only part of the fun! I'll be up half the night unpacking. Who knew I had so much stuff?"

"That's the way it is when you move. You always have more than you thought you had and it always takes longer than you think it will."

"I've never moved before, so how could I know?"

Mr. MacKenzie frowned. "Merry, Matt and I have to get going soon. It's getting dark. Are you okay?"

"Just one more minute, Dad." Merry glanced around at the lengthening shadows, wondering where west might be and if she'd have a sunset view. She looked up at tree limbs silhouetted against the twilight sky. Dry leaves rattled in the autumn breeze, and for a moment she thought she saw...

Great. First night on my own and already I'm seeing ghosts.

Then she spied a man with long, dark hair leaning against the wrought iron fence that surrounded the brownstone's small lot. Dressed all in black, he almost disappeared into the shadows, and she might not have noticed him at all except for his pale skin and intense eyes. Something about the way he cocked his head and stared at her caught her attention. A shiver rippled up her spine.

"You can rest when you're inside. It's getting darker by the minute and you know my eyesight's no good for night driving."

"Have Matt drive home. Where is he, anyway?"

Her father peered toward the heavy oak and beveled glass front door of the building. They'd left it propped open with a marble pedestal from the foyer. "I don't know. Last I saw, he stopped to talk to someone. Must have been the landlady."

A second later, her younger brother raced down the steps babbling, "Dad, did you know Jason Falco owns this building? Do you believe that? Jeez, I'm going to have to visit Merry every chance I get!"

She groaned. "You'd better not, pickle-head. And who's Jason Falco, anyway?"

"You're kidding!" he shouted. "You don't know who Jason Falco is?"

Mr. MacKenzie folded his arms. "Calm down, Matt. It's a fairly common name. It could be anybody. Come on, Merry. Get up."

"Can't... too tired."

Some kind of secret signal passed between father and son. The next thing Merry knew, the couch tipped and they unceremoniously dumped her onto the sidewalk. *Oomph.*

"Hey!" She scrambled to her feet while her brother continued chattering as if nothing had happened.

"He's the lefty pitcher for the Boston Bullets! I swear. I was just talking to his aunt. Oh—she wants the door closed, by the way. It's getting cold in there." As if to illustrate the point, a chilly October breeze blew crisp, brown leaves around their feet.

"Why didn't you say so in the first place?" Merry admonished. "Do you want my neighbors to immediately hate me? Get on the other side of the couch with dad; I can't lift another thing."

Merry marched into her new apartment building, hoping to find the landlord's aunt so she could apologize. No one seemed to be about, but she heard voices from the second floor. As her father and brother staggered and grunted through the front door under the weight of the leather sofa, a young man appeared at the top of the wide, curving staircase.

Long muscular legs in jeans and sneakers had come into view first. Then Merry saw his flat abdomen and broad shoulders under a navy blue knit jersey, and then finally his face.

"Whoa, let me help you with that." He jogged down the steps and grasped the side of the couch her brother had left teetering.

Oh, my lord! What a handsome face it was. Dark, thick brows stood out against his light skin and clear blue eyes. She couldn't identify his hair color easily, since it barely showed under a blue baseball cap. Maybe milk chocolate brown. Merry thought the style was called a buzz cut. The length nearly matched the brown whiskers of the five o'clock shadow on his strong jaw.

"Thanks, man." Matt did a double take and grinned. "I can't wait to set this couch down so I can shake your hand. Believe it or not, my sister's moving into your building and didn't even know who you were."

The handsome hunk just laughed.

Merry put two and two together and decided this must be the famous Jason Falco. *Not bad. Not bad at all.* On the other hand, if her brother insisted on embarrassing her in front of her hottie landlord by pointing out what a baseball fan she wasn't, she'd have to have a little "chat" with him before he left. A slap upside the head ought to do the trick.

She stepped back in order for the three men to pass her as they carried the heavy piece of used furniture into her tiny living room.

Her father surveyed the polished hardwood floor already covered with boxes. "Where do you want this, honey?"

"Um... I'm not sure yet."

"Well, hurry up and decide before I get a hernia."

"Sorry, Dad. Just put it down where you are. I'll figure it out later."

Her landlord straightened to a full six feet tall. "I can help her move things around once she knows where she wants them." And then he winked at her.

Be still my heart!

So there her couch remained—in the middle of the living room.

Immediately, her brother stuck his hand out to the stranger. "It's really great to meet you, Jason. Can I call you Jason? My dad and I are big fans. I hear you can throw a 97 mile-an-hour fastball. And man, your curveball and changeup? Incredible! Do you think I can get an autograph?"

Jason chuckled. "Thanks… uh, sure." He sounded anything but sure as he regarded the taped boxes around the room. "Do you have a pen and paper handy?"

"Leave him alone, Matt. He's obviously off the clock," Merry muttered, not caring if her fan-boy brother collected his autograph or not.

"Oh, yeah. Sorry, man. Hey, some other time…"

"Absolutely," Jason said. He smiled broadly and to her relief, Merry thought he sounded genuine. Fine, then the pipsqueak wouldn't hound her to obtain Jason's DNA. *The DNA that gave him those cute dimples…*

"Well, I'll leave you to get settled," her father said. "C'mon, Matt, we'd better get going." He thrust his hand toward Jason and said, "Thanks for your help. I'll sleep better knowing my little girl is in good company."

Crap. How many ways can my family embarrass me? Merry rolled her eyes. "I'm twenty-five, dad. Not exactly a little girl anymore."

Her father dropped Jason's hand and strolled over to where she stood. "You'll always be *my* little girl." Then he kissed her on the forehead and said, "Call me tomorrow, okay?"

Could she *be* any more humiliated in front of an awesomely cute guy? So much for establishing her image as a hip, sophisticated city dweller now that she had finally declared her independence. She sighed. "Okay, worrywart."

Her father pointed at her. "I mean it."

"I know, I know."

As soon as they were out of the way, she planned to

revel in her freedom, kick up her heels, and have some much needed *fun!* Whether they liked it or not.

———~~~———

Jason watched the close-knit family say their good-byes and Merry's father and brother reluctantly leave. Suddenly he missed his mother. She had tried to create family closeness, but the competition his father had instilled in his sons didn't make for warm relationships. Not to mention the other "little problem" that crippled his family's hopes for a normal *anything*.

As he watched his stunning new tenant wave goodbye to her family, he congratulated himself on offering to stay and help her arrange the large pieces of furniture. *Hot* didn't begin to describe her. Now he could steal some time alone with her.

She looked so different from the rest of her family. Her father had a Scottish look, as you'd expect in a MacKenzie. He was strongly made and his graying hair looked as if it could have been reddish-blond at one time. He and his sandy-haired son possessed ruddy but fair skin and blue eyes.

According to her paperwork, his new tenant's name was Merry MacKenzie, but she couldn't look less like a Scot. Her dark hair, brown bedroom eyes, and full lips, plus her perfectly smooth, glowing dark skin gave her an exotic Mediterranean air. Or maybe Brazilian. God, she made his jeans tight!

"So, where do you want this gigantic sofa?"

She chuckled. "It is kind of a monstrosity, isn't it?"

"No, I didn't mean..."

"That's okay. It's only temporary stuff. I took some

castoffs from our family room and hit a few yard sales, but as soon as I can, I'll replace it with smaller furniture."

"No… I, uh…" *Why am I suddenly a knucklehead around her?*

He had been trained for the limelight for years, so why should he suddenly fall apart in the presence of a pretty girl? Tons of women threw themselves at him on a regular basis. Maybe that's why he reacted to this one differently. He wasn't Jason Falco—star pitcher and reluctant celebrity. He was just Jason, single landlord with a hard-on for his new tenant.

"Look, I didn't mean to insult your furniture, honest. I like it better than mine. I just had some hoity-toity designer decorate my place and it looks like it belongs in a magazine, not someplace where people actually live. This looks awfully comfortable." He illustrated his point by soaring over the arm of the couch and landing on his back on the squishy cushions. He couldn't help the "Ahhh…" that escaped his mouth. He hadn't been able to lounge comfortably for days.

She just grinned at him and didn't say anything.

You're an idiot, Falco. A babbling, bumbling idiot.

Slowly, he rose from his comfortable position and said, "Let's start over." He held out his hand and said, "Hi. I'm Jason Falco, your new landlord. And you must be…"

"Merry MacKenzie," she said, shaking his hand.

"What a charming name."

She rolled her eyes. "It wouldn't have been *my* choice. I share my name with a hobbit."

He chuckled. "Do you have a nickname you'd prefer?"

"No. Just Merry. One of my professors tried to call

me Mac once, but it didn't stick. Thank God for that, because everyone calls my father Mac."

"Well, at least I know what to call him if I see him again. I should have introduced myself. I don't know where my head is at today."

He *did* know what his little head was thinking ever since he'd laid eyes on the beautiful brunette with the cutest, open white smile he'd ever seen.

"No." Merry shook her head. "I should have introduced them and myself since everyone apparently knew who you were. Well, everyone but me. Sorry about that."

He gave her an earnest smile. "Don't be sorry. It's a relief not to be recognized." *Sort of. Now what can I do to impress her?*

"In that case, I apologize for my fan-boy brother. It's weird, but even though he has Attention Deficit Disorder, he can remember all kinds of trivia about things that interest him, like sports." Then she covered her mouth and giggled as her cheeks took on a rosy blush. "Oh, sorry. No offense. I didn't mean to call professional sports trivial."

"None taken." *Granted, it's not like saving lives.* "So, where do you want to do... Um, I mean, where do you want this?"

"How about over there?" She pointed to the longest wall.

"Okay. So do you have a couple of drop cloths or a newspaper or anything? I can stick something smooth under the legs and push it myself without scratching your floors."

She chuckled. "They're *your* floors, I believe. And, yeah, I'm sure I can find something." She pulled the tape off a box marked *Kitchen* and rummaged through it until she fished out a couple of pot holders fashioned of stretchy, colored strips—the kind a child probably crafted. "This should help."

"Perfect." He held up his hands as if they were playing catch. She simply walked over beside him and dropped one beside each leg of the couch. "Can you lift it a little? I'll push it under."

"Oh, sure." Boy, did he feel out of his element with this *unimpressed* woman. He hoped she didn't think of him as a dumb jock.

By the time her major furniture had been placed and set up, he had expended some physical energy and released most of his tension.

I wonder if she has a serious boyfriend? "So, would you like to come up to my place and see what I mean about uncomfortable, hoity-toity furniture?"

"I would, but I'm exhausted. Maybe another time?"

"Sure. Of course. How about tomorrow night? I could make you a welcome-to-your-new-home dinner, unless you already have plans…"

"I'd love that, believe me, but I have to work." She shook her head.

Crap. You're striking out, Falco. "That's too bad. You're a nurse, right?"

"Yeah. I work at Boston General on the evening shift."

"That must not be very convenient for a night life." *C'mon, sweetheart. Give me a hint. I'm dying over here.*

"Tell me about it. I can't wait to have some kind of life now that I'm out from under my father's thumb. In case you couldn't tell, he's a little overprotective." She laughed. "Actually, he's *a lot* overprotective."

Jason chuckled. "He just seemed like a nice, caring father."

"He behaved himself in front of you. If I don't call him tomorrow, he'll be all over my case and chew me out like I skipped school. I don't usually tell people this right off the bat, but we lost my mother when I was sixteen. She had just stepped out for a carton of milk and happened to be in the wrong place at the wrong time. It was second degree murder, but the guy got off with manslaughter. Ever since then, he's barely let me out of his sight."

"I'm so sorry." Jason could relate to a hovering, smothering father. His dad had attended every game and as many practices as he could from Little League on. Jason suspected it had more to do with checking up on his athletic prowess and making sure the family "condition" remained a well-guarded secret than offering moral support.

Damn. He caught himself just staring at her. She had the softest looking skin and he wanted to reach out and caress her cheek. *Later, Falco. Don't blow it—even if it's much later.* And he hoped it wouldn't be. He desperately wanted what everyone else had—a loving family. And he had until Spring Training to find *the one* or give it up for another long, lonely year.

Chad the ghost drifted up from apartment 3A and settled in to haunt his new landlord for the evening.

Jason was back in his pristine penthouse apartment, pacing and mumbling to himself.

"I can't believe I got shot down," he grumbled. "The first time in years a girl has said no to a date with me—and I even offered to cook! That usually crumbles even the most reluctant woman. I probably just asked her at a bad time. She seemed tired. More like exhausted. She had unpacking to do… Damn it, why am I making excuses for her? She said *no* to me!"

Sighing, he halted and let his eyes roam over his showroom penthouse. "I hate this place. It feels like some billionaire's mansion—a *chick* billionaire! And I probably put the rotten designer on the road to fame and fortune by giving her free reign."

Chad grimaced. *I knew he'd regret that.*

Jason suddenly shivered as chills ran up his spine.

Easy, man. I didn't mean to give you the willies by actually touching you, but I like to mock people by pacing right behind them. I didn't know you were going to stop so suddenly. Maybe you should save this crap for your therapist. Don't all rich people have a therapist?

"Now what? I hate to confront people. I'd rather just donate the whole pile to charity and go shopping for myself. Hmm. Since it's off-season and I have a little time to myself, I could ask Merry to go shopping with me to help pick out new furniture. It would give me an excuse to see her again. *Damn*, I'd like to shop downstairs in Apartment 1B. I keep thinking about that comfortable couch in Merry's apartment—and how I'd love to be straddled on it."

Chad grinned. *Ah, now we're finally getting to the good stuff! Lay it on me, brother.*

Jason grabbed the cordless telephone and dialed a long number he knew by heart.

"Hi, Mom. Yeah, it's been a while. How are things back in good ol' Minnesota?"

After a short pause, he said, "I need to vent. I met a girl. A friendly girl who didn't throw herself at me and didn't even know who I was."

He scratched his head. "Yeah, it's rare and weirdly refreshing. But she shot me down. I'm used to women wanting me—well, *almost* used to it, but it's probably just for my money or so they can brag about doing a professional athlete." He chuckled. "Sorry, Mom."

Chad gave an exaggerated sigh. *Oh, you poor baby. I'd have given my left nut to be in your position when I was alive and horny.*

Jason sighed and lowered himself onto the low armless chair. "I'm getting used to being used, and now I've become another kind of player. All of this goes against my upbringing and values. You raised me better than that."

Again, I feel for you, man. You're fuckin' breaking my heart.

"You taught me to treat all women with respect. You drummed into my head that one-night stands aren't okay. But I've had a lot of those—more than I'd care to admit."

Chad drifted to the ceiling and mimed bowing a stringed instrument. *Oh, break out the violins. I think I need a tissue.*

"Dad suggested I ignore women altogether in order to concentrate on the sport. Actually, I want it all—the career and a special relationship—but I'm an athlete and meeting nice, normal women is tough."

He leaned forward and rested his arms on his knees. "Yeah, sure, I guess you're right. Someday when I least expect it…"

Another long pause. "Hey, someday I'll have to do

something else, but for now, I'm okay. If I have to, I can always sell the apartment building."

Chad's ears pricked up at that. *Why would he have to dump the apartment building? He could probably sell the rights to his life story for a million bucks. I, on the other hand, worked my tail off as a real writer and struggled to pay the rent—but I'm not bitter or anything.* Snort.

"I know, Ma. Thanks for listening. Have fun at bingo." Jason smiled. "I love you, too." He hung up, and went straight to his exercise room. Chad floated after him.

I do hope he won't sell the building. I don't think I can stand any more changes. His aunt might ruin it for him, though. Even though her nephew is giving her husband a job and she should be grateful for that, she makes a habit of poking her nose into everyone's business.

Jason squatted on the rubber floor and pumped out some furious push-ups.

Chad hovered directly above him, pumping up and down with Jason's push-ups. This was fun—kind of like a workout but with no effort. *In a way I do feel sorry for Jason... I get the feeling he's not really used to his aunt's ways, and he's worried about her itchy trigger finger. Not that she's going to shoot anybody—I don't think so, anyway. She's trigger happy on the telephone and has threatened to call the police for everything from a little noisy sex to a homeless person walking by.*

I hate to think what having cops at the building would do to Jason Falco. For one thing, it would put him in the newspaper and expose his whereabouts—his safe haven. Good-bye peace and quiet. Hello rabid fans. Chad chuckled sadly and drifted out the window.

—₩—

On Merry's drive home from work the following night, she cursed her rotten luck. The real motivation behind her move to the big city was to meet cute guys and date—maybe even have s-e-x. In a bed! Something she had to go without for the most part while living under her father's roof and ever watchful eye. Backseat sex just didn't cut it anymore.

Yesterday, the most incredible guy asked me out… and I had to work. Crap. Crap. Crap!

It had been a crappy shift, too. They were already understaffed and the assistant head nurse called in sick. *Thanks a pantload.* That meant Merry had to give out the meds for the whole floor and that would make any new nurse neurotic. She hadn't even met the whole staff yet.

What if she made a mistake? She needed this job to pay her rent. She needed to pay her rent to keep her apartment. She needed to live in her own apartment to have a life! Hopefully a cute intern or two would show up *before* she made a med error and was tossed out on her keester.

Even a tiny taste of independence excited her like nothing else had in the last… how many years? Maybe since her training wheels had been removed. Just thinking about her quest ending in failure and retreating home to Rhode Island upset her enough to bring on an asthma attack.

The motivation to leave wasn't *all* about dating. She needed a fresh start. She had been "that weird MacKenzie girl" ever since she was little. For some reason she could smell blood blocks away. It's why she became a nurse in the first place. It seemed only natural that she should take first aid courses.

Merry's thoughts kept her thoroughly preoccupied as she parked her aging Volkswagen in the alley behind her building. Apparently none of the long-term residents owned a car, so she secured a free assigned parking space. *Hooray!*

Strolling away from her car with competing thoughts swirling through her brain, she fumbled in the dark for her back-door key. Suddenly, her feet went out from under her and she found herself hurled to the ground and pinned by some foul-smelling brute. A moment later she realized she had hit hard pavement with her head.

Unable to find her voice right away, or even process what had happened, she lay there, dumbstruck. The moon reflected a glint of metal nearing her face.

"Shhh… Don't scream and I won't hurt you—much." Maniacal laughter followed. A hand fumbled with the buttons on her coat.

Oh my God. What is it they tell you to do in case of rape? Oh, yeah, scream!

Merry inhaled deeply and let out a blood curdling scream. She didn't even recognize the voice as hers. Suddenly her throat tightened and she recognized another threat—her asthma.

She remembered being told to fight but not struggle. They liked it when a woman struggled. *Gouge out his eyes! Punch his nose up into his brains. Fight like your life depends on it.*

As she tried and failed to get near the bastard's face, her assailant grabbed her wrists in one hand and pressed the sharp knife to her neck with the other.

He hissed, "Shut up! I told you to shut up!"

She pushed his arm away from her and freed one hand. Grabbing anything else she could get a hold of, she tried to yank him off of her.

His jeans must have hung low on his hips, because she grabbed onto the waistband of his underwear. *Riiiiiip*.

The perp yelped. His eyes flashed in horror and she realized she had just given him a world-class wedgie.

Dear God, I'm going to die. I'm going to be raped and killed in a back alley on my first night as an independent adult. I'm never going to fall in love, get married, hug my children, or live in a McMansion.

The knife pressed into her flesh, and the warm trickle down her neck meant he had pierced the skin. Should she scream again? Would he just kill her and leave her rather than rape her? Or would he, ewww, kill her first, *then* rape her? *Oh, my freakin' God!*

As she contemplated what would be the lesser of all possible evils, the man flew off of her and landed a few feet away. At first, she didn't see anyone else.

When she blinked, two shadowy figures stood over the gasping pervert. One of them clamped his boot on the would-be rapist's neck and pointed a gun at his face. The other one hurried over to Merry and helped her up.

"Thank you. Both of you. You saved my life!" The man holding her elbow seemed preoccupied with her neck. Awareness rolled over her. She recognized the dark-haired man who had been leaning against the wrought iron fence, watching her move in. Again, he wore all black, but the concern on his face completely changed his ominous air. His dark chocolate eyes were warm and almond shaped, much like her own.

"He missed your carotid artery. You'll be okay."

Merry touched her neck. Thankfully, his diagnosis seemed true. Blood simply trickled from the wound, it didn't gush.

"I saw you yesterday," she said. "Do you live in this building?"

"Nearby," he said, then he turned his attention to the other man, a tall blond with broad shoulders—also dressed in black. "Konrad, here, is one of your neighbors. Hey," he called to the tall blond with the massive shoulders, "leave him to me and take her inside."

"Good idea, Sly," the striking Viking said. His white teeth glistened as a grin spread across his face. His canines seemed larger and more pronounced than in most men. Light facial hair and a short goatee softened his jawline. He had heavy brows of the same color. His ears were slightly pointed and poked though his almost waist-length hair.

The dark-haired man called Sly moved with lightning speed, holding down the assailant.

The guy protested vehemently. "No, please! I'll do anything you ask. Just let me go."

The blond Konrad changed places with Sly and escorted Merry to the back door. She glided along beside him, numb, as if in a dream.

As soon as she had ascended the concrete steps, before she stepped through the door that Konrad held open for her, she turned and caught only a glimpse of the scene she had left behind. Sly knelt beside the stranger and leaned over by his head. Konrad placed his hand on her lower back and hurried her in, closing the door on a male scream that emanated from the dark alley.

Merry left Konrad sitting at her kitchen table and strolled to the bathroom, saying, "The hydrogen peroxide is going to sting like crazy, but I know the importance of preventing infection."

She dug through the box marked *Linen closet* until she found some bandaging supplies. As she swabbed the area, she gritted her teeth and hissed, inhaling a long breath until the worst of the sting abated. A thin bandage did its job staunching the blood.

When she returned, she offered Konrad something to drink.

"No, thanks. I'm fine, but let me get you something while you sit and relax."

Yeah, right. She sat shivering, her arms wrapped around herself while Konrad put the teakettle on and found a mug. Soon he handed her chamomile tea with a spoonful of honey, and she warmed her hands on the steaming mug.

"This is the same comfort drink my mother used to give me when I was hurt or upset as a child. How did you know?" *And the same thing I made for my father when my mother was senselessly murdered during a robbery.*

"Well, you had tea bags and honey in your cupboard."

"Oh yeah." Her thoughts returned to the incident. "Th-that man..." she began. "I..."

"It's been handled by now. He didn't get your clothes off, so I'd guess your virtue is intact. Right?"

She nodded.

A knock at the door of the apartment startled her and she jumped.

"I'll get it," he said.

"Thanks." Normally she'd let her guest sit and answer her own door, but at the moment she liked the idea of someone else facing the unknown behind it.

Her kitchen kitty-cornered off the living and dining area, out of view of the front door, but she heard both male and female voices.

Jason led the pack and soon her tiny kitchen had filled up with several people she'd never met, all of whom seemed concerned for her safety. Konrad filled them in on what had happened.

"Some creep accosted her in the alley. She's okay though," he added hurriedly.

Jason shook his head, wearing a grave expression. "I'll install motion sensors and spotlights back there tomorrow. I'm sorry I didn't think to do it before."

"Oh, Jason," an older woman with short, curly, dyed-brown hair in desperate need of a root touch-up said. "It's not your fault. How could you know anyone would be foolish enough to hang around in the alley at night."

Everyone, including Merry, gaped at her. Did she really blame *her?* She spoke as if instead of merely coming home from work and parking her car right next to her apartment building, she had lollygagged in the alley, waiting for trouble!

"Aunt Dottie, don't be insensitive. It's not her fault."

Thank you, Mr. Hottie. I don't care if she's your aunt or not, that was freakin' rude.

"Damn right," said Konrad. He shot a pointed look at Dottie. "She was minding her own business—something everyone ought to do."

Merry fidgeted. "I had just come home from work

and somewhere between my car and the back door, this pervert jumped me." She nodded to Konrad. "Thank goodness you guys got to me as quickly as you did. I don't know what I would have done if you hadn't been there."

"Died, probably," said Nathan, her rail-thin neighbor from across the hall.

One of the attractive women who shared an apartment on the third floor threw her hands in the air. She had been introduced as Morgaine. She looked nice enough, although her black-lined eyes, black lipstick, and black nail polish made her seem a bit gothic. Jet black hair and a black dress completed the image. "Well, Nathan, it looks like Dottie's not the only insensitive person in the room! Anyone else want to take potshots at the poor girl who was just attacked?"

"I wasn't being insensitive," Dottie blustered. "I just meant it wasn't Jason's fault in case anyone decides to file a lawsuit." Her eyes narrowed on Merry.

"I wouldn't sue him, Mrs. Falco. I'm not like that."

Dottie crossed her arms over her small chest and continued to cast a suspicious look her way. "Well, I noticed that one of the friends you listed as a reference is a lawyer."

"So? She's a defense attorney."

"So? She's still a lawyer."

Jason put his arm around his aunt and steered her out of the kitchen. "Leave the poor girl alone, Aunt Dottie. She's just been through a horrible experience."

"Fine. I will," Dottie said, in a miffed tone. Merry blew out a breath of relief when Jason returned without her.

"I apologize for my aunt, Merry. She isn't usually like that."

"Only when she's breathing," Konrad mumbled.

Apparently the others overheard him and chuckled softly.

Jason heaved a sigh. "She's just looking out for my best interests since we're family." He focused his gaze on Merry and a deep look of concern crossed his face. "Are you really all right, Merry? Do you want me to call anyone? Your father maybe?"

"God, no!" *I'd better squash that line of thinking immediately or I'll be hauled back to Rhode Island kicking and screaming.* "Look." She squared her shoulders. "No one has to tiptoe around me. I'm not a fragile little girl. I'm tougher than I look. I understand that these things happen and assigning blame isn't especially constructive. I happened to step out of my car at the wrong time. I think I've calmed down enough to call the police and report the incident."

"No!" Konrad jumped right out of his chair and stood between her and the wall phone.

He reacted in such a commanding way that Merry wondered what could possibly threaten a big guy like him. Did he need to avoid the police for his own reasons?

"I—I won't bring you into it if you don't want me to, but I should at least tell them what happened."

"And how are you going to do that without bringing me and Sly into it?"

Jason scratched his head. "Who's Sly?"

Merry explained, "There was another man who intervened. Sly's the one who held the attacker down while Konrad took me inside."

"Ohhh…" The group of long-term residents groaned together.

What was that about?

Then Morgaine said, "Yeah, you don't want to do that… call the police, I mean."

Merry looked from one person to the next and the only one who seemed confused was she. "But why?"

"What good would it do?" Konrad rubbed the back of his neck. "I mean, you're all right. You said so yourself. It's not like the cops are going to find him. It's way too late now."

Jason shrugged. "You can do what you want, Merry, but to be honest, I'm not crazy about drawing attention to the building. A police car parked out front will do that. If for some reason they want to speak to me, it'll wind up in the news and I really want to keep a low profile."

Konrad interjected, "He's a celebrity. The last thing he needs is bad press."

Gwyneth, the pretty redhead from 3B drawled, "Sugar, we've all been asked to send any problems to the super, Ralph. He's Dottie's husband. If he or Jason can handle the matter, they will."

"Oh. Okay, I understand. I won't call them, then."

Seconds later, blue lights flickered intermittently through her window.

Gwyneth slapped a hand over her chest. "I do declare!"

"Damn," Konrad groaned. "Dottie must have called them."

"We should have known that would happen," Nathan said. "Well, I'm out of here."

The following day, Merry, more shaken up than she had let on, switched shifts with another nurse so she didn't have to work. Sleep had come hard and left her jaw sore from fitfully grinding her teeth.

She puttered around her apartment, unpacked boxes, and put her special things where she could see and enjoy them. Her new gold silk curtains were now proudly hung at the bay windows. They were a splurge she couldn't stop herself from buying as she excitedly shopped for her first place. She didn't want to cover her hardwood floors as much as accent them, so she bought a five-by-seven faux oriental area rug to group her furniture around.

Other than those two things, everything else had been hers or extra things her family didn't need. Like a second set of dishes and stainless flatware. At one point, her mother decided she wanted new patterns and, thankfully, she hadn't thrown out the old ones.

Merry lined the pass-through from the kitchen to the dining area with plants. Her father had insisted he'd only kill them if she left them behind.

Her Mickey Mouse clock hung on the far wall of the kitchen over the table for two, adding some whimsy to the windowless galley.

The excitement she *should* have felt while decorating her very first apartment eluded her.

"How dare some perv deprive me of this long-awaited thrill. This was supposed to be *my* time."

She had planned to rebel. To make up for the years she'd had to put up with being sheltered. Not only that, but she took care of others when she should have been out all night, kicking up her heels and raising hell.

A knock sounded on her front door.

When she opened it, Jason stood there looking yummier than ever.

"I wanted to stop by to see how you're feeling."

She put on a cheery smile and said, "Oh, fine! Hey, would you like to have dinner with me this evening?" She hoped he'd realize the legitimacy of her work excuse and give her another chance.

"Yeah, I'd love that."

Whew. Spending some time with her hot, new landlord could prove a welcome distraction.

"So, did you have to talk to the police at all?" Merry asked.

"No. Fortunately I was able to avoid it simply by stating the truth. I hadn't seen anything."

"I guess either the cop wasn't a baseball fan and didn't recognize you or wore a good poker face. I would have felt terrible if the whole thing created negative press for you."

"No. Konrad was the only eyewitness—and did you notice he seemed to know the cop who asked the questions? They nodded to each other and Konrad visibly relaxed as soon as he saw him."

"Yeah, I saw that. I thought they might even be related. They have the same large build and facial features," Merry said.

"Nothing was said, specifically, but I got the impression the news wouldn't make it to any reporters."

"That's a relief. I wonder what the others' reaction to Sly meant. Why did they groan when they found out he had been the one left to deal with the criminal?"

Jason shrugged. "I didn't understand that either."

She assumed the other residents knew something they weren't divulging. Sly *did* seem ominous in a dark, dangerous, and freakishly strong way. Adrenaline may have played a part, but she'd never seen a full grown man lifted like he weighed no more than a rag doll.

Jason wandered around her small apartment. "Your place looks really cute."

Merry appraised her work and decided he was right. Her kitchen table wore a new blue and green MacKenzie plaid tablecloth, a nice contrast to the white walls and appliances. Red pillar candles stood at differing heights in the living room fireplace, and a couple of favorite art books graced her coffee table that used to be an old trunk.

"But why don't I have you up to my place? I can provide the salad, wine, music, and ambiance."

"And I'll bet it's a little bigger."

"Well, yeah. It takes up the whole top floor."

"Okay, then. I'll cook and you can set the table."

Now she had to shop for food. *Why oh why did I offer to cook for Jason? I barely know where the stove is.*

He grinned. "Sounds like a plan."

Yeah, she needed a plan. She could put together her famous lasagna and bake some bread sticks. She'd have to cheat and buy the frozen dough this time. Oh, and dessert. Not one, but three. She owed her rescuers some kind of thank you, and since home cooking was all she could afford, that would have to do. Hmm... Apples were in season.

"Well, I'd better go grocery shopping!"

"Until tonight," he said. Smiling, he let himself out and closed the door.

Part of her wanted to stay cocooned in her own safe space, but she couldn't stay locked up forever. She had to go out before dark. The grocery store was only a few blocks away, and rather than face the alley again she tugged on her jacket, found her strong mesh grocery bags, and set out for a brisk walk to the store.

As she locked her apartment door behind her, Nathan appeared to be heading out, too. Wearing black with no reflectors, he wheeled a bicycle. Did everyone in this town wear nothing but black?

"How's the neck?" he asked.

"Oh, fine. It just needed a small bandage, nothing serious."

"Well, you were lucky. I hope it doesn't get infected. Even little scrapes can turn really nasty. They can even cause death."

"Yes, I'm a nurse and know about infections. I bathed it in hydrogen peroxide."

"A nurse, eh? Where at?"

"Boston General Hospital," she said.

His eyebrows rose. "That's where I work too. What floor are you on?"

"Five West. Evening shift." She inwardly squirmed at the golden sky that signaled approaching dusk.

"Ah, you're in pediatric orthopedics. I don't get a lot of business from you."

"Oh? Where do you work," she asked.

"I'm in the morgue. Easy clients. They don't ask for much."

"Ewwww." She immediately regretted her reaction. A morbid sense of humor would probably help in a job like that—and somebody had to do it. She figured he was a real party killer, though.

Merry had carefully arranged it so her job minimized the likelihood of dealing with death. But her neighbor seemed unfazed. In fact, he grinned, as if pleased that his job came with shock value.

She needed to get to the store, so she cleared her throat and said, "Well, I've got to go... Oh, by the way, do you know where Sly lives? I want to bake some kind of thank-you desserts for Konrad and him."

Nathan tipped his head, as if sizing her up. Then he shrugged. "I probably shouldn't tell you this, but you seem like a nice girl. Sly doesn't exactly 'live' anywhere. He keeps his stuff in the basement, but don't tell anyone."

"Oh—I see. He's homeless, then?"

"I didn't say that. He has a roof over his head, he just doesn't *live* anywhere."

The way he emphasized the word *live* made her realize she had missed some sort of big hint. She lowered her voice, and hoped that taking a conspiratorial tone might get him to open up. "What do you mean? I won't tell, I promise."

"I mean, he's not alive. He's undead and only comes out at night. Hates garlic... Ring a bell?"

"Are you saying what I think you're saying?"

"Yeah. We have a vampire in the basement."

Merry thought she heard a short gasp from the top of the stairs and then a soft click.

"Don't worry. You can use the laundry room down there without disturbing him. You might want to wash your clothes during the daylight hours—when he's dead to the world." Nathan laughed at his own joke, but Merry found nothing funny about it.

Hair prickled on the back of her neck and her mouth dried up. *Nathan must be crazy. And lucky me, I live right across the hall!*

She mutely followed him out the door and down the steps. Nathan mounted his bicycle, said good-bye, and rode away. A few feet down the sidewalk he looked back and called over his shoulder, "Don't bother baking a cake for Sly. He won't eat it—liquid diet and all. You can give it to *me*, though."

Chapter 2

DOTTIE PACED ACROSS HER WORN CARPET IN FRONT OF Jason. *Damn it. Why doesn't anyone listen to me?*

"He was probably joking, Aunt Dottie. Either that or he knew you were listening and thought he'd have some fun with you. I've noticed he has an odd sense of humor."

She balled her fists and jammed them on her bony hips. "I know what I heard, Jason. Now if you don't want to investigate it, I'll send Ralph, but someone has to look in the basement. What if there's a coffin down there?"

Ralph chuckled from the other room, then joined them. "I've been down there to clean the lint traps in the dryers, and while I'm there I check the water heater and oil tanks. I think I'd have noticed a coffin, dear."

"Well, I'm not going down there until you check again, so I hope you enjoy doing your own laundry." *Hey, maybe I can get some help around the apartment out of this scare, if nothing else.*

He smirked. "So it's okay for *me* to get bitten by the creepy vampire…"

Uh-oh. Time to backpedal. She wouldn't be much use as a maintenance man if anything happened to Ralph.

Dottie raked her fingernails over her scalp, through her short, graying permed hair. "You're right. I should call the police and make them check it out."

"*Please* don't! I can't have them here all the time. It'll be in the newspapers and call attention to where I live."

"Oh, you're being silly. No one will write a story about where you live. I'm sure they must know that celebrities want their privacy." *Honestly! He's so full of himself sometimes*.

Ralph scowled. "And you think they'll respect that? Dottie, will you listen to your nephew? He owns the building and if he doesn't want the cops to arrive for every practical joke or minor incident, don't call the damn cops! He was nice enough to give me a job and us a place to live. If it weren't for him, I'd have been unemployed for a lot longer than eleven months."

Jason sighed. "I'll check it out for you."

"No. I don't want anything to happen to you, either. Didn't you say you were having dinner with the nurse downstairs?"

He cast her a sidelong glance. "Yeah... Why? You don't want me to send *her* down there, do you?"

"Well... No, of course not. Just ask her about what Nathan said. See if she thinks he was kidding."

Ralph crossed his arms over the T-shirt that barely covered his beer belly. "For God's sake. There's no such thing as vampires, woman. And how is he supposed to do that without letting her know *someone* was eavesdropping?"

She winced. *Someone, meaning me, of course*. No one appreciated her contribution. If they didn't want her to keep an eye on the place and manage it, why did they let her call herself the manager?

"Fine!" Dottie stomped off to her bedroom and blasted her oldies radio station. At that moment "*You Ain't Seen Nothing Yet*" by Bachman-Turner Overdrive served as a warning.

Just wait, you two. Something is going on here. I know it! And as soon as I can, I'll show you evidence and prove my usefulness—one way or another.

—⁓—

Merry's apartment smelled wonderful. The strong aromas of Italian food and cinnamon met Jason's nose as soon as she opened the door.

"Wow, something smells delicious, Merry. I came to see if I could give you a hand when you're ready to bring things upstairs."

"Thanks, that's nice of you. I have the lasagna in a glass casserole dish that's probably hot and heavy..." She blushed.

Oops. Freudian slip much?

"Uh, so if you want to take that, um... You'll need potholders. Here." She shoved the childish pot holders at him.

"I never asked who made these. Do you have a niece or nephew?"

"Nope. *I* made them—at summer camp about a zillion years ago. My father keeps everything." She blushed harder. "The dessert is just apple crisp."

"Mmm... Lasagna. How did you know my number one weakness? And 'just' apple crisp? The only thing that could top that would be apple pie à la mode." She had changed the subject, so he'd tease her about the potholders some other time. "Man, I can hardly wait. I love those two things. You've got me salivating already." His mouth watered over more than the food. They hadn't discussed how to dress, and he'd assumed she'd wear something casual, like jeans and a sweater.

But she wore a clingy red dress. He wondered if she knew how delicious she looked in it.

Merry opened the oven door. "I was going to put tin foil over the pan, but if you're hungry and want to eat right away, there's no need to."

He drew the bubbling dish out of the oven and set it on top of the stove. "No, we can take our time. I didn't mean to rush dinner, and I won't starve to death if we spend an extra half hour getting to know each other over a glass of wine."

She smiled. "Sounds good to me."

Did it? He certainly hoped she was game for involvement with someone whose entire life could be taken over by his livelihood. At times he wished more than anything that he had someone waiting for him at home.

Merry's presence in his building could be the next best thing. She seemed emotionally stable—so far. Certainly more stable than some of his rabid fans.

Loaded down with the heavy dish, Jason let her get the door and lock it behind them. He asked her to extract his key card from his front pocket rather than balance the heavy lasagna pan on one wide open palm and hope not to drop it.

"Okaaay." She gingerly fished the proximity card out of his pocket and held it up to the elevator's scanner. A slight blush colored her cheeks.

The magic card allowed access to the penthouse floor. As they rode the elevator together, he glanced down at her and smiled. She shifted her focus to the floor, but when she looked up again, she showed him her wide sparkling smile—the one that twisted his stomach into a knot and affected lower regions too.

At last they reached the penthouse and the elevator doors opened onto his expansive entry. He watched for her reaction to the pristine condition of his combined living and dining areas. "Welcome to my abode."

Her eyes popped and her smile turned into an open-mouthed, awed expression as she took in the expensively decorated but completely impractical penthouse. She bypassed the kitchen and her high heels clicked across the marble floors to the windows. She still clutched her apple crisp. "Wow!"

He had pulled the curtains closed in all but the one spot that led to his balcony. Even so, the city lights showed through the gossamer, airy curtains and lit up the night like stars. She must have liked what she saw. She seemed positively mesmerized.

Jason set the lasagna dish on his built-in kitchen grill and followed her to the windows. "Pretty, isn't it?" *Not nearly as pretty as the temptress right in front of me.*

"I'll say. I didn't realize our building was higher than those on the other side of the street. I can see the river. You really scored a gorgeous view here."

He chuckled at her use of the word *score*. With any luck, he'd score with the cute Rhode Islander before too long.

"Let me take that dish so you can look around. See the rest of the place." He headed toward the kitchen and set the dish on the curved granite peninsula.

She followed hesitantly. "Thanks. You trust me to wander around by myself?"

"Sure, I don't think you could hide much of anything under that slinky dress."

Her mouth dropped open and she burst into giggles. Even with her tan complexion, her face reddened.

What did I say that for? Now I've embarrassed her and she'll probably wear sweats and bulky hoodies from now on. How could he salvage the situation? Apologize? Laugh with her? No. He just listened to his gut, strode over to her, pulled her into his embrace, and kissed her. He wanted there to be no misunderstanding. He didn't wait for permission. He took possession of her lips and delivered his message resolutely.

Her body molded to his and she wrapped her arms around his neck and shoulders. He didn't want to stop kissing her, but neither did he want to seem overanxious. He pulled back slowly, and still holding her he said, "You're irresistible, you know."

She lowered her head and let out a nervous giggle, but she didn't pull away and maintained a friendly smile. Apparently going with his gut had been the right thing to do. He leaned in for another kiss and this time her lips parted, slightly. He slipped his tongue in her mouth and their tongues touched.

She tasted like apples and cinnamon. She smelled good too—kind of like spicy vanilla. A small moan escaped her soft lips. *I know what you mean, babe.*

Their tongues swirled as if caressing each other. Jason knew he wasn't a bad kisser, but this was the first time he'd felt like his lips were an incomplete puzzle that had found its missing piece. They fit together perfectly.

He didn't know how long they'd been standing there kissing when he reluctantly let her go. She touched her full bottom lip as if it tingled.

He inhaled deeply and let out a long breath. "Man."

"You can say that again."

—∿∿—

Merry wandered through Jason's apartment, barely taking in the details, while he opened and poured the wine. She hadn't expected to be kissed so soon but had hoped things would head in that direction by the end of the night—still, she wasn't about to complain. A twinge of nervousness niggled at her, but how could she find out if this handsome man, who had plenty of money and could probably attract any woman he wanted, wanted her for a fling or more than that?

Merry knew what she wanted. Love, a home, and a family. Sure, a good time at first so she'd have some wild memories to keep her entertained while sitting around in a nursing home, but love, eventually and ultimately. Possibly more than a man like Jason Falco was willing to consider.

Merry's realistic nature acknowledged that love didn't always happen without heartbreak, but her optimistic side hoped to avoid it nonetheless. Her lips still tingled. His line about her being irresistible might have been cliché, but that kiss certainly wasn't.

She suddenly realized she had bypassed an exercise room and had been standing in his bedroom for quite a while. Her attention focused on the king-sized pedestal bed covered in white linens, a white duvet, and loads of white pillows. Why would a single guy need such a huge bed? Obviously, he wasn't planning to sleep alone. But there was enough room in this one for three and the surface sat so low that no one would get hurt if, in all the rolling around, someone slid off onto the white carpet... *Oh!* Damn, wasn't that every man's fantasy? And if he could have anything he wanted... *Eek*.

"Like it?" he said from the doorway.

She started. "Oh, uh... What?"

He held out a glass of red wine to her. "Do you like my place?"

"Yeah! Of course. Who wouldn't?"

"I wouldn't. I think it's cold and sterile."

"Really? Huh, come to think of it, it kind of reminds me of the hospital." She took a sip of her wine and it trickled down surprisingly smooth. She usually thought of reds as bitter, but this mellow brand might help her survive the evening. The idea of kinky aerobics had her shivering inside, yet she wasn't chilly. If anything, her warm cheeks grew warmer.

"I notice that everything is pretty low to the floor."

"I know. Isn't that ridiculous? I had to go and buy myself one chair I could sit in without stretching my legs all the way out. I'm six feet tall. I still can't figure out who the designer had in mind when she picked out this stuff. Dwarfs?"

"It looks like all seven dwarfs could fit in this bed." She glanced back at it, then noticed a gleam in his blue eyes as he smiled. Warning alarms sounded in her head.

But he answered nonchalantly. "The seven dwarfs worked in a mine, didn't they? All this white furniture and bedding would turn gray in a week."

"Well, let's go back to your living room," she said a little too abruptly.

They bypassed the living room and decided to skip the small talk and go right to dinner.

He pulled out the chair for her. That made her smile. *Well, things look as though they're back on track.*

And how! Merry didn't sit, but faced him and pulled his arms around her waist. She delivered another one of her mind-blowing kisses, then swept aside the dishes. She lay back on the table and crooked her little finger at him.

Jason approached her like a panther stalking its prey. He walked forward on his hands and leaned over her. As he kissed her again, she cupped her hand around his hot, throbbing... Mercy! He shivered.

"Is everything okay? Are you going to sit down too?"

Crap. It was just a fantasy. Someday, however, he wanted that particular fantasy to come truc.

Recognizing Morgaine's voice, but unable to hear any response, Chad deduced that she was on the phone—and possibly on the phone-sex line! He could always hope that some kind of *real* foreplay might be in progress, but he pushed his way through the wooden door to find out. He always felt as if he needed to spit sawdust after going through doors. It was better than plaster, though.

"Oh, yeah... Do you like that, baby? Hmmm... I'm really turned on right now."

Sure enough, Morgaine was using her money maker—her super sexy phone voice.

Suddenly the other phone rang.

The witches had two dedicated lines each, and he assumed each had their own clients. But the best thing about their living together was their ability to cover for each other—callers never had to hang up disappointed when they needed to get their rocks off.

"No, baby. I don't have to go," Morgaine said breathily. "I have to *come*."

Gwyneth rushed in and picked up the ringing telephone. Morgaine added some heavy panting, and then... *"Oooh, Ahhh, Ohhhhhhhhh. AAAAAAAGH! AAAAAAAAGH! AAAAAAAAAH!"*

She panted a few times, then said, "That was fantastic! You're *so* incredible. Did I satisfy you too, baby? Yeah? Good." After a brief giggle, she said, "Of course. Call any time. We're always here for you, baby."

As soon as she hung up, she returned to the kitchen where something brewed on a slow simmer. It looked like another batch of her protection potion. Chad had seen her make it before. She kept the black liquid at just below a boil.

He remembered when it bubbled over and made a mess of the white appliances and tile floor. Morgaine declared the batch ruined and threw it out.

Sometimes they slaved over the hot stove for twenty minutes or more as they stirred their spells into all kinds of horrible soupy looking things. Of course, sometimes they were simply making soup. Chad could only tell if they tasted the stuff.

He switched his attention to Gwyneth as she began talking dirty in her sexy Southern drawl.

I love that Gwyneth still has a heavy Southern accent. Those dropped r's and slow drawl are music to my Northern ears. It was hard to believe they were cousins— even though Chad was pretty sure they'd moved from down South somewhere. Chad loved it when Gwyneth used the endearment "Dahlin'" to her better clients. That slow drawl plus the sexy voice could make *him* come. As it was, he tried to avoid the frustration.

It amazed him how the cousins could turn it on and off at a moment's notice. Of course, it was acting! That's why they called themselves phone-sex actresses and could win academy awards. Certainly their performances rivaled Meg Ryan's. *Heh heh. I'll have what she's having.*

Chad knew they had an owl familiar and wondered where it was. Athena was a real owl—kept like a beloved pet. They believed she contained the spirit of some kind of reincarnated ancestor or spiritual guardian. Chad thought it was just a dumb bird.

Her perch was in the bathroom, so if she spilled her food or had an accident, they wouldn't lose another area rug. She didn't fly much, but sometimes got turned on by all the noises and began flapping her wings and hooting.

"Oh, gawd, dahlin'... Oh, that feels so good... Oh yeah, dahlin'. Are you close? Now? Awww... *Shee-it! AAAAAaaa, AAAAAaaa, AAAAAAAAAAAAA!"*

Hoo...Hoo...

Yup, these two are a gas to watch. Chad grinned.

"This is delicious, Merry." Jason hadn't had a meal this good in a long time. Sure, he could grill a steak and microwave a potato, but this... this was ambrosia.

"You make a mean salad, too," she said.

Jason chuckled and scooped another forkful of

lasagna into his mouth. He chewed with his eyes closed to savor the mix of tomatoes, meat, and cheeses. His taste buds zinged.

Wow, a beauty who can cook too. Not like the spoiled debutantes who had been forced on him — speaking of which...

"Merry, there's a charity bachelor auction the PR people roped me into. I really don't want to be auctioned off like a piece of meat, so I was thinking maybe if I give you the money to 'buy' me... Would you be willing to get dressed up and pose as a rich, spoiled brat?"

Merry almost choked on her salad. Then she started to laugh. When she cleared her throat and composed herself, she asked, "When is it?"

"The Friday after next."

"You're in luck. I work every other weekend, but I have Fridays and Mondays off when I work that Saturday and Sunday."

"Is that a yes?"

She shrugged. "I'll think about it."

Well, that was better than an outright no. Now to keep the conversation casual. "Is that why you moved in on a Friday? Was this your weekend to work?"

"Yes. That's when my family was available too. My dad's retired, but my kid brother works Saturdays. On Fridays he gets out of school at noon. Since I couldn't carry all the heavy stuff by myself, I had to take what labor I could get when I could get it."

"So, you're off again tomorrow since it's Monday?"

"Yup. I should probably feel guilty about playing hooky tonight, but when I called, I was still pretty shaken up."

"I didn't realize that. You seem fine." He thought about

her reaction at the bedroom and realized she'd probably feel skittish after a near rape. Now her abrupt change of mood as he'd walked up behind her made sense.

He reached over and grasped her hand. It trembled. "Merry, I'm so sorry you were attacked. I know I said it before, but my uncle is taking steps to correct the lighting in the alley. I promise."

She smiled. "I know. Thank you."

"He'll have it finished before you have to go back to work." He squeezed her hand before he let go. She nodded and looked at her lap.

Wow, she really was upset. I wonder why she didn't let on?

They had finished their meal, cleared the table, and settled on the sofa to talk. Merry set her wine glass on the Lucite table, afraid of spilling it on the white fabric of the sofa.

She had already finished two glasses and really didn't need any more. The wine made her relaxed and her lips tingled faintly. Or maybe she was anticipating another one of Jason's toe-curling kisses.

Jason sat so low to the ground that his legs stretched way out in front of him. Merry had been able to tuck hers demurely under and to one side.

"See what I mean about this ridiculous furniture?" he said.

"It looks cool, but I'm afraid to spill anything on it," Merry said. "Especially red wine."

"I wouldn't mind if you did. It would give me an excuse to toss these and get new ones."

"Why don't you donate them somewhere?"

He looked left and right to the matching side chairs and said, "You know what? You're right. I settled for them just because they were so damned expensive, and I was raised not to waste money. I'm sure there's some office in a shelter or something I can furnish and then get what I want."

"Of course. Maybe you could bring them back to the store if you know where they came from—or save your money from the bachelor auction if you need to."

"Oh, no. It's not the money." He turned to face her and rested his hand on hers.

A slight electric zing traveled up her arm and raised goose-bumps. Her breath hitched, but Jason didn't appear to notice.

"I've heard nightmare stories from some of the guys on my team about those stupid auctions."

"Like what? Blue-haired old ladies with no teeth who want to grope you all night?"

He laughed. "I haven't been through anything like that yet, but it's certainly a risk. No, I'm talking about society women trying to marry for money. They think our off-season is their hunting season. I don't want to get duped into anything less than love."

"So, you consider falling in love the better way to be duped?"

His jaw dropped. "No!" He shook his head, furiously. "That's not what I meant."

"I know. I was kidding."

A moment later, he trailed his finger up her arm, making her quiver.

"Do you believe in love?"

She smiled. "Of course. Don't you?"

"Yeah, I've known some very happy couples. Professional sports can take a toll on relationships, but that doesn't mean it's not worth trying."

"So, it sounds like you're planning to fall in love sometime. What are you looking for these days? Are you playing the field? Trying out relationships? Just want to be friends? You don't have to answer, but I try to be upfront whenever possible, and just so we're clear, this *is* a test."

He leaned back and laughed. "Well, I appreciate your candor."

"Have you ever been in love?"

His expression turned somber. "I thought I was in love once," he said softly.

"Oh, what happened? If you don't mind me asking."

"No, I don't mind. Baseball can take a lot of time away from relationships. Things were shaky anyway and it affected my game. And then I was traded to Boston. She didn't want to leave Minnesota and I didn't have a choice." He took a deep breath and continued.

"I already played the field and that wasn't very satisfying. I guess I'm trying out relationships. Friendships are nice too. I have nothing against going that way if you're not ready to get involved with any-one—especially the first person you met after moving to the city."

She grinned. "I like friendships too, but I have nothing against relationships, either. We could always begin as friends and see where it leads."

"That sounds okay to me. Friends are nice— but..." He heaved a sigh and muttered, "Oh hell," then pulled her into his embrace and lowered his lips to hers. They shared a long, deep kiss. Merry felt her body weaken. Her temperature rose as their tongues sought each other and explored. A deep longing built in Merry's gut and she craved his touch. She slid her hands over his broad, warm back and he caressed hers in kind.

He lowered her to a supine position and never removed his lips from hers. For several minutes, Jason continued his drugging kiss and Merry lost all track of time. Their kissing and caressing may have gone on for an hour or more for all she knew. His tongue occasionally left her mouth and suction fused them together, then she found her tongue chasing his. Her insides liquefied as she realized they were lying next to each other. Anything could happen from there. Anything...

"Jason!" His aunt's voice invaded her dreamlike state.

He sat up. His body leaving hers abruptly chilled and surprised her.

What the... Merry lifted herself to a sitting position. Sure enough, his aunt hovered in the doorway with a key card in her hand.

"I didn't expect you two to be here. Um..." She smiled and her pale skin took on a rosy blush. At last she added, "Well, I thought you'd be downstairs."

"No, we had dinner up here. Is there something you wanted?"

She cleared her throat. "Um, yes. I was going to leave you a note about the women in apartment 3B. There's a terrible racket going on down there. All kinds of hooting and hollering. Even screaming. I want you to talk to them."

He stood slowly and put both hands in his pockets. "Why don't you talk to them, if it's bothering you? I can't even hear them."

Dottie jammed her hands on her hips. "I already did. They obviously don't care if they're disturbing me."

"How about Uncle Ralph? Is he upset by it?"

She rolled her eyes. "Your uncle isn't upset in the least. In fact he thinks it sounds like they're having sex and he seems to be enjoying it."

Jason chuckled. "I'll see if they can keep it down — when they're finished."

"Please do." His aunt spun on her heel and left, slamming the door behind her.

Jason sighed, then looked down at Merry and smiled. "I'm sorry about that."

"Don't worry. It was probably a good thing we were interrupted or who knows what..." She flushed as she realized what she had just revealed about herself, then checked her watch. "Oh, look. It's getting late. We should probably call it a night."

Jason looked disappointed, then said, "Okay. I'll walk you to your front door. Do you mind stopping one flight down? It might be *a little* less embarrassing for me to talk to Gwyneth and Morgaine if you're there."

"If they're really having sex, do you honestly think anything will make it less embarrassing?"

He winced. "I doubt it, but will you come anyway? As a friend supporting a friend?"

She shot him a teasing grin. "Sure, I wouldn't miss it."

"Oh, so you're *that* kind of friend, are you?"

"Don't tell me you can't take a little innocent teasing?" She elbowed him in the ribs.

"Of course I can, as long as you can take it as well as dish it out."

"Bring it on, pal."

———~~~———

Before Jason walked her to the elevator, Merry had offered to talk to the noisemakers in 3B for him. She really did want a relationship based on friendship and it seemed like a small thing she could do for him. So she kissed him good night at his door and took the elevator alone.

Now she stood at the door to 3B, listening to obvious moans of passion, wondering what to say. "Hey... I'm glad you two have such a great sex life, and I hate to put a damper on it, but..." No. Too direct. Maybe, "Hi, it's just little ol' me, dropping off a message..." At last, she decided to try letting them in on something she'd overheard the big, bad manager say. Okay—so she took the cowardly way out and stretched the truth a bit, but that seemed like the only option she could handle. So she knocked.

A long silence followed. She wondered whether to knock again or forget it when, a moment later, the door opened. Gwyneth, the younger one, greeted her with a cheery smile. "Howdy, Merry. What brings you all the way up here?" She wore a long, bohemian-looking, embroidered black skirt and a black crushed-velvet top. Her long red hair looked pretty yet unsophisticated pulled back on the sides with the rest of it hanging in curling tendrils around her shoulders and down her back.

"I wanted to tell you something kind of important. I hope I'm not disturbing you."

"Oh, no. Not at all. Come on in!"

Merry stepped through the door and Morgaine rounded

the corner. "What a nice surprise. How are you feeling, Merry?" Morgaine seemed to be in her thirties with the same bohemian style, but her hair hung loose and straight. A shiny eagle feather tucked behind her ear gave her the atypical appearance of a gothic Native American.

"I'm feeling much better, thanks. It was just sort of unnerving, especially since I'd only moved in the day before. What an introduction to city life!"

"Yeah, you must have felt like you were caught with your pants down." She gasped. "Lordy, I shouldn't let my mouth overload my tail. What I meant was, you musta thought about turnin' around and movin' right out, huh?" Gwyneth's fair complexion turned bright red.

"I admit it occurred to me. But I've waited too long for this to just turn tail and run. It doesn't happen a lot around here, does it?"

"No, and good for you," Morgaine said. "Your attack was the first on our block as far as I know."

"Lucky me."

Gwyneth added, "Now as far as people movin' in and right out, that happens, but only in apartment 3A across the hall."

"Hmm… Maybe it's haunted or something?"

Gwyneth looked to Morgaine, who nodded.

"Would you like to sit down, Merry? We can get you a beer or something…"

"Oh, no, thanks. I have to go back to my apartment and get some sleep. I just wanted to sort of warn you that Dottie's on the warpath about some loud noises coming from your apartment."

The women's eyes widened. "Noise? What kind of noise?" Gwyneth asked.

"She said 'hooting and hollering.' Oh, and 'screaming,' I believe."

The women looked at each other, and Gwyneth flinched.

"And she was telling you this because…?" Morgaine asked.

"Oh, no. She was talking to Jason. She wanted him to talk to you about it, but he was embarrassed. He's a really nice guy and I didn't want to see him squirm, so I said I'd tell you. It's no big deal. I mean, I think it's great that you two are so into each other and have such gratifying sex."

Morgaine straightened and stared. Gwyneth slapped a hand over her mouth. At last the uncomfortable silence shattered when the two women burst out laughing.

Merry cocked her head, confused about what she had said that amused them so much. Eventually the pair settled down and Morgaine spoke.

"We're not lesbians, Merry. We're phone-sex actresses. Sometimes the guys want us to pretend we're getting off too, so they can feel all pumped up about how *virile* they are."

"Virtually virile, she means," Gwyneth drawled.

"Oh! So that's how you make your living?" *Well, that was unexpected.*

"That among other things. It's not like we can really keep it down much. It's what pays the rent. I don't suppose Dottie would care, even if she knew that."

Merry shrugged one shoulder. "Probably not. But maybe there's some kind of soundproofing Jason could look into."

"Some what?" Gwyneth asked.

"Soundproofing—between your two apartments."

Merry glanced around and noticed a lack of carpeting. "In the meantime, maybe you could put down some rugs as a noise dampener?"

Gwyneth nodded. "We could try it."

"Anything to keep the wicked witch of 2B happy, right?" Merry winked conspiratorially.

The women raised their eyebrows, then burst out laughing again.

Now what did I say?

Chapter 3

JASON HANDED A BEER TO HIS UNCLE, TOOK A SEAT ON his low side chair, and stretched out his legs. "How's it going?"

"With me? You know. Same old, same old. I thought I'd see if your life was more interesting."

Jason chuckled. "Well, tonight I got to know one of my tenants better... a lot better."

Ralph leaned forward. "Tell me all about it."

"Merry, the nurse who recently moved in, came for dinner. Jeez, I almost came in my pants while we were making out on the couch."

Ralph laughed. "Glad to hear it. But in a way, that's why I decided to pay you a visit. We need to talk."

"Talk? About my love life?"

Ralph rested his elbows on his knees. "I know this is something you'd probably rather hear from your father, but I'm here and he isn't, so I'm taking it upon myself to have *the talk* with you."

Jason's eyes rounded. "You mean the birds and the bees? Uncle Ralph, I'm twenty-seven years old. I've known about sex since I was eleven."

Ralph chuckled but quickly turned serious. "Not *that* talk. The one specifically connected to our family genetics."

"Oh, yeah. I suppose that's a talk we could have."

"Ever since you were a little boy, girls have followed you around and been fairly forward with you. Your dad asked me to keep an eye on you here and make sure no one got too close—for your own good."

Jason reared back. "What the… So am I never supposed to have the love and trust of a good woman? Just because you two think you know what's good for me?"

"I'm not saying that. I'm just saying you need to be careful. This girl seems like a real sweetheart. The kind of girl you could fall in love with."

"Yeah, and?"

Ralph looked him in the eye. "And that makes you vulnerable."

"I know all about the changes love and sex bring to the picture for those like us."

"She's vulnerable too. This is her home now. If things don't work out, living here might be uncomfortable, but it could be even worse for you if things progress."

Jason folded his arms and frowned. "How's that?"

"If she learns the family secret. You need to be very careful not to show her that side of yourself."

"Even if things don't move forward romantically with Merry, and it looks like they just might, she's already becoming a good friend. She said she'd go to the bachelor auction I was pressured into and bid on me. I really need that to happen. I get into trouble when I'm stressed out."

Ralph slapped his knee. "That's exactly what I'm talking about."

"Don't worry. I wouldn't dare tell her my deep dark secret yet. She might freak and I definitely *don't* want that to happen. But she seems open-minded. Maybe, if we get close first, she'll understand."

"I doubt it. Your mother was one in a million. Your

father was extremely lucky. To expect to find a woman like that is like expecting lightning to strike twice in the same spot."

"So, you're saying that if I get close to a woman, *any* woman, I should *never* share my unique condition?" This little chat was annoying Jason more and more by the minute.

"Yes. Look, as much as I hate to put it this way, you're just a half-breed. You might not experience the same control over your instincts—especially if you let a woman into your life. That's the time we're tested the most. You're not as strong as the rest of us."

Jason shook his head. He knew the instincts his uncle referred to and he experienced the same feelings as much as any other full-blooded family member. But his uncle was right. He didn't have the solid control over his condition that was needed—especially during biological changes. Adolescence had been a double nightmare.

"So, you never told Aunt Dottie?"

Ralph burst out laughing.

Jason waited until his uncle settled down. "You're wrong about Merry. She wants to take stress *off*. She did me a big favor by speaking to some noisy tenants for me… or, more accurately, for Aunt Dottie who had already talked to them. I guess the noise continued. Now Dottie wants to use me as the *muscle,* and I really don't want to be cast in that role." Jason hung his head. "I thought being a landlord would be easy. What was I thinking?"

Ralph took a long swig of his beer. "I'll talk to Dottie. Meanwhile, be extra careful with Merry. Enjoy her friendship, but leave it at that."

"I'm not sure I can."

"Well then, test her first. See how she handles stress herself. You know the fight or flight instinct?"

"What's that got to do with anything?"

"Your father and I had another brother, remember? Until he revealed his secret and his girl ran off. You know what happened after that. Maybe if he'd known that's how she handled bad news…"

Jason paused, mulling it over, then said, "I guess a test might be a good idea. I was thinking I might offer to visit the patients at Merry's hospital and sign autographs. The bonus was supposed to be spending more time with her. But seeing her in action might be a good idea too. So far, everything about her is positive, but there has to be a downside. No one's perfect."

"Exactly."

"So, you want me to test her?" Jason asked. "How?"

"Her job sounds stressful and stress can bring out the worst in anybody. Just watch carefully. See how she handles whatever comes her way."

Jason secretly hoped to see her stay and "fight," not run from stressful situations. At that moment, a knock on his door meant the most imperfect person in the building had returned.

Ralph jumped up. "Don't tell her I'm here. I'll be in your bathroom. I have to go anyway."

Jason said, "We can continue this later," and waited until his uncle was hidden before he answered the door. "Aunt Dottie… Two visits in one night? Don't tell me they're still at it."

"No." She breezed past him, uninvited. "I came to say thank you for speaking to them. And what a good idea… romancing the new girl."

"Good idea? What do you mean?"

"I mean that she won't sue you if you're her lover."

"Jeez, Dottie, is that all you can think about? I don't think she's going to sue me—and we're not lovers yet."

"By the looks of things, you would have been if I hadn't interrupted. Oh, I'm sorry about that, by the way."

"Apology accepted. Maybe you can leave messages on my voice mail or tape notes to my door from now on."

She frowned. "Are you saying you don't want me in your apartment?"

Jason tucked his hands into his pockets and shifted his weight, rocking from his heels to the balls of his feet and back. "Look, it's not that. I appreciate it if I'm away and need this rainforest watered..." He pointed to the massive palms and ficus trees by the windows. "But if I'm home, I should be able to take care of the apartment myself and there are other ways to reach me."

"In other words, you don't want me in here. I suppose you don't want me straightening up the place, either."

"Yeah, I was going to talk to you about that too. I can hire a housekeeper. You already have a place to clean. Plus you do the hallways—"

"Well, it isn't any bother. You should save your money for a rainy day. You can't play baseball forever."

"I know, Aunt Dottie, I know. I'm already taking steps to insure some income in my retirement."

"Like what?"

"Well, there's the investment in this building."

"You won't see a profit from this place for quite a while. It must have cost a mint. Plus Ralph says the plumbing needs to be updated. What if an injury took you out of the game permanently?"

"I know that's always a possibility, but I have other things in the works too."

"Like?"

"I have stocks."

"The stock market is terrible, or haven't you noticed?"

He fidgeted uncomfortably. "Of course I've noticed. But there are other things I can do to make money."

"For instance?"

"Well, my manager told me to keep some notes in a folder in case later I want to write my memoirs."

"Really?" Her eyes lit up. "Can I see them?"

"No!" *Crap, that was about the worst thing I could have said to an old busybody.* He shook his head. "No, it's just a bunch of disjointed notes, not very interesting."

"Wait a minute… You're going to share it with the world, but not me? Maybe I can help. I was a decent writer in high school. You were no Rhodes Scholar. I'm sure I could make it a lot less, well, grammatically incorrect."

"I'll have an editor for that. And if it stinks, they'll hire a professional ghost writer, I'm sure."

"Fine," she said casually. Dottie shivered. "Why is it always so damn cold in here?"

Chad had just caught the end of this conversation. *If only the guy was psychic, he could have a* real *ghost writer. That would be more fun than just watching live humans get themselves into train wreck after train wreck. Although, I have to admit, that's fun, too. I can't wait until his Aunt sneaks in and looks all over for his notes.*

At last her hand reached for the doorknob, but just before she left, she said, "Oh, and I might have a renter for 3A. Some bio-physic-something-or-other professor."

"Good. Thanks, Aunt Dot."

Chad gasped. *3A! That's my place! Well, we'll just see about that.*

As soon as she closed the door behind her, Jason rushed to his computer and changed his passwords.

"All aboard, folks!"

Jason assisted his date onto the Boston Duck Tour vehicle and whispered something to the tour guide.

"I've always wanted to do this." Merry grinned.

"Why haven't you?"

"Well, it's not exactly around the corner from Rhode Island, and it seemed like I was always busy whenever my friend Roz and I thought about going."

Jason took her hand. "C'mon, let's sit in the back-facing seats."

"Isn't it colder out there?"

"Don't worry, I'll keep you warm."

Merry happily followed him to the end of the big yellow duck. They found seats and Jason wrapped one long arm around her back and cuddled her.

"All ready to go?" their *conDUCKtor* asked.

Jason gave a thumbs-up signal.

Merry raised her eyebrows. "Why are we the only ones on the tour?"

"Because I bought all the tickets." He gave her a side-squeeze. "I thought we could talk and get to know each other better without a bunch of eavesdroppers."

"Oh." Merry knew he could afford it, but did he give her the real reason for wanting the whole thing to themselves, or was he throwing money around just to impress her? *Either way works for me.* She chuckled. "Okay, what do you want to know?"

The amphibious bus pulled out of the parking area and onto the street.

"Well, for starters, why do you look more like a Martinez than a MacKenzie?"

"Ah, that's easy. I was adopted. My mother wanted a daughter, had two boys, and then talked my father into adopting me from a local Catholic organization. I know I have Portuguese ancestors, but I don't know any other details about my birth parents."

"That makes sense. Any curiosity on your part about finding your birth parents?"

"None at all. I've wondered about them, but as far as I'm concerned, my dad and late mom *are* my parents."

"Matt is younger, so they decided to have more?"

"My teenage brother was a last minute surprise. He has ADHD and the little wack-job drives me crazy half the time, but I saw to it he did his chores, finished his homework, and went to school unless he had a fever of one hundred and one. He finally graduated from high school this past June—with honors!"

Despite the way she spoke about him, she hoped Jason could tell that she was extremely fond of Matt. "He's the reason I didn't become spoiled. That honor always goes to the youngest."

His jaw dropped. "So you helped raise him?"

She shrugged. "I just did what any good sister would do."

"Man, that's a lot to ask of a kid. How old were you two when your mom passed away?"

"Matt was eight and I was sixteen. I stepped into

the role of caretaker—but couldn't replace my mother. While my family recovered emotionally, and it came time to go to college, I commuted. I continued to live at home while working and finally decided it was time to leave the nest before I was old and gray and wondered what had happened to my life."

"Wow. Even giving up nine years of it to raise Matt was a lot."

"I know. I didn't mind, really. It was important. But if I stayed any longer it would've just become harder and harder to leave as time went on. Especially for my father."

"I'm glad you decided to move—and even happier that you moved into *my* building."

The way he looked at her sent shivers down her spine. He seemed to be feeling a combination of pride, admiration, and something else. His eyes had taken on a soft glow.

"By the way," he said, "I'm thinking of going furniture shopping. Would you like to come along and help me pick out colors that go together? I'm not very good at that."

"Are you sure? You seem like a stylish dresser. So far I haven't seen any striped pants with plaid shirts and polka-dotted sweater vests."

He laughed. "I wear solids so I don't have to worry about prints clashing, and my uniform isn't much of a challenge."

"When were you thinking of going?"

"Tomorrow?"

"That's the day I was planning to go out to lunch and shopping with my friend, Roz."

"Oh, well, maybe some other time. It was mostly an excuse to spend more time with you, anyway."

Merry's cheeks heated. "You sure are a charmer."

"Nah."

"Ah ha! I knew you were too good to be true."

"What do you mean?"

"I've been waiting for some kind of imperfection to show up. Liar, liar, pants on fire."

He raised his eyebrows. Either that was so immature it bothered him or... oh, maybe they *were* on fire, figuratively speaking. She glanced at his crotch. *Yup, a nice big bulge right at the intersection of said pants.*

The giant "duck" rolled into the water of the Charles River. As its tires left the boat ramp, the vehicle floated. The breeze picked up and chilled him, so Jason zipped up his jacket. He'd caught Merry stealing a glimpse at the tent in his pants before he covered it, though. Not that he wasn't proud of his assets, but it was damn cold. *Better hide it before there's any shrinkage.*

"Want to go inside?" he asked.

"Sure, but when we sit down, can it be my turn to ask the questions?"

He smiled. "Turnabout is fair play—as they say."

The tour guide had apparently been told to take the night off from commentary. He smiled as the couple reseated themselves and remained quiet. Then he turned his back and let them have their privacy again.

Jason took the opportunity to cup Merry's cheek and give her a tender kiss. She melted into him and wrapped both arms around his back. They fit as if they were made for each other. Her lips were so soft and kissing her warmed him like no jacket could.

Jason knew he was falling fast and hard, but for some reason putting on the brakes felt like the wrong thing to do. When they finally pulled apart, she sighed and said, "You're very good at that."

"So are you."

"I doubt I've had nearly as much practice as you've had. You must inspire me."

He smiled, then kissed her on her forehead. *Better move on to another subject.* "So what else did you want to know about me?"

"Oh, I don't know. What's important to you — besides baseball?"

"Yeah, that's pretty much a given. I like other sports, too. I played football back in high school. I like to swim. When I finally had to concentrate on one thing, it wasn't hard to decide. Baseball is where my heart has always been."

"Swimming, huh? I love to swim too. I grew up near the beach and my parents felt we all needed to learn to swim as early as possible, for safety if nothing else. Where did you swim in land-locked Minnesota?"

"I guess you don't know our state's nickname. Land of Ten Thousand Lakes?"

"Oh, yeah. That sounds familiar now."

"My family had a place on Lake Superior. You'd be surprised how much it resembles the ocean. Complete with lighthouses, fishing boats, and seagulls."

"I'd love to go there someday. But then, I'd love to go anywhere. I've never been out of New England, except for a couple of trips to New York."

"Seriously?" Jason caught himself, but it was probably too late. He didn't mean to point out how unworldly she was.

"I guess you've traveled all over the country."

He laughed. "Yeah, I've seen quite a bit of this big mud ball we live on."

"More than the United States?"

"Yeah, besides Canada and Mexico, I've been to Europe, Russia, and Japan."

"Japan? You're kidding! When did you go there?"

"In college. Baseball is a huge sport in Japan, and I was curious about the place."

"So you just up and went there?"

"Yup."

"By yourself?"

"Yup."

"And Europe? Where did you go in Europe?"

"All over."

"Really? How?"

He shrugged. "Frequent flyer miles." *If she only knew.*

"Wow. I don't think I'd have the guts."

"Then I'll have to take you with me and show you the world."

She grinned and her perfect, white smile lit up the night. Jason really did want to show her the world—his world. And he wanted her in it from now on.

"Yes, you can come over and see it any time tomorrow. I'm the manager and I should be home all day." Dottie twisted the telephone cord in her hand as she spoke to a prospective renter.

Chad was leaning against the wall, in an incorporeal sort of way, listening in with great interest. *Oh, great. She wasn't kidding. Some poor shlub will rent the place, move in, and I'll have to scare him off. Or maybe I can discourage whoever wants to live there before that. I hope the new landlord will catch on eventually and leave my apartment alone. The old owner finally gave up trying to rent it.*

"It's been empty for quite some time, so I'll just do a little vacuuming and dusting before you get here."

I like my dust right where it is, woman. You leave my dust alone.

"Yes, I manage the place and my husband takes care of any maintenance needed, but I do a little light house-keeping outside the units too."

Naturally. It's so much easier to eavesdrop that way.

"Oh, it's no bother. It keeps me out of trouble." She chuckled.

That's debatable. Wasn't it enough that I let her store a few things in my living room? Now she wants to take away the only place I can go for complete peace and quiet. I can't go to the attic anymore. It's now a penthouse. I can't go to the basement. It's a laundry room and vampire lair. Just where am I supposed to have my hip pad? I refuse to haunt a cardboard box in the alley.

"I'll see you at two o'clock, then. I know you're a professor and probably very trustworthy, but please bring references and paystubs as proof of employment, anyway. Oh, and you know the security deposit is one month's rent, right?"

She ought to make it two and a half. After I get through with him, the place might not look the same.

———～～～———

"It was so nice of you to offer to visit my patients and cheer them up. I'm sure they'll love getting your autograph!" In the hospital elevator, Merry stood on tiptoes and kissed Jason's cheek. "Not to mention I'll probably rise in popularity among the staff."

"Just don't tell them where I live. That's all I ask." He draped an arm around her. "If all goes well, I might come back another evening."

"Hey, if all goes *really* well, I might get on the day shift!"

"Is that what you want to do?"

"God, yes. I'd love to have my evenings free like normal people." *And come home in daylight… especially after the incident in the alley.*

The elevator doors whooshed open and they stepped out onto the corridor that led to the hospital's pediatric orthopedics floor.

"I'll have to go in to report first, but one of the day shift nurses can tell you which patients are well enough to receive visitors. Report only takes about half an hour."

He stopped walking. "Oh. I thought I'd get a chance to go into your patients' rooms with you."

She tipped her head and asked, "You aren't shy, are you? I haven't been here for a couple of days, so I'm not sure which patients would be up for a visit. Of course, if you don't mind waiting until after report…"

"Whatever works for you is okay with me. You go do what you have to do. I'm sure I'll find some casts to sign."

She grinned. "I'm sure you will, too. And a lot of parents will be visiting, so you'll have plenty of people to keep you occupied." She winked. "Don't worry. I won't desert you for long."

They rounded the corner, arriving at the nurse's

station. Merry spotted two of the day shift nurses finishing their notes. Angie always sashayed around like she thought of herself as a femme fatale and Sam, though you'd never know it, was gay. Merry doubted that either one of them would know Jason by sight, so she opened her mouth to introduce him.

Before she uttered a word, Angie looked up and gasped.

"Jason Falco! Oh my God! What are you do—Never mind. What a fantastic surprise!" She rushed around the nurse's station and hugged him without asking if he minded.

Shocked speechless, Merry observed the blonde bombshell hanging all over him and telling him what an adoring fan she was. The green-eyed monster rose higher in Merry's psyche than the Green Monster backfield wall she had heard of, bringing with it uncomfortable prickles up her spine. *Is this how dating him will be? Is that why he just introduced himself as a 'friend of Merry's' rather than my boyfriend? Terrific.*

Sam ambled around the desk and stuck out his hand. As he and Jason shook hands, Angie sidled over to Merry and whispered, "How do you know him?"

Too angry to speak, Merry gritted her teeth and didn't answer. What could she say? He had told her not to mention they lived in the same building. Now she didn't even want Angie to know they lived in the same neighborhood—or the same state! How many unwelcome guests would that bring to her apartment? Angie wasn't known for her ability to keep secrets.

She had to think of a way to send Angie away. Preferably to another planet, but on the other side of the desk would have to do.

"Ah, Ange, would you please make a list of the patients who would like a visit from Jason? I haven't been on for a couple of days, and I'd appreciate someone else who knows their conditions speaking to them first."

Angie hooked her arm through Jason's and said in her syrupy sweet voice, "Why don't I take him around with me? There's no need for a list."

Hell's bells. That backfired.

Jason glanced at Merry and must have seen the annoyed look on her face. He said, "I'm sorry, Merry promised to take me around—if you don't mind."

Merry wanted to kiss him. Maybe this type of behavior was what made him uncomfortable about events like the bachelor auction. Now Merry wouldn't miss it if she had to be wheeled in on a stretcher.

Angie looked crestfallen and dropped his arm. "Oh. All right. I guess you can go around with whoever you want...." She rolled her eyes.

Merry quickly pointed to the family lounge. "There's a place where you can wait for me. Or you can go to the coffee shop and come back later if you'd rather."

"I'd rather not walk into a roomful of strangers in case I'm recognized and stampeded." He smiled as if making a joke, but maybe he wasn't. "So I'll just wait over there." He nodded toward the lounge, stuffed his hands in his pockets, and strolled into the room.

Naturally, an excited shriek followed. "Jason Falco!" someone exclaimed.

—⁓—

The following day, Chad watched as Dottie—appropriately nicknamed—met the would-be new tenant at the bottom of the stairs. "Would-be," since Chad had a plan to discourage new renters. This one happened to be a professor from the high tech university across the river. *Good. Probably someone who doesn't believe in ghosts. I love a challenge.*

Dottie eyed the disheveled looking man wearing ripped jeans and a faded green jacket on the other side of the door and before opening it, she yelled through the thick glass inset window.

"State your business."

"State your business?" Chad rolled his eyes. *She sounds like a cop. Maybe she was a pig back in Minnesota. Come to think of it, I could see her in an interrogation room making suspects squirm with all of her funky questions and crazy conclusions.*

The man's eyes narrowed and he yelled, "I'm supposed to meet the manager to see an apartment. Is it still for rent?"

She paused, frowning, as if she didn't believe him, gave him the once over, then exhaled loudly and opened the door. Chad thought she must have been expecting a pipe-smoking, tweed blazer–wearing, clean-cut, bespectacled man.

She held the door for him and he skirted around it as if she might slam it in his face. She was making Chad's job too easy! If he didn't drive the professor off, Dottie would.

She led him to the elevator and punched the button. Chad wasn't crazy about riding elevators. Being in spirit form, he had to time his ascent and landing just right so he wouldn't wind up on the other side of the floor or ceiling.

He managed the take-off and stuck the landing just fine. *Whew. Why spend the energy to penetrate solid objects like walls, when it's so much easier just to zip into spaces when the doors open? Plus it's fun to see people shiver if I happen to touch them.* He laughed to himself.

He'd have given this guy a nice chill down the back of his neck, but a collar and long, curly hair covered the sensitive skin there. The professor didn't bother removing his jacket.

Chad liked the place nice and cool, and it was a good thing since the owners didn't like wasting oil and kept it just warm enough to prevent the pipes from freezing.

The boxes had been moved from the living room to the closets. While he strolled down the hall, Chad used his telekinesis to open the closet door. That task presented no challenge. He could give it a good slam, too, but would wait until they were in the room so they could see it close with no draft.

He managed to move one of the boxes right into the traffic pattern. *There, now when they round the corner, someone will trip over it and fall splat. That'll be far-out.*

Now that gravity was no longer his problem, he loved watching people fall down. If they were even a tiny bit psychic, they'd hear him laughing his ass off.

I have to let them know the unit's previous owner bought the farm right here in his living room and isn't happy about it. Heh heh. I get what little revenge I can.

He still couldn't get over how they had explained his cause of death. It was officially listed as cardiac arrest. Well, sure. When a bullet enters the brain, the heart stops. *Voila.* Cardiac arrest.

He had been a journalist in the sixties and lived in interesting times. Protest marches, riots, and LSD were some of the stories he had covered. Unfortunately, so were conspiracy theories, and one of those had landed him in hot water with the Feds. *Me and my fucking integrity and first amendment rights.* The public deserved to know the truth, but as he found out, someone didn't agree with that.

The story never came to light. Back then, he used an actual typewriter and had been working on the piece at home. He was dedicated. Laboring under a false sense of security, he hadn't used the dead-bolt and two guys broke down the door. One held him at gunpoint while another confiscated all of his notes and the unfinished story. Chad tried to fight back.

If I ever find out who tipped them off, I'll kick his wrinkly old ass. And, speaking of kicking asses, they were coming back toward the living room.

Making eye-contact, Dottie was grilling the professor about his daily habits—if he played loud music, held wild parties, etc. She completely missed seeing the box in front of her, tripped, flipped, and landed spread-eagle on the gleaming hardwood.

Bull's-eye!

Chad laughed so hard he forgot to slam the closet door.

—◌◌◌—

Jason had shown up at Merry's apartment a little early to prepare her for the bachelor auction. He only had a couple of hours before the event and a vague, uncomfortable feeling had descended upon him. Ever since he had visited her hospital, he wondered if she could tolerate his celebrity and the challenges it would bring. She teased him about it and seemed okay afterward, but they had only run into a forward female fan once—so far.

They had spent a lot of time together over the past two weeks. Now it seemed as if he had known her forever.

If she was the jealous type, this meat market might be painful. He wanted to reassure her that, regardless of what happened, she was his girl. But if she couldn't handle the possible cat calls and attention he'd be receiving, knowing that sooner rather than later would be helpful.

He cupped her cheek and leaned in for a light kiss. She twined her arms around his neck, which invited another.

Jason felt his arousal brimming and knew that soon, very soon, he wanted to take their relationship to the next level. But it would be better to wait until after tonight—after he witnessed how she'd deal with the auction. Jealousy in a mate could be very tiresome, especially with his lifestyle.

But life is funny. As he gazed at her, he realized that *he* might wind up being the jealous one. She was a knockout in her little black dress and high-heeled pumps. Earrings that were thin chains of diamonds gently cascaded almost to her collarbones, and with her hair swept up, her long, graceful neck begged to be kissed.

He was just about to push one of her earrings out of the way so he could trail kisses from her ear to her shoulder when flashing blue lights lit up the windows in her apartment.

"Crap. Not again!"

Merry sighed. "Maybe it's something else. The

college kids across the street are kind of loud. After all, it *is* Halloween."

"I doubt that's why they're here." He strode out into the hall and called up the stairs. "Aunt Dottie, did you call the police?"

She trotted down the single flight of stairs and asked, "Are they finally here? It's about time."

Jason saw them coming up the cement walk and backed into Merry's apartment. "Why did you call them *this* time?"

"I saw someone skulking around outside. He looked sketchy."

"Is he still out there?"

She shrugged. "Maybe. I can't see him anymore, but I want someone to take a look."

Jason sighed. "Well, leave me out of it, okay?" He shut the door.

Merry folded her arms and tipped her head. "Does your aunt know why you're not crazy about the cops coming here every couple of weeks?"

"I'm sure she must."

"Have you ever said anything to her *directly* about protecting your privacy?"

He stared at the ceiling and seemed to mull it over. Then he looked at her, shrugged and said, "I thought I did. Maybe she didn't hear me."

"If there's one thing nursing has taught me, it's to communicate clearly. Confusion that isn't clarified can lead to all kinds of misunderstandings—and sometimes dangerous mistakes."

"Yeah, I guess I can see where being assertive might come in handy, especially in your field. I guess I've gotten used to keeping my mouth shut and letting other people fight my battles for me."

"Really? Like who?"

"Referees, agents, coaches, managers…"

"You're kidding. What do you do if your steak is undercooked in a restaurant? Get one of them to send it back?"

"I eat it anyway. There's no such thing as a bad steak." He grinned.

She leaned toward him and looked him right in the eye. "You do that a lot, you know."

"What?"

"Avoid the question by making a joke. What about female fans who want to manhandle you?"

He grasped her arms and looked her in the eye. "Merry, it happens. I won't lie to you. It's always an uncomfortable situation for me since I don't want to offend them while extricating myself. You never want your fans telling everyone they think you're an ass. I usually joke my way out of it. That's why I want you to buy me tonight. Here." He reached into his pocket and extracted a money clip, fat with green bills. "This should be enough." He had loaded the clip with Benjamins but knew the bidding could go high. He was a celebrity who looked pretty damn good in a tux.

Merry tucked the cash in her clutch purse. "Are you sure you want me to spend all this?"

"It's for charity. Spend it and feel good about it."

A knock on the door interrupted their conversation. Jason rolled his eyes.

"I'll get it," Merry said. "After all, it *is* my apartment." She smiled as if trying to reassure him of her protection.

Jason wasn't sure what he should do. He didn't want to hide in the kitchen like a coward. If someone recognized him, he could always say he had come to pick up his date and no one would have to know he lived there… if Dottie could keep her mouth shut.

Yeah, Merry was right. He really did have to tell his aunt specifically not to alert the world to his location by calling the cops at the drop of a hat, and then reinforce that message as often as necessary.

Merry opened the door and said, "Sly?"

"You know this man?" one of the officers asked.

"Yes. He saved my life a couple of weeks ago." She stepped into the hall and shook the stranger's hand. "I wanted to thank you, but I haven't seen you since that night."

"How've you been?" he asked as casually as if one cop didn't have a vice grip on his arm and the other one wasn't barring the door behind him. Dottie made a disgusted sound and marched back upstairs.

"I'm fine. Thanks to you."

The cop holding Sly asked, "What do you mean he saved your life?"

Sly spoke up quickly. "It was nothing. A misunderstanding that could have gotten out of hand, but it didn't. I intervened."

At first Merry hesitated, and then as if she'd just remembered the cops weren't supposed to know about her near-rape she chuckled and said, "Yeah, that's all it was. I can be a bit of a drama queen. It was just a misunderstanding."

"You sure?" the cop at the door asked.

"Yes, it was nothing, really."

Jason studied the man that must have been Dottie's suspicious character "skulking around" outside. He didn't seem homeless. He was well-dressed in an open-collared black shirt, black trousers, and an expensive-looking black wool coat. "What's the problem, officers?" Jason asked.

"Someone called about a prowler."

Sly laughed. "I was leaning against the fence having a cigarette. Not prowling." He made eye contact with the officer a little longer than necessary and said, "So, I'm free to go, right?"

The cop said, "As long as this woman can vouch for you."

Merry nodded. "I vouch."

"Okay," the cop holding his arm let him go with a warning. "Find another fence to lean against as you have your smokes or, better yet, quit. It's a filthy habit."

"Yes, sir," Sly said and saluted.

The guy seemed awfully cavalier for someone detained by police. After the cops left, he turned toward Merry and said, "Well, nice seeing you again. I'll be on my way now."

"Would you like to come in for some coffee? It's pretty chilly out there tonight."

He glanced at each of them and said, "Maybe some other time. It looks like you and your boyfriend are going out on the town."

Jason placed a possessive arm around her waist. "Yes, we were just getting ready to leave."

"So long." Sly waved. "Oh! Before I forget. You know there was someone else skulking around out there in the bushes, right?"

"There was? Why didn't you say anything?"

"Because the person took off as soon as they nabbed me, and if I said 'Oh, it's not me… it's the other prowler you want,' they'd buy that sometime after they bought the Mass Avenue Bridge."

"Do you know who it was?"

Sly shrugged. "Nope. It was a woman with a knit cap pulled over her hair. She may have been a private detective trying to catch a cheating spouse or jealous ex-girlfriend stalker or something. She had a camera. Well, have a nice night." As soon as he had jogged down the outside steps, he seemed to disappear into the darkness.

"With my luck," Jason muttered, "it's the paparazzi."

Something about Sly didn't feel right. It was more than his attitude or dark hair and pale skin. It had nothing to do with jealousy, even though he seemed overly interested in Merry. There was *something* about his black, glittering eyes. The man oozed danger.

―⁕―

Well, the nutty professor signed the lease anyway. He must be nuts if he thinks I'm going to let him stay here.

So far, Chad had made sure a champagne cork hit the new tenant in the eye, he'd dimmed and brightened the lights at inopportune times, and slammed every door in the place, and all the professor did was explain it away with logic.

Bummer. I'll have to try harder.

He wished he could show himself somehow. *He's not psychic, that's for sure, so I doubt he'd bother with infrared cameras.*

Chad only knew two people in the building aware of

his existence and only one he could speak to—Morgaine, the witch from across the hall. *Maybe when she's in a trance I can talk her into getting this dude to split.*

Of course, there was always the landlord and his girl-friend. Chad had heard them talking about paranormal phenomena recently and it seemed as if the nurse had seen some strange things while working at night in a hospital. Maybe he could try to get her attention and see if she responded to anything.

She had mentioned a room that was used only to house supplies after a number of children had reported seeing the same man, dressed in black, watching them from the end of their beds. He'd have thought the grim reaper might be checking up on their conditions, but she said the man always wore a hat. *Old Grim wouldn't be caught dead in a hat. Ha ha ha.* His pun just occurred to him.

As Chad mulled the situation over, the professor returned "home" to the apartment. *I won't bother learning his name since he'll be freaking out and leaving soon.*

He had brought a female friend with him. She was oddly dressed, though. She looked like a throwback to Chad's generation... the sixties. She wore a long tie-dyed dress and clogs and her hair was long, loose, and mousy brown with gray strands coming in. *I didn't think geeks had girlfriends. Shows how much I know.*

She closed her eyes and stood in the middle of the room.

Ah ha! He brought a psychic! I knew she couldn't be a girlfriend. So far the professor hadn't impressed him as boyfriend material. He spent all his time on the Internet. And he surfed the most boring sites. He grooved on sci-ence and space, mostly. *If he spent even half the time looking at porn, I might consider letting him stay—and that's a big maybe*. But he was of no use whatsoever as far as Chad was concerned.

The psychic was taking a series of deep cleansing breaths and going into a trance.

"Spirits inhabiting this place, can you hear me?"

What should I do? Answer her? Or perhaps it would be more fun to simply stay quiet so she tells the professor that nobody's home and he thinks he's going nuts.

"Give me a sign that you are here. I can help you move on."

Move on? Don't tell me she's going to open up a path to the light and ask me to go into it! Hey, if they wanted me there, they would have invited me long ago. I have a mind to cross my virtual arms and pout, then maybe she'll go away.

She stayed in her trance. He was glad. He hadn't been looking at things logically. If he wanted the professor out, what better way than to use her voice and scare the shit out of both of them? It wasn't the easiest thing to do, but if she was open to it, he might be able to sink into her head and control her speech. *Okay, I've never done this before, so I might not succeed, but it's worth a shot.*

Chad gathered his consciousness at the top of her head and descended. *Man, this is the weirdest feeling. It's all warm and squishy in here! Gross.*

She must not have liked it either, since she squirmed a bit, then straightened and shivered.

Chad glanced down. *Hey—look at me. I have boobs! Nice ones, too*. He chuckled. *All right. Let's see what I can do.*

He tried to align his breathing with hers, first. Then he made her breathe heavily, to add to the drama. As soon as he felt ready, he said in a low, angry voice. "You... must... leave—or die!"

The professor's eyes rounded and looked like they were about to pop out of his head. *Good, I have his attention.*

"Get... out."

The professor stood there, frozen to the spot.

"Get... out! Get out, get out, *get out!*"

He tore out of the apartment and ran for the stairs. Apparently he didn't want to take the elevator and risk that it might be too slow. Chad had to leave the psychic's mind before he started laughing. It was all he could do to hold it in while he squeezed through her gray matter and pushed his way out.

She slumped, straightened, and her body language said she was dazed and a little confused. She looked around the room and spotted the open door. Leaving the apartment, she closed the door softly and apparently forgot all about telling Chad to go toward the light. *Ah, sweet victory!*

Chapter 4

Paparazzi reporter Lila Crum claimed her favorite barstool at the Bay Plaza Hotel and raised her hand in greeting to the bartender. She pulled off her knit cap and tossed it onto the bar. In the mirror, she saw her short, straight, brown hair standing on end with static electricity. She rolled her eyes and patted it back down.

"Hey, Lila. How're things?" Kevin, her favorite tall, lean, not-bad-looking bartender was always interested in her life.

Her shoulders slumped and she leaned forward, resting her elbows on the long wooden bar. "Not good. Bring me the usual, Kevin. I need a double this time, though."

"Uh-oh. Coming right up."

She watched as he poured, making sure he gave her as much rum as she wanted in her Coke. It sucked to be her at the moment. However, she knew that Kevin would serve up some sympathy along with her favorite comfort foods—rum and pretzels. She lived on carbohydrates these days.

"Here ya go," he said. He placed the full glass in front of her without sloshing a drop onto the bar. Good thing. At this point, she'd chase the drop around with her stirring straw until she could slurp it up.

"So, why are you acting like Santa just ran over your grandmother and took off before delivering your presents?"

"My job. I'm about to be fired."

He straightened to his full six-foot-three height and had the decency to look surprised. "Really? I'm sorry to hear that."

She shrugged. "It's not my fault that celebrities are behaving themselves. I've been searching for leads as diligently as I always do, but nothing's panned out."

"Yeah, I haven't heard about any scandals lately, either. I'd call the paper and ask for you if I did."

"I know, and thanks. I really appreciate that." She stirred her drink slowly as she continued to unburden herself. "I thought I had something on Jason Falco. At least I was able to make a few bucks on the side."

"The Bullets pitcher?"

"Yeah. Some woman who thought I was a private investigator said Falco was hanging around with a nurse who worked with her and gave me the coworker's address—wanted me to follow him and find out where he lived."

"How did she wind up thinking you were a P.I.?"

"I was eavesdropping on the staff in a hospital cafeteria. Sometimes I find celebrity sob stories, which make for interesting copy."

"Like who's in rehab?"

"Well, yeah, but that's getting to be a yawn. People don't care about yet another celebrity with a substance abuse problem unless there's an interesting twist to it—like a celebrity kid. So, anyway, I heard this nurse talking to a physical therapist about having just met Jason Falco and she wanted to know where he lived, but the bitch who knows refused to tell her. So I introduced myself. I said I couldn't help overhearing their conversation and that I could find anyone."

"So she just assumed you were a P.I.? She didn't ask to see your license or anything?"

"Well, she might have asked, and I might have just kept talking about how good I was and about how no one could hide from me." Lila found something to smile about, at last. "Anyway, I told her I'd follow the other nurse around until I found them together. Then I'd follow him to his home after he dropped her off. She gave me the woman's address and that saved a lot of time. I hid in the bushes, hoping to snap a picture of the couple together." She sighed.

"No luck, huh?"

"Not yet. I'll get a picture of whoever gets him in the bachelor auction tonight. It would be fair to assume some jealousy on the nurse's part, don't you think?"

"Sounds like the makings of a juicy story. So what's wrong?"

"Unfortunately, I lost my balance and fell out of the bushes. When I landed on something hard, I inadvertently made a noise. The cops came. Someone must have spotted me." She took a long sip of her drink. "I'm losing my touch."

Kevin gave her a sympathetic smile. "I'm sure it happens to the best of 'em."

"That's just it. I *was* the best of them. I thought my job was solid and secure. There's no loyalty anymore. It used to be that if you worked hard, your employer would cut you a break if you had a temporary setback."

"How temporary are we talking?"

"I haven't had a good story in a couple of months." She hid her face by resting her forehead on her arm. *Don't cry. How humiliating would that be? No one likes a sloppy drunk.*

"Is there anything else going on that might cause you to be fired?"

She lifted her face and ran her fingers through her hair. Catching a glimpse of herself in the mirror, she realized she looked old and tired. "You mean like the bottle of Bacardi I hide in my locked drawer?"

He nodded. Lila knew Kevin was no fool. He worked in a hotel bar, for God's sakes. How frequently did he see the same faces? Not often. So she imagined a regular customer like herself might stand out. And almost daily attendance might indicate a drinking problem.

The real problem was she didn't care what anyone thought anymore. She didn't drive, was over twenty-one, and as far as she was concerned, it was her God-given right to get shit-faced every night if she wanted to. Who was she hurting by it? No one. Well, no one but herself—especially if she couldn't get to that bachelor auction later on.

"Am I doing you any favors here, Lila?" he asked.

Fear gripped her. *He'd better not try to cut me off!* "What are you saying?"

"I mean, do you need help? I know addiction can be brutal. I don't want to see anything bad happening to you because I didn't have the balls to say something."

"But... it's not your fault. And if you shut me off, I'll just go to another bar. You can't cut me off all over town." Suddenly a horrible thought occurred to her. What if he could? *"Can you?"*

He chuckled. "No, I can't. And I won't cut you off here, either. No one can get you out of this situation but yourself. But without help, it's almost impossible. Just let me know if you want help, okay? I know some good people in AA."

"Oh." *Whew, that was a close one.* Lila shook her head. "Nah, I'm good." She took another swig of the sweet, tangy liquid that seemed like her lifeline. "Really, the best help you can give me is to keep your eyes and ears open—for other people's problems. I'm fine. *Really.* I can always get a picture of Falco and some random female. Then I can make up an angle between that person and his auction sweetie."

"Or maybe you could include the nurse in your story too and make it like he's three-timing all of them."

Lila laughed. "Three-timing? I love it. Thanks, Kevin. You just gave me my headline!"

———␣␣␣———

Halloween brings with it strange happenings. So to have a bachelor auction on Halloween night with a full moon…? Now there's an extra crazy idea. Chad knew who would show up. The weirdos. If not paranormal types, then the highest of high-maintenance women, and they'd be more motivated than usual. *I smell a supersized disaster. At least trick-or-treating will keep the single mothers at bay. Or some of them with pups may be baying at the moon.*

Jason helped Merry into her coat. As they walked toward the back door where Jason's Corvette waited, a loud crash sounded from the second floor.

The couple gawked at each other for an undecided second.

Jason said, "What the hell…?" and the two of them raced up the stairs.

At the top of the landing, a huge dog lapped up a puddle of water. Slumped beside it was the unconscious body of Dottie Falco.

"Aunt Dottie!" Jason yelled. The dog jerked his head in their direction, then maneuvered around them and bounded down the stairs. Someone on the other side of the front door opened it and he rushed out.

Jason shook his aunt until her eyes opened and she groaned.

Merry said, "Don't move her. She may have hit her head."

As soon as she'd said that, Dottie struggled to a sitting position, fighting off their help. "I'm all right. Did you see that *wolf*?"

Jason glanced at Merry. "Uh, yeah. We saw something like that. It must have been a dog, though. Last I heard, wolves aren't roaming the city."

"Oh, dear Lord, why does everyone doubt me?" she asked, pulling a handkerchief from the sleeve of her pink cardigan sweater. She dipped a corner into the water and held it to her forehead.

Merry cleared her throat. "He was drinking out of that puddle."

"Gaaaa!" Dottie jumped to her feet and backed away.

"What happened, Aunt Dottie?"

Merry liked the gentle tone he took with his aunt. Dottie had a flair for drama, but she had actually fainted so it seemed as if a little compassion was warranted.

"I heard the door open across the hall, so I peeked out the peephole and saw Konrad standing there, stark naked!"

"Are you sure? I mean, maybe he was wearing a

flesh-colored suit and fig leaves for a Halloween party. Where did the dog come from?"

"It was a *wolf,* and I don't know. I had a bottle of holy water nearby, because of… well, just in case, all right? So I grabbed it, all set to toss it onto his disgusting nakedness when I opened the door and there was a wolf! Did you say the wolf was *drinking* the holy water?"

"Where's Konrad now?" Merry asked.

Dottie shrugged, then her eyes flew open. "Do you think he *sicked* that thing on me?" She marched across the hall and banged on Konrad's door. "Open up!" She waited less than three seconds and pounded on the door again.

"He's probably gone out," Jason said. "We're about to go out too. Will you be all right? Where's Uncle Ralph?"

"He went to the convenience store for Halloween candy. I told him not to count on any trick-or-treaters, but I suspect he wants it for himself anyway."

Ralph rounded the corner at the bottom of the stairs and glanced up. "Hey, Jason." He jogged up the stairs and stopped suddenly. "Whoa." He stared appreciatively at Merry. "Well, it looks like you're headed out on a hot date. Has my wife been bothering you?"

"No, not at all." He glanced at his aunt. She stood by quietly. "She just had a little scare. She's all right, though."

"A scare, huh? What else is new?" Ralph spoke quietly behind his hand. "And she hasn't been *right* for years."

"I heard that, Ralph Falco." Dottie folded her arms and scowled.

"You were supposed to. Here." He thrust a bag of bite-size candy bars toward her. "Eat a few of these. You'll feel better. Now let's go inside and leave the kids to their night on the town." He winked at Jason. "Have fun."

In the parking lot, Jason and Merry exchanged a quick kiss before he entered the function hall by the back door, and Merry walked around to the front. Inside, she couldn't believe the crowd of noisy women all vying for seats close to the stage.

A runway had been set up so the stage took on a T formation. She imagined the guys being expected to strut their stuff down that runway and back. No wonder Jason dreaded this! She didn't think he was the type to swagger or strut.

After buying her ticket, which came with a numbered sign shaped like a ping-pong paddle, she tried to find a seat. She held number sixty-nine and smiled, hoping it was an omen of things to come.

People were still arriving. The press in attendance had good seats right up front. She noticed one woman rush in with a camera and press pass at the last minute. When she elbowed her way past Merry, they made brief eye-contact, and the woman looked away quickly—a little too quickly. Then she pushed her way into the crowd faster.

What was that about?

Merry finally spied a seat about four rows back from the end of the runway. She said, "Excuse me" a dozen times as she stepped carefully over the feet of the women already seated in that row. A woman had her large leather Prada bag sitting on the unoccupied chair.

"Excuse me, is this seat taken?"

The middle-aged woman surrounded by real fur frowned as she appraised Merry from head to toe, then said, "Can't you see that it is?"

Merry, surprised by the rudeness, didn't apologize and "accidentally" stepped on the foot of the woman as she passed. The woman gasped and displayed marked annoyance as Merry made her way to the aisle on the other side. *Okay, so Jason was right about the high-maintenance women at these things.*

At last she settled for a seat three rows from the very back of the crowded hall. Maybe if she stood while waving her sign, she'd be seen. Perhaps she should let the bidding start without her and come in only as other bidders dropped away.

Glancing around her, she noticed every type of society woman she could have imagined based on the cliché. Well-dressed, perfectly groomed examples of the "beautiful people" she had anticipated. She only noticed one woman wearing dark jeans and they were topped by a black cashmere sweater with lots of pearl detail. Her jewelry made her attempt to look casual ridiculous. Merry suspected those were *real* diamonds decorating her ears, throat, wrists, and hands. Merry's two items of sparkle were cubic zirconia.

What the heck am I doing here? She felt as if she had walked into a native tribe and was the only outsider. Or more accurately, with her dark coloring, she was the tribal one invading a WASP convention!

Several uncomfortable minutes passed, which she spent watching women greet each other with air kisses and carry on excited conversations about people she'd never heard of and probably wouldn't like if all that gossip were true.

Finally, the master of ceremonies walked on stage to everyone's anxious applause. When he reached the microphone, he welcomed the participants and explained the purpose of the benefit. The money was going to an animal hospital. She remembered Jason telling her how much he loved animals and how he didn't know if he should get a pet considering how often he was away during baseball season. Also, certain pets didn't fare well in the city. She had teased him about raising llamas on the little patch of grass they called a yard. How she missed him already!

A female veterinarian spoke about the amount their last auction had raised and the good use they had made of that money. A shelter in the suburbs had been opened and apparently many of those pets had been adopted.

Merry wondered about the unlucky ones and what became of them. Were they released back into the wild? This woman seemed too nice to "put them down" as the euphemism goes. What did that mean? They insulted the unadoptable until they slunk away with their tails between their legs?

She couldn't help thinking about her birth parents any time the word "adoption" was used. She had always assumed they had been young and in love but unable to support a family. What if they had been one of these spoiled socialites who didn't want the bother of raising children? Maybe her birth mother pretended to be on a world cruise for nine months, then hired a personal trainer to get her slim figure back. Doubtful, but it could happen. *Ugh*. She preferred to think her parents had been a young unmarried couple.

The show started—at last. The first bachelor was apparently some sort of self-made millionaire with real estate all over Boston. She had never heard of him, but most of the crowd certainly had. Wild applause accompanied his model-like parade down the catwalk. At the end, he took off his jacket, tossed it over his shoulder and winked at the crowd. *Oh yeah, he's done this before.*

The bidding began at what the auctioneer called a modest $500.00 and escalated quickly. *Crap, did Jason underestimate the deep pockets of these enthusiastic vultures?*

She extracted the money clip from her black no-name clutch bag and began to count the bills. The woman next to her gave her a dirty look as if counting one's money in public was about the rudest thing she could do. *Tough noogies, nosy woman.* She had to know how much bargaining power she had. Only one thousand dollars. The bidding on the first gentleman, a mediocre-looking guy at that, rapidly approached the thousand dollar mark. *Crap.*

Jason waited nervously backstage. He had volunteered for this gig along with a Bullets buddy who became a free agent at the end of the season and signed with Jacksonville. Apparently his short-stop pal had canceled, so Jason felt very much alone. At one point he peeked around the curtain, partly to see how the other guys were handling this, but mostly to see if he could find Merry in the crowd.

His gut twisted as he realized he hadn't given her enough money. The bidding for the first two guys topped out at twelve and fifteen hundred dollars. Why the hell would anyone pay fifteen hundred dollars for a single date?

He wanted to raise awareness and money for the

shelter, but damned if he wanted to become someone's pet. Somehow he doubted this crowd would be interested in shelter pups, even if they were paper trained. If they had any pets, they probably paid a fortune for a purebred with papers and a dog walker to take care of their pedigree pooches and scoop the poop. Merry would definitely buy a shelter pet. She had told him so, right after asking his permission to have an animal in her apartment.

He didn't like the idea of leaving an animal alone for long stretches, or else he'd have a dog. A Shepherd like his boyhood pal, Duke. He pictured the kind of dog Merry would take home. Probably a mutt version of a goofy sheepdog or something equally as humorous. A smile touched his lips just thinking about her and her huge heart.

Where the hell was she? He had scanned as much of the room as he could see. Maybe she had left as soon as she realized she didn't have enough money. *Oh no*. She wouldn't have gone out to an ATM, would she? He wanted to kick himself, and then realized that ATMs wouldn't allow enough of a withdrawal to make up the difference. So where was she?

She certainly had enough to take a cab home. No, she wouldn't do that unless… Would she think he was making this into some sort of test? That he knew he didn't give her enough money? What the…?

"You're up next, Jason." A hand clamped over his shoulder. He felt as if he had just been told he was going for "a little ride" by the mafia. Now all he could hope for was a major lack of baseball fans out there. Maybe if no one knew who he was, the bidding would stay low.

The gentleman steered him to the place where each bachelor did his walk-on. The MC glanced to his left and his face lit up when he saw Jason.

Even before the last bachelor exited the stage, he announced, "And on deck... We have one of the best baseball pitchers the Boston Bullets has ever seen. I predict he'll make the Hall of Fame along with other lefties like Sandy Koufax and Steve Carlton. But that may not happen for a while, since he's only twenty-seven years old. Ladies, I give you, *Jason Falco*!"

A huge roar rose from the crowd. All he wanted to do was turn and run, but his honest upbringing kicked in and he dutifully marched down the catwalk as he promised he would. He was used to stadium noise and this seemed louder. Perhaps since he was concentrating on something else while on the mound, he could tune it out. Now he felt stupid and afraid! So he tried to concentrate on finding Merry—if she was out there.

Like the others, he stopped at the end of the runway, but he refused to remove his jacket as though he was a Chippendale dancer. Instead, he stood tall with his feet shoulder-width apart and his hands clasped behind his back. He would have resembled a soldier standing at ease, except that instead of keeping his eyes fixed, he frantically searched the crowd for Merry.

At last he spotted her near the back of the room. She seemed so tiny back there, but when she smiled, a grin spread over his face, too. Apparently the women thought it was for them, so they yelled even louder.

At last the bidding started and began at the usual five-hundred dollars. Merry didn't raise her number. He kept her in the corner of his eye as his gaze darted from one raised sign to another. Wondering why she wasn't bidding, he tried to put himself in her shoes. Perhaps she realized it was fruitless. *I hope she'll forgive me for this,* he thought as the bidding rapidly climbed toward one thousand dollars.

At last she raised her number and he heard the auctioneer yell, "One thousand dollars!" The room cheered, but that was no surprise. They cheered every time the amount reached a thousand. Her number sixty-nine amused him. Was the universe trying to tell him something?

Bidding continued with no indication the pace was about to slow down. After it reached seventeen-hundred a few of the avid bidders lowered their numbers, permanently.

Just as the bidding was about to end, a familiar voice yelled out, "Two thousand!"

Stunned, Jason snapped his gaze to Merry. She stood, holding her sign at shoulder level. Her other hand was planted on her hip in a "Don't mess with me, bitches" stance. That made him chuckle to himself.

Oh, no. Another woman jumped to her feet and yelled, "Twenty-one hundred."

As the bidding war broke out, the auctioneer tried to take back control. "Ladies… Ladies!" They ignored him.

"Twenty-three hundred."

"Twenty-four."

"Twenty-five!"

The auctioneer threw his hands in the air, and allowed the two angry rivals to finish his job for him.

Merry edged her way toward the other woman.

What is she doing? Jason hoped she wasn't throwing her own money into the mix. That wasn't what he had intended to happen, plus he was fairly sure she couldn't afford it. But knowing her, even for as short a time as he had, he realized that's *exactly* what she was doing. She'd never ask him to cover the extra expenditure unless they had discussed it ahead of time.

He tried to catch her eye, but the two women were glaring at each other and rapidly coming together toe to toe.

He had to stop her. If she won, of course he'd cover it—if she'd let him—but the more he thought about it the more he realized she'd take responsibility for her own actions, and the bidding was rapidly approaching the three thousand mark!

He cleared his throat. Neither of them slowed their efforts. A female reporter rushed toward the area where she could capture photos of both Merry and the other woman. Jason didn't want attention being called to Merry any more than to himself. Identifying their relationship would put him at risk for discovery. *Man, this was a bad idea.*

Something about the reporter seemed to spook Merry and she glanced up at Jason, looking nervous. *At last!* Before she could look away, he sent her a slight head shake and hoped she'd get the message.

She must have. She frowned at him and whirled back toward her seat—letting her sign whomp the other woman's hip before she trudged away and plopped into her chair, defeated.

The auctioneer jumped back into action and called out "Thirty-two hundred going once… Thirty-two hundred going twice…" He paused, staring in Merry's direction. She folded her arms and looked away—none too happy.

"Sold! To the lovely redhead in the blue suit."

"It's a good thing Jason Falco loves animals, because when my article comes out, he'll be spending a long time in the doghouse." Lila laughed. She had been speaking to her bottle of Bacardi 151, as if it was a living, breathing friend—or lover. Well, so what? Some days it was the only friend she had.

Lila Crum grinned as she developed that night's film in her darkroom. *Three-timing. A perfect headline for a perfectly sleazy article.* She'd followed the woman who won Falco to her home in Brookline. Now she knew where to find them together. If he was any kind of gentleman, he'd pick her up and drop her off at her door.

The photos she captured at the auction tonight would be terrific for tomorrow's paper, and she already had her title: *Catfight at Animal Benefit.*

Wouldn't a snapshot of the debutante's good night kiss be just delicious? Even if he didn't kiss her, if she found the perfect angle, she could make it look like he did.

"I already snapped my first picture when I saw him kissing the nurse in the parking lot. That was too easy! It was like they practically posed for it!" She spoke to her drink and took another swig.

Since tonight was a Friday, and the auction couples were supposed to go out on their dates the following evening, she'd have the whole weekend to get her pictures and put the sordid story together.

"The original *mark,* the woman who thought she was hiring a private investigator instead of a reporter, gave me a hundred bucks as a retainer. That will barely cover the cost of buying your clones for the week." She patted the bottle. "I'll ask her for five hundred before I cough up Falco's address."

She stroked the bottle, then grabbed it and tipped it up for a long sip. "Bleahhhh! Damn, you're strong, but the Diet Coke is so far away."

So tomorrow she'd do her thing. Hide in the bushes outside his auction date's house, grab a picture, and then follow him home.

Her editor would find the juicy story and all the photos to back it up on his desk Monday morning—that is, if Lila didn't oversleep again.

Chapter 5

MERRY SHOOK HER HEAD AT HER OWN INSANITY. JASON wasn't usually an asshole. For chrissakes, he'd been on his best behavior at all times, so why was she giving him the cold shoulder?

Because she wanted to. Maybe she was sick of him being such a perfect gentleman. Maybe she wanted to push him to his limit and see where and how he crossed that line. Maybe it was PMS.

As a nurse, she knew she could always blame it on the full moon and PMS, but as a woman, she knew it had more to do with losing her guy to a rich redhead in a bachelor auction—in other words, all of the above, plus tons of insecurity. What a combination.

"C'mon Merry. We've been driving for half an hour and you haven't spoken to me once. I explained that I had no idea bidding would go that high. Hell, I would have even covered the extra, but I thought you'd refuse it. That's why I gave you the head-shake."

She turned away from him and stared out the window. Whoa, they had just passed Mass Ave and were heading toward Kenmore Square.

That's when she realized he wasn't taking her home.

"Where the hell are we going?"

"Someplace special."

She crossed her arms and frowned. "Who says I want to go someplace special with you?"

"Look, I don't know what's going through that pretty head of yours, but I'm not taking you home until you tell me. Whatever it is, we'll straighten it out."

"Who says I'm crooked?"

He stared at her as if she had two heads. Maybe she did. She felt like two sides of her were at war. Jekyll and Hyde to be exact. *But why that head-shake? In front of everyone!*

Part of her knew he was telling the truth. A big part. The logical part. Besides, it wasn't as if they were engaged or married. He could go out with anyone he wanted, and if she kept acting like a spoiled brat, he just might.

She fell back against the leather seat and sighed. "Okay. You're right. It's not your fault. I don't know why I'm mad, I just am."

"That time of the—?" He halted, but she knew what he was about to infer.

Ebbing embers of anger flared again. "What? How dare you!" If glares were daggers, he'd be shish kabob.

"I was almost married, once," he said softly. "I know the signs."

Why did he have to remind her he had been hurt? Why did she have to care? Why did she suddenly hate any woman who had ever laid a hand on him?

She retreated back into silence. It was safer that way. He was right. She was due for her period in a couple of days and shifts in hormones were making her crazy.

"There won't be a second date with her, Merry. You know that, right?"

She cocked her head and stared at him. He glanced over a couple of times. All she saw in his eyes was sincerity. *Shit*. She still wasn't ready to forgive him.

"How do you know? You haven't even been out with her yet."

He let out a long exhalation and turned left onto Brookline Ave.

"Where are we going? You still haven't told me."

"Look, it's probably not the best time to tell you this, but tonight was a test."

She gasped. "A what?" she asked indignantly.

"A test. You failed miserably. Unfortunately, so did I."

"What the blazes do you mean by that?"

"I mean…" He pulled over to the curb and gave her an intense gaze. "I figured I'd find out how you reacted to me getting some pretty strong female attention. And I thought that if you were okay with it, I'd want to move our relationship to the next level."

Oh, crap. Sails—no wind. She was caught completely off guard and her heart crumpled.

She folded her hands in her lap and figured it was over. He was probably driving her to Rhode Island so he could dump her on her father's doorstep and tell him to come and get her stuff at his earliest opportunity.

"Don't you want to know why I failed, too?"

"Uh, yeah. I can guess, but go ahead."

"What do you guess?"

"That you thought we could stay friends, but you don't even want that anymore?"

There was that look again. She was tempted to check her neck to see if she really did have two heads growing out of it.

"No, Merry. In fact, you couldn't be further from the truth. I still want you—as a friend and as a girlfriend… in a big way. Like a full-time monogamous lover."

"And you call that failing?" Her crumpled heart filled again. With the blood back, it warmed her all over.

"What do you call it?"

She smiled. "Acing it. Passing with flying colors."

At last, he smiled too. "It's about time I did something right." He leaned over and cupped the back of her head. She knew he wanted to kiss her. Something inside still jittered, but it was hard to deny the bridge he was trying to build. It was about time she took a few steps over it and met him halfway.

She leaned toward him. He correctly interpreted her permission and drew her lips to his. They shared a long, tender kiss. Nothing passionate with fireworks and curled toes, but in a way, she needed this more. She needed to calm down and his kiss soothed her.

"Jason, I'm really sorry." She felt hot tears at the back of her eyes threatening to spill. *Oh, for God's sake, Merry. Don't give him any more signs of PMS. He already suspects.*

He smiled but didn't say anything.

"Am I forgiven?" she asked.

"Totally. To be honest, I think I'd have been a little surprised and insulted if you weren't jealous at all."

"Really? Does that mean you don't think I'm a jackass?"

He grinned. "Well… I wouldn't use that word, but you sure can be a—challenge, when you're mad."

She snickered. "A challenge. Nice way to put it. Probably nicer than I deserve." Merry stared at her lap and realized how lucky she was he hadn't dumped her on the spot.

He used the backs of his knuckles to stroke her cheek softly. She closed her eyes and turned into his hand. She sensed, rather than saw, his lips heading for her face. His fingers cupped the back of her neck as his lips brushed her other cheek.

She turned her head to meet his kiss. And what a kiss it was! Long, deep, and languorous. Their tongues met and swirled. She slid her arms around his neck and her abdomen fluttered.

When he leaned back a few inches, he said, "Well, we've made it to our destination. Are you ready to go inside?"

She glanced out through the windshield and couldn't really tell where they were. Some back street and it looked kind of sketchy.

As if he read her mind, he said, "We're at Fenway Park. Don't worry, you're safe. You're with me."

He hopped out, jogged around the car, and opened her door for her. Even right after a fight, he was a gentleman. He helped her out of the car and led her to a back entrance. He knocked on the door, and it opened.

"Hey, Jason," a burly black man said, and shook his hand enthusiastically. "Is this the lady friend you mentioned?"

He mentioned me?

"Yep. This is Merry."

"What a beauty. No wonder you wanted to show her around when the place was deserted. You don't need the competition."

Merry wanted to burst out laughing—and kiss whoever this wonderful man was.

"Merry, this is Bubba. He's head of security here at the stadium and he's giving us a special pass so I can show you my second home."

She shook the guard's hand.

Jason wrapped an arm around her shoulder and escorted her along the deserted corridor. At last, they stopped at one of the luxury boxes. It was like a small, private room with carpeting, comfortable seats, and what looked like a wet bar and snack table.

If not for the full moon, the field might have been invisible, but thanks to ol' Luna he could show her a few areas of interest.

First, he pointed out the pitcher's mound where he spent most of his time when he started.

She rolled her eyes and said, "I think I can pick out the pitcher's mound and the bases."

Then he had to explain what "starting" meant—that he only had to pitch every fifth game or so.

"Must be nice. I wish I only had to work ever fifth night for a few hours and make the money you do."

"Do you know how much money I make?"

"No, and don't tell me. I know sports figures make a lot. Besides, it's rude to ask someone about his or her salary."

He couldn't help but grin. Apparently, she didn't realize it was a matter of public record that he had signed a three-year contract for ninety million. He liked knowing it didn't matter to her.

Next he showed her the "Green Monster."

"I've heard of the 'Green Monster,' but I thought that's what attacked me during the stupid auction."

Jason chuckled. "At least you admit it. No, it's affectionately called the Green Monster because of its size, and… well, it's green. It's hard to see color at night. Some powerful batters can belt a ball right over it and out of the park."

"Really? Holy crap. Have you ever done it?"

"No, but I'm working on it."

While she stared at the field, he stood behind her and stroked her arms. He was trying to make this tour as exciting as he could for a non-fan. Happily, his enthusiasm must have been contagious because she asked a few intelligent questions and didn't yawn once.

He pulled her warm body against his chest and his erection nudged her backside. "See what you do to me?" he whispered in her ear.

She shivered, tipped her head back, and rested it on his shoulder. "Mmm… I guess you really forgave me."

He could almost hear her smile.

He trailed his finger up and down her arm. "You're my girl, Merry. Little disagreements happen between couples. It doesn't have to end things. Besides, you and I are just beginning."

She turned in his arms. Gazing into his blue eyes, she asked, "So, what did you mean when you were talking about taking our relationship to the next level?"

"I think you know." Jason planted soft kisses down her neck to her shoulder. She cupped his jaw and drew him to her lips for a long, deep kiss.

His hands wandered—one up and one down until he held her breast and cupped her bottom. His thumb brushed a nipple and she groaned. When she cupped his balls through his slacks it felt so good he wanted his pants to magically disappear.

After kissing and exploring for a few minutes, Jason walked Merry backward to the comfortable-looking couch, lowering her back zipper as he moved. She found his belt buckle and opened it. He kicked off his dress shoes and then fumbled with the buttons on his shirt as she shrugged out of her dress.

They made out for another several minutes. At last, they nudged each other's underwear off, and the two of them faced each other with only skin between them. Jason swooped in for a long kiss, and then lowered her gently to the sofa.

"You're beautiful," he murmured in her ear.

She took his cock in her hand and stroked. "So are you."

He loved the sensation of her hand gripping his rod, and then she found his ball sac with her other hand and gently squeezed. "Ohhh... I won't last if you keep doing that. Tell you what. Ladies first."

He shifted her onto her back and gently squeezed her breast. Strumming her nipple with his thumb, he took the other one in his mouth. She moaned as he suckled her. She grasped his cock again and caressed it while he did a thorough job on her left breast. Her touch sent prickles of electricity wherever she stroked him. When he moved to her right side, he slid his hand to her mons and she arched into him.

His fingers explored her pussy as he suckled again. Her slick folds indicated her readiness, and even as desperate as he was to be inside of her, he wanted to make it last and show her what he could do.

He circled her clit with one finger. She writhed and whimpered, obviously as desperate as he was for more. He inserted first one finger, then two, sucked her breast deeper and stroked her G-spot. She gasped and rocked with the motion of his finger.

He broke his suction on her breast and slid downward

to lick her. He didn't stop what he was doing with his fingers, since she seemed to enjoy it. In fact, he increased his speed and licked as she arched her back, moaning louder. At last, he fastened onto her button and…

"Oh, God!" she yelped. She vibrated in his arms and cried out. It was all he could do to stay on her sweet spot as she bucked and shattered.

When her body melted, completely limp, he crawled up beside her and smiled with deep satisfaction. She panted heavily and looked dazed. Delighted with her responsiveness, he simply waited for her to recover.

Eventually she managed to focus on his face and spoke breathlessly. "Dear God…"

"Nope. It's just me, Jason."

She cracked a smile and started to laugh. "Sorry, easy mistake."

He grinned and swooped in for a short but meaningful kiss. "Let me know when you're ready for more."

She glanced down at his cock, now hard as a spike. "Soon. How did you do that? I mean, find my G-spot and everything?"

"Years of curling these long fingers around a baseball, I guess."

"Man… I've never—I mean *never* felt anything like that before."

He flipped up onto his knees. "There's more, you know." He dove for his pants and extracted a condom.

"I know… and I want it." She parted her thighs. "Do you mind if I just lie here and let you do anything you want to my boneless body? I promise, next time you'll be first and I'll wait for you to recover."

He chuckled. "I don't mind at all." He rolled the

condom on, tapped her knees a little farther apart, and settled between them.

"I was just kidding," she said. "I won't make you do all the work." She bent her knees, took hold of his shaft, and guided him in.

Even though she was tight, she was so well lubricated he was able to slide in all the way to the hilt. *Ah, heaven*.

He started a slow rhythm, which she matched by lifting her hips. She closed her eyes and let out another long moan.

"Are you okay?"

"Mmm…" She sighed. "Feels good. *So* good."

"Yes it does…" And it did. Better than usual—even though he hadn't been sensitized by oral foreplay. If he had been, he wouldn't have made it this far. Her warm tight channel hugged his girth perfectly. He was afraid he might be too large, but she seemed able to take all of him.

The familiar ball of urgency at the base of his spine demanded he increase his pace. He did so, watching her face for any sign of discomfort. She kept up with his pace just fine. She even opened her eyes and smiled at him—a soft, lazy look pervaded her hooded gaze.

"I love you, Merry," he said. *Where did that come from?* He hadn't intended to make that declaration, but it slipped out with ease.

Before she could respond, he closed his eyes and increased his pace again, now pounding into her. She wrapped her legs around his waist and panted heavily, but not in an uncomfortable way. He spasmed and jerked several times as his orgasm overtook him. He rode the jolts of bliss all the way to the last aftershock, then collapsed beside her.

—w—

Merry had floated through her shift the following
night. She knew Jason was out with Ms. Skinny-dyed-
and-surgically-altered, but she didn't feel insecure.
There *wouldn't* be a second date... because he loved
her. *Her!* Merry MacKenzie of dinky little Schooner,
Rhode Island. They had taken their relationship to the
next level and then some.

She wondered if he had expected her to say the words
when he did. At the time, she could barely breathe,
never mind think and talk. And afterward, they did a
quick clean-up and scooted out when Jason wondered
if security had hidden cameras in those luxury boxes.
Bubba seemed like a nice guy, but was he nice enough
to turn his head? Was any man able to look away from
live porn? *Très* doubtful.

In the car on the way home from Fenway Park,
they made small talk. He asked her if she had plans for
Thanksgiving. Of course, she did. Who would cook
the turkey for her family if she wasn't there? One of
her sisters-in-law would bring a couple of side dishes
and the other would bring pies, but neither one of her
married brothers had room for a big get-together, so everyone came "home" for the holidays. Merry had been
preparing a big holiday dinner with all the fixings since
she was seventeen. Once her older brothers had found
wives, she had some help.

Jason said he'd always gone home for Thanksgiving
and Christmas too, but it was easier when he lived in
Minnesota. Now that he was in Boston, he might choose
one or the other and stay for a few days.

She wondered if he was hinting at an invitation to her house, but she had to think about it. She was sure her family would be okay with it—hell, they'd be thrilled—but would her little brother tell all of his friends and impose upon her ten more mouths to feed? Absolutely. And they'd set upon poor Jason like vultures.

She could always invite Jason and say nothing to her family about his accompanying her. Yeah, that's what she'd do. And now she had an excuse to see him. No key to the penthouse, it was much too soon for that, but she had his cell phone number.

Maybe she'd wait until her day off to call him. Yeah, Monday would be soon enough. What little ESP she had wasn't sensing any dire portents or even warning bells. She'd show him she trusted him completely by not trying to get hold of him first thing Sunday morning. But if he wanted to see her, of course *that* was another matter. She'd not only let him in, she'd throw him down on the couch and have her nasty way with him.

"I'm telling you, Ralph, he said there's a ghost in that apartment. I wouldn't be the least bit surprised. After all, I stumbled over a box that I swear wasn't there when we walked in."

Ralph opened the fridge and grabbed a beer. "Someone probably came in after you and you didn't hear them. Maybe they had something in the box they needed and just forgot to put it away."

"They were *our* boxes, Ralph, and no one else has the key. You never believe me!" Dottie threw her hands in the air.

"About ghosts and vampires? No, I don't, because they don't exist, sweetheart."

"Well that's too bad, but I'm going through with the séance. If you won't come with me, I'll just invite some of the other tenants in the building. I'm sure they'd be interested in knowing if the building is haunted."

Ralph rolled his eyes. "Better ask Jason first. He might worry about the negative attention a claim like that would invite. You'll have every freakazoid breathing down our necks, taking pictures and feeling for cold spots."

"Fine. I'll ask Jason first."

Dottie grabbed the key card to Jason's apartment and stormed out. She slammed the door for extra passive-aggressive emphasis.

Riding the elevator to the penthouse, she hoped Jason would okay the idea. Having a séance would be the most interesting thing to happen to her since she had to sell off her computer to pay bill collectors. Boredom had set in long ago and anything that sounded as if it might have been exciting in 1899 would be a welcome relief.

Fortunately, he opened the door when she knocked. "Aunt Dottie. Is everything all right?"

"Well, yes and no. I'm fine, dear. Unfortunately, apartment 3A is haunted." She brushed by him and squatted on his white sofa.

He stood there, confusion knitting his brow. "Um, excuse me? Did you say haunted?"

"Yes. The professor who lived there and moved out wants his security deposit back. He said we didn't disclose the *fact* that the place was haunted. He had a psychic come in to verify it."

"I see. And is there something you want me to do about this? I'll gladly refund his security deposit."

"Oh, I already did that. Actually, I hadn't deposited the check yet, so I just tore it up. But there is something you can do to help."

Jason scratched his head. "Okkaaayyy…"

"I want to hold a séance. I mean, it would be silly just to take one person's word for it, right?"

Jason shrugged. "I guess… Do you know anyone who can conduct a séance?"

"Yes, and I have it all set up for tonight. I've been assured that she has an unparalleled reputation and the utmost professionalism. In other words, she won't breathe a word of it to anyone—no matter what she finds."

A smile curved one side of her nephew's mouth.

Oh, please. If he starts laughing at me too, so help me…

But all he said was, "Thank you for being sensitive to my need for privacy, Aunt Dottie. I really appreciate that. So yes, go ahead with your plans."

"Oh." Relief washed over her. He wasn't a doubter—just concerned for his precious privacy, as usual.

"Who will be attending this séance?" he asked.

She stood and returned to the doorway, knowing enough to get out before he asked too many questions.

"Well, so far it's you and me. I'll check with the rest of the tenants to see who can come. Apparently the more we can find, the better it will be. Since they've all sworn to protect your privacy too, I figured you wouldn't mind…"

He nodded. "Sure. What time and where is it going to be held?"

"In apartment 3A. Six p.m. I'll get Ralph to set up

a table and some chairs. I'll just have to see how many will be coming, first."

"Knock yourself out," he said with a smile.

Now he's making fun, but we'll see how he feels if the table floats and the electricity goes off. A shiver of excitement trailed down her spine at the thought of something dramatic and extraordinary happening in her otherwise dull day.

Chapter 6

MERRY HAD BEEN DANCING TO SANTANA IN HER KITCHEN when she heard the knock on her door. Her heart leapt, hoping it was Jason. Really, who else could it be? The outer door hadn't opened and slammed, so it must be someone from the building. She rushed to her door and threw it open.

"Dottie?" *Crap. What a disappointment.* "Oh, um… Is something wrong? Was my music too loud?"

"No, dear. There's nothing wrong. Well, not with *you,* anyway." She smiled in an insincere way that made Merry's internal warning lights flash. *What now?* The elevator whirred in the background.

"I just stopped by to invite you to a get-together in apartment 3A tonight. Six p.m. Can you make it?"

Oh, God. She wants to have a tenants' meeting or intervention or something. "What kind of get-together, Dottie?"

"Well, it's a séance. I think I discovered why we can't keep that apartment rented."

Hairs prickled on the back of her neck. "You mean it's haunted?"

"Yes, we think so. Jason and I do anyway. Ralph is…" She rolled her eyes and waved her hand in a dismissive gesture. Her eyes suddenly narrowed at Merry. "You *do* believe in spirits occasionally remaining on this plane, don't you? Because of unfinished business or they don't know they're dead or something…"

"I—um... I think so. There have been some weird sightings at a couple of hospitals I've worked in and I've seen some shows about it."

"Good! It's unanimous." She seemed exceedingly pleased. "We'll see you at six, then?"

"I'm afraid I have to work tonight. But I have tomorrow off. Can we do it tomorrow?"

"Sorry. I booked a medium for tonight."

The elevator stopped and Jason stepped out. "Oh, good. You're home," he said, smiling at Merry.

She grinned.

Dottie backed away from the door and sighed. "Well, I'll let you two lovebirds be alone." She winked at Jason and headed up the stairs.

Merry wondered what he had told his aunt, but simply opened her door wider for Jason to enter. He kicked it closed behind him and swept her into his arms. "Did you miss me?" he asked and lowered his mouth to hers.

She wrapped her arms around his neck and returned his heated kiss. "Mpha... mbbt."

He broke the kiss and leaned away so he could see her face. "What?"

"I said, 'maybe a little bit.'"

They grinned at each other, then Jason lifted her effortlessly into his arms. "I might have thought about you once or twice too."

Carrying her to the bedroom, he nuzzled her neck and said, "There's a lot of time between now and whenever you have to leave for work, and I intend to spend all of it making love to you."

Kissing her tenderly, he lowered her to the bed. A wonderful warm fuzzy feeling swept through Merry as he covered her body with his—like a security blanket. His hands wandered to her breast and his mouth traveled to her neck.

She arched and whimpered as he massaged her breast. Even through her clothing his loving attention felt good, but she couldn't wait to lose the layers separating them.

"Jason," she whispered.

He didn't stop kissing her. "Hmm?"

"Let's take these clothes off. I'm suddenly burning up."

He broke his string of kisses long enough to look up at her and grin. "Can't have that now, can we?"

He reached for the zipper of her jeans and dragged it downward, slowly—sensuously.

She yanked the hem of his T-shirt and managed to drag it off over his head. She couldn't wait to touch him, skin to skin, so she fastened onto his nipple and sucked.

He reared back and groaned. "Oh, baby. What you do to me…"

"Hang on. There are things I want to do to you that I've never done before."

His eyebrows arched. "Really?"

Grinning, he shed the rest of his clothes in nanoseconds.

Merry had read enough *Cosmo* magazines to take advantage of the inside information they were always giving. *What guys really like. How to drive him crazy in bed.* The catchy headlines were always followed with expert advice, often given by the guys themselves.

The issue she had read recently offered some tips on teasing and sensitizing a man before actually getting it on. *Let the torture begin!*

She scraped her nails gently and slowly over his

chest, working her way down. Her mouth followed the path and she licked and nipped at his skin. According to the article, she was awakening his general nerve centers, so everything to follow would be more sensitive. And she intended to give him *everything*.

He closed his eyes and moans of pleasure emanated from somewhere deep within. Confident, Merry let her fingernails rake over his inner thighs, coming close to one testicle and then the other. No actual genital contact, yet. The article said not to be afraid to scrape or apply pressure to a guy's skin. It was much thicker and less sensitive than a woman's, so *be a little rough. They'll love it!*

She hesitated to be too rough with the jewels, though. She knew those were sensitive as heck!

Ha! He was writhing and trying to move his goodies toward her hands. *Not yet, Mister.*

She licked and nipped the skin she had just sensitized, then she blew on the dampened flesh. He shivered.

"Damn it, Merry. You're driving me crazy!"

Yes! Cosmo *didn't lie.*

She licked around his scrotum in a figure eight pattern, as he arched and moaned out loud. She circled his cock with her hand and squeezed, firmly. She was gratified with a groan of pleasure. Or maybe it was impatience. She'd give him what she knew he wanted in a minute.

At last, she took him in her mouth and went down on him. Applying a generous amount of suction on the withdrawal, she took him in again as deep as she could and tried to avoid an inadvertent gag reflex. That was never sexy.

"Fuck, Merry. I'm close." He pushed himself up on his elbows. "You've got to stop!"

She let him pop out of her mouth, looked up at him and smiled. "Are you sure?"

He flopped backward onto the pillow and groaned. "You're amazing, but yes. I want to reciprocate now."

She crawled up his body and said, "So, should I sit on your face?"

"What?" he said, sounding shocked.

"Oh, I'm sorry, was that too forward?"

"No, kind of gross, though."

"Gross?" Merry pouted. "But you just get to lie there, while I straddle and ride your tongue."

"Huh? Wait a minute. What did you ask me, again?"

Confused and disappointed, Merry hesitated, then said, "I asked if you wanted me to sit on your face?"

Jason laughed out loud. "I thought you said something else, another word that sounded like 'sit'."

Merry gasped, then burst out laughing too. "That *would* be gross."

"And way more kinky than I'm looking for."

"Me too!"

He surrounded her back with his strong arms and pulled her down on top of him. "I love a girl who can laugh in bed. I especially love *this* girl." Then he kissed her soundly on the mouth and flipped her over in one fluid motion.

Jason's big, flat bed will be good for something after all. Now I can't wait to try it out. Maybe tomorrow!

Jason delivered a long, fervent kiss and launched into foreplay.

She craved him touching her, filling her. "Tell me what you're going to do to me," she said in a sexy whisper.

Jason grinned. "In other words, you want a play-by-play?"

She giggled. "I thought it might be hot. I feel safe experimenting with you."

He gently cupped her breast and thumbed her nipple as he spoke. "First, I'm going to suck your breasts until you feel it all the way to your toes. Then I'm going to play with your intimate parts until you come just from having my fingers inside you. Then I'll give you the licking of your life until you come again and again. Finally, when you can't take any more, I'll slide my cock inside you and fuck you 'til I die."

She sighed. Who could argue with that? Well, not the dying part, but the rest of it sounded damn good. It was a hotter pre-coitus moment than she'd imagined.

True to his word, he fastened his mouth onto her nipple and sucked while his hand caressed her heated skin. She felt a visceral tug from his suckling, and moaned. She thought if he kept that up, she'd come from his attention to her breast alone.

His fingers trailed down, down, down to her mons and he gently played with her curls. "Oh, God!" He was doing the same thing to her that she had done to him. *Damn tease!* Oh well, she'd just have to "endure" it.

When she writhed and tried to arch her clit toward his fingers, he took mercy on her and stimulated the little bud. A jolt zinged through her entire pelvis and she almost vaulted off the bed. A volcano of climax erupted immediately and she screamed out her joy. When at last she was hoarse and sated, she batted away his fingers. "No more… Can't take it."

He began to slide down the bed, but she grabbed him

before he got very far. "I mean it... I'm done. *Stick a fork in me...* Done."

He chuckled and moved up until he was face to face with her. As he swept her hair off her forehead, he smiled into her eyes. "I do love you," he whispered.

She looked at him through shimmering eyes, but the lump in her throat made it impossible to speak. She nodded instead.

He feathered kisses over her face, neck and collarbone. Eventually her breathing slowed and he asked, "Are you ready for me?"

Merry said in her sexiest voice, "Oh yeah. Want to lie down and let me ride?"

He grinned and promptly dropped onto his back. She climbed up beside him and took his erect member into her hand. *Still hard as a rock under the satiny surface.* Just for good measure, she placed a loving kiss on the tip before throwing one leg over him and sinking down.

Taking his cock into her body, she moaned with the glorious feeling of him filling her completely. Merry's cavern was so wet, he glided in and out easily as he pumped and she rocked. She closed her eyes and lost herself in sensation.

After a good long ride, he added a clit rub and she gasped. "Jason, I..." Her orgasm exploded and she lost all control. All power of speech deserted her except to cry out in ecstasy. Soon after, he climaxed too. When each of them had experienced their last aftershock, Merry collapsed on top of him.

"Are you sure *you're* the one who's going to die in bed?"

"Maybe we both will." He chuckled. "But what a way to go."

—∿∿—

"Now everybody needs to sit around the table and hold hands. At least that's what I've seen on TV. Isn't that how a séance is done, Shandra?" Dottie asked the medium.

She chuckled. "Yes, that's how it's done. Everyone gather 'round and have a seat."

Candles graced the table. Since Dottie had already made sure the electricity was shut off, their glow provided the only light in the chilly apartment. A red oblong tablecloth over a couple of folding bridge tables gave the appearance of one large table, the perfect size for their gathering. Konrad, Morgaine, Gwyneth, Nathan, and Jason surrounded the table and took the vacant seats. Dottie had been with the medium, Shandra, as soon as she arrived and was seated to her right, anxiously awaiting this monumental event.

She grabbed the hands of Shandra and Jason on either side of her and asked, "What do we do next?"

"Simply close your eyes and sit quietly," Shandra instructed.

It was all Dottie could do not to squirm. Shivers seemed to pepper the back of her neck already and nothing had happened yet.

Shandra took several deep breaths and said, "Spirit, please make yourself known." She waited. Nothing happened. She took several more deep breaths and tried again. "Spirit or spirits, if you are here, please give us a sign."

Dottie opened one eye. The candles flickered. Nothing

unusual about that. Her gaze settled on the medium and she watched her closely. The woman began to heave and straighten, heave and straighten. At last, she jerked, opened her mouth and spoke in a voice that didn't sound like hers at all.

"Why are you here in my pad? You're intruding where you don't belong," the voice said. It was significantly lower than Shandra's normal voice.

Dottie murmured, "Pad?" under her breath.

Shandra's voice returned to normal. "Spirit, thank you for allowing me to channel your voice. We are only here temporarily in order to speak to you, then we will leave you in peace. Do you have any messages to relay? I'm here to help." Her head dropped against her chest.

A moment later, her chin lifted and the lower voice answered, "Groovy. Make them leave me alone, man. I need my space."

Groovy? Well, he wasn't from the eighteenth century—unless he picked up conversations and learned some new words.

"Can you tell us who you are?" Shandra continued.

"I am the ghost of Christmas past, and I have come to show you the error of your ways." He made some kind of spooky Oooooo… sound and then laughed.

The medium shook a bit and then spoke in her normal voice. "We mean you no harm. Please let us know with whom we're communicating, so we can better help you."

They waited silently until Dottie couldn't stand it any longer. "Well, if he won't tell us who he is, what does he look like? Maybe we can figure it out. Can you describe him?"

Shandra shook her head. "I can only see his shape. He's tall and thin. His hair appears to be in an afro style."

"Hey, I'm not skinny. I'm fit," said the baritone voice from the medium's mouth. Nathan snorted—or was it just a cough? "I just have a high metabolism—or *had*, I should say. You want to know what I look like? Well, I'm a twenty-six-year-old black man, wearing a tie-dyed tunic, ripped jeans, and several strands of love beads hanging from my neck. Oh, and I also have a bullet hole in my head."

One of the participants made a sound like *Ugh*.

"Great," grumbled Dottie. "We're being haunted by a hippie!"

Jason chuckled.

The disembodied voice answered, "You should appreciate my presence. I may be handy now and then. I can see things the rest of you can't… well, all of you except Gladys Kravitz over there in the flowered moo moo."

"It's not a muumuu," Dottie protested.

"I called it a moo moo because it's fit for a cow."

Morgaine stood and shouted, "Cut the shit, Chad."

Dottie stood too and gaped at Morgaine. "You know this insulting spirit?"

She shrugged. "Well, I didn't know him when he was alive. He talks to me once in a while. Mostly when he's lonely."

"Or bored," Nathan added.

The rest of the participants opened their eyes and stared at Morgaine and Nathan, alternately.

The medium seemed to be the only one not surprised. "How long have you been aware of him?" she asked.

"Since we moved in here. I've lived here eight years," Nathan said.

"And why didn't you think to mention it before now?" Dottie demanded.

Morgaine sighed. "Would you have believed us if we had said, 'Oh, by the way, there's a ghost haunting 3A, and he'll drive out anyone you rent his place to'?"

Dottie crossed her arms. "Maybe. But if he thinks he can get away with tying up an apartment that could be rented, he has another think coming."

Jason cleared his throat. "Aunt Dottie, let's see what else he has to say first."

Shandra held up a hand and regained control. "Most likely, he's here because he has unfinished business. Apparently he does know he's dead, but couldn't or wouldn't move on for some reason. We need to ask him why. Can everyone regroup, please?"

Nathan cleared his throat. "As much fun as this wasn't, I think I'll go back to my 'pad' now." He rose and walked to the door.

Dottie jammed her hands on her hips. "So, how is it you can communicate with ghosts too?

"Helloooo... I work in a morgue. Remember? Anyway, I don't exactly communicate with him. He just likes to hang out with me sometimes."

"Can everyone see and speak to ghosts except for me?"

"I can't," Jason said.

"Nor me," Konrad stated.

All eyes turned toward Gwyneth. "I'm just learnin' how to increase my psychic powers. So far, I can only connect with my dear departed family."

"What are you? Some kind of weird Pagans?"

"Oh, no!" Gwyneth said. "We're not weird—"

Morgaine interrupted. "We're kind of interested in anything 'new age-y'. It's something that's interested me for a while, and now my cousin is following in my footsteps."

Dottie harrumphed.

Before Nathan left, he turned and said, "Just so you know, Dottie, ghosts can be touchy, and if you try to bully him, be ready for consequences."

Her jaw dropped. "Consequences? What kind of consequences?"

Nathan shrugged. "Depends on how creative he is."

Dottie remembered falling *hard* on this very floor. She just knew Chad had moved that box into her path somehow. *Oh, this isn't good.* She grabbed Jason's and Shandra's hands. "What does he want? Maybe we can help him finish his business and then he can leave."

"Ouch, Aunt Dottie, you're squeezing my pitching hand."

"Oh, sorry."

Shandra nodded. "It's possible. The sixties weren't that long ago."

"Morgaine, do you know what he wants?"

"All I know is what he already told you. He wants his apartment left vacant."

Dottie shook her head. "That's not going to happen. Let's find out what that unfinished business is. Shandra, I paid you for an hour, so please continue."

All the remaining participants held hands; Konrad had to reach a little farther to connect diagonally across the table with Gwyneth now that Nathan was gone, but fortunately he had long arms. Long hairy arms, Dottie noted.

"You say his name is Chad?" the medium asked Morgaine.

"Yes."

"Do you know his last name?"

"No. I never needed it just to talk to him."

"Let's see if we can find out more about him. Everyone close your eyes and concentrate on Chad. Try to empty your minds of fear or anger and help him feel comfortable."

Dottie tried her hardest to comply and only a few moments later, Chad was ready to speak. Shandra took a couple of deep breaths and said in the male voice, "My name is Chad Robinson—that's my pen name. My real name is Charles Washington. I was a journalist and reporter for the *Boston Chronicle*."

Dottie took over. "So what's your unfinished business, if there is any? Or are you just being a stubborn ass?"

A low laugh exited the medium's mouth. "Yes, you could say I have some unfinished business. I was murdered. Assassinated, just as I was about to expose a conspiracy against the Kennedys."

Dottie gasped. "President Kennedy? I thought that happened in Dallas."

"No, Herman Kennedy. *Of course* President Kennedy," he said in a snide tone. "Both Jack and Bobby. This is their home state, remember? A lot of prior meetings and planning took place here."

Finally, Jason inserted a question. "Wow. So you know who killed JFK?"

"Yes. Lee Harvey Oswald."

Dottie rolled her eyes. "Oh for God's sake, we all know that."

"But I was shot by the men behind the whole thing. I said it was a conspiracy, remember?"

"Are you sure?" Dottie asked.

"And how did you discover the conspiracy?" Konrad asked.

"I had a source."

Jason piped up, "What's his name? If we can find him, maybe we can learn who the conspirators were."

"A good reporter never reveals his sources."

"But I thought you wanted to know who was responsible for this? I can hire a private detective—"

Dottie jumped in. "Oh, I've always wanted to be a sleuth! Maybe I can go along on stake outs and pick his brain."

"Drive him crazy, you mean. No, I think you'd better stay out of it, Dottie dearest," Chad said.

How weird is it to watch Shandra's lips move and hear a male voice?

"So, you'll let us help you?" Jason asked.

"I kept his name anonymous the whole time I was alive. I don't suppose I have any obligation to continue if you're willing to locate him and find out who put a bullet in my head."

"I'm willing," Jason said. "But will you move on to the light or whatever it is you need to do once this is over?"

"I don't know," he said, sounding honest. "I don't really know how this whole afterlife thing works."

"Maybe I can help you, when you're ready," Morgaine offered.

"Thanks, friend. I'll take you up on that. I'm tired of this scene, anyway. Rattling around in an empty apartment is a real drag."

Dottie cocked her head. "Then why won't you allow…"

"A roommate? Forget it. I need my own space. So, here's the 411 on my source…"

—⁂—

Merry's phone rang long before she would have staggered out of bed. Must be someone who didn't know her habits or they'd let her sleep until ten a.m.

"Hello?"

"Merry? Are you all right?"

Why did her father sound so concerned? "Of course I am, Dad. Why wouldn't I be?"

"I received phone calls from several people who spotted your picture in the Boston newspaper. I drove to the supermarket and picked up a copy to see for myself."

"See what?" she asked, puzzled.

"Your picture with Jason Falco. Only it gives you a different name in the article."

"Really? That's weird. Are you sure it's me?"

"Positive."

"I wonder when that was taken and why?"

"Well, you might want to sit down for this."

"For what? What's going on, Dad?"

"Okay, the picture shows you all dressed up and kissing Jason. It's a little dark, but you're under a street light in front of a sports car."

"Yes, that was Friday night. What of it? I told you we were dating."

"I know, but I just don't want you to get hurt.

There's another picture here. Did you know he's dating other people?"

"Oh, Daddy, that was a one-time thing. He had signed up for a bachelor auction for charity sometime last summer, before he even knew me. He had to take the woman out, but he promised me there wouldn't be a second date."

"Uh-oh. So it sounds like you think he's dating you exclusively? You're not aware of the other one?"

"I just told you I was. She's a thin redhead, right?"

"Uh, yeah. The second one is, but there's a third picture here. A young woman with long brown hair. He's hugging her."

"Oh. Well, you never know when those pictures were taken, and it might just be a fan or something. Everyone seems to think they know him and they feel like they can walk right up to him and hug him, even though he's never seen them before in his life. That's why he doesn't like to go out in public."

"Hmm... I hope you're right. Under your picture it says, Live-in girlfriend, Allison Flores, no longer lovey-dovey."

"Allison who? What rag are you reading, anyway?"

"The *Boston Telegraph*. And, um, here's the part you might want to sit down for..."

"Oh, no. There's more?"

"Just about the name."

"Yeah, what's with that? She must have made one up."

Her father cleared his throat. "Or been very psychic. Allison Flores was your birth name."

Merry dropped back onto her pillow with a thump. Shock waves rendered her temporarily speechless.

"Honey? Are you there?"

"Yes," she said in a small voice. "How on earth could some reporter know that? *I* didn't even know that!"

"Well, it's true. We liked the name Allison, but not with MacKenzie. Allison MacKenzie sounded kind of long and clunky. We looked at your tiny smiling face and the name Merry popped into your mother's mind. Merry MacKenzie felt right. So when we changed your last name, we changed your first name too."

"Oh." *Allison*. She had always liked that name. And *Flores* would explain her Latin features. She had never thought about having had another name since she was adopted as an infant. But how the hell did someone learn about her other name?

"Dad, do you think the records have been unsealed and someone has been trying to find me?" It might be a long shot, but what else could explain it?

"Or maybe they *have* found you but aren't ready to introduce themselves yet. Either way, I'd like you to keep me informed."

"Sure. I'll let you know if anything comes of it." Merry let that roll around in her mind for a minute. Should it feel creepy that someone might know who she really was but wasn't willing to reveal himself to her? Regardless of whether it should freak her out or not, it did.

"You know I love you, Pumpkin. If you need me, I'm right here for you."

Uh-oh. She was regressing into little girl mode and he sensed it. Time to put on her big-girl panties and deal. "I know that, Dad. Listen, I'm going to talk to Roz. She might know how to approach this."

"Rosalyn Wells? That's right, she's a lawyer, isn't she?"

"Yeah, she does both criminal and civil law. I think adoptions are done in civil court."

"Talk to her. And let me know if she needs my help to figure this out."

Jason hadn't expected a P.I. to have a nice office in a high rise downtown. He had thought a shabby store front in the seediest part of town was likely where he'd find his sleuth. What was probably true, though, was that he'd watched too many detective shows on TV.

He rode the escalator to the second floor. Not much of a view from there. Preoccupied with what he would say to the P.I., he almost missed seeing Merry on the opposite escalator, going down.

"Merry!"

She looked his way, frowned, and faced forward.

Huh? What's her problem? "Merry!" he yelled as she moved further away.

At last she swiveled and yelled back over her shoulder, "Blow it out your ass, Falco."

What the hell? She had seemed fine yesterday. More than fine. Warm, cuddly, and responsive. He sighed.

Women. I wonder what I've done now.

He thought about turning around and catching up with her. Would she tell him what was on her mind or would she give him one of those "If you don't know what you did wrong, I'm certainly not going to tell you" responses?

Maybe he should let her cool down. After all, she had admitted to PMSing recently. Whatever minor infraction he had committed, she'd probably feel foolish about it as soon as her hormones returned to normal.

Deciding to continue on, he arrived at a long hallway with floor to ceiling glass offices on either side. *That's ballsy for a private dick. I guess he's not afraid of retribution via gunfire.*

Finally, he located the office with *Joseph Murphy LLC.* inscribed on the door. Heading inside toward the receptionist, he took in the trappings of the small but neat office. It offered comfortable contemporary furniture in the waiting area, tables, magazines, and a newspaper. Great, if he had to wait, at least he'd have something to read.

"I'm Jason Falco. I have an appointment with Mr. Murphy," he told the receptionist.

She stopped filing her nails and lifted her bleached blonde head. "Joe will be right with you, Mr. Falco." Then she scowled at him and went back to her manicure.

Hmmm... Not even a smile. Not very friendly, although she calls her boss 'Joe.'

Jason found a seat on the white leather couch and reached for the paper. It was folded open to one of the inside pages. And there he discovered his picture! Actually, three pictures of him. One with Merry, kissing in the parking lot at the bachelor auction; one with his "date" on her doorstep the following night. And one with a fan who stopped him on the street for his autograph. To his horror, the headline read—Three-timing Falco!

Oh my God! No wonder Merry gave him the cold shoulder! He glanced up and saw the receptionist glaring at him. *Oh, crap.*

Anxiously he scanned the article to see what kind of

details they may have divulged. *Please don't have my address in there.*

Under the picture of Merry, the story read, "Live-in girlfriend, Allison Flores, no longer lovey-dovey."

He held up the newspaper to show the receptionist. "This whole article was completely fabricated."

"Sure it was…" she said with a sarcastic smirk.

"It was! First of all, I'm living alone and I don't know anyone named Allison Flores. This is my girlfriend, Merry. Then, I had to take out the second woman as an obligation because she paid for me in a bachelor auction. And this third one—"

"Yeah, yeah. Save it for someone who cares. I'll see if Joe's ready to see you." She buzzed her boss and announced Jason's presence.

"You know what? Maybe I will talk to him about it. I want the hide of the reporter who wrote this."

"He'll find her, but he won't skin her for you. You'll have to do that yourself."

Jason's lips thinned into a hard line and his nostrils flared. "I just might."

Merry's best friend Roz sat across the kitchen table from her and handed her a tissue.

"Merry, open this door!" Jason pounded again. "I know you're in there."

Merry blew her nose and yelled, "Go away!"

Roz gave her that pathetic smile. The one that says, "I know what you're going through, and thank God it's not happening to me."

"Please! I need to talk to you," Jason yelled.

"Give him a chance, Merry. You said yourself he didn't seem like the two-timing type. And what about the woman using a made up name for you? Chances are the whole story was made up."

Merry thought about it for another minute. It was very possible that a good explanation existed, so why didn't she want to hear it?

Maybe he'd lie and just break her heart again later. Maybe she wanted to show him what would happen if he did cheat on her… if she let him live.

Roz grasped her hand and squeezed. "Merry, just open the door and talk to him. I'm right here if you need me."

It was harder to say no to two people than one, so she heaved a sigh and shuffled to the door. For some reason, she decided to look through the peephole, even though she knew full well who stood on the opposite side.

Jason's posture slumped and he stuck his hands in his pockets. He turned toward the elevator and started to leave.

She opened the door quickly and said, "Wait. I'll talk to you."

Jason spun and strode back to her. "Merry, the newspaper article is a lie." He stood before her, but thankfully didn't reach for her. She would have backed away. She wasn't ready to forgive him—or the reporter. Not yet.

"Someone set me up, Merry."

She tilted her head. "And why would anyone want to do that?"

He shrugged. "I don't know. Maybe to sell news-papers? Because people like to see celebrities stumble and fall to prove they're human and no better than they are? I have no idea. All I know is that I'm not three-timing you or even two-timing you."

"I know about the woman who won you in the auction, but who's the other one?"

"No idea. She said she was a fan. She grabbed and hugged me before I had a chance to react. I practically had to peel her off, but that wasn't my fault. For all I know, the reporter paid her to do it."

"Either that or she was in the right place at the wrong time."

"Merry, I swear...!"

"So did I—when my father told me about the article."

"Your father saw it?"

"Yeah. So did the neighbors back home."

"Shit. But it's all a lie!"

Roz poked her head around the corner and said, "Is everything okay?"

Merry shrugged.

Jason looked surprised. "Oh, I didn't know you had a friend here."

"Yeah, imagine that. I have someone who cares about me."

"You know that's not what I meant. Besides, I care about you too—a lot, and you know it."

She heaved a sigh. Then she looked into his sincere face and said, "I know. I care about you too."

"Then could you please stop torturing me for something I didn't do? I swear you're the only woman I'm dating and that's how I want to keep it. I can't leave with you feeling this way."

She stepped forward into his grasp, and they held each other tight.

"Now that's more like it," Roz said.

Merry had almost forgotten she was watching them. "Oh." She let go, but kept her arm around his waist. "Jason Falco, this is Rosalyn Wells. My best friend from home."

He extended his hand but kept one arm around Merry's waist as if she might try to escape. "Nice to meet you, Rosalyn. Did you drive up here from Rhode Island?"

"No, I live near the Allston line, and feel free to call me Roz."

"Part of the reason I moved to Boston was to be closer to Roz," Merry said. "We've been best friends since grade school."

"I'm glad you live in Boston, then. I might not have met Merry otherwise."

"Unless you believe in fate," Roz said.

Merry tipped her head up to look in Jason's eyes. He smiled. "Maybe I do. I can't imagine my life without Merry in it anymore. You scared me, babe."

She wrapped her other arm around him again and squeezed. "You scared me too."

"I told you things like this might happen. Please talk to me before believing any crap like that. I'll always tell you the truth, I promise."

They exchanged warm smiles and a short but very sweet, tender kiss. "I love you," he whispered in her ear.

Roz cleared her throat, "Well, I should be going…"

"No, you don't have to," they both responded at once. Then they chuckled.

"I didn't mean to interrupt your visit," Jason said. "Merry knows where I am when she's free."

"No, I really have things to do," Roz said. "But if you want to find this bitch reporter and threaten her with libel, I can hook you up with a colleague of mine."

"Why wouldn't you handle it yourself?" Merry asked.

Jason showed a spark of recognition. "Oh, you must be the lawyer Merry gave as a reference."

"Yes. I graduated from Suffolk Law a couple of years ago. I'm still low woman on the totem pole at Payne, Richards, and Stewart. In the same building where Merry saw you earlier."

"What kind of law do you practice?"

She and Merry exchanged glances. Merry nodded.

"I used to do civil work, mostly divorces, but now I'm a public defender, and for some reason I get the weird cases."

"Weird?" he asked. "What kind of weird?"

"Weeeeiiiird. The kind of cases most people find hard to believe. I'd give you an example or two, but... well, never mind. That's not important. I have a colleague who's very good at intimidation. I could recommend you to him."

Jason smiled. "That won't be necessary, but thanks."

"I don't know," Merry said. "I'd like to see you do it. People shouldn't get away with that kind of thing. It's rotten, destructive, and just plain wrong."

"You know how I feel about rocking the boat, Merry. I'd rather not."

"Then I will," she said.

Chapter 7

LILA SAT AT HER FAVORITE BAR STOOL AND TOASTED herself—in more ways than one. Kevin polished glasses and occasionally glanced her way.

"So you saved your career?"

She smiled proudly. "Yep, I shertainly did."

"I hope it was worth saving."

She narrowed her eyes. "Wha's dat shupposed to mean?"

Kevin draped the dishcloth over his shoulder and leaned on the bar. "I mean, it doesn't seem to be making you happy."

Shocked, Lila lightly rocked back on her stool. "Not happy? What are you, nuts? Here I am shcelebrating, and you think I'm unhappy? Maybe you need glashes."

"Look, Lila, I've known you for about two years, right?"

"Uh huh... and?"

"And I worry about you. In that time I've seen you go from bad to worse with only brief moments of what some people call happiness. I call it oblivion."

I'm feeling positively giddy. What's his problem? Lila tried to stand to make an angry point, but her ankles wobbled and she wound up on her ass. "Owww... Hey, where'd the floor come from?"

Kevin must have jogged around the bar, because the next thing she saw was his extended hand. "Come on, Lila. Get up. Customers are gawking."

"Let 'em look. I don't need your help. I can shtand

by myshelf." She shuffled to a sitting position between
two bar stools and leaned against the bar. Using the
rails for leverage, she took a deep breath and pushed.
When she tried to lift herself, her feet slipped out
from beneath her and she sat down hard, legs splayed.
"Owww... I need a whoopee cushion." After a short
delay to process it, she realized what she had said and
began to laugh. Her laughter escalated to hysteria. Soon
she was weeping with laughter and her sides hurt as
much as her tailbone.

Strong arms hauled her up, dragged her over to a
chair, and plopped her onto it. "Stay there," Kevin said.
"I'll bring you some coffee."

"I don't want coffee. It'll kill the buzz." She rested
her head on the table and decided the word "buzz"
was a pretty funny word. "Buzzzzzz... Buzzzzzz..."
Suddenly, she sprang to her feet and said, "Time to get
up!" Staggering, she made her way toward the door.

"No, Lila!" Kevin yelled. "Don't go."

"Awww... Why? You gonna mish me?" She leaned
against the strong oak door for support.

The sensation of the door pulling away from her and
her body falling were the last things she remembered.

Merry had just walked in the door when her telephone
rang. Who could be calling her at midnight? *Oh no. I
hope nothing's wrong at home.* She trotted to the kitchen
and grabbed her phone.

"Hello?"

"Merry, it's Jason."

"Hi!" Maybe her lover missed her warm body and

wanted her in his bed for the night. That would be much better than an emergency.

"My dad is sick and I have to go home to Minnesota for a few days."

Her bubble burst. "Oh." She didn't mean to sound so crestfallen, but a few days apart? She couldn't help wondering, was his dad really sick? Or was Jason sick of her?

"What's the matter, honey?"

"Nothing," she said.

"Come on. Nothing always means something."

"Well, it's just the timing. I had hoped to see you. I have a little surprise, but it can wait." She opened the cage and stroked her new pet rabbit as he waited for his food.

"Ah, I see. Well, I need to see my dad. Can you come with me?

"Come with…?" Stunned but pleased that he'd asked, her insecurity abated. "Actually, I can't. I have to work, but I'll keep my cell phone with me in case you need support. What happened?"

"Heart attack. My dad's a typical type-A personality, so it's not terribly surprising."

"Oh, I'm sorry."

"My plane leaves tomorrow morning. I'll come down and say good-bye before you leave for work, okay?"

"Uh, sure. What time in the morning?"

"Eight-thirty. I'll have to leave by six. Oh, I forgot. You'll be asleep."

"That's okay, Jason. You can wake me."

"No. You need your sleep. I'll call you when I've seen my dad. That way you'll know my plane landed safely and how long I might be away."

"Sure. That'll be fine."

"I'll miss you," he said softly.

"I'll miss you too."

But since her period had just arrived, she wouldn't miss having to work around that so early in their relationship. At least she had spoken to a doctor at her hospital about those birth control pills that cut your periods down to only four times a year. He'd given her a sample as well as a prescription, so she was going to start on it right away... and while she was at it, maybe they could get tested for AIDS and the two of them could dispense with the condoms.

"Hey, Jason? How would you feel about getting an AIDS test when you get back?"

"Is that my surprise?"

She laughed. "No. Just a thought. If I get tested too, maybe you could ride bareback, if you know what I mean...?"

"Oh, yeah. I know what you mean, and I like how you think. Maybe I'll get my doc in Minnesota to give me a test and I'll bring my results home to you."

"I'd like that a whole lot." And *he* would like the fact that she'd only have PMS four times a year instead of twelve! That *and* "Buns" were his surprise.

Merry and Roz sat together at the dance club with long faces. Apparently the guys had decided that Roz was Merry's wingwoman and they approached in pairs. The ugly dude asked Roz to dance, while the guy who thought he had a shot with Merry seemed to expect her to jump at the opportunity to dance with him.

So far, everyone paled in comparison to Jason. They seemed way too young. Lots of college students lived in the area. The older men were either drunk or sleazy or both. Merry had refused repeat dances with everyone and was running out of excuses. Her feet hurt, she was tired, she was starting to sweat and hated sweating, etc.

"I'm thinking about leaving, Roz," she shouted over the loud music. "Are you with me?"

"One hundred percent."

They grabbed their evening bags and headed for the exit. When they had escaped outside, Merry's ears were ringing. "Jeez, that music was loud."

"What?"

She raised her voice and spoke to Roz's ear. "Is this an off night, or are most clubs like this?"

"I'm sorry to say, this is fairly typical. You won't find many Jasons in the world, let alone in a place like this." Roz's words seemed muted and far away.

Merry stuck her finger in her ear and wiggled it. "I hate to say this, but I'm maybe an eight and all these threes and fours think they're God's gift. Am I delusional?"

A couple of men passing by gave her a once over. One of them called over his shoulder. "You're a ten, babe. If only I wasn't married…"

Oops. She must have been talking louder than normally, but who could tell?

Roz shook her head and chuckled. "No. You're not delusional, except that you think you're an eight. You're a solid nine, and the only reason you're not a ten is because you're moping."

"I am moping, aren't I?"

"If your face were any longer it would hit the sidewalk."

Merry sighed. They continued to walk in silence until they reached Roz's car. Once inside, Merry sagged against the seat.

"I'm an idiot, aren't I?"

Roz glanced in her direction as she turned the key. "What do you mean?"

"I mean, I thought this whole living in the city experience would be so much different. I admit, I'm not as excited as I should have been tonight, but honestly, where were all the good-looking GQ models? Do they go to different clubs or what?"

Roz laughed. "Yeah, honey. The gay bars. Listen, I'll tell you something my mother once told me. 'For every perfect-looking guy, there's at least one woman who's sick of putting up with his crap.'"

Merry chuckled. "You're mother is probably right about that."

They pulled into the busy street and drove back to Merry's neighborhood. On the way, they passed Brookline Ave. Merry remembered her tour of Fenway Park and the wonderful man who'd not only *forgiven* her jealous outburst, but made sweet, tender love to her on the couch in a luxury box.

"Did I ever tell you about our trip to Fenway Park?"

"Yes, and did I ever tell you how envious I am?"

A sigh escaped, then hot tears threatened to surface from the corners of her eyes. *Oh, no. Don't react like a big baby over this.*

It wasn't as if she needed her boyfriend's consent to go dancing with a girlfriend. In a way, she was glad she did. Now, at least she knew what she *wasn't* missing. Still, she felt guilty.

"You won't tell Jason about this, will you?" Roz asked.

"Why not?"

"Why would you? He doesn't need to know you visited a club out of curiosity. It would only hurt him and it certainly didn't amount to anything—except maybe cure you of your ridiculous idea about what single life in the city is like."

Merry inhaled deeply. "I suppose you're right. I can't help feeling guilty, though. He's home with a sick parent and here I was, kicking up my heels—or trying to."

"Hey, he might not be as saintly as you think, either. Didn't he have any girlfriends back home?"

Merry's green-eyed monster grabbed her by the throat. "You don't think he'd… No, I can't picture it. He even asked me to come with him. And he says he loves me."

Roz smiled knowingly. "And you love him."

Merry simply stared at her friend.

"You do, don't you?"

She faced forward and let the traffic mesmerize her. She wasn't ready to admit it before, but now… "You may be right. I was holding back because of this 'ridiculous' city-life idea, as you called it."

"Well, I'm damned glad we burst your bubble."

"I feel like an idiot."

Roz shrugged. "Yeah. Welcome to the human race."

—∿∿—

Chad knew that Morgaine, besides doing phone sex, was also a first class phone psychic. When he wanted to get her attention, she usually knew it and tuned in to him. Sometimes, however, he suspected that she tuned him out on purpose and pretended not to hear him rattle her beaded curtain, or stomp around, or move light objects.

Like today. He wanted to know what was going on with his investigation, and she was ignoring him.

He had already hidden one of her earrings. It was her favorite pair, too. Dangly copper with Aztec-like designs. She'd said they conduct electricity to her head and third eye. *All the better to tell your fortune, my dear…* Plus she thought the copper looked groovy against her black hair and black clothing. He saw her searching frantically for the missing one.

Maybe she already knew what he wanted and couldn't tell him anything more than what he'd heard already. *That would be just like a psychic, but damn it, the least she can do is ask Jason what's happening.* Had he hired a private investigator like he was supposed to? Do they have any leads? Do they need any more information?

Well, we'll see how well she deals with having her phone lines crossed. That ought to get her attention. Oh good—it's ringing and she's across the room. Let's see, which one is it? Ah, the psychic line. Let me make a slight adjustment, and… there. That call is now coming into the phone-sex line. He couldn't wait to see the result of his prank.

Morgaine picked up the telephone and in her sexiest voice, she said, "Hello, lover. This is Venus. Tell me what I can do for you." Silence greeted her.

"You're awfully quiet. Some first time callers need a bit of encouragement. Is that what's going on? I'll do anything you want, and I mean *anything*."

Click.

"That's odd," she said.

Gwyneth spoke from the kitchen. "What's odd?"

"Someone on the sex line hung up on me. I must be losing my touch."

"Y'all were probably just disconnected. Don't pay it no nevermind."

"Yeah, maybe." Morgaine waited another minute for the caller to try again. When nothing happened, she strolled into the kitchen. "What are you making?"

"I'm tryin' out a recipe for one of those Yule log things."

"Yule isn't until December twenty-first. Why are you making it now?"

"Well, they're tricky. I figure I have plenty of time to practice so I can get it right for the actual day."

"Smart."

The phone rang.

"Oh, there he is, Morgaine. I'll bet he's a shy one who had to screw up his courage." Then she laughed. "Maybe I should reword that."

Morgaine strode toward the phone. "No, you said it perfectly."

Breathlessly, she crooned into the receiver. "Hey, baby. I knew you'd call back. Now don't be shy. We can just talk for a while if you want—if this is your first time…"

A female voice responded. "Uh, no. This isn't my first time."

Morgaine wrinkled her nose.

I've heard her say she doesn't like doing lesbian phone sex and didn't advertise that way, but occasionally it happened and heck, she needed the money. Chad perked up his ghostly ears expectantly.

"Oh, I didn't recognize your voice, sweetheart. Forgive me. What do you need from Venus today?"

"Huh? Is Venus in conjunction with something?"

Morgaine glanced at the phone and double-checked the lines.

Yup. It's the phone sex line, babe. Chad hovered over the desk so he could hear every word.

She sighed. "It's all right. I'm a go with the flow type. Venus can be in conjunction with you, sweetheart. Is that what you need? A little licking? Some finger action? I can strap on a dildo and—"

"What? Excuse me? Do I have the right number? I'm looking for Madam Morgaine, telephone psychic."

Morgaine gasped. "Oh! I'm sorry. No, you must have the wrong number. I—I thought you were my—girlfriend. What number did you dial?"

The woman repeated the number of the psychic line.

Chad knew the two lines were nine-hundred numbers but in no way similar. On purpose. Just to prevent this little problem.

Hmmm, what could have happened?

He blew a breath of cold air down her cleavage.

Morgaine suddenly realized there was a *ghost* of a chance that the source of the problem might be Chad and her lips thinned to a hard line.

"Ma'am, I think there's something wrong with the phone lines. Could you call back later, please?"

"Okay…" the woman said, sounding confused.

Morgaine hung up, rose, and jammed her hands on her hips. Then she yelled at the ceiling, "You fuckwad, Chad! What the fuck…?"

"Really! Such language, and from a nice Southern girl."

"I'm from Maryland, you idiot."

"That's south of Boston." He laughed. *"It's about time I received your undivided attention. I want to know what's happening with my murder investigation."*

"Rot in hell, you self-centered, inconsiderate spook!"

"Hey, I don't appreciate the racial slur."

"It wasn't a racial slur, you jerk. It was an insult aimed at your ghostliness. If you were alive, I'd…"

"Yeah? Well, I'm not. So what are you gonna do now?" Chad purposely came close enough to chill her and she shivered.

Gwyneth poked her head around the kitchen corner. "What's goin' on?"

"It's that friggin' ghost. He messed up the phone lines on us, just because I couldn't talk to him right away."

"Well, that's no good, honey. You need to talk to him. Ask him nicely what he wants and tell him we'll help him if he puts the phone lines back the way they were."

Chad backed off. *"Listen to your kiss-ass cousin, Morgaine. She knows how to respect her elders."*

"You're not my elder. I'm thirty and you're frozen somewhere in your twenties—going on twelve." Morgaine crossed her arms. "Besides, elders are wise and you're just a wiseass. I can't help you. I don't know anything more than you know already."

"Go talk to baseball-boy. Ask him if he hired that private dick. I want to know what's happening on my case."

"Fuckin' A… Okay, I'll ask."

"Are you sure you want to do this, Merry?"

Roz put her hand on Merry's shoulder, slowing her

determined march toward the paparazzo's apartment in Dorchester.

"I have to. First of all, what she did was just plain mean, and second, I want to know where she came up with my birth name."

Roz shrugged. "I'll admit it's a hell of a coincidence. Did you tell Jason what you're planning to do?"

"No, he has enough to think about."

"He might have even more to think about if he knew you were in this neighborhood. I don't have a good feeling about this place."

Merry glanced around her. The street was lined with three-story tenements in various stages of disrepair. Chain-link fences surrounded most of the yards. Graffiti decorated the boarded-up, broken windows on one house that seemed to be abandoned. When Merry saw a small face in an upstairs window peering down at her, she shivered. *What a place to raise children.*

"Look, I was attacked in one of the nicest areas of the city. It can happen anywhere."

Roz glanced all around. "I almost feel sorry for the woman, living in a place like this."

Merry glared at her best friend. "You didn't say what I thought you just said. Did you?"

"No. You misheard me. I said, the woman's a bitch."

"Good. Now, harden your heart or something. We're coming up to her house."

Merry glanced at the paper on which Roz had scrawled the woman's address. A dilapidated grayish blue house with grayish white trim stood behind the obligatory chain-link fence. A gate ran across it and was padlocked. "Damnation! We came all this way and we can't even get to the front door? Isn't that illegal?"

Roz shrugged. "It might be against some fire code or something. Maybe she gets her mail at a post office box and never has visitors."

Merry faced the gate with her hands on her hips. "Well, she's getting visitors today."

"What are you thinking? You're not going to climb over that fence are you?"

"No. The gate. It's smoother on top."

"Holy crap, Merry. Are you nuts? What if she shoots you for trespassing?"

"I'm not going home without talking to her." Merry fitted her boot between the grates and boosted herself as high as she could by straightening her arms and locking them. Then she swung one leg over. Now straddling the fence, she paused.

"What's wrong?"

"Nothing."

"Then why are you stopping?"

"I'm stuck."

"You're what?" Roz examined Merry's clothing. "I don't see anything caught on the fence."

"It's not that. Either I'm going to break a wrist or perform a female castration on myself."

"Holy mother... Well, you got yourself into this. Think of something to get yourself out."

"This is a very delicate operation. Let's see, I could..." She shifted one hand quickly so she didn't twist her wrist on the dismount. Then she swung the other leg up behind her and braced that knee at the top.

At last, she sprang away from the gate and landed on the concrete walkway on the other side. "There!"

"Very impressive." Roz crossed her arms and stayed where she was.

"Now you try it."

"Hell no! I might want to have children someday."

"If I can do it...."

Roz gestured to her own body with both hands. "In case you hadn't noticed, I weigh a little more than you. I don't think I could support my weight on my hands like you did."

Merry tipped her head. "Of course you can. Just lock your elbows."

"Yeah, and break my wrists. Look, Merry, I love you and everything, but I can't do this."

"But you were going to be my witness. I can't do this without you." Merry knew she was whining, but didn't care. Whatever it took. She *had* to confront this woman.

"Look, I'm sorry. Maybe I can witness your conversation from here. Just refuse to go inside. That might not be a bad idea, anyway. You wouldn't want to give her access to her gun."

"What makes you think she has a gun?"

At that moment, the front door opened and revealed a tall, fit man with brown hair askew. "Can I help you?" he asked.

"Oh, uh... Is this where Lila Crum lives?" Merry asked.

The man eyed both of them with suspicion and crossed his arms. "What business do you have with Lila?"

"It's personal," Merry said, as she trotted up the steps.

A female voice from inside the house called out, "Kevin, who are you talking to?"

The man continued staring at Merry and said, "She isn't feeling very well right now."

"This won't take long. Can you ask her to come to the door?"

"For fuck's sake, Kevin!" the voice yelled. "I asked who you're talking to."

Merry yelled around him. "Look, I just want to talk to you for a minute."

"Go away," yelled the voice. "I don't want to hear about your religion or anything else you're selling."

The guy at the door didn't appear to like being ordered around. His lips thinned as he glanced back into the house. "They're not selling anything, Lila. Get out here and talk to them." He left Merry there with the door open and strolled out of view.

Merry turned to Roz and shrugged as if to say, What do I do now?

Roz shook her head vehemently, so Merry waited on the doorstep.

Before long the guy reappeared wearing a jacket and called back over his shoulder, "I'm going, Lila. *You're welcome* for last night."

"Wait!" the woman yelled.

The guy rolled his eyes and waited next to Merry. She just had to ask, "Are you her boyfriend?"

"No. I'm her bartender." He called back into the house, "I have to get home. I need to change and get to work so the fun can begin all over again."

"You do this for all your customers?"

"Nope. I've never done this before and probably won't do it again."

The woman, presumably the very rumpled Lila Crum,

stumbled to the door. She pushed her scraggly brown hair off her face and blinked a couple of times as if to clear her vision. "Sorry, Kevin. What did you say about last night?"

"I said you're welcome."

"For taking me home, or…"

"Or what?"

"Did anything else happen?"

He looked exasperated. "You don't remember anything, do you? If you mean did I take advantage of you, the answer is no. I helped you to your bedroom and tucked you in. Look. You're still wearing your clothes."

She looked down at her wrinkled brown shirt and black jeans and nodded. "So where did you sleep?"

"On your couch."

"Oh. Well, uh—thanks."

"Yeah, like I said, you're welcome." Then he charged down the stairs and halted on the walkway. "Shit," he muttered. "Lila, will you unlock this damn gate?"

"Oh, sure." She disappeared into the house and returned with a set of keys. As she handed the key ring to Kevin, she finally turned her attention to Merry. "How the hell did you get in?"

"I had to climb over the gate. You might want to leave it unlocked. A person could get hurt that way."

Her eyes narrowed. "You're trespassing. That means I can shoot you."

"I wouldn't if I were you. See that woman there?" She pointed to Roz. "She's a very talented lawyer and my best friend. I doubt you'd want her to witness my murder."

Kevin had unlocked the gate, but Roz wisely stayed on the other side.

"Well, maybe I'll just shoot you both."

He rushed back up the stairs and wedged himself between Merry and the homicidal reporter. "You're not shooting anybody, Lila."

Lila peered around him. "Who are you, anyway?"

"You don't recognize me? You took my picture... and you printed it in the newspaper."

Kevin stepped away and Lila eyed her curiously. "Oh! You're Allison," she finally said, smiling as if they were long lost friends.

"That's debatable." Merry crossed her arms. "First of all, how did you come up with that name?"

"What do you mean, 'come up with' it? I do my research. I don't invent the facts. I just report them."

Merry laughed, then quickly cleared her throat. "Let me say this differently. How did you research my name?"

"I talked to some guy hanging around outside your building. Long black hair... black eyes... black clothes... kind of pale."

Merry recognized the description of Sly, but that only confused her more. Lila continued, so she must not have felt the need to protect her source.

"I figured you two were related since he had the same last name. Flores, isn't it?"

Merry took a step back. "Is it?"

Lila nodded. "Yeah. I'm pretty sure he said his name was Sylvestro Flores. I have it written down somewhere."

Merry was so stunned she almost forgot what she had originally wanted to confront her about. *Almost*. "So, where do you get off trying to ruin other people's love lives? Are you so miserable that you want everyone else to be miserable too? Jason Falco is a decent, honorable man, and you had no business—"

Lila laughed. "Oh, for fuck's sake. You can't be serious."

"I'm as serious as a gas attack."

Kevin chuckled. "Uh, I think that's supposed to be 'serious as a heart attack'."

"Oh." Merry felt the blush rising from her neck to her face.

Lila laughed hysterically. When she could speak again, she said. "Look, don't bother lecturing me. I have first amendment rights and I can print whatever the hell I observe and I saw him cheat on you with my own eyes."

"Bullshit," Merry yelled. "He wasn't cheating. You were at that bachelor auction and you knew he was obligated to take that woman out. And the other woman you saw was just a fan who happened to recognize him as he was out getting some fresh air. It's because of people like you that he has to avoid being seen in public."

Lila leaned against her house. "Oh, isn't that sweet. You decided to stand by your man."

Merry wanted to jump the woman right there and scratch her eyes out. She took a step forward and Kevin jammed his body in front of her again.

Roz came rushing up the walkway, shouting, "Don't touch her, Merry. So far, you're okay and all we needed to do is warn the woman."

"Warn me? About what?"

Roz straightened to her legal-eagle pose. "Leave Merry and Falco alone, or I'll slap you with a lawsuit for libel."

"Why is she calling you Merry?"

"Because that's my name, doofus."

Kevin shifted uncomfortably. "Look, I don't like the possibility of getting in the middle of a cat fight. If you've said what you came to say, you should go, now."

Roz nodded. "I agree. Let's go, Merry. She's been warned."

Merry hesitated long enough to give the bitch the evil eye. "Fine," she said between clenched teeth. "But I'll be watching you." She pointed at Lila as she joined Roz.

Lila's eyes lit up as though she enjoyed the challenge. "Oh, you do that."

———

"Come on, Morgaine. You've been stalling all week. I know you don't like interacting with the nosy bitch, but I'll be right there with you. If she gives you any trouble, I'll trip her and you can enjoy watching her fall ass over teakettle down the stairs."

Morgaine tittered. "Chad, all I can say is I'm glad you're on *my* side. Okay, let's go." She tossed her book onto the coffee table and wrapped a black shawl around her shoulders.

"Sorry about the draft."

She shrugged. "You can't help it. I understand."

"Do you mind taking the stairs? It's only one flight, and the elevator's kind of a pain in the ass for me."

"Sure. No problem. I wish I could just go to the penthouse directly, but his aunt made it clear that we're not to bother him." She opened the door and hesitated a moment before she closed it. "Are you out?"

"Out and hovering over the stairs. You realize you wouldn't have hurt me even if you had slammed it on my foot, right?"

"Oh, that's right. Well, pardon me for being courteous."

"I was just busting your chops. Let's do this thing."

Morgaine descended gracefully down the steps to the second floor.

Chad really liked Morgaine. He couldn't figure out why she didn't try to date more. *She's certainly pretty enough by anyone's standards—in a gothy way, but still… I guess her need to stay close to the telephone cramps her style.* It was a shame Dottie made them curtail their noisy phone calls. That was part of the fun. Now they'd lost customers and didn't know what they'd do to make ends meet.

Morgaine was training Gwyneth on the psychic hotline and hoped to train herself to act as a medium. That was the deal. She'd help Chad, and he'd help her. He hoped they'd be able to pull it off. It was one thing to open your mind and listen to a spirit who's trying to communicate with you. It's quite another level of difficulty to open your mouth and let them use your vocal cords. He wasn't sure this psychic thing was really a good gig for them.

What's worse is sometimes you have to summon the spirits, and God knows where they are. I mean, I'm hanging around my old apartment because I don't know where else to go. Outdoors is a really bad idea on windy days and if you think rain or snow feels lousy hitting you on your skin, imagine what it feels like passing right through you. Brrrr… "Oh, good, we're here."

Morgaine raised her fist to knock and hesitated.

"Come on, my witchy friend. You can do this."

She heaved a sigh, but before she could bring her knuckles down on the door, it opened. Dottie stood there as if she had been looking out the peephole the minute they arrived. She probably had.

"Morgaine! What brings you downstairs?"

She fidgeted and looked uncomfortable. "I… um. I need to get in touch with Jason."

"What do you need Jason for?"

"Tell her to mind her own business. Tell her to go jump in the river. Tell her to—"

"I need to ask him about the investigation."

Dottie's eyes lit up. "Oh, yes. The private detective… We *must* get that ghost out of our building."

Morgaine waited, but Dottie didn't appear to want to share any more information. Either that or she didn't have any.

"Would you help me speak to Jason about it, please?"

"Oh, you don't need to do that. I know Jason found someone very good and hired him."

Morgaine sighed again. "Look, Chad is badgering me to give him some kind of news or an update about what's going on."

"Badgering you? Since when have I badgered?"

Morgaine looked to her left side and said, "Yes, you've badgered me, Chad. You've been a royal pain in the ass about it, so don't sound so surprised."

Dottie stared at her and raised one eyebrow. "You're arguing with the ghost right now? He's here with you?"

"Yeah, sorry about that. He's driving me nuts."

"Oh, well we can't have that, can we? Come in, dear. Jason's not home."

"I wondered why I hadn't seen him. So why didn't she say that in the first place? And what does she expect to gain by inviting you in if she doesn't know anything, and—"

Morgaine looked at the ceiling and said, "Shut up, Chad." Then she accepted Dottie's invitation, followed her inside, and sat on the flowered slip-covered couch.

Dottie glanced at the ceiling nervously. "I don't think I want him in my home. You have to invite them in, don't you?"

"That's vampires. Ghosts can go wherever they damn well please. What a moron."

Morgaine shook her head. "If I could keep him out, I would, believe me. Unfortunately, he'll just pull some nasty stunt to get my attention if I try to ignore him."

"Oh, dear," Dottie muttered. "Well, maybe I can call Jason and find out the private detective's name and number. I'm sure we can get you some kind of information if we try."

She looked at the ceiling and raised her voice. "I'm just going for the phone book, Chad." She inched over to the roll-top desk as if the unseen presence had a gun trained on her.

"This could be fun, but as long as she's cooperating, I'll leave her alone and let her do her thing. I'd almost rather she'd stop and be her rude self again. Then I could blow a cool breeze down her neck and frighten her out of her wits. Now that would be enjoyable."

She flipped through a few pages of a private phone book with a black leather cover. "Okay, this is his mother's number. I'm sure he's staying with her while his father's in the hospital."

"Oh? What happened to his father?" Morgaine asked.

"Heart attack." She looked at the ceiling again. "So you be nice to him when he gets home. Apparently it's been quite an ordeal."

"Yeah, yeah. Get on with it, pokey."

She dialed ten numbers and waited. And waited. They *all* waited. Finally her eyes lit up and she said, "Hi, Jason. You're just the one I wanted to speak with. How's your father?"

"Who the fuck cares... I want to know who shot me. Can you hurry it up, please?"

Morgaine frowned. Fortunately her eyes focused in the opposite direction, so she might as well have been frowning at the toaster.

"Oh, good. I'm glad to hear that," Dottie said. "Listen, dear... I'm sitting here with Morgaine, the girl from 3B who can hear our ghost. And, well... apparently the ghost is here too."

"Chad. My name is Chad. Or Charles. Or Mr. Washington. Look, just because they took away my body doesn't mean you can just forget my name. I'm an entity with an identity. Hey, I like that. Tell her that, Morgaine!"

Morgaine shook her head.

"Oh, I'm all right, but the ghost is pestering Morgaine to find out what's going on with the investigation. I was hoping you could tell us something."

Dottie grabbed a pen and paper. "Yes, I'm ready. Okay... Joe Murphy. 555-4329." She appeared exceedingly pleased. "Thank you, Jason. I'm sure that will help to satisfy our spirit visitor. So, when are you coming home?"

"Hey, Morgaine... maybe you can ask her to invite the detective over and you can practice your medium lessons. That way I can give the detective some leads and ask him questions directly."

Morgaine nodded toward Dottie as if to tell Chad to wait for her to get off the phone. Damn manners.

She continued blathering on to give her love to all the other family members while Chad yawned and drummed his virtual fingers on the desktop. He was just about to blast her with a gust of cold breath when she finally, finally hung up.

"I'm sorry to make you wait, dear," she said to Morgaine. "But I think we have what we need." She waved the telephone number as if it were a clue to her own mystery. "I've been dying to talk to him anyway."

"Ah ha, just as I thought. The woman couldn't resist sticking her nose into it, could she?"

Morgaine put on her nicest smile and said, "I don't suppose you could invite the detective to come here? Perhaps that way, Chad could speak to him through me?"

"Oh." Dottie straightened, looking somewhat offended. "You're a medium too, I suppose." Then she glanced around the apartment and whispered, "Is he still here?"

"I think so. I can't see him. I can only hear him, since I'm clairaudient, not clairvoyant. I'm still just learning to be a medium." Morgaine cocked her head. "Chad, are you still here?"

"Tell her I'm so fucking here that I'll kick her through the ass if she thinks for one minute she's going to take away my right to participate in my own cold case and let her try to manage it."

Morgaine nodded. "Yes, ma'am. He's here."

"Okay, I'll call the detective and we'll see what we can arrange that will be convenient for all of us." She paused with the receiver in her hand. "I don't suppose he has any appointments I should work around, does he?" She laughed.

"That does it." Chad blew a big gust of cold air right in Dottie's face and she shivered, casting her eyes nervously around the room. *"Finally, an appropriate expression of fear. It's about time! I was ready to sing my rendition of R-E-S-P-E-C-T."*

Chapter 8

MERRY COULDN'T BELIEVE HOW MUCH SHE MISSED Jason. Had they only been together for a few weeks? It didn't seem possible, although she had to admit that certain fine details of his face were fuzzy in her memory.

When she opened her door and threw her arms around him, every nuance came rushing back. His subtle scent, how his stubble softly scratched her cheek, his dimples when he smiled. She wanted to drink in his essence and etch every single detail into her memory. The straightness of his nose, except for the slight bump from when it had been broken, the clarity of his blue eyes...

"God, I missed you," he whispered into her hair. "You were all I could talk about while I was home. My family really wants to meet you."

"I missed you too!" How and when did his presence disarm her so completely? She'd always felt a strong pull, but now the yearning seemed overwhelming. If she had been a spy and he James Bond, she'd hand over the art, cash, and/or passwords. Anything he asked for. All she wanted was to be in his arms.

And to her relief and delight, the feeling seemed mutual. He hugged her close against his hard chest as if he needed to fit her against him so tight a gust of wind couldn't come between them.

"I'm sorry. I should have asked about your father before getting so carried away."

"He's going to be fine. And now that I'm here, so am I."

Merry raised her eyebrows. "Did anything happen to make you feel otherwise?"

"No, not really. Well, nothing specific. You know what it's like to go home after you've been away for quite a while and your life is…"

He trailed off. She must have been wearing a puzzled look because, no, she didn't know what it was like. She had barely flown the nest. Her little wings hadn't carried her far away for very long.

"Well, you know what they say. You can never go home again…"

"Why? What happened to make you feel that way?"

"Nothing traumatic, like having my posters of Britney Spears ripped down and thrown out or anything…"

He poked her with his elbow. It took a moment, but she finally identified his remark as a joke and tried to laugh. Not very convincingly, though.

"I'm sorry. I was trying to be funny. Actually, my old bedroom is now my mother's quilting room. She left a daybed in there for guests, but the décor is drastically different.

"No, that's not what I'm talking about at all. It's just that—things change while you're gone. You think everything is right where you left it and then you're shocked that the movie theatre moved from downtown to a multiplex on the outskirts and the wild piece of land you thought of as 'your favorite view' gets developed into a condominium community. I guess you'll know what I mean in a few years."

Merry's shoulders slumped. Just because she didn't

move out of her father's house as soon as she turned eighteen didn't mean she was... Damn, she couldn't even think of a word for it. *Unworldly*, that was it. She had stayed home in Schooner, Rhode Island, taking care of her family. She'd seen the theatre close and reopen in a bigger and better venue, but it hadn't fazed her at all. And the available land had been developed too. She simply didn't feel nostalgic or care that much. Or maybe nostalgia hadn't had a chance to set in.

It was time to let go of her defensiveness. She tamped down her feelings as well as her issues. They were hers alone and didn't need to become a burden to Jason. He was in a different place and to recognize it would be the wise thing to do.

"I understand," she said.

He swept her into his arms and kissed her hair. "You do? Because I wanted you with me so badly. I wanted to show you all my old haunts, and I wanted to share you with my family to show them the part of my life that's better now than they remembered. I really want to take you home with me for Christmas and already told them to expect you."

Merry tensed.

"Uh-oh." He slapped his forehead. "I know you're close to your family. The words came out before I had a chance to think them through. But seriously, think about it. All I could talk about was you. My family wants to know you. It's only natural."

Silence seemed to dare either of them to speak. At last, he simply picked her up off the floor and left her apartment, yanking the door closed with a slam. Too stunned to speak, Merry wrapped her legs around his waist and held onto his neck as he carried her into the elevator.

"Now, I need to get one thing straight between us, Miss MacKenzie…"

"What?" she asked, breathless.

"Do you love me?" He gazed into her eyes. She noted an expectant lift of his eyebrows and something else. Something she'd never imagine a man like Jason Falco would show. Was it fear? Doubt? Did her answer matter enough to make him insecure?

She pulled him to her tighter and held him as close as she could without smothering him. A confession of love followed by CPR wasn't very romantic.

At last she whispered furiously, "Jason, I love you so much, I can't see straight."

Somehow, the two of them wound up on the elevator's new carpet, feverishly kissing, stroking, sucking, and nipping. Reality disappeared. The only thing that existed was this moment, the touch of his skin; the taste of his mouth; how dizzy she felt and yet how grounded and right everything seemed when he held her and she inhaled his scent.

They lay side by side. His long legs protruded from the elevator. He didn't seem to notice the door trying to close, brushing his blue jeans and opening again. Closing and sliding open. Closing and sliding open.

Merry climbed on top of him. Glad she had gone braless that morning, she leaned over and rubbed her hardened nipples back and forth across his chest. An unquenchable fire sprang up and she moaned.

With his abdomen flat against her, his arousal prodded her belly. She scooched lower until seated flush with his hard-on. He didn't know she wasn't wearing panties, but he soon would. She ground down in circles on top of his erection.

Jason groaned, but in a good way. "I want you so much. God, I can't stand to wait another minute."

The doors stayed open and a strange voice said, "Apparently not."

Oops.

Whipping her head around, Merry spotted Sly. Wearing his usual all-black attire, he stood just outside the elevator. His hand blocked the door and prevented it from closing again.

"Really, Allison. I'd like to say I raised you better than that, but the truth is I never raised you at all."

"Um… What do you mean?"

Jason tried to sit up. Merry scrambled off his lap and stood. She smoothed the wrinkles out of her skirt.

Jason levered himself uncomfortably off the floor and stood beside her. "Merry, why did he call you 'Allison'?"

"I—um… need to ask him some stuff."

"It's a long story," Sly said. Then he focused his gaze on Merry. "I understand you wanted to see me?"

"Yeah. I guess Konrad finally gave you the message."

"No, he told me right away, but I had to wait until your evening off."

"Oh—yeah. I guess you would, if what I was told is true."

Jason scratched the back of his neck. "Does someone want to tell me what's going on here?"

Sly lowered his voice and breathed heavily a couple of times. "Luke, I am her father."

"Funny."

"No, really," Merry said, wide-eyed. "It might be true."

Jason raised his eyebrows and glanced at one, then the other, then back again. "Damn. I can see the resemblance, but…"

Merry cast a hopeful gaze at Sly. "So how…? Um, why…? Oh my, I have so many questions!"

Jason kissed the top of Merry's head. "Why don't you two talk?" He pulled a key card from his pocket and handed it to her. "I had an extra one made for you."

Merry's mouth dropped open. "My own key?"

"I'll be upstairs when you're, um… ready."

"I bet you will," Sly said.

"Thanks, Jason. And you…" Merry pointed an accusing finger at Sly. "You don't get to have an opinion on the matter. I have an overprotective father already, and one's enough."

Sly lifted his hands in a "don't shoot" gesture and took a step back.

"I *will* see you later," Merry said and kissed Jason on the lips—hard.

"Mmm-hmmmph."

When she broke the kiss, Jason retreated into the elevator and Sly let go of the doors so they could slide shut.

"So, you're telling me it's true? You're a… a vampire?"

Sly pulled his long, dark hair off his neck and fastened it behind his head with a silver elastic. Then he leaned against the back of Merry's leather sofa and crossed his ankle over his knee. "If I weren't, you wouldn't be alive."

"Oh, you mean that super-human strength thing?

That's true too? I guess it must be. I wasn't sure how you managed to toss that assailant off of me like he was a sock monkey."

"Strength, speed, heightened senses. All of it. But that's not the first time I rescued you. I was turned right before you were born. It was the only way I could get your mother to the hospital fast enough."

"Wait a minute, are you telling me that because you couldn't hail a cab you had yourself turned into a vampire?"

Sly smirked. "Not exactly. Your mother was attacked by a vampire. She fought, but by the time he let go of her, she had lost so much blood… I was afraid she'd die and take you with her. I begged the vampire to help me and he said there was only one thing he could do."

"But that's a lie. He could have rushed her to the hospital…"

Sly gave her a sidelong glance and lowered his head. "He was a vampire, Allison. He didn't care about your mother or me or you. He selfishly offered to turn me, probably for his own amusement. He acted like a cat playing with a mouse. But I didn't have much of a choice."

"Oh."

An uncomfortable silence followed. At last, Sly followed up with, "I didn't believe vampires existed until I saw one with my own eyes."

"I'm with you there." Merry shook her head as if clearing it. "So what happened? To my mother, I mean?"

"It was too late to save her. They took you by C-section—and just in time. You were going into distress. As it was, you were a month early. You had to spend a couple of weeks in the hospital in an incubator. It gave me time to think about what kind of father I'd be."

"You thought about keeping me?" *I wasn't rejected.*

"I wanted to, believe me. I wrestled with the decision. You were all I had left of your mother, and I loved her dearly."

"You must have! You were willing to become a vampire to try to save her."

He nodded. "When I realized I'd never be able to drive you to school on a sunny day or attend any of your daytime events—and you'd have to grow up in a dark home with a father who might be tempted to snack on you in desperate times…"

She snapped to attention. "You wouldn't!"

"No, I wouldn't. But I didn't know what to expect back then. I didn't know what I was destined to become. Some vampires are pure evil, and who knows why?"

Merry settled back into her chair. "I'm so sorry. I mean, about what happened to you and what you had to go through all these years because of a selfish, uncaring… Well, you know."

"Yes, I know. As it turns out, vampirism doesn't make a man an undead asshole. It's the illusion of power and omnipotence that does. Very small people, when they get a taste of power, seem to abuse it."

Merry nodded. "That makes sense. But you're not an asshole. Um… are you?"

Sly laughed. "Depends on who you ask."

"You sound well-educated. What did you do, before the, uh… incident?"

"I had an engineering background and founded a

small company. Without me there to run it every day, my partner took over and kicked me out on my butt."

"But that's awful!" Merry realized she had already formed an alliance with Sly. Here she was, taking his side in an argument that had nothing to do with her and happened long ago. *Uh-oh. Don't be gullible, Merry. His story might be horse shit.*

"Look, Allison…"

"Call me Merry."

"Do I have to?"

She sighed. "I know, it's kind of a weird name—especially if I'm in a shitty mood. People who don't know better will use it as a reason why I should be cheerful absolutely all of the time."

"What about the people who do know better? What do they do?"

"They stay out of choking reach."

Sly laughed with a hearty resonance that warmed her. "I can see a lot of your mother in you."

"Really? What was she like?"

"She was a spitfire. Full of piss and vinegar, as they say."

"Ewww. Who says that?"

He shrugged. "It's just a saying. It means she spoke her mind, and nobody used her for a doormat. She was passionate about everything she did. She stood for good causes. She believed in doing the right thing, even if it wasn't the easiest thing."

"You mean she was some kind of an agitator? Or zealot?"

"No. She wasn't the militant type. Far from it. She was a social worker—more of an advocate. If there was an underdog who needed her help, she was there. If there was a cause that needed a sign to be carried, your mother was there, waving it."

"I advocate for my patients and their families all the time."

Sly nodded. "It doesn't surprise me."

"And something else makes sense now. I've always been able to smell blood, like a mile away."

Sly nodded. "In my desperation, I tried to turn your mother as I felt her life slipping away. You may have received a drop of my vampiric blood."

Merry was stunned by all these revelations, yet she had to know more. "What was her name?"

"Alice."

A stab suddenly hit Merry in the chest. "You named me after her?"

"Yes. There was no kinder, purer heart on the planet. She deserved someone to carry on her name, if not her legacy."

Merry hushed, temporarily. "No wonder you want to call me by that name. But just so you know… my mother called me Merry, because I was such a happy baby."

Sly smiled. "I'm glad. Your biological mother and I were thrilled to learn you were on the way. Perhaps you picked up on our vibes and knew how much you were loved." He adjusted uncomfortably. "I hope you didn't grow up thinking you were unwanted."

"I never knew why I was given up, but at least I knew I was wanted very much by my family—the family who raised me."

"They knew you were special. I made sure you were in good hands."

"Made sure? How?"

"Let's just say I kept tabs on you. I saw your adoptive parents take you home. I watched the Schooner newspapers. If I'd heard anything negative, I'd have taken action against whomever didn't treat you right."

"How did we wind up in the same place? Was that some kind of crazy coincidence?"

Sly shook his head. "I began advertising Boston apartments for rent in the Schooner paper as soon as you graduated from high school. I always knew you wouldn't be content to stay in a small town. I was thrilled to see you had been accepted to nursing school! I knew you'd make a wonderful nurse. I can't tell you how proud your mother would be."

Merry sniffed.

"I began placing ads again as soon as you graduated. I checked out each place. Made sure you'd be safe and that I could stay in the vicinity to protect you. Morgaine was the one who guaranteed that you and your family would be the only ones to see the ads. She put a spell on each one."

Merry couldn't speak. She was aware that her mouth hung open, but she couldn't shut it. It was almost as if she had reverse lockjaw. "I—I don't know what to say. I don't like being manipulated, but if you hadn't done that, I'd have never met Jason."

"Please watch your heart. I've heard things. It seems he likes to love 'em and leave 'em."

"No, he's not like that with me. You don't have to worry."

"I hope not. I might have a hard time staying out of it if he hurts you."

"So do you think that's your role? To hover and make sure nobody hurts me?"

"No need. The MacKenzies took good care of you. I just kept myself handy, in case they didn't."

"Okay, this is going to sound weird..."

"Weirder than discovering your father is a vampire?"

"Yeah. Well, maybe. I always had the feeling that I had some kind of guardian angel looking out for me."

Sly grimaced. "I'm not much of an angel, although I imagine myself as a secret crime fighter sometimes. I suppose I could be thought of as an avenging angel."

"So what did you do to the perp—No, never mind. I don't want to know."

"No, you probably don't."

Merry took a deep breath. "What would you have done if my family hadn't taken good care of me?"

He shrugged. "Whatever I had to do."

"Including...?"

"Including anything."

—◦◦◦—

Jason parked himself in front of his computer and opened his email. He'd told his family in Minnesota that he'd let them know right away if Merry had accepted their invitation. But she hadn't. He wasn't ready to take her "no" for an answer yet, damn it.

He minimized the page and stormed off to unpack, throw some laundry in the washer, and do any other mindless chore he could think of until he could talk to Merry again.

As he opened his suitcase and transferred what clothes

were still clean back into his dresser and closet, his mind drifted and ruminated and obsessed.

My mother always said when it was right, I'd "just know." A few minutes ago I did, but now... Why did Sly call himself her father? Who is that guy? He can't be much older than she is. And why did she seem okay with it? "I guess all I have to do is ask her."

Instantly, he felt better. *Of course. Stupid of me. All I have to do is ask her when she comes up to see me later.* She would tell him the truth. That's one reason he knew it was right. No games. She had always been honest with him. Hadn't she?

He slung the bag of dirty laundry over his shoulder and headed for the elevator. As he passed his computer desk, he noticed the page he had been working on was open and stopped suddenly. *Didn't I minimize that?*

Setting down the laundry bag, he reread the page. A few words had been added to the end of what he had typed.

They read, *Do you want my advice?*

Startled, Jason glanced around the apartment. Who the hell could have come in while he was in his bedroom and want to give him advice?

"Aunt Dottie," he yelled.

When there was no answer, he did a quick search of the place.

Empty.

If it wasn't Dottie, then who? Chad? Nah...

Just for peace of mind, he grabbed his lucky bat from its place of honor on the wall of his exercise room. Then he walked from closet to closet, throwing doors open and quickly adopting his "batter up" stance.

Nothing. "Crap. I must be losing my mind."

Everything was too low to the ground to hide beneath, but just for the hell of it, he bent over and scanned the floor anyway. *Maybe some anorexic child is hiding under there?*

A bizarre thought reentered his mind. "The ghost?" He shook it off. "I *must* be losing it—big time."

He set the bat down and returned to retrieve his laundry. Just as he was about to pick it up, he heard the gentle tap tap of his keyboard.

Snapping to attention, he read the words *while* they appeared on his screen.

You're not losing it. It's me, Chad.

"Fuck." Jason took an unconscious step away from his desk.

Then the words, *So, how's my investigation going?* typed themselves.

"Uh… Okay, I guess. Damn, this is weird, Chad."

So what? Talk to me.

"I hired someone. He's supposed to be the best. Dottie said you were anxious, so she was going to set up a meeting. I don't know when it is, but I'll find out. I promise." Aware he was beginning to babble, Jason stopped himself.

The words *Good boy* appeared on the monitor.

A nervous chuckle escaped. "So, were you the one who wanted to give me advice just now?"

Don't want to, but you probably need to hear it.

Jason took a deep breath. "Okay… Let's have it." He flinched, thinking he could have worded that a little better.

Your girl is going through some heavy shit. She was there for you, man. Now it's your turn. Don't be uncool.

Too stunned to speak, he simply nodded his head.

A knock at the door provided a welcome interruption.

He hoped it was Merry. This "heavy shit" Chad spoke of had him intensely curious and feeling more than a little protective.

When he opened the door to find Dottie standing there, his hopes crashed, but he was still glad for the distraction.

"Hi, Aunt Dottie." He almost asked how everything was in his absence, but figured she'd tell him anyway. Part of him didn't even want to know.

"Hello, Jason, dear. Welcome home. How was your trip? How's your father?"

"Much better. They have him on a special diet and exercise program, and he's already—"

"Yes, that's nice. Good to hear. Now, about that ghost of ours... I made the appointment with the private detective. I'd like to be part of the meeting, if you don't mind."

Jason's warning bell sounded, but agreeing to it would get her out of his hair faster.

"Sure. When is it?"

"Friday. Ten a.m. You should be able to make that, right?"

Since his schedule was flexible, consisting of working out in the early morning and seeing Merry after she woke up at ten most mornings, it was perfect. "That's fine. I'll come down for you at about nine-thirty."

"Oh, no. The meeting is going to be held here. Chad wants to attend. Morgaine will be there too since she seems to be able to communicate with him but I don't want that nasty Nathan fellow involved."

"The guy from 1A who works in a morgue?"

"Yes, there's something about him I don't like. I can't put a finger on it. Can you do anything about him?"

He almost groaned aloud. "*Do* anything? Like what?"

She shrugged. "Talk to him?"

"About changing his personality?" Jason shook his head. "I honestly don't think you can ask someone to be something they're not."

Dottie jammed one hand on her hip. "Well, does he have to be an asshole?"

"Aunt Dottie!" He laughed. "I've never heard you talk like that."

"Oh, you may hear me use even more colorful language if I continue to feel insulted and disrespected around here. I honestly don't know why people don't like me. I'm such a nice person. And I've never done anything to them…"

The elevator whirred behind her. *Oh, please be Merry!*

"But you're right," she said. "First things first. And the most important thing is getting rid of that damn ghost."

"Uh, Aunt Dottie. You might want to lower your voice. I'm pretty sure he's here."

She gasped. "Here? Now? How do you know? Is Morgaine around?"

"No, it's just you, me, and Chad. He typed a message while I was on the computer."

Her face scrunched and she bit out, "Oh, sure. He finds a way to talk to you." She stormed over to his computer, but Jason beat her to it and turned it off. "What did he say? He talks to everyone except me. Me, he attacks!"

"Attacks? How?"

"He practically froze me in my perfectly warm apartment. And let's not forget the box incident. I know he stuck that there just so I'd trip over it."

"I'm sure he's not attacking you, Aunt Dottie. He just wants to get your attention."

"Oh yeah? Well, he has a hell of a nerve scaring me out of my wits. And what could he want from me, anyway? A sandwich? He's dead!"

Thankfully the elevator door opened and Merry stepped from it. Dottie eyed her hand—the one holding Jason's key.

Chapter 9

OH, NO. WHAT AM I GOING TO TELL HIM? MERRY STOOD JUST inside Jason's apartment even after his aunt left, hesitating to move further.

He strolled over and stroked her arms as he scrutinized her face. "You look a little freaked out. Is it because I gave you a key, or is it something else?"

"Uh… No. I mean, yes. I mean…" She took a deep breath and stalled. *What the hell do I do? He'll think I'm nuts if I tell him the truth.*

He wrapped one arm around her waist and escorted her to the couch. "Here. Sit. Let me get you a glass of wine. Then we can talk."

She nodded and sank down onto the low white sofa. Maybe she could stall for time if she spilled red wine on his white couch? Nah, he'd probably tell her not to clean it so he could throw it out and start over.

Sly had asked her *not* to tell Jason about his place in the basement. For a vampire to find a lair that wouldn't be discovered and build a false wall with a hidden entrance took a lot of time and trouble. Plus, he had friends here. Konrad in particular, but he went to Morgaine for spells, too. Spells? Real magic? Really? Was anyone in this building *normal*?

He promised that he never killed in their neighborhood, well, except for the one time he and Konrad had saved her—probably. He hadn't come right out and said it, but she could extrapolate. He'd said he only hunted vermin. When she asked, specifically, if he meant animal or human, he simply looked away and changed the subject. *Avenging angel? Crime fighter? I guess it could be worse.*

When Jason returned with her glass of wine, she was no better prepared to talk. She didn't want to base their relationship on deception, but what in the world could she do? Was anyone ever *completely* honest with their partner? Maybe this could be considered one of those little white lies? Everyone tells them to protect the ones they love.

"So, tell me. What's going on?"

She inhaled deeply. "I—I guess it's possible that I just met my biological father."

Okay, so this was a little different—more like leaving out certain facts. That wouldn't even be lying, technically. It was like not telling him about going to a club with Roz once, right? No, that was to prevent hurt feelings.

"What else? I know there's more."

She dropped her head in her hands.

He settled in beside her and stroked her back. "Maybe I should help? There's something I need to ask you too."

Whew. Maybe the subject wouldn't come up at all if he had his own issue to discuss.

"Are you freaked out because I gave you a key to my place? Because if it's too soon—"

"No. That was sweet. I won't use it unless you're here, of course. But it was a very kind gesture. Thank you."

"It wasn't meant as an empty gesture, Merry. It's more like a symbol. I know you've felt a little insecure with the attention I get as a professional athlete, and in the future I'll be preoccupied with the game, but I want you to *know* you're special. I'm always here for you. And I trust you to come to me if you ever have any doubts. And I'm here for you if you want to talk about problems of your own. Okay?"

She nodded dumbly. *Problems of my own? If I didn't have to lie to you, I wouldn't have a big problem right now.*

"Okay, so it isn't the key. Tell me what's wrong."

She took a big gulp of wine. "What makes you think something's wrong?"

He raised one eyebrow. "Because you look like you've just seen a…" He shook his head. "Bad example. Look, I can just tell. So, spill it."

He wants me to trust him. I want to trust him. Can I? Should I?

He heaved a deep sigh. "Okay, let's play twenty questions. Does it have something to do with Sly?"

Uh-oh. Letting him grill her could be worse than coming forth with a limited amount of information. What if he asked the wrong question? *Tell him something, anything!*

"Okay, yes. I found my birth father. It's a little freaky."

"Yeah… are you sure it's him, Merry? I mean—he's so young. He doesn't look like he's much over thirty."

"Yeah, I guess he was very young when I was born."

"Like five? That *would* be freaky."

She laughed. "No, he wasn't five. Some people just don't show their age. That's not what I meant by freaky. All your life you've known one person to be your father, and then along comes this other person who knows things no one else could know and, well…" She shrugged. "I feel like I'm being disloyal to my dad, somehow." She could tell he wasn't buying it.

He cocked his head. "It takes a lot to knock you off balance—PMS aside—but I imagine meeting your birth father could do it. But it's more than that. I know you."

"Oh! How sweet—and how brave." She brightened. "That reminds me… I wanted to tell you about your surprise."

"Are you changing the subject?"

"No. You said PMS. I started on the new extended use pill. It's a birth control pill that's taken every day for three months, so your body is fooled into thinking it's not that time. Now you don't have to put up with my PMS every month—and I found out there's an herb that can help lessen the symptoms. Now my hormones won't turn me into a rabid dog every twenty-eight days. Isn't that great?"

He smiled. "It is unless you save up all that misery and turn into the bride of Frankenstein if you forget a dose. Will I have to sleep with one eye open?"

She tapped him playfully. "No, smart-ass. It won't be any worse than any other PMS I've had. I can give you back your key at the first sign of trouble if you're worried."

He wrapped an arm around her shoulder and kissed her temple. "No, I'm not worried. I was just goofing around. It's a nice surprise, but don't feel like you have to do that for me."

"Believe me, I'll be doing it as much for me as for you. There's no joy in feeling like a body snatcher has taken over and you've turned into some kind of mad alien."

He laughed. "Is that what it's like?"

"Pretty much."

He shook his head. "Well, I've always thought you girls had it easy in some ways, but I may rethink that now. So, I guess it's good that you don't have it now, considering…"

Crap, he's going back to Sly. Quick, think of something else!

"Um, I have another surprise. Guess what? I adopted a pet!"

"Really? That's great. What kind?"

"A cute little white bunny rabbit."

"Rabbit?" He reeled backward as if she'd said she now owned an anaconda or Bengal tiger.

What the heck? "I thought you loved animals."

"Oh, I do! I do."

"But…?"

He shrugged. "But… nothing. It was just kind of a surprise. I thought maybe you'd say a dog or cat."

Hmmm. I'd better let that go. "And there's something else, but it isn't quite so pleasant. I hope you won't be upset."

He leaned back. "Ah, now we're getting to it. Go ahead. You can tell me anything. I won't get mad."

"Really?"

"I promise."

"Whew. Okay, well, you know that paparazzi reporter?" His face fell. "Uh-oh…"

"Hey, I haven't even told you anything yet!"

"I know, I know. I'm not mad. Go ahead. Whatever it is, I want you to tell me."

She bit her lip and hesitated. Jason stroked her back

again and she relaxed somewhat. "I tracked her down—just to talk to her—and my friend Roz came along."

He groaned. "I thought you might. How did that go?"

"Not very well. I told her what I thought of her fabrications. She claimed to just report her observations. I told her to leave us alone."

"And what did she say to that?"

"Basically? Something like, 'Make me.'"

To his credit, Jason didn't react badly. He nodded but didn't seem upset. Maybe she could trust him with other things that might push his buttons—if she had to.

"So, do you think that's the end of it?"

She shrugged. "Maybe? I hope so."

He fidgeted. "You don't sound one hundred percent sure."

"Well, no one has called me with any more incriminating rumors about you." Ha, so there. Put the shoe on the other foot and let *him* squirm for a while.

"You know what? I feel kind of sorry for her," he said.

"Why? Have you met her, too?"

He chuckled. "No. Confrontation isn't my style, remember?"

"Yeah." She smiled. "I like that about you." *Good, maybe he'll leave Sly alone.*

"And I like that you can stand up for yourself." He took her glass of wine and set it on the table. Then he closed the gap between them and kissed her.

Whew! Crisis averted…for now. As they kissed, she took great pleasure in the fact that he made sure she was as satisfied as she could possibly be, each time they made love.

Perhaps for the first time in her life, she felt as if raw

sex and lovemaking were both present in every coupling. Not that she'd had much experience before this.

"Jason?"

"Yeah?"

"Can I sleep with you tonight?"

His grin lit up his whole face. "I'd love that."

———

Today was the day everyone would gather in Chad's apartment to talk to him about the conspiracy. Yes, the whole building had been included—except Sly. The Falcos still didn't know he "lived" in their basement. They must not—since Dottie hadn't had a major spaz in a while.

Speaking of the devil's daughter, she's waiting impatiently with the detective, glancing around the candlelit room, as if I'm going to materialize in front of her. Like I would if I could. I'd rather appear to those less prone to fainting.

Chad remembered the old TV show, *Columbo*, and thought Detective Joe Murphy, sitting at the head of the table, facing the door, looked like a modern-day version of Peter Falk in the starring role—but without the trench coat, or the lazy eye, or the mop of... *okay, he looks nothing like him.*

Yeah, he'd seen the TV show. Nathan used to watch it all the time. They both identified with his whole "crazy like a fox" routine. As a matter of fact, he still let Chad watch crime dramas with him. Chad decided that Joe looked more like the guy with the cockatoo on his shoulder... Beretta.

Nathan wasn't watching much TV these days. During

decent weather, he spent more time outdoors, soaring above the earth. *I think he prefers being a bird—an animagus raven.*

Chad imagined it must be a peaceful feeling and envied the freedom he could experience all the time if it were possible. Nathan was only able to shift for about two hours, tops, but was working on lengthening his "free as a bird" time. Everyone needed a hobby. After a hard day at the morgue, he appreciated the break.

He talked to Chad sometimes. Nathan couldn't hear him, but he could see him. So Chad would nod and point to what he wanted. Sometimes it was like playing a game of charades.

I wish I could feel that free. Well, I can, sort of. Having no body, no bills, and no boss kicks ass. Of course, sometimes it was boring as hell. *Probably more boring than hell, actually. If there is a hell.* For all Chad knew, this was his hell. He'd been trapped in this building for over half a century, and for all that time, all he could do for entertainment was get his kicks vicariously.

Now that he'd learned a few tricks—like telepathic communication and moving objects with his mind—things were a little better. The séance was the most communication he'd had with the living for a long time.

Morgaine could hear him and Nathan could see him, but it was like hanging out with one person who's blind and another who's deaf—and no one else. *I suppose it's better than nothing.*

I wonder what would happen if they got together? Morgaine and Nathan, I mean. Nah. They're way too different. They don't even like the same TV shows.

Morgaine's into the reality shows. I swear they can make a TV show out of anything these days.

And Nathan was into fictional dramas. He was even hooked on a couple of soap operas. *If I let that slip, he'd kill me. Ha! Well, he can't do that, but I'm sure he'd probably stop watching them just to spite me. Then I'd never know what happened with Robert's amnesia and Bethany's secret baby. Can't have that.*

Finally, the rest of the participants started arriving. Merry and Jason had just stepped off the elevator. Morgaine and Gwyneth left their apartment and were crossing the hallway. Konrad and Nathan were walking up the stairs, making small talk. *I overheard Dottie telling Joe that her husband, the super, opted out of the séance, preferring to "keep an eye on the building." Like it's going somewhere?*

Chad's theory about those who protested most about not believing in the supernatural were usually blustering out of fear of it. *I might like to test that theory with the super sometime—or not.* It sounded like fun, but he didn't need another convert to Dottie's *oust the ghost* movement.

Everyone took their places around the table. Morgaine explained what they needed to do. Chad hoped the girl was up to the task. She was still having a hard time relinquishing control to him, but they'd only had a couple of practice sessions.

"Now if everyone will hold hands and close your eyes…"

As soon as the co-residents were linked and completely still, Morgaine did the deep pranic breathing required to clear her chakras and make room for Chad's energy—*or some such crap. She tried to explain it to me in spiritual terms. Funny that I'm the spirit, and I still don't get how it works.* All he knew was that it did. If everyone cooperated and didn't disrupt her concentration, they might be able to pull it off.

Well, here goes nothin'. He eased into her, and she jerked ramrod straight. *My energy must not be as flexible as I thought.*

"Chad, if you can speak now, the detec—"

"Hello. Chad speaking."

Dottie gasped as he channeled his voice through Morgaine. *Well, what did she expect? That I'd sound exactly the same using Morgaine's larynx as I did using Shandra's?*

If he somehow figured out another way to do this, he'd try it. Sharing a body wasn't the most comfortable feeling in the world. *I'd better nip her crazy reactions in the bud.*

"Shut your piehole, Dottie, and let me speak to the nice detective. If you open your trap once, I'm gone. Understand?"

She scrunched her eyes shut and nodded.

"So, Detective, do you mind if I call you Joe?" he said.

Joe smirked. "Sure. If it's good enough for the Vice President, it's good enough for me."

"Ah, a politically aware detective. Perfect! Because my murder had to do with politics—big time."

Joe narrowed his eyes. "Tell me, Chad, who do you think killed you?"

"What the hell? If I knew, I wouldn't need you, would I? Detective, with all due respect, that's why you're here. To find out."

He shrugged. "I just thought you might have some idea. You know… leads I could investigate."

"Not really. I was minding my own business, typing the biggest article of my career for the *Boston Telegraph*, when two men in ski masks burst in. They didn't say a word. Just worked me over like professional hit men.

"One of them yanked the paper out of my electric typewriter—we used those things back in the old days—and the next thing I knew, I heard a gunshot and everything faded to black. When I came to, the place was upended. Couch cushions unzipped and tossed, all of my books scattered on the floor, even the kitchen cabinets had been rifled through."

"So, were you dead yet?"

"Oh, yeah. Dead as a doornail. I didn't know it right away, though. I just felt dizzy and a little stunned."

"When did you figure out you were dead, and what made you think you had been murdered?"

"Well, Joe, when I reached for a book and scooped up nothing but air, I became alarmed and suspected that something might be wrong. I tried again, and noticed my hand traveled right through the books. Next, all of me traveled right through the couch, and I couldn't pick up the cushions. And as far as knowing that I had been murdered? Well, the bullet hole in my head seemed to suggest it."

"So you could see yourself?"

"I could see my body on the floor. I—the spirit or soul that is me—my essence—leaned over my twisted body and didn't really feel like crawling back in there, what with the blood pouring from that painful looking hole and everything."

The detective nodded. "Understandable."

Nathan piped up. "Good move. You probably would have been a vegetable, slumped over in a wheelchair, unable to feed yourself or wipe your own butt."

"Yeah, thanks, man. I really needed that image."

"So, who discovered your body?" the detective continued.

"The police."

"How long did it take them to show up?"

"I don't see the relevance to this case."

He shrugged again. "No relevance. I was just curious."

"Great. I finally get a detective to take me seriously, and he wants to know how Boston's finest were performing in the sixties?" *Jesus. Take a couple of deep breaths. Don't piss off the guy who's being paid to help you.*

Morgaine took the deep breaths for him and he continued.

"So, what have you done so far to catch my killers?"

"Catch them? This happened fifty years ago. I'd probably have to dig them up if I wanted to cuff 'em and bring them in. In case you didn't know what a cold case is, it's when the trail has gone cold, and this is the coldest case I've ever worked on."

It was all Chad could do to hold his temper. *Damn, I wish someone had a bong going. I'd float around in the smoke and hope for a contact high.*

Morgaine took another deep breath and Chad said, "Look, you asked for leads. Don't you want to know about the article I was writing?"

"Sure, I was getting to that."

"Yeah, after you racked up an extra hour to charge Mr. Baseball."

Jason raised one eyebrow.

Joe cleared his throat and shifted in his chair. "So, what was the article about?"

"Like I said, a conspiracy. A big one. The Kennedy assassinations."

"Yeah? You know who killed JFK?"

I'm not falling for that one again. "Hey, I had a source. I already told baseball-boy all about it. Didn't he give you any information before now?"

"Yes. But I wanted to hear it from you."

"Fine. His name was Spider. We met in a parking garage downtown next to the X-rated movie theatre."

The detective nodded. "I remember the place. It's a damn shame they tore it down. Nowadays, perverts without DVD players are out of luck."

Oh, the things I could say to that...

"So, do you have any other name for him besides 'Spider?' I doubt I'd find him in the nineteen-sixties Boston area phone books under that name."

"No, but much later, a dude who looked like an older version of him claimed to have the same knowledge. His name was Dean Warner. The FBI negated his claims."

Detective Murphy rubbed the stubble on his chin. "Yet, if the information was false, why were you killed?"

"Exactly! Now you're getting it."

Morgaine's head fell forward, and Chad realized she needed a break. He yanked himself out of her body and let her know she could rest, but he'd be back.

"Something's wrong with her," Gwyneth cried.

Konrad rose, scooped her up, and headed for the door. "Open the apartment door for me, Gwyneth. I'm taking her home. This shit-show is over, folks."

—ᴧᴧ—

Lila hung back in the shadows. The chilly November air made a few minutes of espionage seem like hours. What was everyone doing in there? She had seen people walking upstairs, but the place was dark with the exception of one dimly lit window on the third floor.

"There's something weird going on in there," she muttered to herself.

"Back again, are we?"

Startled, Lila jumped and felt as if her heart had lodged in her throat on the way down. "Who the…? Oh, it's you. Sylvestro, right?"

"Call me Sly."

"Okay, Sly," she said, feeling a little sly, herself. Maybe she could get some more information out of him and the evening wouldn't be a total waste. "How's Allison?"

"Allison who?"

"Give me a break," she said. "The woman we talked about last time I saw you."

"Oh, I should apologize. It was a case of mistaken identity. As it turns out, her name isn't Allison after all. I'm sorry if I gave you misinformation."

"Oh. Well, mistakes happen. I've since learned that her name is Merry. Is that right?"

He didn't confirm or deny. He simply stood there, staring at her. Then he leaned forward and sniffed the air right in front of her.

Lila stuffed her hands in her pockets and leaned away, trying not to let her teeth chatter. Something about him gave her pause. Last time, she didn't pick up any sinister vibes, but now… *Maybe he knows about the article and is pissed—like everyone else who knows this sainted Merry seems to be.*

She'd have to try a different tactic. "So, do you know why the building is so dark? I think people are home. At least, while I was waiting for someone, I saw people come and go."

"Who were you waiting for?"

She waved away the question like it was no big deal. "Just an old friend. I thought I saw him last time I was here."

"Last time you were skulking in the bushes?"

She chuckled. "Well, okay. He's not exactly a friend. He's a friend of a friend. You know how that goes."

Falco and I are both friends of the media-reading public, right. And if no publicity is bad publicity, he should thank me. When the baseball season starts up again, everyone will be watching to see what "bad boy Falco" is up to. Hey, cool. I should be able to spin it that way and get another credible story out of it.

"And you thought you'd find this guy here? What's his name?"

"Oh, I'd rather not say. You might alert him to the fact that I'm watching for him—for my friend—and I really don't want to bother him."

"Why would I say anything? Are you stalking him for your friend or something?"

She slapped her knee and laughed. "Ha! Stalking. That's funny."

"You think stalking is funny?"

"No, of course not. Just the fact that you think I'm doing it." She elbowed him.

Sly grabbed her elbow faster than she could blink and his expression changed. His posture straightened and his eyes darkened. Suddenly, she didn't feel safe—at all.

He leaned toward her and held her stare as he whispered. "I suggest you leave, immediately. There's nothing and no one in that building that concerns you."

"Okay," she replied in a high voice that cracked. Then she turned tail and dashed for the nearest subway.

After running two blocks, she slowed. Why should she be afraid and suddenly leave? She had never been intimidated into deserting a stakeout when tracking down a story before. Hell, she wasn't afraid of anyone or anything!

Something was definitely weird there, though... not just the building, but also the fact that it came with a sly guy who seemed determined to protect it or its residents, or both.

"I need a drink," she muttered out loud. Then she trotted to the subway that would bring her to her favorite watering hole. Maybe she could make nice with Kevin, too. Having about one friend, total, made her all alone in the world if she lost him.

Somehow, she thought he'd forgive her. She knew he liked her—and not just as a good customer. He let little tells slip. Things no one else would notice. His pupils grew larger when he looked at her. He couldn't help giving her a smile from across the crowded bar every once in a while, even if he was busy with other customers.

Oh, yeah. He liked her all right. Maybe it was time to explore that a little more. She had never been one to trade sexual favors for anything, but her liquor bill seemed to be growing out of control. That didn't mean her drinking was out of control. *Not at all*. Just that she either had to settle for cheaper dives or wait until she sped home to drink.

Yeah, that wasn't going to happen.

Chapter 10

CHAD FLOATED ABOVE MORGAINE AS SHE SAT AT HER desk, swiveling back and forth in her chair. She'd promised to help him communicate with the private detective—on paper. It was easier.

"So I'm supposed to make a list of all possible enemies, no matter how small the insult or how insignificant the damage might seem to me."

"Make a list of everyone you ever pissed off. Anyone who might have a bone to pick with you, no matter how ridiculous it may seem."

"That's what the detective said. I know. It seems strange, since I gave him the best lead I had already. Somehow, I don't think my dry cleaner did it."

"So I guess your dry cleaner goes on the list?" Morgaine picked up her pencil and asked, "What's his name?"

"Wong. Dwight Wong."

"You're kidding."

"No. I made a joke about his name and voila... he's on the list."

She chuckled, but wrote it down.

"Morgaine, you're a good kid. Funny, I call you a kid even though I was about your age when I was bumped off. But as far as company goes, you're pretty good. Emphasis on the 'pretty.' I don't know why you choose to scare off guys with your harsh, gothic look or share

your king-sized bed with your cousin instead of some handsome dude. I know you're not lesbians. Believe me, I've been waiting and hoping."

Morgaine laughed. "Okay, so who else did you piss off?"

Chad pondered for a minute. *"Everybody."*

"Everybody? Come on, you couldn't have offended *everybody*."

"Hey, after all this time together you know me, right? And you doubt it?"

Morgaine shrugged. "I suppose I should put myself on this list, then."

"You didn't know me back in the sixties, babe. Hell, you weren't even born yet. We're only talking about those folks I pissed off while I was alive—to get a list of suspects."

"And he's going to chase down every one of these leads? Even Dwight Wong?"

"I guess he wants to wight my wong."

Morgaine rolled her eyes. "Okay. I believe you. You pissed off everybody."

Gwyneth breezed in from the kitchen. "Would y'all mind sayin' *annoyed* instead of pissed-off?"

"Why?"

"That expression annoys me."

"You mean it pisses you off?"

"No, I mean it annoys me."

Morgaine dropped her pencil. "You heard him, Gwyneth?"

Gwyneth stood up straight. "I did! Jeezum crow, I heard the ghost."

Her cousin jumped up and hugged her. "I knew

you could do it. All you needed was to awaken the psychic within."

"Oh, great. Now I have to watch my language in front of Ms. Southern Belle?" Chad grumbled.

"If you don't mind," Gwyneth said, politely.

"Give me a break, Belle. I'm dead and I'm pissed off about it. What are you going to do if I curse? Slap me across the face?"

She crossed her arms and pouted.

Morgaine patted her on the shoulder. "You'll get used to him. I did."

"I suppose."

"Now, where were we?"

"We were about to write everyone's name—at least everyone you knew in the sixties—on this list." Morgaine picked up the pencil again and said, "So, go ahead. Name everyone you knew."

"Fuck that. Look, I'll give you a couple of ex-girlfriends and everyone I owed money to. I can't remember the names of every cabbie and waitress I stiffed."

"Fire away."

"Arlene Lynch, Madam Kowalski…"

"Madam?"

"Not that kind of madam. A psychic, like yourself."

"How did you piss… I mean, *annoy* a psychic?"

"Easy. I told her she was a fraud. That no one could talk to the dead and her whole psychic act was bunk."

Gwyneth and Morgaine looked at each other and raised their eyebrows.

"Okay, okay. So I made a mistake. One of us had to be wrong. Just like people who believe in heaven and

hell. The believers are gonna feel so faked out if they end up like me."

A knock at the door interrupted the task at hand.

Gwyneth answered it.

Merry stood there with damp hair, wearing exactly what she was wearing last night.

"Ah, the good ol' walk of shame." Chad smirked and floated toward the ceiling.

"Merry. Nice to see you. Would you like to come in and set a spell?"

"Yup. Nothing out of the ordinary here. Just a friend coming by to say 'Howdy.' Southern manners…"

Gwyneth looked up. "What about Southern manners?"

"They're not much different than WASPy Boston manners. If there's an elephant in the living room, you suddenly become deaf, dumb, and blind."

"Elephant? What are you talkin' about? And by the way, I ain't dumb."

Merry gave her a sidelong glance and looked as though she was reconsidering Gwyneth's hospitality. "Are you talking to Chad?"

She brightened. "Yes! Isn't it excitin'? I just discovered I could."

"Thrilling. Yawn. Learn to swear without the phone in your hand, and then we'll talk."

"Oh, hush, you." She did a quick double take at Merry's wrinkled brow. "Oh! Not *you*, hon. Please, come in. I'll just have to ignore him."

"That's what I have to do most of the time," Morgaine said as she left her desk and strolled over to the women at the door. "Otherwise people would think I was yelling at them."

"Is he that bad?" Merry asked.

Morgaine shrugged. "Not really. He's just a little sarcastic. Come on in. Sit down. Let me get you something to drink. Do you like tea?"

"Sure. But you don't need to go to any trouble. I was just wondering…" She took a seat on their flowered couch. Gwyneth sat next to her and Morgaine retreated to the kitchen.

"What is it, hon?" Gwyneth asked.

"You sound like you're talking to a six-year old, Belle."

Gwyneth cringed, but ignored him.

"I was wondering if you guys could tell fortunes? You know, like read palms or tea leaves or something?"

"Oh, yes. We both read palms. Morgaine reads tarot and tea leaves. I'm still learnin' the meanin's of all the symbols."

"That must be fascinating!"

"Oh, it is."

Morgaine called out from the kitchen, "Do you want us to read your tea leaves, Merry? I'm already making the tea and it would be a good chance for Gwyneth to practice."

"Really? I'd love that!"

Gwyneth winked. "I bet y'all want to know if a certain tall, handsome baseball player loves you."

"Oh, no. I know he does." She smiled, sounding confident.

"Can't you tell by the goofy grins on their faces every time they're together?"

"Well, you'd better be careful, anyway." Morgaine called. "I've heard he's a heartbreaker."

Merry cleared her throat. "Actually, I stopped by

hoping we could schedule a date night? Since he doesn't like going out in public, I thought getting our fortunes told might be a cool thing to do right here in our own building. I'll pay you, of course."

"Since I'm just learnin', I wouldn't feel right acceptin' y'all's money. Even though I'm so poor I can barely pay attention." She laughed. "Y'all can pay Morgaine, if she wants."

"You bet your badonkadonk I want to be paid for it," came Morgaine's voice.

Gwyneth giggled. "We're a little poor now that we've lost our customers who wanted noisy phone sex. But I won't charge y'all until I'm more confident."

"Cool. Maybe Morgaine can read one of us and you can read the other?"

"Okay. I think we can do that. But, for today, do you have a particular question you want answered? We usually start by havin' you make a wish, and then we try to say if it's gonna come true."

"Yeah, there's something kind of bothering me. When I was in high school I had my fortune told by a psychic who said that someone was talking trash behind my back. And it was true. I'm kind of wondering if someone's been hanging around, spying on me and Jason."

"Spyin'?"

The tea kettle whistled.

"Well, yeah—for lack of a better word."

"I do declare! I'd rather jump barefoot off a six-foot step ladder into a five-gallon bucket full of porcupines than see anything bad happen to you."

"I don't think *that's* necessary, but the situation scares me a little."

Morgaine rounded the corner with a tray loaded with teacups, cookies, and a steaming tea pot. "You're not talking about Sly, are you? Because we know he won't hurt you. He looks scary and he hangs around here a lot, but he's a pussycat."

That brought a guffaw from Chad. *"Interesting description. A pussycat who laps up blood instead of milk."*

Gwyneth stuck her hand on her hip and stared at the ceiling. "Chad, are you still here?"

"Yup."

"Well, go away."

"Make me."

She rolled her eyes and looked defeated, mumbling, "Just remember that an arrogant bug is a cocky roach."

Morgaine shook her head and sat beside Gwyneth. "Chad, will you at least be quiet so Gwyneth can concentrate on Merry's reading?"

"I suppose…" Chad conceded with a sigh.

Hoo. Hoo.

"You too, Athena."

Merry glanced around. "Who's that?"

"Just our pet owl, honey," Gwyneth said.

Morgaine wiggled to get comfortable. "Okay, I think we're good to go. Merry, drink your tea while thinking of your wish. You'll need to imbue it with your thought energy."

As Merry sipped, Morgaine clued Gwyneth in on things to look for that would indicate a covert situation or someone operating behind the scenes unbeknownst to them.

"The Ace of Spades pointing up, a bat, a bee, a duck… Of course, you have to see if it's in close proximity to another symbol. There may be something positive to neutralize the negative or there may be bigger clues to indicate real danger like a knife or crossed bones."

Gwyneth nodded. "Okay, but if I forget, I'd better ask twice than lose my way once."

"How do you know all this stuff, Morgaine?" Merry asked and blew on her tea to take another hot sip.

Morgaine and Gwyneth looked at each other, some sort of communication passing between them. At last Morgaine said, "I think she can be trusted, don't you?"

Gwyneth nodded. "If she can accept the existence of a ghost in her midst, she can probably accept a couple o' witches."

Merry's eyes rounded. "Witches?"

Gwyneth reached over and patted Merry's knee. "Oh, don't worry, darlin'. We're the good kind."

"Actually," Morgaine continued, "we're what's called hereditary witches. Our grandmother was that odd woman who lived in the woods at the edge of town, cultivating herbs and making healing potions for anyone who came to her for help. Some didn't trust her and their kids gave our mothers a hard time in school, saying they were Devil worshipers and things like that. Nothing could be further from the truth."

"Oh. Is that why you moved up here?"

"Well, that, and I attended college here. I wanted to study herbal medicine. The money ran out long before I got to graduate. Still, I learned why Granny's medicine worked so well."

"But you decided to stay."

"Yes. I liked it. Summers aren't so sweltering hot. Gwyneth moved up here to help me pay the bills, and we decided to concentrate on Wicca. There's no degree needed, just dedication, study, and practice. Plus, healing with herbs and magic doubles a practitioner's chance of success."

"That's fantastic! What kind of clients do you have? I imagine they must be into New Age, natural healing too."

The two witches exchanged glances and chuckled. Then Gwyneth said, "You have no idea…"

Merry cocked her head, but returned to finishing her tea and asked what she was supposed to do next.

Gwyneth had her turn the cup upside-down onto the saucer, place her hand on top and make a wish. Merry closed her eyes and frowned as she concentrated. Eventually, she opened her eyes and let Gwyneth take the cup from her.

"Holy shee-it!" Gwyneth exclaimed.

"Whoa. I thought little Miss Goody Two Shoes didn't swear!"

"I don't. Hush your mouth, Chad. Morgaine, look. This'll put a quiver in your liver." She pointed inside the teacup.

"Tell me what you see, sister."

"Sister? I thought you were cousins. Or maybe you're both. Doesn't that happen back where you guys come from?"

"Shut up, Chad," Morgaine demanded.

"Yeah, Chad," Merry echoed. "Leave them alone. This is important to me and I want them to be able to concentrate."

"Oh, all right."

"I see bats, bees, and ducks all over the place."

Morgaine bent over the cup and nodded. "Right. I see them too. But look! Here's a bear."

"What does a bear mean?" Merry and Gwyneth asked at the same time.

"It's a powerful protector. And look how close it is, Gwyneth. The two are obviously connected."

"Do you think it's Sly?" Merry asked.

"If not him, it's me. I'll fix you up with some protective talismans and, if you'll allow it, I'll cast a spell to see you through this time. Oh look! There's an arrow. There's the answer to your question." Morgaine pointed to something in the cup and all three women peered at it.

"Yeah, I see it," Merry said. "I'm almost afraid to ask. Is that a good sign?"

"Yes and no. It depends on where it's pointing. Yours is pointing up, which means your expectations will be exceeded. If it were pointing sideways, your expectations would be met, but there would be no surprises. If pointing down, you'd never get your wish."

"So that means my wish will be granted?"

"Yes, but maybe not *how* you expect it to happen. If your expectations are good, no matter what happens, you'll have a positive outcome. If you expect the worst, though..."

"That's what I'll get."

Gwyneth cried, "Oh no. You aren't one of them folks who expects everything to go wrong, are you?"

"No! Oh, I didn't mean that at all. I was just finishing Morgaine's sentence for her."

"Whew!" Gwyneth said and sagged. "Because if there's one thing I've learned from Morgaine, it's that you reap what you sow. We're all bundles of energy and we attract the kind of energy we carry around with us. Positive attracts positive. Negative attracts negative."

Merry nodded, but didn't look as though she quite grasped the concept or its importance.

"I had to work hard on my attitude when I got here," Gwyneth continued. "I was kind of a mess, but I've learned so much from Morgaine. And now, things are really gettin' better for me."

Merry smiled. "I'm glad. But um…" She waved at the teacup. "I'll pay you to finish the reading."

"Oh, yeah! Sorry." Gwyneth took the spoon and stirred the leaves. Then she stared into the cup with intensity. "Lordy, Morgaine! I think we'd better read our *own* tea leaves. There's too much stuff showin' up in here and it's all too close to home. Dayum!"

"I thought you didn't swear, Gwyneth."

"Shut up, Chad," both witches yelled.

Jason stood alone on his balcony. He barely noticed the city lights as he ruminated over whether or not it was time to let Merry in on his well-hidden secret. The reason he was so protective of his privacy. The reason the paparazzi was such a pain in the ass, not to mention his aunt Dottie.

Fuck it. He always thought better in his other form, so he yanked off his shirt, bowed his head, and closed his eyes. As he hung onto the narrow metal railing, he felt his body shift. A moment later his talons gripped the railing's edge and he spread his wings. *Ah, sweet freedom.*

He knew he made a magnificent display. A majestic falcon soaring above the city. A bird of prey. Master of the skies. Hunters were pretty rare in Boston's Back Bay, so he felt safe. Silhouetted against the light of the nearly full moon, he let his thoughts run free.

Falcons were monogamous. Now that he had found his mate, he couldn't lose her to anyone else. How could he ask her to wait two months until he returned from spring training? And why would she come with him if they weren't married? The answer was simple and frightening. She might not and that was a chance he wasn't willing to take.

How and when would he tell her what he really was? She deserved to know, especially if he wanted to spend the rest of his life with her—and he did. There was a chance he might inadvertently shift in front of her and that, at this stage of their relationship, could be a disaster.

Having only half shapeshifter blood made it harder to control his shifts. His brother had had much more practice since a demanding career hadn't consumed him. Plus he had the extra motivation of needing to make a normal life for his wife and kids. His sister-in-law knew about the family secret and almost didn't marry his brother as a result. That's why he had to be sure to pick the right moment to tell Merry.

Their children would only have one-quarter shape-shifter blood, so might never shift at all, like his brother's kids—so far. Jason couldn't imagine his brother having that talk with them. Not only did he have to tell them about the birds and the bees, he had to tell them about the birds and humans.

Jason thought surely his Uncle Ralph must have told Dottie about the Falco family secret, but now he realized his uncle, wisely, had not. His father, a typical Alpha male, was so self-disciplined that he could probably go years without shifting if he wanted to. Only extreme stress could make him shift against his will. He hadn't even shifted during his heart attack. *Thank goodness,* his mother had said. They were right in the middle of a dinner party.

The full moon also contributed to the urge to shift at inopportune times. Merry had asked him to accompany her to her home on Thanksgiving, and having just been home for a week, he had accepted. That was *stupid*! He hadn't checked the calendar to see what phase the moon would be in. Since Thanksgiving came late this November, it landed right on the first day of the three days considered the full phase. He had feared shifting in front of her during the last full moon—at the bachelor auction! Only keeping his cool under fire had saved him.

His "workouts" with Merry may have helped him relieve stress. He had been resisting his falcon shifts more easily. He flew high enough during orgasm to rival any falcon flight he'd ever tried, and he didn't even miss soaring above the city.

Still, not only did he have to divulge to her his shape shifter secret, but he also had to tell her what being a *falcon* shapeshifter meant. Once falcons chose a mate, they were completely monogamous. He had assumed he and Merry were exclusive, but he had to be certain. To find out otherwise could drive him into a jealous rage, in which case he'd probably shift and peck out the eyeballs of his rival.

And just in case, she also needs to keep her bunny in its cage.

So he had a lot on his mind. The woman he wanted to marry needed to know what she was getting into. He had to meet her family and impress the hell out of them so they would approve of him taking her so far away from home so soon—if she agreed to accompany him home for Christmas.

What could happen during Thanksgiving, though? Her family seemed very supportive and loving. It would probably be a wonderful experience. *That's the attitude*, he told himself. He was worried for nothing—hopefully.

Peering down over the city with his mind more settled, he glided joyously along the river to the ocean and back. He had found his one and only. It was time to celebrate, not ruin it with needless worry.

———

They got an early start on Thanksgiving morning. Merry and Jason, all bundled up in layers to ward off the chill, climbed into his small sports car. He revved the engine and let it warm up.

Merry glanced at his handsome face. "So, are you ready for this?"

"As ready as I'll ever be."

"Well, try not to worry. They're going to love you."

"But they don't even know I'm coming. Are you sure it's fair to spring another guest on them?" He backed out of the alley and pulled onto the street.

"I'm the one who does the cooking, so they won't care unless we can't find another place around the dinner table and someone has to eat sitting on the floor."

"Are you serious?"

She laughed. "Of course not, silly. Relax. Everything's going to be fine."

Merry glanced at the other beautiful brownstones as they drove by.

She had planned well. She had given her father the grocery list and had him buy everything she needed ahead of time. Now all she had to do was arrive by eight a.m. to season the turkey and get it cooking.

"So what is Thanksgiving at your house usually like?"

"Well, I don't have to get up early or anything. I usually have everything ready to go the night before and once I put the turkey in, there's plenty of time to prepare the extras. I make the stuffing separately, so the turkey won't take as long to cook. Potatoes will be peeled by my little brother, and that activity comes with the added bonus of keeping him out of trouble for a while."

"Is he really apt to get into trouble without something to do every second?"

"No, but structure is good for him."

"You know him better than I do. So what's next? After you get the food prepared?"

"My sisters-in-law will arrive by eleven with more side dishes to keep warm in the oven and pies for dessert." She had thought of everything, right? So why was she so nervous?

Jason headed toward Storrow Drive, which would take them to the southeast expressway, then to route 95—and home to Rhode Island.

Jason. He had to love her family, and they had to love him. *Had to!* They were all too significant to her for anyone to feel less than enthusiastic about her choice.

Yes, she had made her decision. No more looking around. Even if she wasn't one hundred percent sure the timing was right, the man was. And that was more important, right?

Part of her wanted to experience independence for longer than a few weeks before finding the man she wanted to spend the rest of her life with. The other part of her couldn't get over the fact that she'd found the man of her dreams so quickly and easily. Not to say this euphoria was going to last. She knew the passion would someday become a simmer, but she couldn't imagine the fire going out—ever.

"So, does Roz make an appearance? Since you two are from the same town, I imagine she'll be there for the holiday, too."

"No. She doesn't usually come over. It's just family."

Merry thought about how Roz had dated off and on, hoping that each new man was "the one." Sadly, none of her relationships had worked out. She was intelligent, successful, and despite being a little chunky, beautiful. Roz deserved no less than an amazing man who loved her completely. Yet Merry was the one who ended up with exactly what they'd both yearned for. True love.

She couldn't help feeling a little guilty for barely setting foot in the dating waters and coming up with an incredible hottie. But Roz would understand and be happy for her—wouldn't she? Of course she would. That was probably the test of true friendship.

Merry tried to shake off her insecurity and drag her mind back to the moment. Jason still seemed tentative. What was going on in that handsome head of his? She stared out the window and lapsed into silence.

—∧∧∧—

Jason's mind had whirled with questions all the way to
Schooner, Rhode Island. One in particular. Should he
pull the ring out of his pocket before, during, or after this
visit? Before would give them the chance to announce
it to her family if she said yes. But what if she said no?
That was entirely possible, since they had only known
each other for six weeks.

Merry pointed out her family's driveway, so he had
a split second to decide. Even if he decided not to decide right now, that was making a decision. *Crap. Why
couldn't it be as easy as knowing whether to throw a
fastball or a changeup?* Realizing that Merry might
throw him one hell of a curveball if he did it in front of
her family, he bypassed her driveway.

"Hey! Where are you going?"

"We're early," he said. "And there's something I
want to tell you. Is there someplace we can park for a
couple of minutes? Maybe someplace with a view?"

She tilted her head and scrutinized him like she was
trying to read his mind.

"Uh, yeah. Keep going until you get to the stop sign
and turn left. There's a view of the ocean down there."

"Perfect."

"Is something wrong? Do you want to back out?
You can always drop me off and someone can drive
me back…"

"No! I mean, no—nothing's wrong."

Her forehead wrinkled, but she didn't say anything
more until he found the spot she must have had in
mind and cut the engine. The harbor seemed deserted.

Fishing boats floated nearby. The seagulls seemed disinterested and bored. He didn't care to hunt them as much as pigeons and mourning doves. The latter were delicious. Probably because in urban areas birds were fed by humans. Seagulls ate whatever they could scavenge and diarrhea made them poop on everything in sight. At least *he* had the decency to aim at a tree branch or rooftop.

Maybe this was a bad idea. He still hadn't told her his little secret. Only she might not think it was so little.

"Well? You wanted to talk to me about something?"

"Uh, yeah." He removed his seat belt and faced her squarely. "I know we haven't known each other all that long…" he began and paused. Now what? He had rehearsed this in his mind, but the words seemed inadequate now.

She nodded, then tilted her head, waiting for more.

"Jesus. Words are failing me," he said, and took a deep breath.

"Look, whatever it is, I love you. Nothing will change that."

Deciding to *just do it*, he pulled the little turquoise box from his jacket pocket and handed it to her.

Her eyes widened in surprise.

She really didn't expect this. Damn. Why didn't I wait? Well, it was too late now. The cat was out of the bag—or the box was out of his pocket, as it were.

She opened the top and gasped at the sight of a two-carat diamond solitaire in a gold setting.

"Holy crap!" she exclaimed. Then she clapped a hand over her mouth and giggled. "Sorry. That wasn't a very romantic response, was it?"

He laughed, grateful that she'd broken the tension. "I was kind of hoping for a yes or no, but if you need time…"

She shook her head but didn't say anything.

He waited with his heart in his throat. If she said yes, he'd tell her. If she said no, there'd be no need to.

She smiled. "Well, what I mean is, I don't need time to make up my mind. I don't want to put you through that. But I'd like time to get to know each other for a while before…" She stared at the ring, but didn't take it out of the box.

"Is that a yes?"

"Can it be a maybe?"

"No."

Her eyebrows arched.

"The anticipation is killing me."

He hadn't planned to push her, but as it turned out, he had to. A yes meant he had more to say before they told her family. A maybe meant he had to decide, again, whether or not to tell her the rest, and *maybe* shift in front of her if she didn't believe him. Although the decision could be made for him. He could feel the stress building and his hands gripped the steering wheel more tightly.

"I guess if you're okay with a long engagement…"

"I was hoping to take you to Florida with me in February when I go to spring training, and we'll have to be married to live together."

She gasped.

"Well, if we want to keep my image squeaky clean. You know how role models have to avoid controversy. It's a, you know, kind of moral thing to some people." *Jesus, Jason. You're babbling. Get a grip.*

"Oh." Now she seemed even more stunned. "I, um… That's so fast. Are you sure? I mean, how long is spring training? A couple of weeks?"

"No. A couple of months."

She groaned. "Damn. That's a long time to be apart. I'd miss you like crazy."

"Tell me about it."

She shrugged. "I don't know what to say."

"Say yes."

She giggled, but it sounded like a nervous giggle. Now what should he do? Maybe it was a sign. If she couldn't handle a fast wedding, maybe she wasn't ready for the rest of it.

"I guess you need time to think, after all." He reached for the ring.

She swiveled away from him, holding the box out of reach.

"Oh, no you don't. No Indian gimmees."

He laughed. "Well, are we going to sit in this car all day, or are you going to put it on?"

She sighed. "If I put this on, we'll have a lot of questions to answer. Can you handle that?"

He nodded. *If she puts it on, I'll have a lot of explaining to do. Why the hell didn't I wait?*

"I love you, Merry."

She plucked the ring from the box and slid it onto her ring finger. Stretching her arm out in front of her, she admired it and grinned. "It's gorgeous."

Relief washed over him, but it didn't last long. Now he should tell her the rest.

She leaned over and kissed him. He cupped the back of her head and pulled her back for a longer, deeper kiss that he hoped would convince her she'd made the right choice—no matter what.

"I love you," she whispered.

"Good. Hold that thought, because I have to tell you something about myself that you deserve to know if you're going to be my wife."

"Oh? What is it?"

"How much time do we have?"

Her expression turned to concern and she checked her watch. "We're supposed to arrive in five minutes."

"Five minutes? I thought we had longer than that. When did you say we'd get there?"

"Eight o'clock."

"Oh. I thought it was eight-thirty for some reason."

"Well, it was, but I decided to move it up a bit. I thought I'd try a new recipe and wanted to give myself extra time."

"In that case, the rest of this conversation will have to wait."

"You're kidding!"

"No, I think it's best."

"Wait a minute. You ask me to marry you. I accept. *Then* you tell me there's something I have to know about you. And now you won't tell me what it is?"

Jason leaned back against the seat and frowned. *Damn. She's right.* She'd probably go crazy all day if he didn't tell her *something*.

"What is it? You owe the Mafia money? You murdered your ex-girlfriend? Your AIDS test was negative, but you have syphilis? *What?*"

"Look, it's nothing bad, all right? Think of it like this: I'm really Superman, and you only know the Clark Kent version of me."

After a long pregnant pause, she burst out laughing.

Between Jason's extreme embarrassment, her waffling, and the prior stress of proposing taking its toll on his emotions, he felt himself beginning to shift. *No, no! Not now!*

The next thing he knew, his talons gripped the steering wheel and his wings flapped wildly.

Merry screamed, jumped out of the car, and darted between the buildings, out of sight.

Fuck! If only he were out of the car. Peregrine falcons could fly up to two hundred miles an hour, and he could track her down before she reached her family. But try as he might, he couldn't shift back.

Chapter 11

"MERRY!" JASON'S VOICE YELLED FROM OUTSIDE AS HE pounded on her father's front door for the third time. "Merry, come to the door. We have to talk."

She held onto her younger brother's arm in a death grip. "No. Don't answer it."

"But it's Jason. Your boyfriend. Remember him?"

Do I? Not really.

He pounded again. "I'm not going away until you talk to me, Merry."

Matt strained to reach the doorknob. "Just because you had a fight doesn't mean—"

"I'm not opening that door until you're gone," she said to her brother.

Jason knocked again. "At least let me give you your purse. You might need your inhaler."

"See, Merry? He's trying to be nice. At least talk to him."

She hissed in her brother's ear, "I will not speak to him with an audience. Leave or I'll never open it." She waited an anxious, silent minute. At last, Matt skulked out of the living room. *Whew*.

Opening the door, Merry snuck around it and stood on the stoop, lost for words. Jason leaned against her doorframe with the saddest, most pathetic expression she'd ever seen. The nurturer in her wanted to rush into his arms and comfort him. Then she remembered she didn't know this man—if he *was* a man. Never having been exposed to anything so bizarre in her life—except a vampire father and a haunted apartment building—all she could think of to do was protect herself. Protect her family. How could she expose them to… what? A magician? Shaman? Some kind of weird animal spirit possession?

He reached out to her. She hesitated, then walked into his arms and started to shake.

"Are you okay, sweetheart?"

She couldn't speak, so she shook her head vehemently.

"I'm—I'm so sorry. I didn't mean for you to find out like that."

"Find out what? I don't even know what I just saw. Are you some kind of magician?"

"I'm a shapeshifter."

"A shape-who?"

"Shapeshifter. You may have heard of us in Native American legends. But they're not just legends. We exist, and my alternate form is a falcon."

She reached for the railing. "I have to sit down."

"Here, let me help you." He supported her forearm as she lowered herself to sit on the top step, then he sat next to her.

"I wouldn't have believed you if I hadn't seen it with my own eyes. Do you shift into any other shapes?"

"No. Only a peregrine falcon."

"Why did you wait this long to tell me?"

"I was afraid of losing you."

"But you asked me to marry you. When were you planning to tell me?"

"Merry, I screwed up. I should have told you before I proposed. I thought we had more time than we did.

I never should have come with you for Thanksgiving. Stress and the full moon affect shifters."

"How?"

"It's harder to resist the desire to shift under stress. You've heard of the fight or flight response, right?"

"Yes."

"Well, my tendency is for…"

"Flight," she finished for him.

"That's right. Listen, I—I think it's better if I just go home. I can come back and get you when you're—"

"No. I'll ask my dad or Matt to take me home. I need to think."

He offered a sad smile. "I understand, but I'm glad you think of Boston as your home now."

"Yeah," she murmured absently. "I worked too hard to get out of Schooner. I, uh… I'd better get back inside."

He helped her up. "You know I'm head over heels in love with you, don't you? That I'm not dangerous or crazy… that I'll be right there waiting for you when you get back."

She nodded, opened the door, and he handed over her bag.

As she took it, she said, "Thanks. It was sweet of you to think of my inhaler. I'm surprised I didn't need it half an hour ago."

Jason called his manager from the road. He was a young, single guy, so maybe he wasn't all tied up with a big family Thanksgiving dinner. Fortunately, he answered his phone.

"Hey, Jason! What's up?"

"Hi Brian, I need to find a batting cage and beat the shit out of some balls."

"Whoa, that doesn't sound good. Did something happen?"

"Yeah, but it's hard to talk about."

"What's her name?"

Stunned, Jason hesitated, then asked, "How'd you know this has to do with a woman?"

"It always does."

He sighed. "Look, I just need to get some aggression out and I'll be fine. I figured you might be able to call around for me and see if there's a place open or willing to open, even though it's Thanksgiving Day."

"Sure, buddy. Let me call some of my contacts and get back to you."

"Thanks, Brian. I owe you."

"Just give us a winning season and call it even."

Yeah, right. If Merry doesn't come around I'm fucked… and not in a good way.

Merry had taken the ring and tucked it into the zippered compartment of her purse. She would give it back, of course… or not, depending upon her decision. So many conflicting thoughts and feelings warred inside of her. Her family hadn't seen it. She managed to hide it in her bra before she walked into the house, but she didn't want to take a chance of losing it.

All day her family had asked what was wrong. Thank goodness her father had been in the shower when Jason showed up and didn't know anything about it. She swore Matthew to secrecy with the threat of instant death if he breathed a word of it. So all anyone knew for sure was that she seemed more moody than usual. If anyone pushed it, she could always blame it on PMS again, but thankfully no one did. Now that she was on the seasonal pill, that would be a fib, and she was a lousy liar.

All day she'd been going through the motions woodenly. Even during the meal and the football game, all she could think about was what had happened in Jason's car. Did it really happen?

Before she moved to Boston, she was bored. Now boredom was beginning to look really attractive. However, she was *not* moving back to Rhode Island. Not, not, not!

At last all the guests had gone and her father cornered her in the kitchen. "You seem so preoccupied, Merry. What's wrong? Did Falco break your heart?"

She exhaled, defeated. "Not really."

He balled his fists. "I knew it! Merry, I want you to come home. You're far too young and impressionable to live alone in a big city."

"I'm not alone," she protested. "I have Roz and I've made several friends in my building, plus Jason didn't break my heart. He just—surprised me." *The ring. Maybe if I see the ring again I'll know I didn't dream up the whole thing.*

"Surprised you how?"

Merry knew that if she didn't give her father some kind of explanation, he'd harp on her about coming home until he either drove her crazy or talked her into it.

She trudged to where she'd left her purse, saying, "I'll be right back."

In her old bedroom, she opened the zippered compartment and fished around. When she didn't feel cool metal, she panicked. *The ring! It's gone!*

She turned it upside down and dumped the contents on her bed. No ring fell out. *How could this happen? Oh, lord. I'm losing it. I just know I am.*

The hot sting of tears welled up in her eyes and a lump formed in her throat. It wasn't just about how to tell Jason she'd lost it—if indeed she'd ever had it— maybe it was a sign. Maybe she had lost Jason. Her heart ripped in two at the mere thought.

She burst into tears and her father appeared in the doorway seconds later. "There's something bothering you. Something terrible, and I *demand* you tell me what it is."

"Oh Daddy..." she sobbed. "Jason gave me this beautiful diamond engagement ring, and I've lost it!"

"Engagement...!" His posture stiffened, then relaxed. "I understand now. Where did you last see it?"

She tipped her purse toward him. "It was right in this compartment. Now it's gone." She blubbered until he came over and sat next to her on the bed.

"Maybe it's a sign," he said. "I still think you should come home."

Merry cried, "No! If it's a sign of anything, it's a sign of how much I love Jason, and how much I don't want to lose *him*!"

"Oh," her father said, sounding disappointed. "Why weren't you wearing the ring?"

"I—I said I had to think about it."

"That was very wise. You've only been together a short time. And maybe if you come home and think about it…"

"Stop it! Stop saying that! I'm not moving home and that's final!" *I swear, I've never punched an old man before, but if he keeps this up…*

Thank goodness the guests had gone home. If they heard her yelling at Mac like that, they'd all be crowding around her.

Her father bristled. "You do *not* have to be so rude about it, young lady."

Merry doubled over and sobbed again. Her father patted her gently on the back. "Look, I know you're upset. We'll just forget you said that, all right?"

"Gaaaa! No! We won't! I meant it. Look, I'm sorry if I was rude, but I'm twenty-five frickin' years old. I need to be on my own for a while. That's the only reason I hesitated about marrying Jason."

Was it? Was that the only reason? Good lord, she had accepted a ghost and witches living in the same building with her—not to mention a vampire birth father—and even considered them friends. Her eyes and mind were opening, probably as a result of finally being on her own. Unsheltered. Perhaps whatever had happened with Jason was something she could try to understand and get used to.

She fished frantically all through her purse and felt something in the lining. "Wait. I think I may have found it."

She pulled the lining inside out and noticed a hole about the size of a nickel in the bottom. It may have fallen through it! She tore the lining along the seam and dove into the compartment again. "Eureka!" she cried. The ring was only a little worse for wear, a piece of lint lodged in one of the prongs.

She immediately slid it onto the ring finger of her left hand and yanked out the lint.

Her father grabbed her hand and whistled. "My, my. That's a rock you don't want to lose! You'd have had a pretty hard time paying back what that monster cost."

She giggled with relief. "It's not a monster, dad. It's a symbol of love. *Big* love." She rested her head on his shoulder.

Mac put an arm around her and kissed her temple. "Okay. I guess my little girl is happy, and I'll just have to be happy for her."

She threw her arms around his neck. "Thanks, Dad. That's all I want. I know it's soon… but it's right."

Now if I can only apologize to Jason for freaking out, I hope he'll understand and forgive me. He has some explaining to do, though. Why the heck did he keep this from me for so long? And what exactly is it? There's so much to talk about.

"I've got to go home, Dad. I've finished the dishes. Will you drive me?"

His eyebrows rose. "Isn't your car outside in the driveway?"

"No. Jason dropped me off. He was going to come with me, but…"

Mr. MacKenzie held her gaze, and she fidgeted under his intense scrutiny.

"Well, he changed his mind. He also had an invitation from his aunt and didn't want to hurt her feelings. And you guys didn't even know he was coming, so he didn't have to worry about letting you down." *Okay, that was sort of true. He'd told her that Dottie had assumed he'd spend Thanksgiving with them, and by now he probably had.*

"He intended to come with you and then changed his mind? You must have been disappointed. So *that's* why you were pouting all day."

"Well, yeah. Of course. So, will you drive me home?"

"Only if I can speak to him."

"Dad, for God's sake, will you stop protecting me? I'm a grown woman! Now do I have to take a cab to the train station or should I ask Matt?"

He sighed. "One of us will take you back to Boston," he said, albeit reluctantly.

Chad followed Dottie to her apartment to see what devilry she was up to now. Plus he felt like taking a ride on their ceiling fan.

"Ralph, what's Jason's deep, dark secret?" Dottie asked sweetly.

Ralph whirled around. His eyes rounded and fixed upon her. "What do you mean?"

"There! That expression tells me everything. You know, don't you?"

Uh-oh, Chad said to himself. *The old man's in for an interrogation. He really needs to work on his poker face.*

She folded her arms and waited.

Ralph puttered to the kitchen. "I'm making myself a sandwich. You want one?"

"Don't you dare try to change the subject," she cried, bunching her fists and striding after him. "If something untoward is going on with our nephew, I have a right to know what it is."

"Untoward? What the hell does that mean? And what gives you that right? Don't you think that if he wanted you to know, he'd have told you?"

Untoward. Adjective, meaning unfavorable or unfortunate. Chad enjoyed his expanded vocabulary. He'd worked hard to become a journalist. As a black man in the sixties, it had almost required memorizing the dictionary. And even then, he suspected he might have been hired by the newspaper as the token black man. *Untoward circumstances will force Ralph to divulge a secret he's been sworn to keep. Untoward.*

"I want *you* to tell me," Dottie whined. "We promised each other long ago we wouldn't have any secrets from each other."

Oh, Christ on a cracker! The dude's really in for it now. I can't believe he agreed to something like that. Hell, I wouldn't promise to tell any woman everything. A guy who does that is asking for a flowerpot to the head.

"That was thirty years ago when I was stupid in love and would have promised you anything."

Oh no! Talk about brutal honesty. Chad was trying hard not to laugh. *I don't want to miss a word of this.*

She reeled back. "Don't you love me now?"

"Of course I do! Would I put up with your antics if I didn't?"

"Antics? I have no antics… Hey! You're trying to change the subject on me, aren't you?"

Chad shook his head as he observed from the stationary ceiling fan. *Nice try, man. But you* know *she's never going to drop it.*

She jammed her hands on her hips. "Well, it isn't going to work. I know you're keeping something from me and I won't stand for it!"

"You'll have to, Dottie. I don't know what you heard or where you heard it, but I have no idea what you're talking about. He could have meant anything. Maybe he's a secret cross-dresser. By the way, what *did* you hear, and where'd you hear it?"

She shrugged. "I overheard Jason talking to himself. He was wondering how to tell Merry about his deep dark secret."

"Well, that's what you get for eavesdropping. You'll have to ask Jason if you really must know, but I think that would be too damn nosy, and you know what a private person he is. Do you *want* him to evict us?"

"Don't be ridiculous! He won't evict his own relatives."

Famous last words, lady. If I were him, you'd have been tossed out on your ass a long time ago.

"Hi Roz, it's me. Do you have time to talk?" Merry twisted the phone cord and bit her lower lip. She hoped her best friend could give her some perspective.

"Sure. Where are you?"

"I'm still in Schooner. Matt's driving me back to Boston in a few minutes. I need to talk to someone I can trust before I leave, though."

"Sounds serious. Do you want me to come over?"

"No, that's okay. By the time you got here, it would probably be time to leave."

"All right. So what's up?"

"Jason asked me to marry him."

The shriek on the other end of the phone almost blew out her eardrum.

"Jesus, Roz. You might want to save your excitement. I found out something about him that's giving me fits. I don't know what to make of it."

"Uh-oh. What is it?"

"I can't tell you… Well, not specifically. Not until I find out more about it. I'm really, really confused right now."

"Crap. How am I supposed to help you if you won't tell me what it is?"

"I don't know," Merry moaned.

"It's awfully soon to talk about marriage, don't you think? I mean, you only met him in October, right?"

"I know. And at first, he said he wouldn't push me to make a decision. And then he did anyway. So I said yes, and then I found out this awful secret."

"He told you about this… something—whatever it is—*after* you said yes?"

"He didn't exactly *tell* me. He more like showed me. All I know is that I have to talk to someone."

"Why? Does he have two dicks or something?"

She laughed. "No, believe me, the one he has is quite enough."

"Maybe the person you should be talking to is Jason."

"I know, I know. But he's not the only one with a problem. Part of it is me."

"In what way?"

"I'm not sure. When I'm with him, I just sort of melt. You know? I'm afraid I won't be able to stand up for myself."

"Why? Does he boss you around?"

"No! It's not that. I just want whatever he wants, because I want him to be happy."

"That's called love. It sounds like you've already made a decision."

"No, I haven't. I don't even know how I feel about this. I *do* know how I feel about him."

"And...?"

"And yeah, I love him. Still, I'm confused. I really need to figure out what the whole other thing means to me before I just give in to what he wants, which is a short engagement."

"How short?"

"He wants me to go with him to Florida in February for spring training, as his wife."

"Wow. That *is* short. And you said yes?"

"Yes."

"But that was before you knew about this... thing."

"Yes."

"What is it? Some kind of visible growth that's genetic?"

She chuckled. "No. Well, not a growth. I don't know about the genetic part. Maybe it's the side effect of some kind of scientific experiment?"

"Say what?"

"Never mind. I can't go into that. Not yet."

"Okay. So back to the proposal. How do you feel about the engagement now?"

"I don't know," Merry wailed. "I don't know how I feel about *anything*!"

"Boy, you're flip-flopping all over the place."

"I know. It's like... Well, not like I've lost myself or anything. More like I'd never *found* myself. Now I have, but can I trust it?"

"I was wondering how this was going to play out. I mean, you *just* busted out on your own. We talked about going clubbing, kicking up our heels, and then you go and meet this gorgeous hunk and fall in love *immediately*. Aren't you apt to feel gypped out of the whole singles scene? If not now, how about ten years from now? Twenty years? The rest of your life?"

"I don't know. From what I've heard from you and the girls I work with, it's not that glamorous. Oh, I know. They complain about their husbands, but they wouldn't want to go back to being single for anything."

"We're not talking about them. We're talking about you. How do *you* feel? Take it slow. Think about each situation. Spit out words that describe as many things that you're feeling as you can. Maybe we'll see something emerge. Start with how you feel about being with Jason now, then move on to how you feel about being with Jason forever."

Merry sat silent. *Crap. Was it that easy?*

"Okay… I'll try it." She took a deep breath. "I feel lucky, loved, appreciated, incredibly special…"

"Anything else? Anything negative?"

"No. I think those are the words I'd use for how I feel about being with Jason now. I mean, I was worried about his fame and how that could drive me nuts, but he's pretty much put those fears to rest."

"Yeah, I guess if he proposed, he means it. Okay, so now think about being with Jason for the rest of your life. How does that make you feel?"

"Um… lucky. Incredibly special. Like I couldn't have done any better in life. A little scared, but I think that's normal."

"Hmm…" Roz said. "I'm suddenly envious and want to ask you if he has any brothers?"

Merry chuckled. "He does, but he's already married."

"Damn."

"I'm still upset that he didn't tell me about this complication *before*."

"Yeah. You need to confront him about that, but you might want to keep the big picture in mind. Maybe he was just afraid you'd say no and wanted to know what you'd say before you knew about the... thing. That could make him do it ass-backwards, but it was only a mistake and probably forgivable."

"I guess so. But why would he think I'd say no if I knew first?"

"Does he know how you feel about him?"

"I thought so."

"Okay, well, I guess you'll have to ask him why."

"Yeah." She sighed. "It all boils down to my having to talk to him, doesn't it?"

"I'm afraid so."

"Damn. Well, at least I have the questions, even if I don't have the answers. Thanks for helping me put it in perspective—I think."

"Glad to be of help. Now, for God's sake, tell me what happens! This is like a TV show, and I don't want to miss an episode."

Jason rushed to his cell phone and snapped open the cover on the second ring. *Please be Merry. Please be Merry.*

"Jason? It's Aunt Dottie. Is everything all right between you and Merry? I looked out the back window this morning and saw you two leaving together, and just now I saw her walk in the front door with a young man."

A young man? Jealousy stabbed Jason in the heart so hard he could barely speak. "Uh... Thanks."

"For what? I was asking you if you two had a fight or something?"

Jeez, she really is the nosiest Aunt Busy-Body this side of the Rockies.

"Do you want me to go downstairs and ask her to come up when she's free? Maybe if she's still mad at you, I can invite her to my place and you can casually drop in?"

And give you a front row seat? I don't think so.
"Thanks, but I'll go down to her apartment myself."

"Are you sure? I wouldn't want the—"

Jason snapped the phone shut, not even caring if he was rude. He had to get down there and see about this young man from her hometown. There was more he hadn't told her and he prayed she was past the initial shock.

Soon he had to tell her that other men had no place in her life. Peregrine falcons formed monogamous pairs, and now that their mating process had begun... *Damn, I've got to get down there, now!*

He hurried to the elevator and pushed the button for the first floor multiple times. Then he took some deep breaths. He *had* to calm his panic. Shifting in front of her and whomever she was with wouldn't help matters at all. On the other hand, no matter how hard he tried to stay in control, he could fly into a jealous rage, literally, and peck out the "young man's" eyeballs.

Quickly rethinking his plan, he almost stepped off

the elevator, but the doors closed. He felt trapped and spun into full-blown panic. The next thing he knew he shifted. His wings tried to flap but he was caught in his own crewneck sweater snare and fell to the floor. The elevator slowed as they approached the second floor. *Oh no!*

The doors slid open and Dottie stood there. Upon spying him in his alternate form, she jumped about a foot in the air. Shock drained the color from her face. He tried to struggle past her but he couldn't move more than an inch.

"What the hell...? Ralph!" She reached in and hit the emergency stop button. "Ralph! Come here right now!"

When her husband didn't appear immediately, she dashed to her front door, opened it, and yelled, "Ralph, goddamnit, come here!"

Having a moment of privacy, Jason concentrated as hard as he could. He visualized himself in human form—and shifted back. *Whew*. Fortunately, he made it into his clothes before Ralph and Dottie appeared at the elevator doors.

"Where's the bird?" Dottie demanded.

"What bird?" Jason asked.

"Oh, don't give me that innocent routine. There was a bird in this elevator not one minute ago, and he was wearing your sweater."

Jason glanced down at his sweater.

Ralph stared at Jason for an uncomfortable moment, and then began to laugh. Jason joined in, knowing what his uncle was going to do. He was going to make Dottie think she was hallucinating. He was sorry he had to play it that way, but it was his uncle's choice.

"Aunt Dottie, I think you've been working too hard. Maybe you and Uncle Ralph should take a vacation."

She stomped her foot. "I haven't been working too hard. I barely work at all. And I'm not crazy. I know what I saw."

By that time the other neighbors had heard the ruckus and appeared in the hallway. Jason stepped out of the elevator but left the emergency stop on.

"Sounds like somebody's got their feathers ruffled," Gwyneth drawled as she and Morgaine descended the stairs.

Ralph held up one hand as if to stop them from coming any further. "Everything's fine. It's just a family matter."

Dottie glared at her husband. "Everything's not fine. There was a bird in this elevator. It's bad luck when a wild bird enters a building. Haven't you ever heard that?"

The other residents stared at each other in surprise. Eventually, Konrad asked, "Where's Nathan?"

"What's he got to do with anything?" Dottie asked.

"I'm right here," Nathan said from the bottom of the stairs.

"You didn't let your *pet bird* out of its cage, did you?" Konrad shot him a pointed look.

Nathan cocked his head. "No. He's been right here in my apartment all evening."

Jason strolled to the top of the stairs. "Everything's okay, folks. Thanks for your concern, but you can go back to your apartments now." That's when he saw Merry peeking up the stairs, trying to stay hidden.

"Merry," he called and rushed down the stairs two at a time. Buns hopped into the hallway. She grabbed her pet, retreated into her apartment, and shut the door.

I'm not going to just walk away, Merry. You're mine, damn it!

He knocked. She didn't answer.

"I'll wait here all night if I have to, Merry," he yelled. "You're my girl and I deserve a chance to explain, damn it. We *need* to talk!"

A moment later, Matt wandered into the hallway. "Don't pay any attention to my sister," he said, speaking a little louder than necessary.

"Why not?"

"She gets psychotic sometimes. Besides, you're Jason friggin' Falco! You could have any girl you wanted. Maybe you should teach her a lesson and go out with someone else."

Merry's door almost flew off the hinges as she opened it hard enough to bounce off the opposite wall. "Time for you to go home, Matt."

"Damn! I finally get to see Jason again and now I have to leave? I'm *never* going to get his autograph," her brother wailed.

"I have something better than an autograph," Jason said. "Why don't you both come up to my place and I'll get it for you before you leave, Matt, then Merry and I can talk."

Matt looked like he was about to bust a gut with excitement. "Better than an autograph? And I get to see your penthouse? Heck, yeah! I can't wait."

Merry closed and locked her door behind her. The neighbors had cleared out. *Thank goodness*. She didn't trust Matt not to tell her father if he saw some of the black-clad wild characters she lived with. Then he'd have yet another reason to try to yank her back home.

Matt followed Jason to the elevator like a puppy. The elevator hummed with electricity: its own, Matt's, and the jolt that raced through Merry when Jason took her hand and kissed her knuckles.

When the doors whooshed open, Matt stepped out as if in a dream and said, "Whoa!"

"Like it?" Jason asked.

"Are you kidding me? This place rocks!"

"Well, go ahead and look around. I'll be right back."

"Don't touch anything!" Merry added.

Matt clasped his hands behind his back and wandered across the open expanse to the balcony. Merry couldn't wait to get rid of him so she and Jason could talk.

She had stewed all the way back from Rhode Island. Why hadn't he told her the truth earlier? Why was he rushing her into marriage? How on earth could she know what marrying a *whatever he was* would be like?

Not to be selfish, but this would impact her life in a big way. If she married him, she'd be faithful. She knew that about herself. That meant giving up her brand new freedom for the rest of her life. He had to be "the one," or she was screwed. They certainly had a lot to talk about.

Jason returned a few moments later with a baseball glove and a magic marker. Matt rushed over to him.

"Is that yours?"

"It's a prototype of a lefty mitt I'm supposed to endorse. See? It has my name on it already, but if you want, I'll sign it to you."

Matt looked as if he might keel over. "Jeez, yeah! That would be totally cool."

Jason wrote, *To my buddy Matt* and scrawled his

signature. "There. You have the very first one. They aren't even for sale yet."

"Wow." Matt handled the glove like it was made of glass. "Thanks, man!"

"You're welcome, and thanks for understanding if I keep your sister here when you decide to go home."

Merry steered Matt toward the elevator. "He's already decided. He was just leaving."

"I was?"

"Yes," she said firmly. "You were."

"Okay. Okay. I'll see you later, Jason."

"Any time, pal."

Merry groaned.

Chapter 12

MERRY SWIVELED BACK TO TALK TO THE MAN WHO wanted to marry her. He was striding toward her as if she might escape.

"That was very nice of you to mmmuphmm…"

Jason had grabbed and kissed her before she could finish her sentence. *Oh well, he probably knew what I was going to say.* She draped her arms around his neck and returned the kiss. He tilted his head and deepened it.

Sometimes Merry felt as if she lost her balance with his kisses. It was as if time stopped and the whole world fell away. At that moment, she felt as if she had found herself and come home. Whatever little oddities she had to adapt to, it couldn't be worse than learning to live with a hole in her heart where Jason should be.

When they finally pulled apart, he cupped her cheek and stared directly into her eyes. "Does this mean you still love me?"

"You scared me. We need to talk, but I'm willing to hear what you have to say."

"Good. I'll get you a glass of wine."

"No thanks. I want to be sure I hear every word and won't wonder tomorrow morning if I made up the whole thing in a drunken stupor."

He chuckled, then led her over to his "comfy chair," as she called it. He sat down and patted his lap. Merry sat atop a nice-sized bulge and did a little wiggle.

He groaned. "If you want to talk, you'd better not start *that*. I'll get completely sidetracked and you deserve a good, thorough explanation."

"You're right. I'll try to behave myself so you can tell me everything."

He smiled and shook his head. "You're almost too good to be true. I mean it."

"Has this ever happened to you before? I mean, turning into a…?"

"Peregrine falcon," he supplied.

"Uh, yeah… Has it happened in front of anyone who wasn't ready for it?"

"No. I've been pretty lucky. And I'm working hard on controlling my shifts. My dad was big on teaching us self-control."

"So your dad is a…"

"A shapeshifter. Yes. We're human, but peregrine falcons in our other form. My father, brother, and myself."

"But your mother isn't?"

"No. If both parents had been shifters, I would have had pure shifter genes and better control, but I'm only half shifter. My mother loved my father enough to take a chance on him, and we love her even more for handling the weirdness."

Merry looked at him sideways. "How much weirdness are we talkin'?"

"Well, we liked to shift in the backyard to fly. That meant getting naked before we left the house."

"What did the neighbors say?"

"Thanks to a private yard with loads of trees, they never found out. Mom was still worried about small planes and helicopters passing over at the wrong time. And we had to promise to stay away from jet engines."

Merry chuckled. "That's a good idea in any form. So what else was weird for her?"

"Besides the fact that she could never join in? Well, we'd bring the occasional pigeon home for dinner."

"Pigeon? Yuck, that's disgusting!"

"No, it's really good. My favorite is mourning dove, but there's plenty of both in any city. We lived in the suburbs, but had a few special places my father would take us to hunt. And don't freak out, but we used to love rabbit, too."

Merry's hand flew to her chest as she gasped. "You wouldn't hurt Buns!"

"No. He's your pet. Even in falcon form I'll be aware of the difference between Buns and a wild rabbit. I promise I won't do anything to hurt him."

"But… other cute animals? Chipmunks? Kittens?"

"We really didn't bring anything cute and furry home to Mom. She would have been furious. So we stuck to mostly pigeons, but she didn't even want them. Once she put her foot down and said she wasn't going to pluck our pigeons and cook them for us, so we had to settle for store-bought chicken. If you ask me, she's the weird one. Who wouldn't prefer fresh game?"

Merry wrinkled her nose. "Okay, so you like fresh game. How about quail or pheasant?"

"Sure. I like just about anything except owls and eagles."

"I should hope not. Aren't they endangered?"

"Not as endangered as we are around them, because *they* eat *us*!"

"Oh! That must be frightening if you run into them on

your… flights? But don't you have the upper hand since you can turn back into a person when you want to?"

"Yeah, usually. You should see their eyes when they suddenly have a mouthful of heavy human." He laughed.

"But if you're up in the air, the fall could kill you!"

He shrugged. "Like I said, I've been lucky. But under stressful conditions, it's a lot harder to handle the shifts."

"So I guess you really *have* been lucky."

He hung his head. "I couldn't shift back for quite a while this morning. I'd never have shocked you like that if I could have avoided it."

"What was so stressful this morning? I mean, yes, I was having a hard time with the pressure to marry you so quickly, but why would it matter if it's before spring training or after?"

Jason pursed his lips. Eventually he answered in a voice that sounded so serious it scared her. "If we go forward and we're bonded, I could die without you."

She shook her head and tried to look into his eyes. "I don't understand."

He fell silent and pensive, as if trying to find the right words to explain.

"It sounds as if you mean that litcrally," she continued.

"I do." He took in a deep breath before he continued explaining. "We began a mating process, you and I, and because falcons are one hundred percent monogamous, you'll be my partner for life."

"Are you saying you were a virgin before you met me?"

He chuckled. "No, I'm not saying that. But I've

always kept dating superficial so that bonding wouldn't happen until I was ready."

"Wait a minute, didn't you tell me you were in love once before?"

"Almost. I thought I was, but I didn't know what love was back then. And almost doesn't cut it for falcons. You either are or you aren't. Plus, she and I never had sex."

"So why didn't this mating process begin with someone else if you've had sex?

"I didn't stay with anyone long enough. I had to protect my heart until I found the right girl. The minute I fell in love with you, and made love to you, we were bonding. As our relationship progressed and deepened, you may have felt it too."

"I—I guess so. I really panicked when I thought I'd lost you—the you I thought I knew."

He caressed her arm. "I understand. But I'm the same man, and you'll never lose me."

"So tell me everything I need to know if I'm going to be your wife. Wait, not just what I *need* to know. Tell me everything."

He took her hand and nodded slowly. "Falcons mate between March and May. It's not a choice. We don't decide when it's right for procreation. It's an instinct."

Confused, Merry tipped her head. "Are you saying that come spring, we'll be boinking like bunnies?"

He laughed. "Only if you want to." Then his expression grew serious again. "This is where being a shifter complicates things. We not only have physical instincts, we have human emotions too. Falcons who can't mate when their bodies tell them to can create havoc with the extremely stressed human half."

"God, the shifts must be really hard to control then."

"You betcha. Can you imagine that instinct hitting full force while I'm in Ft. Meyers, Florida, and you're in Boston, Massachusetts?"

"I guess that's a long flight, either by plane or wing, and if you shift during the trip… Oh no! What a tragedy that would be."

"You *do* understand. My only other alternative would be to give up my livelihood, which would kill me in a different way. My whole life has been about this sport, and I love it. To give it up would be like giving up a piece of my soul."

Merry nodded, and then something occurred to her. "So, if we're bonded, you can't have sex with anyone else?"

"No, and I wouldn't want to."

"Works for me." At last, she could relax completely. *No worries when he's on the road—no matter how many female fans show up at his hotel room.*

"Once I have a full-blown sexual relationship, the mating instinct sort of turns itself on and can't be shut off."

"So now that you're *fully blown* and your instincts are *turned on* in more ways than one… what does that mean? Is this a done deal? Do I get any say in the matter?"

"Well there is one more step, but it has to happen in the spring. If I come to you in falcon form, holding a symbolic gift, even just a pebble, it's a sign. It signals the nesting instinct. Quite often falcons begin their mating this way."

"So what happens if I don't want to get pregnant right away?"

"Just stay on the pill."

"Hey, I'm open-minded and stuff, but are you sure

about all of this? I mean, how do you know what will happen if I'm not with you in the spring?"

"I've seen it happen. I had another uncle besides Ralph. He wound up mating with a woman who wasn't so open-minded. She left him, disappeared, and couldn't be found. The result wasn't pretty."

"What happened?"

"He killed himself, but not before going stark raving mad."

Merry gasped. Could she live with herself if she did that to Jason? Was it her fault if she didn't go with him and something horrible happened?

"Oh, my God! So this is really a case of do or die."

He nodded, then one corner of his mouth curled up. "Or you could say we have to *do it* or die."

She laughed. At last the worst of her worries had been relieved and she *could* laugh again.

"So do you have any more questions?"

"Yeah. You said your Uncle Ralph is a shifter, too. What I can't picture is Ralph choosing a woman like Dottie. I mean no disrespect, but, um... she isn't the most open-minded person on the planet."

Jason blew out a deep breath. "No, she isn't. I'm pretty sure she doesn't know."

"How the hell has he managed to keep a secret of that magnitude from his own wife?"

"Veeeery carefully."

Merry elbowed him. "Very funny. That joke's older than you are. Oh, wait. That brings up another question. Do you have a normal lifespan? Are you immortal or something?"

He laughed out loud. "No. Immortality doesn't exist."

Hmm... I know someone who says it does. Merry wondered again if she should tell him about Sly. Since they were speaking open-mindedly...

Jason continued to talk before she could think of how to tell him. "Falcons have a life span of about thirteen to sixteen years. That's why we stay mostly in our human forms. We live longer."

"Especially your Uncle Ralph!"

He chuckled and nodded. "Especially my Uncle Ralph."

"How does he do it? I mean, Dottie is continuously stressed out. Why doesn't that rub off on him and cause him to shift?"

"He's one hundred percent shifter, so he has great control. And he tunes her out a lot."

"Sheesh. Okay, I think I only have one more question."

"Shoot. No, *don't* shoot, but ask away."

"If someday I get pregnant, will I lay eggs or have babies?"

He burst out laughing and didn't stop until she hit him.

Somehow, Jason needed to seal the deal. He probably wouldn't feel secure until she put his ring back on her finger, but the boat had stopped rocking. He had brought her muffins for breakfast and taken her out to lunch, a museum, and dinner, but they hadn't spent the day together as he'd hoped—in bed.

They kissed in the elevator all the way up to his apartment. He hoped she wanted him as badly as he wanted her. He *needed* to make love to her. As much as he didn't want to come off like a caveman, he was having trouble controlling the passion that grew within him all evening.

Without letting her pull away, he continued to kiss her and walk her backward at the same time, guiding her toward his bedroom. Fortunately, she must have known what he had in mind and began fumbling with his belt buckle. That's all it took.

He wanted to rip her blouse off, but forced his shaking fingers to undo the buttons one by one. By the time they reached the bed, she had managed to undo his pants and plunge her hand down his boxer briefs.

Dear God! His cock strained at its confines and he hurried to undress himself the rest of the way. Merry unzipped her skirt and let it fall to the carpet. She stepped out of it just as Jason straightened. A red G-string met his gaze.

"Damn, Merry. You're *killing* me." He tackled her. After they landed and bounced a couple of times, she giggled.

"Then prepare to die, because I've barely started." With that, she unhooked her matching bra.

He growled and slid his arms around her to take it off. As soon as that barrier was removed, he lowered his head to the breast nearest him. He licked it mercilessly before taking the hard, distended nipple into his mouth to suck. She arched and a low moan of pleasure emanated from her mouth as she clutched his shoulders.

His fingers trailed down her soft skin and hooked her tiny thong. Sliding it off, he opened her to many more pleasurable possibilities. Overcome by sensations, he nipped her other breast and suckled deeply as she undulated beneath him.

His hand found her mons and cupped it possessively. *Mine. All mine.* The building fire inside roared in his ears. He'd never felt anything like this. Amazed and dazzled by the irrational effect she had on him, he'd stop at nothing to win her over. Expensive gifts, weekends in Paris. All the things he told himself she'd see right through, he'd offer anyway.

His whole body burned with the need to couple, and soon. Her body churned restlessly against his as if she felt it too.

"Merry, I want... no I need..." his breath hitched and he could barely speak.

"What do you need, lover?" she asked, her voice soothing as silk.

"I need... you. All of you."

There. He'd acknowledged his deep desire to merge with her as one. Sex was part of it, yes, but his heart and soul were on the line too. He gazed into her eyes, hoping she'd see the full truth of his few words.

She stared back at him without blinking, then puckered up. Jason assaulted her mouth with all the passion a kiss could convey. He wanted to venerate her. To sear her with his brand as a sign that she was his—*all* his. She squirmed and he realized he could be frightening her.

He broke the kiss reluctantly. "I'm sorry, I didn't mean to be rough. It's just that..." He began to shake and couldn't finish his sentence.

"Jason, are you all right?"

"No. I need to be inside you. *Now*."

With a look of concern, she opened her legs. Even though he wished he didn't have to rush her, sweet relief flowed over him like cool water. He positioned himself between her legs and plunged into her to the hilt. He moaned as she cried out.

"Oh, God! Did I hurt you?"

"No." Her shallow breaths begged to differ.

"I'm so sorry." He kissed her softly and waited for a go ahead sign before he began the familiar rhythm of joining.

"I'm fine. Really."

He kissed her again. "I love you," he said as he withdrew and thrust. "I'll always love you."

She closed her eyes but didn't answer, not that he had asked or even implied a question. He kissed her neck, shoulder, temple, and nipped her earlobe as he rocked back and forth. He finally closed his eyes too and reveled in the feeling of her channel tugging on his cock as if she wanted to keep him deep inside of her.

He felt his orgasm building to a fevered peak. His rhythm had accelerated. When did that happen? He slammed in and out of her, all the while trying to maintain control and losing.

"Merry!" he cried and jerked with the release of his seed in deep spurts.

She shuddered and shrieked out while climaxing at nearly the same time. He rode her until she whimpered and all the tension had drained from her body.

When she opened her eyes, they shimmered. "Jason," she whispered. "I love you so much."

"Are you sure I didn't hurt you?"

She grinned. "If you did, you can hurt me like that again sometime."

He nuzzled her neck and breathed in their mixed scents. Her willing commitment would happen. She *would* be his soon.

~m~

The next evening, Jason and Merry made their way up to the third floor to Gwyneth's and Morgaine's apartment. He said, "I'll admit I was kind of amused when you asked me to go for a tarot card reading date. But then I thought, why not? It sounds like fun."

"Good. I thought it would be easy to date right in our own building. And I think they're looking forward to it too. Gwyneth wants to practice her fortune telling with cards and tea leaves, and Morgaine's an expert in a lot of interesting things. She'll be there to supervise."

"I was wondering how they learned this stuff. Witches, huh?"

"Yeah, I hope it's all right that I told you."

"Since you've been open-minded about my idiosyncrasies, who am I to judge? I figured I owed you the same courtesy." *Can people predict the future?* He didn't know, but it might be interesting to hear what they had to say.

He had spent the past hour at Merry's place, intending to "pick her up" like a proper date should, but they got good and distracted. Fortunately they didn't specify a particular time for their readings, or they'd be late, late, late.

They stood before the door to apartment 3B, but before she knocked, Merry asked him, "Are you going to be okay with whatever they have to say? I don't want to put you in a situation where you might freak out and shift."

He smiled. "I'll be fine, but thanks for the thought."

Gwyneth opened the door without their knocking.

"Wow," Jason joked. "How did you know we were here, Gwyneth? You must really be psychic."

She shrugged. "I felt y'all's energy and saw y'all's auras."

"Oh." *Yeah, right, you heard our voices.*

As soon as they'd stepped inside and closed the door, she smiled at them knowingly. "You two just had sex, didn't you?"

Jason's jaw dropped.

Merry sucked in a gasp. "How did you know that? Are you really *that* psychic?"

Gwyneth laughed. "Not this time. Y'all are just flushed and glowin'."

They stared at each other wide-eyed, then Merry laughed.

Jason scratched his head. "You caught us."

"Have a seat. Morgaine will be right out. Do y'all want some sweet tea? Maybe y'all need somethin' to cool off?" she asked with a wink.

Merry answered quickly. "May I have one of those beers you offered me before?"

"Of course. Jason? How about you?"

"Sure. Sounds good."

As soon as she left the room, Jason placed a hand on Merry's knee and whispered, "Is this really a good idea?"

She shrugged. "It's too late now. She'll think we don't trust her if we leave."

"I'm not sure I do. I'm getting some kind of weird vibe here."

"She's just teasing us. Probably getting a laugh because we thought they were having sex with each other instead of over the phone."

No, it's something more than that. He glanced around at the décor, half-expecting to see pentagrams painted on the floor or dripping candelabras in the corners. The place seemed surprisingly "normal." A few crystals in a dish sat on the coffee table, a bookshelf displayed some new age titles, and a set of wind chimes with stars and moons hung silent in front of the closed bay windows.

Gwyneth returned with two open bottles of beer. Looking over her shoulder, she called out, "Morgaine, are you comin'?"

"Don't bother her if she's working."

Merry gave Jason a poke in his ribs. "Ow... What?"

It took a second, but he figured it out. Maybe he wasn't supposed to know? Heck, as long as Aunt Dottie didn't bother him, they could make their livelihoods as lively as they wanted to.

"So how did your own tea-leaf readings go?" Merry asked. "I know you were concerned about what you saw in my teacup. Did it affect you in any way?"

Gwyneth smiled. "No, thank goodness. No danger in our cups, but..." Her countenance grew more somber. "There was an indication of trouble for a loved one. It was probably just confirming what we saw before."

She raised her eyebrows. "You consider me a loved one?"

"Well, of course, honey. Who could *not* love you?"

Jason smiled at Merry and squeezed her knee.

At last, an unseen door clicked open and Morgaine emerged. *What's that thing on her shoulder?* An owl swiveled its head and spotted him.

Jason leapt to his feet. "Jesus Christ!"

The owl took off, flying right at him, screeching its head off.

"Not now!" Jason yelled. He dashed for the door, covering his head.

The two female hostesses stood immobile and open-mouthed for a moment. Then Morgaine bellowed, "Athena!"

The owl ignored Morgaine's command, and Jason fumbled with the doorknob. Merry dashed over to him and batted the owl away. He had just opened the door when he shifted. His clothing fell off and prevented the door from closing completely.

Feathers flew everywhere. Standing between him and a frantic, hungry owl, Merry took a winged beating and cried out. He did his damnedest to shift back, but the fight or flight instinct was too overpowering. Jason flew off into the hallway and prayed that either Morgaine would get her predator under control or Merry would be able to rip his clothes out of the way and shut the door on his assailant in time to prevent a catastrophe.

When Chad heard the crazy commotion outside his apartment door, he squeezed through the wooden door and found a flurry of activity going on.

A wild owl was dive bombing a falcon in the stairwell. Merry, Morgaine, and Gwyneth were rushing down the stairs shouting at them, and each tried to grab the owl.

Dottie stepped out of her apartment, screamed, and hurried back in, slamming the door. She glued her huge round eyeball to the peephole, though. By the time they made it to the first floor, Nathan had stepped out of his apartment to see what was going on, froze in horror, and ducked back in, but left the door partly open. Then he reemerged in his raven form.

Now there were three of them, flapping all over the place.

A female figure with a camera around her neck held a pad of paper and a pen. She peered through the glass of the outer door and watched the whole thing wide-eyed and open-mouthed.

The owl finally cornered the falcon and was readying to snatch it with lethal-looking talons. Then Nathan in his raven form did something so brave, Chad never thought he'd see the day. He rammed right into the owl, knocking her into the wall so hard, it temporarily stunned her.

Both raven and falcon flew into the sanctuary of the first floor apartment and a second later, the door slammed shut and the double locks clicked.

The woman outside the front door rushed to the right and must have jumped because by the time Chad squeezed through the glass, she was hanging onto the windowsill in order to peer into Nathan's apartment.

What Chad saw through the window didn't entirely surprise him. A naked landlord and naked Nathan leaned against the door, staring at each other.

Bummer. Their secret's out.

Jason spotted the woman in the window about to snap his picture and took off running. A bright light flashed before he made it very far.

"Nathan, I need clothes!" he yelled.

"Borrow whatever you like. Everything's in my bed-room closet."

He wasn't kidding. His bedroom held very little fur-niture. A bed and a bookcase to be exact. Throwing open the closet door, Jason revealed a few items on hangers, very neat and orderly. Everything black—apparently Nathan's favorite color, being a raven and all.

"Nathan," Jason yelled. "I don't see any underwear, and there's no time to look around."

Nathan appeared in the doorway, wearing only black jeans. "I go commando. It helps me avoid getting caught in my clothes in case I have to shift in a hurry. And take one of my black shirts. Leave the top couple of buttons open."

Jason grabbed a pair of slacks and hopped into them. "Smart. We should probably talk at some point."

Nathan shrugged. "Do we need to?"

"You saved my life, man. I'd like to thank you and talk to you about how you control your shifts so easily. You popped into human form faster than I did, and I really wanted to get out of my tasty falcon body."

"Oh, in that case, fine."

"What did you think I wanted to talk about?"

"Oh, I don't know… eviction?"

Jason chuckled. "Not hardly. I owe you my life."

Nathan's lip rose in a half smile. "I guess you do. But don't expect us to become best buddies or anything, no offense. I'm just not into that 'bromance' stuff."

Jason pulled a shirt off the hanger. "That's good, because neither am I. Still, it's weird to find another shifter in the same neighborhood, never mind same building."

Nathan smirked. "You've never heard 'Birds of a feather flock together'?"

"Well, yeah, but what does that have to do with coincidence?"

"Paranormals tend to attract other paranormals. Why do you think you were attracted to this building?"

Jason straightened. "Because of you?"

Nathan nodded. "Maybe. And maybe I'm not the only one."

Shocked, Jason braced himself against the closet door. "Are you saying there are other shifters in this building besides the three of us?"

"Three? Oh, then you know about Konrad."

Confused, Jason asked, "Wait a minute... Konrad's a shifter too?"

"Oops. I thought he was the third one you were referring to. Who *did* you mean?"

"You, me, and my uncle."

"Ah, Ralph is your uncle. He's a falcon at times, too? I wondered why you hired the pair of them. He's next to useless, and she's a complete liability."

"Yeah, well, they're family. But whatever you do, don't tell Dottie. I don't think she knows, and I'm sure she'd freak."

Nathan laughed. "Damn. That would be so much fun."

"I'm serious."

"Yeah, okay. What are you going to tell her just happened?"

Jason slapped a hand over his eyes and slumped against the door. "I have no idea."

"Have you tried the 'you must be hallucinating,' routine?"

He nodded. "Unfortunately. She caught me in the elevator in falcon form, stuck in my sweater. I hate to make her think she's going nuts."

Nathan snorted. "Stuck in your... Oh, that's priceless."

"Yeah, well, that's one reason I'd like to talk to you. It seems there are some things I need to learn that you can teach me."

Chuckling, he said, "I guess so. New to this, are you?"

"No, but I'm only half-shifter. It's harder to control sometimes when new circumstances add stress. It's happened a few times recently. I've been able to keep stress to a manageable minimum before this, but now..."

Nathan nodded. "It's been harder since you acquired a girlfriend, right?"

"How did you know?"

He rolled his eyes. "Women. They can complicate the shit out of everything."

Just then, another camera flash through the bedroom window temporarily blinded them.

Jason glanced at what Nathan was wearing—jeans only—then at himself—pants and an open shirt. That, plus where they were standing—beside a queen-size bed—added up to *bad news*.

"Shit!"

Chapter 13

MERRY DIDN'T QUITE KNOW WHAT TO DO. SHE LOITERED in the hallway outside her front door, knowing Jason was inside her neighbor's apartment, but should she knock? What if he was hurt? Did Nathan know more about helping a shifter than she did?

She had already told Morgaine and Gwyneth that a reading was probably out of the question in the foreseeable future and to keep their pet in the apartment at all times—hidden—and on a tether.

Maybe the future wasn't meant to be foreseen. Perhaps hers would never be easy to predict now that she had landed in the capital of the state of weirdness.

Mentally counting on her fingers, she ticked off each resident's "special gift." Morgaine and Gwyneth were witches. A ghost lived across the hall from them. She lived next door to a raven and her boyfriend and his uncle were falcons. Oh! And she mustn't forget about her vampire dad in the basement.

She remembered Konrad's seemingly superhuman strength and wondered what *his* story was. He was friends with Sly, so he must be something-or-other. Another vampire? Maybe one who shifts into a bat? Sly had laughed at her when she asked if he could do that.

So how did she end up here, anyway? Oh yeah. The ad in her weekly small town newspaper. Boston sounded so exciting, and the ad had been placed there for three weeks in a row—until she answered it. Sly had asked Morgaine to use some kind of spell to be sure she saw it and no one else did, but that was impossible, wasn't it?

What the hell... In this weird place, *anything seemed possible*.

As she waited patiently, contemplating her life turned upside down, Jason flew out of Nathan's apartment, only this time in human form and half dressed.

"Stay here," he shouted when he caught sight of her. Then he yanked open the front door and vaulted over the railing.

"What the...?"

Nathan appeared in his open doorway and leaned against it, appearing entirely too casual under the circumstances. "Nice night, isn't it?"

"What was *that* about?" she asked, pointing toward the front door.

"You mean Jason?"

"Yeah, he just ran out of here like he was being chased by a grizzly bear."

Nathan laughed.

"What's so funny?"

He shrugged. "He wasn't being chased. He's doing the chasing, and if a mere five-foot-five woman thinks she can outrun a peregrine falcon, she's sorely mistaken."

"Five-foot-five woman...?" Suddenly Merry remembered the flash she thought she had seen through the front door, and a horrible foreboding invaded her gut. "Oh, no!" Her eyes narrowed and she balled her hands into fists.

"You know her?" Nathan asked.

"I hope to God it's not who I think it is."

"Why? Who is she?"

"Lila Crum." She practically spat the name. "Did you happen to see the newspaper a few weeks ago?"

"No, why?"

"This paparazzi reporter made up a rotten story about Jason and tried to ruin his career and our relationship."

"That blows. I don't read the newspaper. Too depressing."

She stared at him a moment. "But you work in a morgue."

He laughed. "Death isn't depressing. Most of the folks we get were old or sick and death was a release from a painful prison."

"I guess... So what do you think Jason's going to do when he catches up to... whomever?"

Nathan shrugged. "You know him better than I do."

"What would you do?"

"Oh, I'd peck out her eyeballs. Then I'd probably take her camera and drop it in the river. Or the ocean. Yeah, the ocean would probably be... Are you all right?"

Merry hadn't realized it, but her face had probably lost its color and the room was beginning to swirl. Nathan reached her before she passed out and lowered her gently to the floor.

"Breathe slowly. You're hyperventilating."

Merry blinked and exhaled, then purposely slowed her breathing. Her vision cleared. "I'm okay. Thanks."

"Think nothing of it." He stood and watched her while she shakily struggled to her feet.

"So, do you think Jason would do that? Hurt someone, I mean?"

He shrugged. "What do you care? I thought she tried to hurt you."

"Not physically. No eye pecking. Nobody deserves that. Besides, I feel kind of sorry for her."

Nathan made a noise that sounded like *pshah*. "The paparazzi? They deserve whatever they get."

"She's a human being, or *was* once. I think she lost a big piece of her humanity. The part that cares about other people's feelings."

"And some people have more than their share of humanity and care too much. You, for instance."

"Me? I don't care too much. I care just right."

Loud cursing outside signaled someone's approach. Merry opened the front door and Jason hurried inside, buck naked, dragging Lila with him.

"Jesus! Look at you."

Nathan sighed. Sounding bored, he asked, "Where'd you leave my clothes?"

"Marlboro Street. About two blocks down. I'll go back and get them later."

"No need. I feel like taking a walk. I'll just go get my keys." Nathan disappeared into his apartment, but left the door ajar.

Lila grinned. "Oh, so you share clothes as well as a bed?" Then she turned her evil smile toward Merry. "I'll bet you didn't know your boyfriend had a boyfriend."

"He doesn't," she said, and crossed her arms.

"Oh yeah?" Lila laughed. "When I get through with him, you're the only one who'll believe that."

Nathan reemerged shrugging into his black jacket. "Look, lady, I don't know what your damage is, but this guy doesn't deserve whatever crap you're dishing out."

"Defending your lover, are you?"

"Blow it out your blowhole, lady," he said calmly and pushed past her to leave.

"Hey, see if you can find her camera while you're out there," Jason called after him. "She threw it in some bushes."

Merry worried her upper lip. "Jason, what are we going to do with her?"

"We?" he asked. "She's my problem."

"Well, yes, but she seems intent on destroying my reputation too. Unless you don't think a nurse's reputation counts."

"Of course it does." He looked pensive. "Can you get my key so we can take her up to my place? It would be harder for her to escape through a window from the fourth floor. Besides..." He looked down at himself. "I need some clothes—again."

Once in Jason's apartment, an uncomfortable silence passed between Merry and Lila while he dressed hurriedly. When he reemerged from his bedroom, Lila was sitting in his comfy chair. Merry stood in front of her with her arms crossed.

"Can I have something to drink, please? Something strong?" Lila asked with surprising politeness.

Jason frowned. "First of all, get out of my chair. You can sit on the couch."

While she moved, he looked to Merry. "What's your opinion on giving her alcohol?"

Merry sighed. "Well, we don't want her to go into withdrawal. If it's been a few hours since her last drink, she might. Who knows how long she was lurking outside the building."

Jason sat in his chair and nodded.

"Hey, you sound as if you think I'm an alcoholic."

"Aren't you?" Merry asked. "Your bartender friend seemed to think so."

"Kevin? He'd never say that. Besides, he's not my friend anymore."

Casually, Merry said, "Really? Then I guess you don't need a drink and can do without one now."

"Damn straight. I can take it or leave it. I—I'd just prefer to take it."

"Prefer to or need to?" Merry asked. "I need to know how to keep you safe."

"Don't you dare diagnose me!"

Merry shrugged. "Fine. No drinks then. Why don't you tell us why you're doing this?"

"Doing what?"

"Trying to ruin my reputation," Jason said. "And possibly my relationship with my future fiancée." He frowned and waited.

She smirked. "*Future* fiancée, huh?"

Merry sat on the arm of his chair. "No matter what you print, I'm not going to believe it, by the way."

Lila shrugged. "Whatever. I report what I see, and I've seen some weird shit around here. Why wouldn't I report it? Give me one good reason."

"Because it's destructive."

"Hmm… Nope. That's not enough. Perhaps I should have said, give me *seventy-five thousand* good reasons."

Merry leaned forward. "Was that a bribe? Why, you brain-damaged, parasitic…"

Jason put his hand on Merry's arm. "Stop. I'll pay it."

She sat up straight. "You're kidding!"

Jason held Lila's gaze. "The money comes with certain conditions, though."

"I'm interested. Keep talking."

"The story dies right here. The pictures are destroyed. And you never come near this building or the people who live here again."

Merry interjected. "And you go to rehab."

"Whoa!" Lila stood and clenched her fists. "I told you, I *don't* have a drinking problem."

"Thou doth protest too much."

Lila started toward Merry. Jason jumped up and stood in front of her. "You touch her and not only will the offer be rescinded, but I'll sue you and your paper for libel, defamation of character, and attempted bribery."

Lila stopped in her tracks.

Ah ha. We know what to use for leverage. Jason wanted to avoid the stress and publicity of a trial at all costs, but she didn't know that.

"I'll lose my job."

"Maybe you need a new line of work, anyway. Look, Merry's idea was a good one. I'll pay for a full treatment program. If you sign out early or against medical advice, the money stays in my bank account, and I'll sue the paper for millions."

"What makes you think you'll win?"

"I have an excellent lawyer. He's never lost a case." That wasn't necessarily true either, but it sounded good. He must have convinced her, because she remained quiet and appeared to be thinking it over.

"Look, Lila," Merry's voice softened. "I know of a

couple of excellent thirty-day programs. I've recommended them to a couple of people I know and they were damn glad they participated. Each got more than they expected—not just a chance to sober up. It improved their whole lives."

After a long hesitation, she asked, "How will I know I'll get paid after the thirty days?"

Jason crossed his arms. "I'll leave a check made out to you in a sealed envelope with the hospital administrator. The instructions will be written on the outside of the envelope. He'll only give it to you upon completion of the entire program. Otherwise, it comes back to me."

She narrowed her eyes. "What's the catch?"

"Only that I take you to the facility myself," he said. "And I need to see that you're admitted before I leave. You can watch me put the check in the envelope and hand the envelope to the administrator."

"Maybe he's a friend of yours and will tear up the check as soon as I turn my back."

"You can ask him or her if we're friends. Since I play baseball and don't know anyone in that business, I'm certain it won't be a problem."

Merry strolled over to her and placed a hand on her shoulder. When she didn't shrug it off, she said, "You're being given a very generous offer. If you're smart, you'll take it and when you get the money, disappear to some beautiful location and get a new job."

Lila exhaled and lowered her shoulders.

She's going to go for it! "Oh, one more thing…" Jason said.

"What now?"

"If you ever try to extract any more money from me,

you'll go to jail. I have my phone set to record all calls just in case you or anyone else of like mind manages to get the number. And if you ever write to me…"

She shook her head. "I won't do that. I'm not stupid."

"Good. Then we understand each other."

She nodded. "Can I go home now? I'll have to pack."

Merry held up one hand. "Not so fast. You could break your word and run the story. We're about the same size. I have clothes you can borrow."

"And what am I going to do in the meantime? Sit here until tomorrow when the admissions department opens and the hospital administrator shows up?"

"That sounds like the best option," Jason said. "I'll make the arrangements tonight."

"And I'll wait up with you," Merry said.

Concerned for Merry, Jason shook his head. "You need your rest. Don't you have to work tomorrow?"

"Yeah, but I don't trust her. She might knot together all your sheets and tablecloths and lower herself to the ground. Somebody has to baby-sit."

Lila put her head in her hands. "I need a drink. And maybe several more between now and tomorrow."

Merry nodded. "I figured you might."

"Pick your poison," Jason said, and strode to his bar.

"Lots of rum and a tiny bit of coke."

"Hey…" Merry brightened. "I know just the person to watch her. He stays up all night anyway."

"Who?" Jason asked.

"Sly."

"Do you know where to find him?"

Merry shifted her weight from side to side and avoided eye contact. "I think so."

"Fine. Can you do me a favor, though?"

"Anything."

"Stop at the third floor on your way down and tell the girls that if they can't guarantee their pet never leaves the apartment, I'd like them to find a new home on a nice farm for their owl."

"Already did."

Merry tiptoed down to the basement. She hoped that the frigid night air had kept Sly inside. Did vampires feel extremes of temperature? Weren't they already cold dead?

"Sly?" she whispered.

No answer came. She was about to call his name louder when she rotated around and came face to face with him. Instinctively, she recoiled and sucked in a deep breath.

"Don't be afraid, Merry."

"Sorry. You just surprised me."

"I tend to do that to people. You were looking for me?"

"Yeah. I was wondering if I could ask you to do me a favor? A big favor."

"Depends. If it's to eat garlic bagels with you during the day, I can't."

She chuckled. "No, it's nothing like that. I just need you to watch someone for me tonight. She's up in Jason's penthouse and until we can get her to rehab in the morning…"

"Ah, the nasty reporter," he guessed.

"How did you know?"

"We've met. It's hard to miss the alcohol on her breath."

"That's right. You told her my name was Allison.

Well, she knows better now, and she's threatening to ruin Jason's and my reputations."

"I don't particularly care what she does to him, but if she's out to embarrass or humiliate you in any way, I can take care of that—permanently."

"Oh, Christ, no! I don't want you to do anything but prevent her from sneaking out of Jason's apartment during the night. I'd stay up with her myself, but I have to work tomorrow. Working as a nurse on only a couple of hours sleep is a dangerous idea."

He nodded and leaned against the support column. "Did I ever tell you I'm proud of you?"

Surprised, a grin crept across her face. "I don't know, but it feels good to hear it."

"I'll need to get back down here before sunrise. Does your boyfriend know where I sleep during the day?"

"I don't think so."

"Does he know what I am?"

"No. And I'd have no idea how to tell him..." She shrugged.

"Good. Please keep it that way."

"I will."

"Promise?"

"I promise."

"All right, then. Shall we go?" He gestured toward the cellar door.

She hugged him without even thinking about it. He held her awkwardly at first, then embraced her in earnest and patted her back.

Just as she suspected... He was freezing cold.

"You'll be nice to Jason, won't you? He's very important to me."

Sly rolled his eyes. "I suppose I'll have to be."

She shot him a warning look.

Sly had never seen the penthouse and looked forward to checking out the celebrity's digs. Since he and Merry stopped at her apartment to pack some clothes for Lila, the reporter was good and inebriated by the time they finally arrived. He barely had a chance to glance across the marble floor and high ceilings before she staggered over to him.

"Ish thish my babyshitter?"

She reeked of rum. Being sensitive to odors anyway, the smell overwhelmed him and he held her at arm's length.

"Hey, I know you. You're the neighbor." She swayed slightly as she pointed to him. "You told me a fib. You shed Merry's name was Allishon."

"Sit down and be quiet," Sly said. "You're already getting on my nerves."

"You're a shitty babyshitter."

Jason strolled over to him and offered his hand. Sly didn't dare shake it or he'd discover how cold he was. But at the same time, he didn't dare not to. He promised Merry he'd "be nice" to him and she was watching closely.

At last he took the proffered hand and shook it, apologizing at the same time. "Sorry about my cold hands. I was outside."

Jason snatched his hand back. "Jeez, it must be freezing out there. What were you doing outside?"

He shrugged. "Just appreciating the stars. The sky

is clearer on crisp evenings. I'm something of an amateur astronomer."

Jason frowned and nodded like he was thinking, *Ooookaaaay*... "I have a nice view of the sky from my balcony, but I wouldn't stay out there tonight. I think the weather predictions are for snow."

"Oh, good," Lila interjected. "I hate shnow. Shuddenly being inshide for a month doesn't shound sho bad."

"I'm actually glad to meet you, Sly," Jason said. "Maybe when the rum princess passes out, we can get to know each other better."

"Ha, ha. Rum princshessh. I like that better than plain ol' 'rummy'."

As if the power of suggestion was all it took, she staggered over to the low couch and fell like a tree.

"How much did you give her?" Merry asked.

He sighed. "I have no idea. She said I didn't know how to make a decent drink and she'd do it herself. She wound up drinking right out of the bottle. What took you so long?"

"Crap." She looked down at the barely conscious Lila and shook her head. "I was packing for her. I called around to see if anyplace was still open so I could buy her some underwear, but at this time of night I would've had to go downtown to a sex shop."

Jason chuckled. "Damn. Maybe if you had, you'd be tempted to buy a few things for yourself."

Sly stiffened.

Jason and Merry exchanged those knowing, sexual looks, and he didn't like it. Didn't like it at all. Celebrities broke hearts and he'd better not toy with Merry's.

Lila interrupted the charged silence with a soft snore.

"I'll stop on the way to the rehab and let her buy some stuff."

"I don't think that's a good idea," Merry said. "I'd suggest checking her in directly, and then you can go buy her what she needs. About six pairs of cotton panties and some sports bras ought to do it. Or I can drop some off for her later."

Jason stared at the inert body. "Do you think she'd run if I stopped? I don't know what size to get."

"Probably not," Merry admitted. "She's going to feel like absolute crap in the morning. She'll probably have what I call the 'never agains.' But she might barf in your car if she has to wait very long."

"Sheesh. I'd better take her straight to rehab, then. You sure she won't bolt if I stop at a red light?"

"She's more apt to run when they wean her off the anti-seizure medications. She'll feel better enough to move quickly, but old habits die hard. She might want to drink for quite a while. Sometimes it takes almost the whole thirty days for the cravings to pass. Did you make arrangements for a locked unit?"

"Yeah. There's a bed waiting for her at the first facility you suggested. They said the first two weeks they're locked in and only go out onto the grounds if they earn it after that. Even then, they're supervised."

"Ask them to make it three in lock-up."

"You sound like you know what you're talking about," Sly said.

"I had to learn this stuff in nursing school and do a semester of clinical practice in a psych ward. I learned that it takes three weeks to break a bad habit, and *hopefully* replace it with a good one."

"You don't think she'll be ticked off if we tell them to treat her differently?"

Merry looked over at Lila again. "Oh, she'll be pissed. It's called tough love. If she gets the help she needs, she'll thank you for it... eventually."

"Three it is, then."

Merry hugged Sly. "Well, I'd better say good night. And really, I can't thank you enough." Then she strolled over to Jason and kissed him with an astounding lip-lock for what seemed like hours.

"Ahem."

The couple pulled apart, *finally*. He knew Merry was sensitive about overprotective fathers, but honestly! Did he have to witness them fawning all over each other?

Okay, okay. So he hadn't really been a father except to plant the seed, but his protective instincts kicked in anyway, just like a real dad's would.

Or maybe he couldn't help but be reminded of the passion he'd never have again, and just like seeing any other couple madly in love, it hurt.

Chapter 14

MERRY DEPARTED TO SLEEP IN HER OWN APARTMENT, and Sly settled in on the comfy chair. Jason considered asking him to move to the other one, but in Merry's mind Sly was going to become his father-in-law... even if Merry was the only one who believed his cockamamie claim... *Oh, hell. Let him have it.*

Sly leaned back and looked quite comfortable. "Nice place. You must be doing well for yourself."

"Well enough."

Sly nodded and continued to appraise the place. "Yup. Real cushy."

What is this? Was Sly making sure he could support "his daughter" in the style to which she would become accustomed? Or was he collecting information for a future shakedown?

"So, what are your intentions toward my daughter?"

Jason couldn't stand the charade anymore. He burst out laughing.

Sly raised an eyebrow. "Is that a funny question? Am I supposed to find that amusing?"

"No. Forgive me, it's just that..." He threw his hands in the air and let out a deep breath. "Would you like a drink?"

Sly smiled and his eyes glinted. A chill ran down Jason's spine.

"No, thank you. I'm fine."

"Okay." Jason scratched his head and figured he'd better answer the man's question, no matter who he thought he was. He might not be as stable as he appeared under that calm exterior. "So, my intentions toward Merry are completely honorable, I assure you. I've already asked her to marry me."

"Really? She said nothing about this to me."

He shrugged and sat on the low chair since it was the only seat left in the grouping. Lila took up only part of the long sofa, spread eagle and face down, but he didn't want to wake her. Managing a drunk was much easier this way.

"Maybe she was waiting for a better time." He gestured toward Lila. "We had other things to deal with tonight."

"Indeed. I take it the reporter caught your little shifting act earlier."

Surprise zinged through him like an electric shock. Too stunned to speak, he simply stared at Sly.

"Merry does tell me her important news, so I was surprised she didn't mention something as meaningful as a wedding."

Way to turn the tables, guy. "I, uh… I'm sure she will."

"I didn't see her wearing a ring. Did she accept?"

Still recovering from shock, he wondered why Sly was *not* making a big deal about his being a shapeshifter? Was he really only concerned about the wedding? Had he heard him correctly?

"Well?" Sly tipped his head.

"Huh? Oh, yeah. She did and then she said she needed more time—to take care of a few things. We're waiting to tell people until we hammer out the details."

"I see." Sly sounded skeptical.

"What does that mean?"

"Oh, nothing. I just want to be sure nobody is stringing my daughter along. I'd hate to see anyone hurt her."

The menacing look in his eyes chilled Jason to the bone.

"Because if anyone were to hurt her, I'd have to *do* something about it."

"Wait a minute. Are you threatening me? I'm not going to hurt Merry. In fact, she's more apt to hurt me. I'm head-over-heels in love with her."

"Good," Sly said, seeming satisfied. "Then may I make a suggestion?"

"Sure." *Why the hell not? This conversation can't get much weirder.*

"Hold your wedding after dark. I'd like to attend. Candlelight weddings are beautiful anyway. Don't you think?"

"Pardon me, but am I missing something here? You seem to have concerns about our wedding, but haven't batted an eyelash over my shifting capabilities."

"I was getting to that."

Damn. Time to change the subject, quick. "Well, before you move on, I have some concerns of my own."

"Oh? What would those be?" His face and posture didn't change—as if he couldn't imagine anything on his end being out of whack. Was this guy for real?

"Well, first off, you seem way too young to be Merry's father."

Sly smiled. "Why thank you. I try to take care of myself."

"That wasn't meant as a compliment," Jason said. "I'm serious. You couldn't be a day over thirty years old by the looks of you."

"And again, you flatter me."

"No!" Indignant, Jason jumped out of the low chair and paced. "Something's wrong here. Either you're not Merry's birth father and have convinced her that you are for some reason of your own, or… I can't think of another possibility."

Sly leaned forward and clasped his hands. "Well, I'm sorry you can't think more creatively. There *is* another explanation. I haven't convinced her of anything but the truth."

Getting nowhere, Jason exhaled audibly. "Okay, say I believe you, why didn't you come back into her life before? Why now?"

"Because I wanted to get to know her but didn't want to interfere in her upbringing."

"I don't get it." He shook his head.

"What's to get?" Sly asked. "It's simple. I was a sudden widower with an infant I couldn't raise properly on my own. Giving her up was one of the hardest things I've ever had to do, but I did it for her."

"Okay, that sounds very sensible and noble, but how old were you at the time?"

Sly stood and crossed his arms. "You're still doubting me. Perhaps I should leave. You can take care of your own—problem." He nodded toward the inert body on the couch.

Lila turned over and draped her arm across her face. Her snores grew louder with occasional bursts of pig snorts.

Jason's righteous anger deflated. "I'm sorry. Look, I know Merry, and she'll be furious if she thinks you left because I treated you badly. Please stay."

Sly scrutinized him. "No more talk about my age, all right?"

"Fine. We'll talk about something else." The words no sooner left his mouth than he regretted them.

Sly smiled. "All right. Tell me what kind of shape-shifter you are."

"I thought you knew."

"I saw a feathery fight in the lobby, and then the door across from Merry's slammed. Seconds later, I saw you and Nathan in his apartment, naked, leaning against the door. It was a simple matter of putting two and two together."

Jason let out a nervous chuckle. "Well, you're the only one who came up with four. This broad," he pointed to Lila, "thinks I'm gay and that Nathan and I are lovers."

Sly laughed. "Ridiculous."

"Yeah, totally. After all, I'm with Merry."

"Oh, I didn't mean your being gay was ridiculous. Just being with Nathan. He's a piece of work."

Jason was just about to get back on his high horse when Sly said something to de-saddle him again.

"So which bird were you?"

"The falcon."

"How did you explain the shifting to the rum princess?"

"I didn't."

He nodded. "She probably thought she was hallucinating."

"One more reason to sign herself into rehab."

Sly nodded again, but said nothing.

"How did you see the whole thing? Were you out there together?"

Sly snorted. "As if I'd voluntarily subject myself to her rotten company. I keep an eye on the building because my daughter lives here."

"I see." He really didn't understand half of what was going on. Perhaps waiting for the details to shake out and concentrating on the matter at hand would be the best thing to do. "I can't wait until Lila's out of here. Thanks for watching her, if I forgot to say it before." *And I can't wait until you're out of here, too, whether you're doing me a favor or not.* "By the way, where do you live?"

"Nearby," Sly said. A corner of his mouth curled up, and suddenly Jason didn't want to know.

The elevator whirred and stopped on the top floor.

"Are you expecting someone?" Sly stood.

"No. It must be Merry."

Jason strode to the elevator just as Dottie stepped off.

Oh, no. What now? "How did you get up here?"

"Jason, I need to speak to you about earlier…" It was just like her to ignore his question and ask one of her own. She glanced over toward Sly. "Who's this?" Then she strolled over to the couch, gazed down at Lila, raised her voice and echoed herself. "Who's this?"

"Shhh… Aunt Dottie. You don't want to wake the devil."

"She looks a little rough around the edges, but not exactly devilish. What happened to her? Does Merry know she's here? She didn't say anything to me about it."

"One question at a time, Aunt Dottie."

Sly glided over to her, took her hand and kissed her knuckles. "I'm Sylvestro Flores… and charmed to meet such a lovely lady."

Dottie's mouth dropped open—with no words following, for once.

Jason hoped Sly's presence might slow her tirade about the wild bird fight, so he let them continue talking.

"Flores? Isn't that what they said Merry's last name was in the gossip column?"

"Yes," Sly said. "She's my..."

"Sister!" Jason interjected. "Yes, Merry was adopted and she recently found her only blood relative."

Sly gave him a look that could only be interpreted as reluctantly complicit. "Ah, yes. My sister. We are finally getting to know each other after a lifetime apart."

"Well, then what are you doing up here? Shouldn't you be down in Merry's apartment? I know she's down there. I checked."

He and Jason exchanged glances. Sly picked up Dottie's hand again and gazed into her eyes. Dottie's jaw slacked and she stared at him without blinking.

"You need to go back to your own apartment. There's nothing going on here. Nothing happened earlier tonight to concern you. You just came up here to say 'hello' and 'good night.' I was introduced to you as Jason's friend, Sylvestro."

A moment later he released her hand and she blinked a couple of times, appearing confused.

"You know, it's funny, but I came up here just to say 'hello' and 'good night.' Now isn't that silly of me? I didn't need to swipe Ralph's key card to do that."

"No, you didn't. Maybe next time you can call on the phone."

"Sure." She shook her head, looking confused. "But it's nice to see you anyway."

"Nice to see you too, Aunt Dottie."

"And it was lovely to meet you," Sly said, bowing, but never losing eye contact.

"Yes, you too," she said, smiling sweetly. Then she wandered to the elevator and left—the look of confusion having been replaced by contentment.

Neat trick. But how the hell did he do that, and how do I know he won't do it to me? "Was that mind control? Hypnosis?"

"Something like that."

"Do you do that often?"

"No, only when necessary. It seems to have come in handy this time, don't you think?"

Jason had to reluctantly agree. Maybe someday he'd ask Sly to teach him how to hypnotize his pesky aunt with no more than a look.

Chad watched while Detective Joe Murphy stood outside in the snow, buzzing Jason's apartment for the third time with no answer.

"He's not home, dumbass! Try the witches' apartment!" Damn, I wish ordinary people could hear me yell. If he'd had some kind of major breakthrough, Chad wanted to know about it!

"Shit." He surveyed the other names and buzzers. "Where did that medium live? Across the hall from the so-called haunted apartment, right?"

God, I hope he's bright enough to figure it out. Only two apartments on the third floor. One buzzer has two names on it and the other apartment's name plate is blank. C'mon, genius.

"Here goes nothin'," the detective mumbled.

"Yes? Can I help you?"

A soft feminine voice answered *before* Joe hit the buzzer and he jumped, startled. Gwyneth had been standing next to the intercom expecting him for five minutes.

Get used to it, Detective. Psychics, remember?

"Uh, this is Detective Joe Murphy. I have an update regarding Mr. Washington's case. May I come in?"

"Oh, of course!" sang the sweet voice of the younger cousin.

Joe entered the building when she buzzed the door open, then paused. It looked as if he was deciding whether or not to take the stairs. He had already seen the elevator and probably wanted to check out the rest of the beautiful old building. The elegant touches of sculpted crown molding and the gleaming mahogany banister would appeal to anybody who had a taste for the finer things in life.

Despite being a man of about forty, he jogged up the stairs and stopped to admire and whistle at the gorgeous crystal chandelier hanging between the first and second floors.

"Mmm… I could get used to living like this. Maybe once I debunk this ghost business, I can move out of my office and into that vacant apartment. I'll bet the retainer the landlord paid me would cover a security deposit."

Ha! I knew he wasn't a real believer. The cousins' door opened before he reached it. Gwyneth stood there to greet him. *Maybe she can convince the arrogant prick that he doesn't know everything.*

"Good mornin', Detective. How nice to see you."

"Good morning. It's Gwyneth, right?"

"Yes. How sweet of you to remember me. Can I get you somethin' to drink? A cup of tea or a beer?"

He grinned.

A polite, pretty young thing with red hair brushing her fanny? Like anyone could forget her. Hell, if I were fifty years younger—and alive… sigh.

"Is your cousin home?"

"No, I'm afraid not. She was called back home last night. We had some sad news. Her grandmama, my great-aunt, just passed, bless her soul."

"I'm sorry to hear that. You didn't go with her?"

"No. We have a home business and I have to stay here to take care of our customers."

"Oh, I see. Well, my condolences again on the loss of your great-aunt. Was she ill?"

"Yes, I'm afraid so. Oh, she lived a good full life. Seventy-four and she didn't suffer in the end. She had extensive knowledge of herbal medicine and knew what to take to stop the pain. Unfortunately, she may have taken a little too much yesterday and phhhht."

"Well, it's good that she didn't suffer." He scratched his head. "I'm sorry Morgaine's not here since I know she thinks… um, I mean she's the one who can communicate with your ghost."

"Well, guess what? So can *I*!"

"Really? I thought she was the only one."

"She was, but I worked real hard on developin' my psychic powers, and now I can hear him too."

"Excellent! Maybe I can relay the information through you to your landlord and the, um…"

"Spirit of Chad? You don't believe in ghosts, do ya, Mistah Murphy?"

"Not so much." He smiled weakly.

I guess no one bothered to ask him before this? Or if they did, he lied. Chances are he wouldn't have been hired for this interesting and lucrative case if he hadn't.

"That's all right. We're used to that. When we meet a skeptic who needs our help, we just do what we do and let the results speak for themselves."

"I can respect that."

She gave him a genuine sweet smile. "That's all we want. If you treat us with respect, we're happy to help."

The telephone rang.

"Oh!" She covered her mouth and looked embarrassed. "I'm very sorry. It's the business line. Could I ask you to wait in the hallway?"

"Of course," he said. "I understand completely."

Ha! I doubt it.

Joe exited the apartment with Chad floating close behind. He waited until the phone stopped ringing, then glued his ear to the door.

"Well, hello, sugar. What can I do for you today?"

A brief silence followed, then, "I'm not wearin' a stitch."

What sounded like heavy breathing followed. "Ohhhh…" she moaned. "Suck my big tits. You like 'em big, don't ya, darlin'?"

Gee, I wonder if Detective Murphy is smart enough to figure out what their 'business' is.

"Oh yeah. Squeeze them. Suck them. Ohhhh… Oh, yeah, baby. Let me take your cock in my hand. I want to rub that cock all over my breasts until you are good an' hard. Then I'm gonna take it in my mouth. I'm just dyin' to suck your luscious cock."

Joe's eyes nearly bugged out of his head.

Now he understands. Or maybe he thinks she's planning a hot date, not making a living with phone sex, although she's not big-breasted so the caller obviously doesn't know what she looks like. Joe kept his ear glued to the door and listened intently. *Don't worry, Joe. You'll hear lots more.*

"Oh, thank you. I just couldn't wait another minute. I'm goin' to suck your cock now. I'm gonna suck it so hard and so deep, you'll think you've died and gone to heaven."

Slurping sounds followed. *Her favorite trick is sucking on one of those thick candy canes. Handy since she can mumble around it and sound as if she really does have something naughty in her mouth.*

Joe grinned. Lewd talk coming out of the sugary sweet Southern belle obviously amused the hell out of him, but it also made a sizable bulge in his pants.

If he bothered to imagine what was happening on the other side of that phone, his willy might wither.

"You wanna come now? Okay darlin', where do you want me when you come? Oh, yeah. That sounds good. I love that position. I'm gettin' on my hands and knees now."

Chad couldn't help messing with the private dick. He blew a breezy chill down Joe Murphy's neck, which proved as good as a cold shower. The detective shivered and glanced over at the door across the hall.

Ha! I can almost hear his thoughts. "No. It couldn't be. A ghost? For real?"

Backing away from the door, Joe whispered, "Okay, I know you're here. As soon as Gwyneth is, um—finished, I have something to report. Say a word to her about my listening through the door and I'll shut right up and go home."

He looks pleased with himself, probably thinking, "That ought to cover all possibilities, if there actually is a ghost." I doubt he means it, though. Chad was sure he'd have to do some more convincing, but he did want to hear what the P.I. had to say first.

When Gwyneth opened the door she appeared no different than before.

That sweet young thing could have been selling magazines over the phone for all anyone could tell—except I know better. And now, so did Joe Murphy.

"I apologize for the interruption. Please come in and make yourself comfortable."

"Is your ghost here?"

She cocked her head.

"Hi Gwyneth. I've been following this bozo around since he walked in. I was with him in the hall and now I'm here with both of you."

"Why, yes. He said he was in the hall with you and then he came into the apartment right behind you."

Joe glanced over his shoulder, then strode to the armchair and took a seat.

"Are you sure I can't get you somethin'?" she asked.

"You could probably give him what you were giving your customer."

Her gaze moved to the ceiling. "Now, don't be crude, Chad. He does *not* want that!"

Joe cleared his throat. "I think I'd like that cup of tea now."

"Sure thing, darlin'. I'll be just a minute."

As soon as she was out of sight, Joe whispered furiously, "If you want any information, you keep your mouth shut about earlier."

He looked as if he felt like an idiot, whispering to the air. Chad chuckled. *At least I convinced him my existence is a remote possibility, and this conversation with Gwyneth might be real.*

The telephone rang again.

"Oh fiddlesticks!" Gwyneth blurted from the other room.

She scurried around the corner, but before she could ask him to leave, he jumped up and said, "I'll wait in the hall."

Sure you will, buddy. So you can eavesdrop without her knowing.

Her cheeked reddened, but she smiled. "I'm so sorry. It's not usually like this."

He held up one hand in a gesture that said "think nothing of it" and retreated to the hallway.

Joe took a couple of minutes to think about it and must have decided, *What the hell… if the ghost is real and he wants his update, he'll keep his invisible mouth shut.* He leaned his ear against the door again.

"Have I been a bad girl? Oh honey, do I need a spankin'? Yeah, I think you need to spank me so I'll learn my lesson."

Plenty of slapping sounds followed. Joe shook his head and mumbled, "Unbelievable."

I don't know what's so unbelievable about it. Different strokes for different folks and all that.

"Oh! Ow! Ow!" Smack, smack. "I'm sorry, honey. I'll never do it again. Now what did I do?" Smack,

smack, smack. Sniffle. "I'm so sorry. I promise. I'll never fuck another man." Smack, smack.

At least not until the next phone call. Heh heh. Chad floated over Joe's head, intending to put his own ear to the door. His aim was a bit off and his ear traveled *through* the door instead.

He sighed and pulled his head out of the wood in order to remain on Joe's side of the barrier. *If only he realized… These girls help men act out their needs. Maybe this guy caught his wife in bed with someone else and by pretending to spank her with Gwyneth acting as a stand-in, he can satisfy that need without actually doing it to his wife.*

Or maybe he has a fantasy of catching his girlfriend with another man, but doesn't have the guts to tell her about it.

Obviously, she knew what turned on each customer, and this one's fantasy involved spanking. Joe covered his mouth with one hand to stifle a snicker. He wandered away from the door and sat on the stairs. *From the sizable bulge he's sporting, I'd guess he's getting turned on too.*

Smack, smack. They could still hear the sound effects without an ear to—or in—the door. *Now what'll he do? Pretend to be deaf? He must know she wasn't spanking herself.*

Joe took a chance and opened the door a crack. Bent over the leather chair with a fly swatter, he saw her give the seat a couple more good whacks.

"Ow, ow! Please, forgive me. I've learned my lesson," she pleaded into the phone. A sigh followed. "All right. Uh-huh. I aim to please. Just a measly little ninety-nine cents a minute. Uh-huh. I'll talk to you later, darlin'."

She set down the receiver, and Joe quickly closed the door.

When she opened it to invite him in, he asked, "Is everything all right?"

She beamed. "Everything's just peachy, Mister Murphy."

"Call me Joe."

Yes. Anyone who witnesses such intimate secrets ought to be known by their first name.

"Okay, Joe. Now where were we?"

"I wanted to tell your ghost about a breakthrough in the case."

"Oh, yes. How could I forget?"

"After all that, how could you remember?"

"Chad, honey, are you still here?"

"I'm waiting with bated breath."

She listened for a moment, then smiled and said. "He's as anxious as a cat in a roomful of rocking chairs."

"Huh?"

"Oh, sorry. He can't wait to hear what you have to say."

"Well, I know it wasn't the government. I checked my sources with every agency and contrary to Chad's suspicions, it wasn't the CIA, the FBI, or even the PTA, for that matter."

"Oh, groovy. A smart-ass detective making light of my murder."

"Huh? What did you say, Chad?" She listened again for a moment.

"I said to tell him to shove his jokes up his ass."

"Oh, my! I can't repeat that."

"Just ask him what he does *know."*

Gwyneth nodded. "Okay, I'll ask him. Mister Mur... I mean, Joe, who do you think did it if not the government?"

"Come on, you incompetent wretch. Maybe you could throw me a bone of hope before dashing my fantasies of you ever uncovering the conspiracy of the century and finding the murder suspect. After all, I gave you the motive."

"I didn't say it wasn't *some* government, just not ours. Ask him if he heard the attackers' accents?"

"Of course not. If I had I would have told you already. All they did was bust in, grab the papers off my desk and out of my typewriter, shoot me, tear the place apart, and disappear."

She listened. "No, he says they never uttered a word. Just took the papers he was typin', shot him, and left the place a mess."

"Ask him about their physical description. Anything he can remember. Their height, build, eye color... anything."

"Gaaaa...!"

"Now, Chad honey, be patient. He's tryin' to help you."

"I told him this before. Two of them. Tall, thin builds, and wiry. They wore ski masks and all black clothing."

"Uh-huh. Well, see now? That just might help the detective." She focused on Joe and said, "They were all black and wiry. Wore ski masks." Then she gazed at the ceiling again. "How about their eyes, Chad? Did you see their eyes? I find the eyes are the windows to the soul."

"Yeah. Their eyes were blue. Ice blue."

"Blue. That's fairly uncommon, isn't it?"

"Wow, I'll say. Black men with blue eyes who ski? I'll have this case wrapped up in no time."

"Dear God almighty. I said they were wearing black, not that they were black. Tell him he's a moron."

"Oh, I'm afraid there's been a misunderstandin'. He said they wore black, not that they *were* black."

Joe nodded. "That makes more sense. Is it possible they were Scandinavian?"

"I don't friggin' think so. But, yeah, I guess they could have been. Hell, they could have been blue-eyed Eskimos."

"He said they could have been Scandinavian—or blue-eyed Eskimos. I'm sorry. I guess that doesn't narrow it down much."

"Blue-eyed Eskimos?" Joe cocked his head and frowned. "Oh, I get it. He's being sarcastic. Does he do that a lot?"

"Oh, yes. All the time. But don't pay him no mind. He's just frustrated. Can you imagine what it must be like? Bein' a ghost trapped on this plane until you find your killer? He must think this mystery will never be solved. You are his last hope, Joe."

Joe stood. "Tell him I'll do my best, ma'am. I don't have many contacts with foreign governments, so this may take a while longer. Ask Chad if he wants me to continue?"

"You bet your bippy. If the residents ever want me to stop haunting this building, you'd better."

Gwyneth cocked her head. "He says he's not goin' to leave us alone until he knows who did it."

"Good. I mean, if that's the case, I'll continue to investigate, and please let Mr. Falco know about my visit when he returns. Thanks for your help."

"It was an honor, Joe. You come back any time, you hear?"

He smiled and let himself out. On his way down the stairs, he whistled.

Chapter 15

CONVINCED THAT SOMETHING FUNNY WAS GOING ON, Dottie Falco crept through the hallways floor by floor. She pressed a shot glass against each resident's door, rested her ear against it, and listened.

The girls upstairs must have been asleep, thank goodness. She didn't need an amplifier to know what went on in that apartment. She skipped 3A, figuring if she couldn't hear the ghost when he was speaking, she couldn't hear him floating around the empty apartment—or whatever it was he did in there. Besides, the place gave her the willies.

On the second floor, she carefully, *very* carefully, tiptoed to Konrad's door. Remembering the incident on Halloween, she'd been wary of him ever since. *Flesh-colored Halloween costume, my butt*. And no matter what anyone said, that animal she had seen was a wolf. She had grown up in northern Minnesota, for God's sake. She knew a wolf from a dog. Its fur wasn't as thick as a timber wolf, but if it was an indoor pet, it wouldn't need as thick a coat. Damn Jason's soft spot for animals.

She placed the shot glass between her ear and the door and listened intently. What was that sound? Panting? It was at times like this when she regretted not replacing the nine millimeter Beretta Ralph had found and given away. How *dare* he assume she'd only be dangerous with a gun. *Now* look what she had to resort to for protection. She glanced down at the rolling pin in her other hand. *How cliché.*

Whatever she thought she had heard ceased. No sound came from Konrad's apartment. She waited another few minutes to be sure. Nope. She couldn't hear a thing through the door. The apartment might be unoccupied at the moment and the panting was her imagination—or perhaps the wolf had fallen asleep. Still intensely curious about what waited on the other side of that door, she shuddered.

Conversely relieved and disappointed, she moved on. Light from a bright moon reflecting off the snow lit the first floor hallway through the glass front door. At the bottom of the stairs, Nathan's door stood ajar! *What the…?* She approached carefully, lingering on the last step, listening for any sound at all. Nothing.

If he wasn't home and simply forgot to lock his door, what a stroke of luck that would be! She had always been curious about the dark, gloomy mortician—or whatever he was. She knew he did something with dead people at a hospital. Just thinking about it made her skin crawl.

She took another two steps, paused behind the door, and listened carefully. Still nothing. Not a sound. So, like a thief in the night, she slipped past the door to the opposite wall and flattened herself against it.

If anyone comes home right now, I'm toast. She glanced at the front door. *No, I'm not. I live in the building too. I'll just say I had a dizzy spell and had to lean against the wall for support. I might even get some sympathy for a change.*

At last she steeled herself for the big moment. Taking a deep breath, she stole inside apartment 1A. The place was dark except for the light leaking around the drawn window shades. *Why didn't I bring a flashlight?*

She didn't get two steps into the apartment before wild fluttering feathers beat her about the head and shoulders.

"Ack!" She dropped the shot glass and rolling pin. She tried to pivot and run while covering her head, but the door slammed in her face. Panic gripped her as she swatted away the mad bird, only to be grabbed by a pair of strong hands an instant later.

"What the hell are you doing in my apartment, Dottie?" Nathan yelled.

"Being attacked by your damn bird! Where is the vile thing?"

Now that her eyes had adjusted to the lack of light, she scanned the room's ceiling and corners. Only when there was no sign of the offending bird did she look at Nathan and discover he was... *Eek!* Naked!

"Where are your clothes?" she demanded.

"I was asleep, and you haven't answered me yet. What are you doing here?"

She lifted her chin. "I was doing a late night check on the building and everything was fine, except your door was open. Anyone could have walked in."

"And did, apparently."

She broke free. "Where's that bird of yours?" Marching further into the apartment she said, "I want to see if it's the same one that's been flying around the halls lately. No wonder it gets out all the time, leaving your door open like that..."

By the time she reached his bedroom, he was next to her again, clenching her arm tightly.

"The tour is over, Dottie. Now get out."

"Not before I take a good look at that bird." She flicked on a light, took a quick peek, and twisted away. "And for God's sake, put on some clothes!"

The light in the bedroom illuminated his meticulously made bed. "I thought you said... Mmmuph!"

Nathan had slapped a hand over her mouth and held her arm bent behind her back at a cruel angle. "Now do you see what your nosiness has gotten you into? There's absolutely no need to go tiptoeing around the halls at night, and if I leave my door open, it's not an invitation to come on in and snoop. Do you understand?"

He yanked on her arm and pain shot to her shoulder. She nodded frantically.

"No, I don't think you do." His voice took on a deadly serious calm, more menacing than any growl or loud protest. "Now, don't move."

He released the arm he had been pulling and blood flowed back into it. She wanted to sigh in relief, but his other hand still squashed her mouth. She had to free herself so she could bolt. Opening and closing her jaw, she bit down.

"Ouch! You bitch."

She took off toward the door but didn't get more than a few steps. Something tripped her and she tumbled to the floor. *Oomph.*

Nathan landed on top of her. "Thanks, Chad."

"Chad? That nasty ghost is here?"

"Yeah. Now hold still."

Dottie wriggled beneath him. "Get off of me, you naked pervert!"

"It's time you learned to mind your own business,

lady. What happens in the hallway may be public, but you stick one toe inside anyone's apartment and you're trespassing."

She tried to respond, but as soon as she opened her mouth, something soft rammed past her teeth. She struggled but couldn't move her arms. He had them pinned. Panic set in and she thrashed back and forth for all she was worth. That's when her vision blurred and she passed out.

"What do you want me to do with her?" Sly looked over at the limp body lashed to a rickety chair in the basement—*his* basement.

Nathan leaned against one of the stacked storage boxes. "Just watch her. When she comes to, we'll make her sweat a little before we let her go."

"Are you out of your ever-lovin' mind? If she comes to down here, I'm screwed. She's not supposed to know I live here."

"She doesn't have to know. You have your place hidden, right?"

"Yes, but what am I supposed to do with her in the meantime? If the sun starts coming through those windows, I'll have to crawl into my hidey hole."

"I'll be back long before that."

Sly shook his head. "Why me? Why do I always have to baby-sit the problem people?"

"Isn't it obvious?"

"What? You mean because I'm a vampire?"

"Of course. If she gives you any trouble…"

"You want me to drain her if she doesn't cooperate."

It was a statement, not a question. A statement he hoped conveyed his disgust.

"Not really. Just scare her a little. Face it, you're an intimidating guy."

"I'll be sure to add that to my resume."

A faint moan escaped their captive, and she righted her posture.

"Oh, crap. She's coming to."

"Just keep an eye on her for me until I fix my door with a hidden spring-loaded latch. I won't be long."

Dottie's eyes fluttered open, then darted around the basement. When she spotted Nathan and Sly her eyes popped. Soon after, she must have figured out what they'd done because her eyebrows bunched together and a litany of muffled sounds leaked through the gag.

"Now, now, Dottie," Nathan said. "My friend here is going to hang onto you for a little while. It's for your own good. Once you know just how upset people are about the invasions of their privacy, we'll take off the gag and allow you to apologize."

More sound blasted through Dottie's gag and Sly was pretty sure he could guess what she was trying to say.

"Bapherredz! Umpie mi if mimih!"

"I'm sorry, Dottie. This was none of my doing," Sly said.

"Ey dong caah. Et mi goo." She squirmed rigorously.

"I *would* untie you except that Nathan is probably unsafe until you calm down."

"Heh dethufs ta dah."

"No one deserves to die, Dottie. But, in my opinion, you deserve a stern talking to—at the very least. What you did was breaking and entering."

Her expression and posture deflated.

Nathan clapped Sly on the back. "Thanks. I knew you were the right para—I mean, man for the job. I'll only be a few minutes, I swear. The snow is coming down pretty heavy. I'll just run to the subway and make a quick trip to an all-night hardware store."

"How quick? I can't think of any all night hardware stores around here."

"There's a big one in Somerville. I'll fly over and it won't take more than an hour to grab what I need and ride the subway back."

Sly groaned. "An hour? Hell."

"Come on, man. Have you forgotten who gave you your key?"

"You were supposed to keep your mouth shut about that."

"Well, now we both have a reason to keep the bitch locked up until she learns to mind her own business."

"Have you forgotten whose window you peck on at night to let you in?"

"We are so screwed."

Dottie nodded.

"Nathan? If anything happens to my welfare because of this, I'm coming after you."

"Fair enough. I might not make much of a meal, though. I hope you like feathers in your mouth."

"Just hurry up."

Dottie's eyes rounded in alarm, then she fainted again.

Sly frowned at the slumped over bound and gagged body. "High-strung, isn't she?"

"Just a tad."

Merry stood in front of Jason's long expanse of windows trying to gauge how much snow had already fallen.

"I think there's about eight inches out there so far."

Jason sidled up behind her and nuzzled her neck. "There's about eight inches right behind you. Want to do something about it?"

She grinned and reached back to cup his erection.

His arms surrounded her and he moaned softly next to her ear. "Do you have any idea what you do to me? All you have to do is stand in one spot long enough for me to admire your beauty and I get hard."

She pivoted to face him. "I'm glad you enjoy the view. I like what I see too."

Suddenly, pitch blackness enveloped them.

"Did you do that?" Merry asked.

Jason laughed. "I'm a shapeshifter, not a magician. Looks like we lost power, Merry."

"Oh, I thought maybe you'd arranged the whole thing."

"I couldn't have timed it better if I did."

His lips found hers in the dark, and they shared a long, languorous kiss. Any reservations she might still have melted away whenever she experienced one of his masterful kisses. Maybe he hadn't made love to many women due to his condition, but he sure had kissed a few.

Merry secretly liked knowing he had limited his experience sexually. Before that, she felt like the young naïve girl some people made her out to be. But falling in love with Jason had changed all of that. Now, every spare minute was spent making love, and she couldn't have been happier about it.

He took her hand and navigated them to the gas fireplace. Perfect for just such occasions, she thought. One push of the thermostat and a glorious flame illuminated the room. The romantic ambiance added to her arousal. She nipped his ear lobe.

"Getting frisky, are we?" he asked and smiled.

"You bet I am."

As if planned, they sank to the carpet and let their hands and lips explore one another's bodies, through their clothes.

"I love you, Merry," Jason said between nibbles to her neck and collarbone.

Merry sighed. "Love you too."

He knew how to please her. Thinking about how he satisfied her, multiple times, melted anything that was left of her guard. She couldn't be happier when he made love to her, and they could go on for hours or days, for all she cared. Jason could make her forget she had a job.

It was as if he found buried treasure in the form of the black bra and panties she wore when he uncovered them and he groaned. Merry made a mental note. *Must go shopping for lingerie. I want more of those reactions.*

He explored her body thoroughly. He pulled aside the lace that hid her breasts and blew on her nipples. They hardened immediately. He placed his warm mouth on one and suckled, then the other. As he stroked her sensitive inner thighs, she writhed with pleasure.

When his hand glided to her apex, he barely touched her and she arched, silently pleading with him not to tease. He obliged her fully, zeroing in on the trigger of her most intense sensations and brought her to a shattering orgasm. She gritted her teeth and tried not to cry out as she usually did. He stayed on that sensitive spot until she tore his hand away.

"I... can't take... much more."

Jason pulled her close and kissed her with such fervor that their chests rose and fell together.

"I'm only letting you rest so you won't leave me to get your inhaler."

"I'll have to keep one in your bedroom."

He smiled and kissed her hair. "Please do."

"It's your turn now."

"Music to my ears. Where do you want me?"

"Lie back."

Jason grinned and assumed the position. As she rolled up onto her knees, he said, "Turn around. I'm not quite finished with you."

Her eyebrows arched. "The sixty-nine position?"

"Yeah."

She had barely recovered, but did as he asked. "Go easy on me or I won't have the energy to do what I want to do for you."

"Sounds promising. You got it."

She took his length in her mouth and swirled her tongue around from base to tip as if following the stripe in a candy cane—a very thick one.

He moaned appreciatively.

"Oh, you liked that! Let me do it again." And she did, several times.

His rock-hard erection pulsed and perhaps to distract her, he tongued her slit. Still sensitized, she jumped. He grabbed her buttocks and dug his fingers in to hold her still before he bore down on her clit.

She shattered—again. Her control exploded in shards all around her. Luscious spasms radiated out from her core and beyond her body, like heat waves might pour off a sidewalk on a hot summer day.

He continued to pleasure her until she begged him to enter, to be inside of her. Jason rolled her gently onto her back and positioned himself to enter. He penetrated her almost reverently.

Merry's pulse skyrocketed, and she ached with need. His slow, deep thrusts tore at her patience, yet gradually gave way to a faster, more frantic pace that could make lovemaking an Olympic sport. Both of them threw all of their energy into it. The joy of bringing *him* to climax and anticipation of another deeply rewarding orgasm powered her on. Her moans increased in volume and frequency.

She gripped his moist shoulders as if they might fly off the floor. The pleasurable friction of their bodies along with the growing love and trust between them led to another explosive release. She let her control go and cried out, spasming in both agony and ecstasy.

Jason collapsed beside her when they had both reached a thorough climax and milked every aftershock.

He gathered her in his arms and gazed at her, a golden glow from the fire reflected in his eyes. He tenderly covered her mouth with his. When at last he let go of her lips, he took in a deep breath and pushed back the hair around her face. "I am desperately in love with you, Merry MacKenzie, and don't you forget it."

"Why would I ever want to?"

They kissed and cuddled until their breathing returned to normal.

Exhausted to the point of slap-happiness, they cracked stupid jokes and laughed until sleep overtook them.

"Darling?" he asked her the next morning.

She sat at his breakfast bar, wearing one of his T-shirts, and chuckled. "Yes, dearest?"

"Come home with me for the holidays. I want you to meet my family."

"What about meeting mine?"

"Name the day." Jason reached for a frying pan and hoped that making her breakfast would put her in a conciliatory mood.

"Um… Christmas? I have to do the cooking."

"Is that carved in stone? Anyone can cook. Look at me." He poured some oil into the pan and lit the burner. "I'm cooking right now."

"Christmas dinner is a little more difficult than scrambled eggs."

"Please. It's important to me. Important to my family. They're all dying to meet you."

Merry smiled. "You've talked to them about marrying me?"

"And little else."

She sighed. "I know we should both get to know each other's family, but the time crunch makes it hard. In a *normal* relationship, there would be plenty of time for getting acquainted."

His mood plummeted. "I'm aware of that," he said and turned his back. How many times would he have to listen to everything being different in so-called *normal* relationships? He broke an egg a little too hard and bits of shell dotted the bowl.

She remained silent while he fished the pieces out with a spoon. He didn't hear her slip off the stool or come up behind him, but her arms glided around his waist and he whirled around to meet her upturned face.

"I'm sorry. I hate to keep reminding you that our relationship isn't typical. Maybe that's a better word than normal."

He smiled. "Much better." He ran his fingers through her hair. "It's not all that unusual for professional athletes, though. Unless they marry their high school or college sweethearts, they have precious little time to date. Most women would find that difficult."

"I guess I'm not most women."

"Are you saying you wouldn't miss me for two whole months?"

She frowned. "Of course not. I'd miss you like crazy."

Frustrated with this no-win conversation, he had to change the subject. "So, Christmas. All relationships require compromises. Even typical ones."

"That's true..."

He sensed a "but" coming so he tried to derail her.

"How do you like your eggs? Wet, dry, or in between?"

"You see? There's still so much for us to learn about each other."

Jason braced his hands on the counter. "Merry, I can't take this."

"Huh? Can't take what?"

He couldn't see her face, but she sounded genuinely surprised. Didn't she know how much anxiety she created each time she spoke of slowing down or delaying? Just as he was about to admonish her, his cell phone rang, thank God.

He held up one finger to Merry and flipped open his phone.

"Hello?"

"Jason? Is Dottie up there?"

"No. Is she missing?"

"Yeah. It's the weirdest thing. Her side of the bed is still tucked in like she never came to bed last night. I pooped out early and left her watching a movie, but here it is morning and she's nowhere to be found."

"That *is* weird. Maybe she decided to visit one of the other tenants and got wrapped up in a long conversation. You know how she can talk."

"I thought of that, but can you picture her spending any length of time with any of these tenants?"

"Come to think of it, no."

"That's why I'm worried. Oh, and there's another thing."

"The power outage?"

"Yes. You don't happen to have a generator tucked away somewhere do you?"

"No, I'm afraid not. Why, is it getting cold in the building?"

"Freezing. Someone left the back door open."

"Shit. You don't think Dottie…"

"I don't know what to think."

Jason watched Merry's brows knit in curiosity. "Look, we're about to have breakfast, but I'll come down and help you figure out what to do in a few minutes."

"Okay, but don't be long. I'm afraid the pipes might freeze and burst."

"What's wrong?" Merry asked.

"Apparently Aunt Dottie's missing and the back door was left open last night. Uncle Ralph's afraid the pipes might freeze since there's been no heat in the building."

"Crap. Now I feel guilty for sleeping in front of your nice warm fireplace."

"Don't. Just remember all the perks you'll get from living with me. Winters in Florida, a temperature-controlled penthouse… You'll never have to suffer." He winked.

A look of determination stiffened her spine. "Let's go downstairs and check on everyone. We can reheat breakfast later."

Jason sighed. "Uncle Ralph? Are you still there?"

"Yeah."

"We'll be right there. See you in a minute."

Nathan's eyes drifted open. An immediate awareness of unfamiliar surroundings startled him awake. Floral wallpaper met the white crown molding of the ceiling. It looked like the same crown molding in his apartment, but he sure as hell didn't recognize the wallpaper. A pink wicker lamp swagged over the bed. Plus something smelled like wet dog.

Where the hell am I? He rolled and bumped up against a warm lump. Rolling the other way, he encountered the same thing.

He bolted upright. "What the…?"

On one side of him, Konrad wiped his eyes and said, "Easy, buddy."

On the other, Gwyneth stretched and said, "Well,

good mornin', sugar. I'm glad y'all made it. We thought you was a goner last night."

"A goner?" Nathan tried to remember the last thing that had happened to him. He hadn't found what he needed at the first store and had to travel a ways to another one. By the time he located the spring locking mechanism for his door, it was so late he was afraid Sly would clobber him. He had shifted and flown back in the freezing cold with the home improvement bag in his beak. After that…?

Konrad sprang out of bed fully dressed. "Well, I guess you don't need me anymore, so I'll head downstairs." He strode out of the room.

"What happened? How did I get here?" Nathan demanded.

"Y'all are one lucky shapeshifter, Nathan. Konrad found you half frozen on the back steps. He carried y'all up here for Morgaine and me to heal you."

"What did you do to me?"

"Well, there was nuthin' we could do other than warm you up. Morgaine isn't here, so I asked Konrad to help me by puttin' his body heat on the other side of you. Then we piled all kinds of quilts and covers over all three of us. You must've been toasty warm in the middle."

"Oh…" The drawn window shade blocked some of the light, but clearly sunrise had already happened. *Damn. Sly is gonna be pissed!*

Nathan leaped out of bed and realized he was naked. He whirled away from her and covered his privates with his hands. "Yikes. Sorry about the flash."

Gwyneth sat up and the covers fell away, exposing her naked torso, red curls tumbling over her shoulders.

"Don't apologize for what mother nature gave y'all. There ain't no need to be ashamed or embarrassed in front of little ol' me. I think you have a fine body."

He took in the view over his shoulder. Hers was mighty fine too but he didn't have time to stand around and admire it. "Well, um—thanks. And thanks for saving my life, but I have to get downstairs. You don't happen to have any men's clothes I could borrow, do you?"

"I'm afraid not, sugar. You can wear my robe, though." She pointed to a long floral printed dressing gown hung from a hook on the back of the door.

Nathan shrugged. "Better than nuthin'."

He struggled into the tight garment and pulled it around as far as he could. He'd have to hold it closed over his privates since only an inch overlapped. "I'll return it as soon as I can. And, uh…" One last look at her unabashed nakedness later, he mumbled, "Thanks again."

"Stay warm, now." Gwyneth waved as he took off running.

On his way to the basement, he bypassed his apartment, too worried to stop and throw on some jeans. If Sly hadn't thought to cover Dottie, she'd be half frozen by now too.

At the bottom of the basement steps, he halted. A workman paused in his effort to wrap the water pipes with heat tapes and glanced over at him. No one besides this man occupied the basement, at least no one he could see. Sly had probably holed up in his wall, but… *Where the hell is Dottie?*

What could he say? *Uh, excuse me. Did you see a gagged woman tied to a chair down here?*

The workman and Nathan stared at each other for a

few seconds. At last, Nathan cleared his throat. "Sorry to bother you. Has anyone been down here besides you?"

The man shrugged. "Just the landlord, I guess. He's the one who called me."

Shit. I'm toast.

"Can I help you?"

Nathan heaved a sigh. "Not unless you have a vacant apartment I can rent."

The man gave him the once over as Nathan stood there in Gwyneth's bathrobe and said, "I don't think so."

Chapter 16

"I WANT THEM OUT!" DOTTIE YELLED. "ALL OF THEM! This place is full of dangerous psychotics and nut bags with illegal pets."

In as soothing a tone as he could manage Jason said, "Aunt Dottie, I know it may seem that way—"

"Seem? Baloney! It is!"

Shaking inwardly, he hoped his voice would help calm himself, even though he doubted it would change her tone. The last thing she needed right now was to watch her nephew shift into one of those feathered predators.

Ralph returned from the kitchen with a glass of Scotch and handed it to her. "Dottie, try to remember who owns the building. If Jason doesn't want to evict anyone, we don't have the right to make demands like that."

She took a giant gulp of the liquor. "Gaaah!" Then she rasped, "That burns all the way down."

Good, maybe that will shut her up. Jason took a deep breath. "Try to hear me out, Aunt Dottie. I have something to tell you."

"I knew it! It's your deep dark secret, isn't it?"

Shocked silent, Jason froze with his mouth agape. Fortunately, Ralph jumped in front of him to block her line of sight and perhaps distract her from him.

"Honey, he asked you to listen. Now I'm sure he wants to recommend we take that vacation he offered us before. That way he can deal with things on this end the way he thinks they should be handled. Isn't that right, Jason?" He twisted his torso to watch his face without Dottie seeing it.

Jason nodded and inhaled a deep breath. *Thanks, Uncle Ralph. That's a much better idea than trying to explain away everything she's seen.* "I was thinking of buying a vacation getaway in the islands. Someplace where no one would recognize me and I could really relax with Merry in the off season. I'd like you to check out a few places for me."

Ralph stepped aside. "There, you see, Dottie? The only secret is where he'll be spending his vacations so he can have complete peace. And I think it would do us a world of good too."

"Humph. I doubt that's his only secret."

"Please, honey. Don't insult our nephew by calling him a liar. He's been more than kind and understanding."

"I think *I'm* the one who's been more than understanding. I've put up with wolves at my door, birds in the hallway, and a vampire somewhere in the basement where I do our laundry."

"Aunt Dottie, there's no such thing as vampires, and I saw no one in our basement when I found you. Neither did you. Doesn't that tell you something?"

"Well, how did I get gagged and all trussed up like a holiday turkey? Did I imagine that too? Or maybe I tied myself to that chair and knotted the rope behind my back where I couldn't reach it."

"I'm going to talk to Nathan. I promised you that and I will, as soon as I know you're all right."

She took another swig of the Scotch. "I'll feel better when I've had about three of these, but you're not going to convince me I'm hallucinating—and I'm not going anywhere. You need me here to protect your interests."

Jason sucked in a deep breath. "Look, I'm sorry to have to tell you this, but I've avoided inviting my buddies over due to your frequent—um, how do I say this? Alarming reports?"

"What in heaven's name do you mean?"

Jason looked to Ralph.

"Please don't deny it, honey. You're an alarmist. You jump to conclusions and the first thing you do is look for Jason. I don't blame him for worrying about having friends over. If they were here when you... Well, let's just say I don't blame him."

"But you *do* blame *me*. Yet you're the one who doesn't want me to call the cops!"

"No, Aunt Dottie. Nobody's blaming you. I know you think you're helping, but..." What else could he say without calling her a pain in the ass? "Look, I really would like you and Ralph to take a little vacation in the islands. It's on me." Maybe he could get her to go if he gave her a mission she'd enjoy more than looking for real estate. "Um, I wasn't going to say anything yet, but while you're down there, can you look for a private honeymoon hideaway?"

Dottie's jaw dropped. "You're getting married? Why didn't you tell us?"

Jason shrugged one shoulder. "She hasn't put on the ring yet. She's still thinking it over."

"Oh." Her posture slumped.

"I'm pretty sure she'll accept, though. I know her. She has a kind heart, and I don't think she'll let me down." He sent a pointed look to Ralph.

Ralph smiled and clapped him on the back. "I don't think she will, either. Congratulations. Now doesn't that sound like fun, Dottie? We have a honeymoon to plan and we can take a second honeymoon in the process."

At last Dottie let a weak smile cross her lips. "I suppose. It's been a long time since we've gone anywhere."

Thank God, now if I can just get her out of here soon. "I'll make the plane reservations. Do you two have passports?"

Dottie nodded. "Yes. We applied for them when they changed the laws and we needed them to visit my sister in Canada."

"Great. I'll see what kind of island tour I can get at the last minute." He leaned toward Ralph and said in a low voice, "Can I count on you to keep an eye on her while I do that?"

He nodded. "I'll look after her. She needs a good nap."

"Okay. I'll go talk to Nathan now." *And I hope he has a good explanation. I don't want to evict the guy who saved my life.*

Nathan heard a knock on his door. He stopped packing his bags long enough to answer it and found his landlord standing there.

"We need to talk."

"Come in," Nathan said morosely. "Have a seat."

Jason sat in the chair Nathan pointed to and waited quietly for him to get settled.

Nathan was pretty sure he knew what Jason came to say, though. "I'm sorry, Jason." Nathan perched on the edge of the sofa and clasped his hands between his knees. "I swear I thought she was a burglar. What was she doing walking into my apartment at midnight?"

"I don't know. I barely reassured her enough to stay put and now Ralph is plying her with Scotch. I'm sending them off on a vacation tomorrow. So, tell me what happened."

To anyone else, it would sound bizarre, but a falcon might understand. "I had caught a mouse in the alley earlier in the evening and had just shifted back into my raven form to enjoy my meal when the door opened. The light behind her obscured anything but a silhouette. You know what it's like when you're in bird form, right? You think like a bird first and a man second. Instinctively, I sensed a threat and flew at her head and beat her with my wings to drive her off."

"Okay. So couldn't you have let her think you were a pet bird? You know I allow pets, so you'd be well within your rights to own one."

"I was under duress and not thinking as clearly as I could have. I shifted into human form, hoping to scare the shit out of the burglar, and I didn't know it was your aunt until she had seen too much."

"She said you had a gun."

"I do. I never would have used it. I may joke about death, but I'm not a killer."

Jason nodded. "Do you have a permit for that gun?"

"Why?"

"In case she calls the cops on you no matter what Ralph and I do to calm her down?"

"Shit."

"I know my aunt, and she'll want to. I hope we can talk her out of it."

Nathan gulped. "Double shit."

"So you gagged and tied her to a chair and left her in the basement with a guy she thought was a vampire?"

"Shit. Shit. Shit."

"What were you planning to do with her after that?"

"I admit I didn't think it through well at all," he said sheepishly.

Jason shook his head. "Fan-fucking-tastic. Now what do we do?"

"We?" Nathan lifted his head and stared at his landlord, wide-eyed. "I'd planned to pack my bags and leave before the eviction notice was delivered. I figured I wasn't fast enough and you were here to tell me to get out."

Jason tilted his head. "I know how hard it is to find affordable apartments in this town, especially on short notice. You didn't think I'd turn my back on you after you saved my life, did you?"

"Well, uh—yeah. I..." *Damn. I can't believe he wants to stick up for me.* "I don't know what to say."

"Say you'll apologize profusely if that's what it takes."

"*Me* apologize to *her*? She's the one who walked—"

The look on Jason's face was all he needed to see. "Yeah, of course. I'll try anything. I just doubt it will be enough."

"We'll cross that bridge when we come to it."

—∾∾—

Merry met Roz at a local fast food restaurant. She needed a heart-to-heart with someone she could trust to be honest with her.

"You know how Jason wants to marry me before spring training, right?"

"Yes, have you accepted?"

"I'm pretty close."

"What was that thing you couldn't tell me about before? Can you tell me now?"

Merry dropped her head in her hands. "Jeez! I want to, but I'm not sure I can." She reached across the table, grabbed Roz's wrist, and searched her face. "Will you believe whatever I tell you without accusing me of losing my marbles?"

"Uh, probably. I've never known you to lose your marbles—or your mind for that matter. We are talking about your sanity, right?"

"Yes."

"Well, then yes, you can tell me anything without my questioning the amount of your marbles."

Merry took a deep breath. "Here goes nuthin'. Jason is a shapeshifter."

Roz's eyes widened and she fell silent.

"I knew you wouldn't believe me," Merry wailed.

Other people in the restaurant glanced over at them. Both women waited until everyone returned to minding their own business, then continued their conversation in hushed tones.

"I'm familiar with the term," Roz said, "but only in fiction. Are you telling me he's a werewolf or something?"

Merry suppressed a laugh. "No. He's a peregrine falcon. There are some nice benefits to his being that particular bird."

"Oh? Like what?"

"Well, first and foremost, they're monogamous."

"That's terrific. You'll never need to worry about his fooling around on you, even when he's on the road or if you see stupid, damaging headlines in gossip columns."

"I know. That part's really great, but there's a down side."

"To monogamy?"

"Well, yeah. I mean, now that he's made his choice, apparently he's begun some kind of process that can't be stopped. In other words, it's me or no one."

"Well, that sucks—for him. You can take your time about it though, right? I mean, I can understand his wanting to make it happen sooner rather than later, but he isn't still pressuring you to marry him right away, is he?"

"Kind of. There's more."

"Uh-oh. What else?"

"The reason he wants to marry me before spring training is so I'll be in Florida with him when the urge to mate hits in March. Apparently it's a falcon instinct at that time of year. If I'm not there, the human in him may be so stressed out, he could lose *his* marbles. Even if he doesn't, he could shift without warning in order to fly to me wherever I am. That would end his career."

"*Wow!* That's a lot of pressure."

"Tell me about it."

"So what else will change if you marry a shapeshifter? Does anything happen to you?"

"No. I won't change at all. He likes to stay in human form, so things shouldn't be that different."

"Okay. So what are you worried about if that's the case?"

"I feel like I'm letting you down. We had all these dreams of going clubbing on my weekends off and leading the *Sex and the City* lifestyle for a few years. Here I am looking at marriage to the first man I met on day one in the city!"

Roz chuckled. "Merry, don't worry about me. Hell, if I found a hottie like Jason, I'd leave you in the dust."

"Oh, nice. Thanks."

"Hey, I'm just being honest. And that's part of your problem, hon. You're too nice. You love him, right?"

"More than I thought possible."

"So why are you worrying about me? You can't please all of the people all of the time. Sometimes you have to make a choice. I know you. You'll bend over backwards trying to take care of everybody and make sure everyone is happy."

"You're right. I hate that about me."

"Don't hate it, just accept it. It's who you are. You're a caretaker. Look how long you took care of your father and brother."

"I know. I put my life on hold for years! And I *just* set out on my own."

Roz stared at her tea. "So where were you going?"

"Going?"

"Yeah, your journey. Your life. You wanted *Sex and the City*. Well, you *have* sex and the city. Where did you *ultimately* want to wind up?"

Merry shrugged. "Well, eventually happily married to the man of my dreams. Maybe have a kid or two. I'm not sure I want to drive a minivan, but the rest of the American dream sounds pretty good."

"Okay. What about your job? Do you want to continue working?"

"Of course. I have no idea what I'd do with myself all day if I didn't."

"Can you do that if you travel between two homes?"

"As a nurse, I'm lucky in that respect. I can work

per diem. Sort of like a substitute teacher. I sign up as available on the days and times I want to work and they call me in when they need someone."

Roz leaned back against her chair. "With the huge need for nurses everywhere, you should be able to work pretty much whenever you want. That sounds perfect. So what's stopping you?"

Merry shrugged. "I don't really know. I wonder what people will think about the whirlwind—"

"There you go again! Stop worrying about everyone else. You're making me a little crazy, Merry. Ever hear the saying, 'Don't look a gift horse in the mouth?' Well, it seems like you're looking a gift falcon in the beak. Unless there's something else about his nature you haven't told me."

"No, I've told you everything I know."

"And has Jason told you everything?"

"Yes. I grilled him pretty thoroughly. He said if I ever have any more questions, just ask. He won't hide anything from me again."

"That's right. He didn't tell you before he proposed. What did he have to say about that?"

"He wanted to. He was afraid of losing me. He admitted he screwed up."

A tear shimmered in the corner of Roz 's eye. "I wish I had someone who loved me that much, be they falcon or human. Not a werewolf, though. I don't think I could handle something that shreds human beings, even once a month."

The blond head sitting behind Roz turned around.

"Konrad!" Merry exclaimed. "I didn't know that was *you* sitting there."

He smiled. "Fancy meeting you here. Mind if I join you?"

Roz whispered, "How about it, Merry? Are you all talked out?"

All talked out? Is that what she was doing? Just letting me talk to hear the sound of my own voice? Merry knew better than that, though. It seemed as if the more they talked the more she knew what she wanted. Roz probably realized she'd figure it out. But would it have killed her to just offer an outsider's opinion?

"I'm good now, Roz . Thanks for listening."

"Anytime. Just invite me to the wedding."

"Invite you? I want you to be my maid of honor."

Konrad rose. "So, you and Falco are getting married?"

"Don't say anything about it to anyone, okay? I think he should know before anyone else does."

Merry had parked her car in the alley and stepped through the back door just as Ralph and Dottie wheeled their suitcases off the elevator.

"Hi Dottie, Ralph, are you going somewhere?"

"Yes. Jason is sending us on a scouting mission," Ralph said.

Dottie's uncharacteristic sweet expression said she was happy about it.

"Oh? What kind of scouting mission?"

"I don't know if we're supposed to tell you or not. He might be saving it for a surprise." Ralph winked.

She squinted. "Hmm… Now the curiosity will drive me crazy. Is Jason home?"

"I think so. He made all the arrangements this

morning." Ralph checked his watch. "We'd better get going. Don't want to miss our flight."

"Let me hold the door for you." Merry hurried back and opened the door she had just come through.

As the couple rolled and hefted their suitcases outside and down the steps, Ralph said, "Thanks. We'll see you in a couple of weeks."

"Have a good time." Merry had never seen Dottie so quiet—or Ralph so happy. Something weird had to be going on.

She had planned to see Jason anyway to give him the news of her decision. He'd probably be over the moon. *Should I change into sexy underwear? Nah. If we're going to be married, he may as well get used to seeing the regular stuff.*

She proceeded straight to the elevator, used her key card, and punched the *P* button for his penthouse. Suddenly she couldn't wait to tell him. Had the elevator always taken this long to reach the top floor?

Her mind raced with all the details they'd have to arrange. Pick a date. Apply for a marriage license. Arrange for a church or chapel, find a minister or Justice of the Peace, or maybe a cruise ship captain? By the time she reached his place, she had ruled out the cruise ship idea. Their privacy could be invaded if he was recognized, and she wanted him all to herself.

The elevator doors slid open and she strode into the apartment. Not seeing him, she called out, "Where's my gorgeous lover?"

A grunt echoed from the exercise room. *Oh good. He's here!*

She rushed toward the noise and burst into the room.

A guy she didn't recognize stood behind Jason as he lay on the exercise bench, pressing a barbell over his head.

"Oh, sorry to interrupt," she said.

Jason grinned. "Grab this thing, will you, Henry?"

The other guy helped him set the weighted steel bar into the holder. He sat up without using his hands.

"Merry, this is a buddy of mine, Henry Gilson. Henry, this is my girlfriend, Merry."

"Correction," Merry said with a smile. "I'm his fiancée." She flashed the beautiful ring she had finally put on her finger.

Jason's eyes opened wider. He leapt off the bench, crossed to her, and kissed her soundly. Gazing into her eyes, he said, "That's the answer I was waiting to hear."

Henry extended his hand. "Congratulations." After he shook both their hands, he said, "I'd better get going. It sounds like you two have something to celebrate."

Jason held Merry close. "We sure do. Thanks for coming over at the last minute, man. I was getting flabby."

His friend laughed. "If you're flabby, I'm obese."

"Well, thanks for spotting me. I'll call you in a few days if you wouldn't mind helping me out again. I don't think Merry could handle two hundred and fifty pounds."

Henry laughed. "Yeah, call me anytime, man. We can't let anything happen to our star pitcher."

Chapter 17

JASON NUZZLED MERRY'S NECK AS THEY PLANNED their wedding. He couldn't believe she had finally agreed—to everything.

She pushed his head away and giggled. "Cut that out. If we get sidetracked, none of this is going to happen."

He sighed. "Oh yeah. It would be just terrible to get sidetracked with sex, wouldn't it?"

"Are you being sarcastic?"

"A little bit."

"Okay, I'll get off your lap then."

She tried to stand, but he wrestled her down and pinned her to his growing erection. "You're not going anywhere, sweetheart. I'll cooperate. We'll plan first and have celebration sex afterward. How's that sound?"

"Perfect." She smiled and kissed him.

Now that she had said yes, a huge weight had been lifted. "Let's see. I guess we need to figure out who, what, where, and how. We know the why. You're marrying me for my money, right?"

"Oh, absolutely." She rolled her eyes.

"Now who's being sarcastic?"

She chuckled. "Okay, okay. Let's start with when. That seems to be the most urgent thing since we have a deadline. Let's figure that out first."

"How about tomorrow?"

She gasped. "You can't be serious!"

ASHLYN CHASE

He laughed. "You're so fun to tease." Of course she wanted the beautiful white wedding. What woman didn't? But pulling it off in a short amount of time would challenge the best wedding planner. He'd have to agree to give her some time, despite his urgency.

"How about right after the holidays?" he asked.

"Which holidays? Christmas and New Years? Or Groundhog Day and Valentine's Day?"

"Valentine's Day is too late. We need to be in Florida by mid February and you *do* want a honeymoon, don't you?"

"Hell yeah."

"So how about January?"

"I guess we could get everything arranged by late January. It's a good thing we're not trying to do this in June."

"For many reasons," he said, hinting again at the end result if this didn't happen.

She nodded and stroked his cheek. "Okay, how about the second Saturday after the holidays, which is my weekend off?"

Her continuing her job blindsided him. "You're going to work up until the last minute? I thought you'd need some time to get everything ready."

"Well, I should give them plenty of notice. It's not easy to replace nurses. There's a nursing shortage, you know."

"But that's not your problem."

"I know I haven't been there very long, but I've already made some nice friendships among the coworkers on my shift. I don't want to leave them in the lurch."

"Then we'll have to hire a wedding planner to help you get everything done."

"No. I don't want one. I've heard too many horror stories."

"Really? Like how many?"

"Okay, one. A friend back home hired a wedding planner. She said the woman kept talking them into things and drove up the costs until her parents had to take out a second mortgage to pay for it."

"I'll pay for it. Your father doesn't have to worry about that."

"We'd better ask him if that's okay. He's a proud man, Jason."

"We could always elope."

She gave him the stink eye.

Damn, this is becoming complicated. "Okay. How about if we pay him a visit soon. Maybe we can talk to your family's minister at the same time. I don't want any media circus, though."

"So no inviting Lila, then."

"God, no!"

Merry laughed and Jason rolled his eyes when he realized he'd been had. Then her expression sobered. "You know what they're going to think, don't you?"

"How lucky you are to have such a devilishly handsome and smart fiancé?"

"There you go again."

"There I go what?"

"Being sarcastic."

"Who's being sarcastic?"

She grinned. "Okay, okay. So they might think that—or they'll think we're getting married in a hurry because I'm pregnant."

He gasped. "You're pregnant?"

"No, silly! But everyone is going to think I am."

He kissed her shoulder. "Can't we just tell them the truth?"

Her eyebrows rose. "That you're a shapeshifter who might go nutty without me?"

"Hell no. Just tell them that I'm nuts *about* you and I want you to go to Florida with me in February. Tell them I can't live without you and won't live with you unless we're married."

"Can't live with me, can't live without me, huh?"

"You said it, I didn't. Just remember it's our decision, no one else's."

Merry sighed. "Yeah, I'm just anticipating all the possible problems before they happen."

"They might not happen. In fact, if you go into it with that attitude you might cause them to ask questions. If you just act happy and excited, they probably won't question it at all."

"Yeah, right."

"Okay, how about this. Let's compromise. Give your job a three week notice as soon as you can. We'll get our marriage license on your next day off and we'll call a minister to book the church as soon as that's done. Then send out the invitations right around Christmas. Once everything is in motion, I think people will accept that it's going to happen. If anyone is rude enough to ask if you're pregnant, say no. And speaking of Christmas…"

"Yes?"

"Let's invite everyone here for Christmas. That way you can meet my family and I can meet yours and no one's feelings get hurt."

Merry nibbled her top lip as she mulled it over. "Okay. I think that might work. And speaking of invitations…"

"Let's keep it small. Immediate families."

"I meant invitations to the wedding."

"So did I."

"You're kidding. How about close friends?"

"A few."

"The people in our building?"

"Vegas is looking better and better."

She shook her head. "Uh-uh. Eloping is not an option. Only daughter, remember? My father would kill me if he didn't get to walk me down the aisle."

"Which father?"

"Oh, that's right! We'll have to hold the ceremony after sunset."

"You're kidding."

She tilted her head and looked up at him, batting her eyelashes. "Please?"

He groaned. "It's a good thing I love you."

"I could say the same for you. Now, can I think about the fun stuff?"

"What do you mean?"

Her eyes twinkled. "Shopping! I have a wedding dress and lingerie to buy." She hopped off his lap and jogged to the elevator.

"Hey, don't I get celebratory sex?"

"Sorry. No time for hanky panky."

"Damn. It starts already?" As the elevator doors began to close he called out, "You'll make up for that on the honeymoon, sweetheart."

"Count on it!"

The case has been solved! Chad cheered. *I can't believe it. Columbo came through. I guess he deserves his reputation as a first class sleuth, after all. Now we're just waiting for the landlord to meet with him.*

Jason greeted Joe Murphy at the front door and shook his hand.

"Come in. I hope you don't mind, but I invited some of the other tenants."

"Gwyneth and Morgaine, I hope."

"Yes. I figured they could help with the translation between you and Chad."

"Perfect." Joe followed Jason to the elevator.

Chad noticed a spring in Joe's step. *Maybe he's pleased about seeing Gwyneth again. Or he could just be strutting like a peacock because he solved a challenging case. Maybe both. Hell, I don't care if he brought his own trumpet to blow. I can't wait to find out who was responsible for my murder.*

Jason pushed the button for the third floor. "We're meeting in their apartment, if you don't mind. I guess they feel more comfortable there. They said it helps to connect in their um… sacred space, I think they called it."

Joe shrugged. "Whatever floats their boat."

Jason chuckled.

As soon as they arrived at 3B, the door opened. Jason had just lifted his fist to knock, but didn't have the chance. *You gotta love psychics.*

"Come in, gentlemen," Gwyneth said. "How nice to see you again, Mister Murphy."

"Nice to see you again too, Gwyneth. You look lovely."

"Why, thank you."

She blushed that peachy color only redheads can turn. Chad thought he saw a little mutual attraction going on there.

Morgaine was already seated. A teapot steamed on the coffee table in front of her. Four unmatched bone china cups and saucers had been laid out. Honey and milk took center stage along with a plate of cookies.

"Can I pour either of you gentlemen a cup of tea?" she asked.

"Thank you," Joe said.

Jason shook his head. "I have to go after this. I'm taking Merry out to do some Christmas shopping."

"Morgaine, please don't tell me you're going to do the Southern manners thing again and chit chat the afternoon away. I'm dying over here."

She chuckled. "Be patient, Chad. You've waited over forty years; you can wait another four minutes."

"Is Chad getting restless?" Jason asked.

"Oh, he's been fussin' about this all day," Gwyneth said. "'When are they gonna get here? Can't you call and tell 'em to hurry it up?' He's been drivin' us crazy."

"Maybe I shouldn't have planned this get together when he was listening," Morgaine said.

Joe frowned. "How can you tell if he's around, anyway?"

"We ask him to announce himself. It's only polite." Morgaine handed Joe his tea. "Eavesdropping doesn't show respect, and we expect to be treated with the same respect we show others."

"That's good. Otherwise it might prove very inconvenient to have him around. Of course, now that I have an answer for him, he shouldn't be around much longer, right?"

"We hope he can move on to Summerland after that," Gwyneth said.

Joe raised his eyebrows. "Summerland? Is that some kind of rest home for spirits?"

Gwyneth and Morgaine laughed.

"Aren't you just precious? Bless you're heart. No, Summerland is what we call the place spirits get to. Kinda like what some people call Heaven. And we believe in reincarnation after that."

"Okay, okay. The Wicca lesson is over, girls. Get to the point, will you?"

Morgaine sighed. "I'm sorry gentlemen, Chad is trying to push us along."

"That's fine," Joe said. "We can chat more after he's gone."

"What makes him so sure I'll be gone? None of us know what's going to happen after this." He seems *downright anxious to get rid of me, though.*

Joe gazed at the ceiling. "So, Chad. It's a good thing I researched the international angle. I managed to obtain some fingerprints from your old case file and a friend of mine ran them through Interpol. The guys' names were Hans Gottlieb and Franz Keiser."

"Hans and Franz. You've got to be kidding."

"What was that, Chad? Did you have a question for Mister Murphy?"

"No. For God's sake, don't stop him. I was just adding commentary. Now tell him to keep talking."

"No, he didn't have a question, pardon me for interruptin'. Continue, Mister Murphy."

"That's quite all right, Gwyneth." He paused and gave her a soft smile. "Back in the fifties these men were Swiss bankers."

"Swiss bankers? I was murdered by Swiss bankers? What the fuck?"

"Now, Chad. Don't be rude."

"What's he saying?" Jason asked.

"Oh, nothin'. He just uses some crude language sometimes."

"Well, so do you, sweet cheeks."

Gwyneth rolled her eyes. "Please go on, Mister Murphy. I'll just ignore him."

"All right. Well, this may take a little explanation."

"Ya think?"

"These men became involved in the IMF."

"Is that like the FBI or the KBG?" Gwyneth asked.

"No. It's the International Monetary Fund. Basically, it's like a world bank. It was originally set up to stabilize exchange rates and facilitate a way to improve the world by making loans to participating countries when they most needed it. Most of the countries belonging to the United Nations are part of it."

"Really? I wonder why I never heard of it. Chad, you shut your mouth."

"I wasn't going to say a word."

Joe cleared his throat. "Okay, well, back in the sixties, there was some talk of President Kennedy shifting our debt from the world bank to our national bank."

"I see." Gwyneth nodded slowly then switched to a head shake. "No, I don't see. What's that got to do with Chad's murder?"

"Well, the world bank stood to lose a lot of money in

interest from us. There were other things being discussed at the time. Some very unpopular decisions were made— like lending money to dictatorships as long as the regime was friendly to U.S. interests. In 1964, the world bank financed Brazil's overthrow and the new dictator."

"I do declare! Isn't that right around the time President Kennedy was shot?"

"Yes. So, you understand the timeline. That's important. With the IMF's headquarters in the USA and America having the only veto, our country wielded quite a bit of power."

Morgaine squinted. "So the rest of the governments blamed us for lending money to violent men to overthrow their own countries' governments."

Joe nodded. "It's created quite a negative image ever since. Historically, the president of the IMF is from the United States, whereas the managing director is European. That policy has been in question for years and may change, but since 1944, that's the way it's been."

"So what are you saying?" Jason interjected. "That Chad knew something about this and was about to expose the plot to assassinate our president by the peaceful, neutral Swiss? Or at least someone thought he did?"

"I'm glad he asked the dumbass question so I didn't have to."

"I don't know what he knew. He never gave us specific information from his article. All I know is that some of the prints from Chad's apartment belonged to these two guys. Tell him he can rest easy now, though. They spent several years in jail for embezzlement later on."

Jason took a deep breath. "Did you hear that, Chad? All is well. Justice has been done."

"Justice? You call a few years in a white collar prison justice for murder? I want more. I want them hanged. I want them drawn and quartered. I want a firing squad. Where are they now?"

Morgaine sighed. "He's not happy. He wants to know where they are now."

Joe's brow knit. "They died of old age. Please remind him that if he were alive, he'd be seventy-six years old."

"And enjoying my grandchildren or relaxing on the golf course or fishing. I missed all of that."

"And we understand that, Chad," Morgaine said, "but there's not much more we can do. We can't dig them up and hang their skeletons."

Joe's eyes widened. "Is that what he wants?"

Morgaine shrugged. "Chad, honey? There's nothing we can do about the past. Maybe if you move on you can confront them in the next life. That often happens in reincarnation."

Gwyneth added, "And don't forget about karma. Karma may have paid them a visit too. I mean, why did they have to embezzle? Maybe they lost all their money."

Morgaine nodded. "Or perhaps they had miserable marriages or someone in their immediate family died horribly. You never know how karma will work or when it will catch up with you, but it always does."

"I want to know how it worked, then. I want to know how they paid the price for taking my life."

Morgaine rubbed her eyes. "That might be difficult to find out, Chad. Maybe they just lived with a tortured conscience for the rest of their lives."

"Crap. Not good enough."

Gwyneth laid a hand on Joe's knee. "Is there any way you can find out what happened to them, Mistah Murphy?"

Joe bit his bottom lip. "I can check their obits and get the names of family members. Maybe a little more digging will give us a few facts, not much in the way of whole stories, though. Unless I can find some close family."

Jason cleared his throat. "I'm not crazy about the idea of paying for any more digging. That could go on forever and maybe require trips to Europe. Chad, you wanted to know who killed you. Now you do. We kept our end of the bargain. Now you keep yours."

"I'm not going anywhere."

Morgaine stared at the ceiling and shook her head in exasperation.

Joe asked, "What did he say?"

She looked Joe straight in the eye and lied. "He said, 'What if I can't?'"

Joe squinted as if thinking deeply, then said, "I have an idea."

Ralph picked up his cell phone on the third ring. "Jason? Is everything okay?"

"Yeah, everything's fine. How's your trip going?"

"Fantastic. This was the best idea. Dottie's never been so relaxed. It really has been like a second honeymoon for us. I really have to thank you for that."

"I'm glad to hear it. Listen, I called for a couple of reasons. First, tell Dottie that 3A is rented."

"The alleged ghost is gone?"

"No, but he accepted a roommate."

"You're kidding. Who?"

"The P.I. I hired. He's still investigating, but I didn't feel like footing the bill anymore. So Chad is letting him rent the apartment and Joe will keep digging in his spare time. Hey, it's a pretty creative solution, right?"

"I guess so. Do you mind if I just tell Dottie the ghost is gone, and we have a new tenant?"

Jason chuckled. "No, I don't mind at all. I'll ask Joe to keep Chad a secret. Joe can't hear or see him, so he won't even know he's there."

"Sounds like the ideal roommate."

"Yeah, he scored a pretty sweet situation. I think he has a crush on one of the girls across the hall."

"Aren't they lesbians?"

"Merry doesn't seem to think so."

"Speaking of Merry, how is she?"

"She's great. She said yes, Uncle Ralph."

"Finally! Hallelujah."

In the background, Jason heard Dottie asking what Ralph was so happy about. Ralph muffled the phone, but his voice still came though. "Jason said Merry accepted. They're getting married soon."

After a pause Ralph said, "Dottie's giving you a thumbs up. She's on the patio. When will it be?"

"January twenty-second."

"Thank God it's before spring training. You must be relieved."

"I'll say. So have you found a place for our honeymoon?"

"Yeah, this place we're at now is great. Yesterday we visited an island known for its history, but I wouldn't recommend it. I'd say some of that pirate blood must still be running through the native's veins."

"Uh-oh. That's not good. So where are you now?"

"St. John's. It's very private. Just like you wanted. You can sail, snorkel, and they even have a campground if you want to rough it."

Jason laughed. "I'm sure that's just what Merry had in mind for her one and only honeymoon. How's the resort?"

"Nice, but there's an even better one nearby. We checked it out earlier today. Dottie's having the best time quizzing all the managers."

"I'll bet she is. Hey, maybe travel writing could turn into a good sideline for her. She said she was a good writer."

"That's something I hadn't thought of. But what about my job? You'll still need a maintenance man, won't you?"

"Of course. Your job is secure. I just think it might be a good idea if Dottie had a hobby."

"You're absolutely right. So, what's Merry going to be doing after the honeymoon while you're in spring training, besides, um, the expected?"

"She found something called the Traveling Nurse Corp. She's looking into either that or the possibility of a per diem job. She doesn't have to worry. Nurses are needed wherever we go."

"And you're okay with her working?"

"I'm okay with whatever makes her happy."

"I guess she makes you pretty happy, right?"

"Very. I couldn't be more fortunate."

"Has she met your folks yet?"

"Ah, no. That's the next hurdle. We're getting her family and ours all together on Christmas. That way everyone can meet everyone and we can announce the big news."

"You aren't telling anyone before that?"

"No, we decided to keep it a surprise."

"Oh, boy. Good luck with that."

"What? You sound worried."

"No, no. I just hope your father's on his best behavior."

"He should be. He knows what's at stake."

"Yeah, he does. That's why I'm worried. If her father has any reservations… well, you know how your father can get."

"Oh boy."

"And didn't you say Merry's father is overprotective of his little girl?"

"Oh boy."

"Uh-huh. Like I said, *good luck*."

Chapter 18

MERRY HAD DECORATED HER LITTLE APARTMENT WITH a small live Christmas tree and garland while Jason bought an artificial pre-lit tree that blazed like the sun. Just as well. She had asked him to host the family get-together at his place on Christmas Eve since hers was so small and underwhelming.

She offered to do all the cooking and had planned the menu, then realized what a major task she had taken on. Trying to please everyone, she wanted to include both sets of family's holiday traditions and foods. Thank goodness her thoughtful fiancé wouldn't hear of her doing it alone and told her to hire an extra pair of hands.

So here she was, in Jason's penthouse, counting out the number of plates, cups, and saucers. She was relieved to see the caterer had brought a few extra, just in case of breakage. Not that she expected dishes thrown like Frisbees, but one never knew.

"So, let's see…" she mumbled to herself as she mentally inventoried the menu. "Ham, sweet potatoes, eighteen-pound dressed turkey, cranberry sauce, potatoes au gratin, asparagus, carrots, a green salad, three pies… Six people are never going to be able to eat all this food. We'll have leftovers for a week."

Jill the caterer smiled. "Some folks think that's the best thing about holidays. My mother made the most delicious turkey sandwiches and turkey soup after both Christmas and Thanksgiving."

"Maybe I should get her recipes. And some for ham, if you have any. Trying to incorporate two sets of family traditions will test the weight limit of this buffet table."

Jill laughed. "Everything will be fine. I brought extra potatoes au gratin so you can cut up the leftover ham and have a casserole later on. That's why I don't just mash the potatoes."

"You're brilliant. Thank you."

"Well, everything is all set, and I should be on my way. You'll find the ham sliced almost all the way through in the warming drawer on a cutting board. The vegetables are in the warming trays. The turkey is in the oven, all cooked and with the heat off it'll stay hot while you get everyone settled and the champagne poured. Would you like me to carve the turkey before I leave?"

"Oh, no. That's my father's job. He'd feel deprived if he didn't have the honor of hacking up the bird."

Suddenly a horrible thought struck her. *What if carving a large bird was offensive to a family of falcons? Oh, dear God.* She hadn't thought to ask Jason. Was it too late to cook pigeon? And, oh God, her family would have a fit if their traditions had to be changed.

"What's wrong?" Jill asked. "You look nervous."

Merry steadied herself and inhaled deeply. "I *am* nervous. I'm meeting my future in-laws for the first time."

"Oh that's wonderful! Congratulations."

"You don't understand. They don't know we're getting married yet. We decided to tell them all at once, tonight. Oh, Lord, what were we thinking? Jason says his parents will be thrilled, but my father... This was *such* a bad idea."

The elevator began to whir. Merry gasped. "They're here! Oh my God. How's my hair? How's my makeup? Do I have anything in my teeth?"

Jill laughed. "You're gorgeous. Now just relax, everything will be fine."

"I might need my inhaler," she squeaked, and was about to run to Jason's bathroom for her spare.

Jill grabbed her shoulders. "Calm down. Take some slow, deep breaths."

Merry did and her nerves settled.

Jill pulled on her wool coat and wrapped a scarf around her neck. "I'll take the elevator down as soon as it gets here."

The doors swooshed open and three people stepped off. The love of her life, plus a middle-aged well-coiffed woman wearing a camel-hair coat, and her equally dignified, well-dressed husband.

This is it. The first impression.

Before Jill slipped away, however, Merry grabbed her and gave her a quick hug. "Thanks for everything," she whispered.

Jill nodded and exchanged places with the family who'd just exited the elevator. Everyone wore congenial smiles, but they slowly grew into grins. Maybe she had already made a positive impression.

—∞—

As soon as all the guests had arrived and everyone except Matt had a full glass of champagne in hand, Jason raised his glass. *It's now or never.*

"I'd like to thank you all for coming tonight. I know you had to travel from out of state, but we wanted to tell you our wonderful news all together."

He took Merry's hand, and they grinned at each other. Finally, they turned to their families and said at the same time, "We're getting married!"

Matt leapt in the air and let out a whoop. Merry had expected as much, which was why she didn't want Jason to give him a glass of anything liquid yet.

His parents seemed overjoyed. His mother grabbed and hugged him and then hugged Merry in turn. His father beamed as he shook Jason's hand and kissed Merry's cheek. As Merry expected, her little brother jumped between them and hugged them both.

"If my sister's going to be Mrs. Jason Falco, I want season tickets!"

"Now, hold on a minute…" Mr. MacKenzie crossed his arms.

"Dad…" Merry answered in a warning tone.

Damn. I was afraid of this happening.

"It's not that I'm not happy for you, I just have a couple of concerns."

Jason remained completely calm. "Please, Mac, say whatever's on your mind." *But think carefully about how you say it, Mr. Overprotective. My father has a short fuse.*

"Now, don't take this the wrong way. I just don't want to see my little girl get hurt. You're a famous star and that could be a problem for a new wife. I'm thinking about that news story that called you a three-timer."

"Sir, that was completely fabricated by a paparazzo trying to save her job by printing a sensational story."

"She made up the whole thing, Dad."

He gave Jason a sidelong glance, then asked Merry, "Are you sure?"

Mr. Falco bristled. "Are you calling my son a liar?"

His wife put a hand on his arm. "Calm down, dear."

"*Everyone,* hold it right there," Merry said. "Yes, I'm sure, Dad. I wouldn't put myself in this situation if I didn't trust Jason, completely. And I do."

Thank God Merry jumped in.

"My son is incapable of being unfaithful," his father added. "In fact, your daughter is more apt to break *his* heart if—"

Jason held up one hand. "Back off, Dad. I can deal with this." *And probably a whole lot better than either of you old geezers.*

Mr. MacKenzie continued as if he had been asked to. "What about your whole big spiel about needing your independence, Merry? How many times did you insist you needed to live on your own to discover who you were? Are you telling me you know everything you need to know about yourself and you're ready to make a life-changing decision like this in a couple of months?"

"I know, I know. Believe me, I questioned that too. But Roz set me straight. She asked what I ultimately wanted out of life. I had to admit that ultimately, I wanted to be happily married to someone I love as much as I love Jason. And, Dad, he loves *me* just as much. I was luckier than anyone could have expected to find him so soon."

Mr. MacKenzie relaxed slightly. "Okay, you're using the word *ultimately*, so it doesn't sound like this is going to happen right away. A long engagement would be good for the two of you. You're probably still getting to know each other."

Merry inhaled deeply and spat out the rest of it. "We've set the date for January twenty-second."

Mr. MacKenzie gasped. "*This* January?"

Merry nodded.

"You've got to be kidding!"

Jason cringed when his father interjected, "Since when did you become the authority on relationships? The kids are in love, they're consenting adults, and they can get married any time they damn well please."

His mother held onto his arm and gave a little tug as if trying to lead him out of the room, but he didn't budge.

Mac crossed his arms. "But you see? You just called them kids. They're only in their twenties. Who knows what they want at that age?"

"*They* do," his dad bellowed.

Merry faced her father squarely and held him at arm's length. "I want you to hear me right now, and hear me good. I *know* you want the best for me. Well, this is it. Marrying Jason Falco is what's best for me."

Mr. MacKenzie's eyebrows rose. "You're pregnant, aren't you?"

"No! I'm not pregnant." She sighed. "I knew you'd think that."

Time to step in again. "I have to leave for spring training in February, Mac. We'd like to be together and the only way that will happen is if we're married."

Her father faltered. "Well, at least you're not talking about just shacking up…"

"He has his reputation to think of," Merry said.

"Whatever happened to that reporter who was causing you so much trouble?"

Jason smiled. "There's a happy outcome to that story."

Merry raised her eyebrows. "Really? Have you heard something recently?"

"Yeah, I haven't had a chance to tell you yet. The administrator called and said she would be completing the rehab program soon and that someone named Kevin would pick her up."

"Oh, that's good. I had the feeling he was sick of her. It looks like he's giving her a second chance."

"Yes, and there's more. She wanted him to return the envelope I left for her, unopened."

"Wow! It seems like she's really embracing the program."

Jason nodded. "You can feel very proud of your daughter, Mac. She could have written off the woman, but instead she recognized her alcohol addiction and saw that she received good care for it."

Mac beamed. "I've always been proud of my Merry. She deserves the kind of devotion she shows the rest of the world. That's why I think she ought to make sure that this is what she wants. Maybe you can visit—"

Merry scrunched her eyes shut and raised her voice. "*Stop*, Dad. Just stop. We're getting married January twenty-second. Now, do you want to walk me down the aisle or don't you? Because I have another father I can ask."

Dear God, don't tell me she's talking about Sly.

An uncomfortable silence ensued with Mr. MacKenzie's hurt evident in his eyes. At last, he said, "Well, I guess you really have found your independence. You don't need me at all anymore."

"I never said that, Dad. I *do* need you. I need you to believe in me and trust that I know what I'm doing. I need you to know that you raised me well and that it's time to let go. I need you to love me, unconditionally."

He nodded.

It occurred to Jason that maybe he was worried about paying for a big wedding. He certainly wasn't a rich man. But he was proud. How the heck should he approach that subject? One glance at his father and the answer, *In private*, popped into his mind so loudly it was almost audible.

"And to answer your question, of course I want to walk you down the aisle. I think I've earned that right and I don't want to give it up to anyone."

Jason heard Merry exhale. "Thank you, Dad."

Jason's father smiled and raised his glass. "Now that that's settled, I'd like to make a toast to the happy couple."

Everyone echoed his sentiments, clinked glasses, and Matt said, "Hey, what about me?"

"You'll have to be content with sparkling cider, Matt." Merry disappeared into the kitchen to get him a glass.

Jason suspected it was because Matt was on Ritalin, not just because he was only seventeen. When she returned with his glass of cider, he clinked everyone's glass again and said, "To season tickets!"

———✧———

Merry arrived at the Old North Church in a stretch limo with her father and Roz. The same limo would whisk her and Jason back home to change and then away to

Logan Airport and St. John's Island in the Caribbean. Two receptions would be held later in the year. One in Minnesota and one in Rhode Island.

Her heart fluttered with excitement.

A gentle snow had fallen earlier in the day, but now that evening had arrived, the dusting served to whiten the dirty snow banks without the bride needing a pair of white boots to wade to the church steps. The sidewalk had been scraped clean.

Her father jumped out of the limo's passenger side and opened Merry's door. He looked so handsome in his tux, and he beamed as he extended a hand to help her out. Her shoulder-length veil, winter white velvet gown, and long white gloves showed off her dark hair and glowing tan skin to their best advantage. A string of white pearls had been a gift from Jason earlier that week and she wore them proudly.

Roz had hugged her and told her how happy she was for her about a hundred times that day. She looked almost as radiant as Merry felt. Her gown was midnight blue velvet and highlighted her blue eyes. She wore her medium brown hair in an up-do and her pearl drop earrings reminded Merry of those in the famous painting *Girl With A Pearl Earring* by Johannes Vermeer, sometimes called the Dutch Mona Lisa.

"You look beautiful, sweetheart," her father said.

"Thanks, Dad. I feel beautiful."

"Are you nervous?"

"No. Happy, excited, but amazingly calm."

"Good. Me too."

It's about time!

He jogged around to the other side of the car and helped Roz out while Merry waited on the sidewalk. Her breath created fog in the chilly January air and amused her for the few seconds she had to spend in it.

She hoped everyone would be cozy and warm inside. The old church could get drafty on cold winter nights. Jason had pulled some strings and landed the historic site for their wedding with permission for Merry's family pastor to perform the ceremony. She glanced up at the tower where the Revolutionary War soldiers watched for the famous signal "One if by land; two if by sea" and imagined two lanterns hung there to herald the approach of British ships.

"Ladies, arc you ready?"

"Ready when you are, Mac," Roz said.

Merry smiled. "Lead the way."

At the top of the few steps, he held open the outer door. Inside the vestibule, two larger white doors faced them. They were closed to keep out the chill. Beyond that, her anxious groom would be waiting beside her brother. Matt was so ecstatic when asked to be Jason's best man, he had to sit down before he passed out.

Jason's own brother hadn't been sure if he could make it or not. Eventually he committed to attending, but by then the arrangements had been made. Merry couldn't imagine things working out more perfectly since she knew the brothers weren't close, and Matt would walk around with a permanent grin for the rest of his life.

Mr. MacKenzie escorted the ladies to the side and slipped through the door. He returned with Merry's older brother, Rob, while her other brother, James, threw open the doors and wedged them with a door stop.

Merry took a deep breath. *Any second now*. She started toward the door, but her father held her back.

"Not yet, honey."

The wedding march resounded from an old organ. Rob extended his arm to Roz and the two of them walked through the doors and down the aisle. Merry had checked out the church with Jason and knew it was filled with enclosed booths. These booths had been purchased by families for their exclusive use in generations past and still wore brass name plates claiming them.

The guest list had been so limited, she imagined only a few of the booths at the front of the church would be filled. She had confessed to Roz that even though Jason had wanted a small wedding, she had thought the sight of only a couple of rows filled would be sort of sad.

"It's time, honey," her father said, and smiled.

Merry nodded. As they approached the open doors from the side, she heard a loud rustling. She imagined the guests standing and turning to get a glimpse of her walking down the aisle, but it sounded like more than a handful of people.

Please, Lord, don't let me trip.

To her amazement, the church was filled. Some guests she knew and some she didn't. Scanning the room of smiling faces, she realized that in her surprise, she had almost forgotten to smile herself. Then she caught sight of Jason at the front and beamed. *Damn, he looks gorgeous. How did I get so lucky?*

She glided, dreamlike, toward him. The closer she came to the front pews, the more people she recognized. Aunts, uncles, and cousins. Old neighbors from Rhode Island. Baseball players from pictures Jason had on his walls. And right up front stood Jason's parents, Ralph and Dottie, and his brother's family.

Pleased beyond reason, Merry saw that on either side of them were all of her strange new neighbors. Morgaine, Gwyneth, and Joe Murphy on one side. Sly, Konrad, and Nathan on the other. Sly's shiny black hair had been cut and styled. It was swept back from the sides and widow's peak and he looked quite handsome—in a dangerous, vampiric way. She wondered for a fleeting moment if Chad was around. The place was packed.

Someone had sold her out. She glanced over at Roz. Her maid of honor winked at her. *Ah ha*. Her best friend had been in cahoots with her husband-to-be and planned a surprise—the big wedding she had always wanted.

Merry kissed her dad, and took her place beside her happy groom. When she linked her arm through his, she gazed up at him through the tears shimmering in her eyes. He grinned at her and kissed her forehead. At that moment, Merry knew for sure her ultimate dreams were coming true.

Epilogue

IT WAS ALMOST TIME FOR JASON TO RETURN FROM practice, and Merry had just arrived home from her shift at the local children's hospital. She opened a bedroom window and let the warm Florida air inside.

As soon as Jason flew over the windowsill and landed on the bed, she started to peel off her clothes. When he appeared in falcon form in front of her, carrying a piece of something in his beak, it could only mean one thing. The last step of their bonding was about to take place, and Merry's panties dampened. She didn't even look to see what he'd brought.

"How was the game, lover?"

He shifted and folded his hands behind his head. "Fantastic. I just wish it had happened in the regular season. You're good for my batting average."

She gulped when glancing at his erection. How could a man become so unbelievably hard so fast? When it came to her man, there didn't seem to be any occasion he couldn't rise to. She chuckled to herself as that thought ran through her brain.

"What's so funny?"

"Nothing. Have I told you how proud I am of how well you've learned to control your shifts?"

He smiled and held his arms out to her. "Maybe, but you can tell me again."

"Well, I am. You must have worked hard."

"I did. Nathan put me through the paces so many times, I thought I was learning a whole new professional sport."

As soon as she was naked, she dove into his arms where all rational thoughts vanished. Jason could melt her mind in seconds. Heat rushed to her nipples as their lips fused. His strong hips braced hers and she grabbed his smooth buttocks as they rolled together.

His scent seemed to intensify, swirling around her in clouds of rugged, primitive man. His tongue swept her mouth in deep swirls as his hand found her breast and massaged it. Waves of hot, wanton need undulated through her.

As he broke the kiss, his body slid downward. Merry shivered, unable to tear her gaze from him, knowing he was about to consume her bare breasts. As joyfully anticipated, he latched on and sucked. Immediately her womb clenched and she arched further into his mouth. He suckled her thoroughly, then gave her other breast the same attention, creating shivers of sweet sensation.

"Oh, God. What you do…" Coherent words went the way of coherent thoughts.

"Are you ready for this? I mean, this is the final step in our bonding."

"Bring it on, stud."

Jason ran his hand over her pussy and inserted a finger into her aching passage. She moaned as her cream lubricated his path. He pulled back, inserted two fingers, thrust in and out of her core, and returned to sucking her puckered nipples.

"I love… I want…"

Jason let her breast pop out of his mouth and asked, "What do you want, darling?" He slid downward again and without stopping his fingers he added his tongue to the onslaught.

She gasped. "You... I want... you!"

He stopped licking long enough to say, "You have me, baby. I'm yours."

Her breathing grew ragged as she rolled her hips to keep him flush to her lower body. He continued his skillful strokes, making love to her most intimate parts. Decadent sounds reached her ears. That was all it took to launch the rippling sensations that signaled her impending orgasm.

Suddenly bolts of electricity shot through every nerve ending. Her thighs tensed and her body spasmed. She screamed her release with complete abandon. She crested and came again and again, generating white heat. Beads of sweat popped out on her brow.

Jason rode the wave of her climax until her body weakened. When he finally stilled, she melted into the mattress. Even though she was spent, her legs continued to tremble.

"I love how hard you come," he said, smiling.

Between heavy panting, she managed to say, "It's all you, lover."

She placed her hands on either side of him and pulled until he walked up on his knees and positioned his lower torso over her face. She took his erection in her hand and guided it into her mouth.

Jason reared back and moaned. She knew he loved fucking her mouth, and she loved giving him pleasure almost as much as receiving it. She held onto his hips as he pumped them. Before long he pulled out and panted.

"Can't handle any more of that?"

He chuckled. "Not today." He slid down until they were face to face. "I couldn't stop thinking about you— about getting home to you."

"How did you know today would be our final bonding?"

"Instinct. Pure, primitive, driving need."

While he kissed her, she spread her legs and he positioned himself at her opening. In one long thrust, he drove into her. Both of them moaned and sighed. The feeling of his cock filling her warm center made her dizzy. She lifted her hips and locked her ankles behind him in wicked invitation.

She clung to him as he rocked her world. Her breath shuddered with each withdrawal, and with every thrust she almost sobbed her joy.

Her legs fell away to allow him deeper penetration. Jason ground his pelvis into hers, creating the perfect amount of friction against her clit. His strokes grew bolder, faster, yet their bodies stayed together like they were secured with elastic bands.

Lost in sensation, her nipples tingled. His balls slapped against her ass. The building tension in her pussy promised another mind-blowing orgasm was on its way.

"God, I love you, Merry," Jason said, and gasped.

His motions became erratic and signaled his orgasm. She tipped over the edge and let go of her own, crying out her pleasure. She rode her climax to the end, and savored every aftershock.

As they lay together, boneless and motionless, she sighed.

"Is everything okay?" he asked.

"Everything's perfect," she said with a smile. "You're perfect."

He laughed. "No, I'm not."

"I love you anyway."

"And I love you—always have, always will."

"I almost forgot. What did you bring me?"

"Take a look."

Merry rolled onto her side and picked up the smooth pebble from where it fell. "It's blue, almost like the Caribbean sky."

"That's because I brought it back from our honeymoon in the Caribbean. It's a piece of Larimar—and it's only found there."

"Oh!" Merry cradled it in her hand. She couldn't have been any more thrilled if it was the rarest diamond on the planet. "I love it. Can I have it made into a necklace or a brooch?"

"You can make it into anything you want."

"This will make a perfect reminder of how and where we began our marriage, and because you gave it to me here, it'll always symbolize our final bonding." She ran her thumb over the smooth stone. "It's beautiful."

Jason kissed her neck. "I can't imagine anything more beautiful than to spend my life with you."

Acknowledgments

A million thanks to Rose Knox, bookstore owner, brainstormer, beta reader, and friend. Rose steers me toward the nutty, hot, romance novels I devour while keeping me away from the ones that would give me indigestion. She's largely responsible for my addiction to romance.

Major thanks to Emily Bryan—a *wonderful* author who critiqued my scenes and laughed in all the right places!

Big thanks to my friends Daniel Walsh and Pam Claughton, enthusiastic baseball fans, for answering hundreds of stupid questions from this faithful football follower.

Thanks again to Susan Grimshaw, bookseller for Borders who mentioned my concept to my Sourcebooks editor, Deb Werksman. And to Deb, for taking a chance on me! I was terrified, but she had more confidence in me than I had in myself.

Hey, Deb, I did it! I freakin' did it! What's that you say? You want me to do it again? Oh, boy. Can I have a day off for good behavior?

About the Author

Ashlyn Chase describes herself as an Almond Joy bar. A little nutty, a little flaky, but basically sweet, wanting only to give her readers a scrumptious, satisfying reading experience.

She holds a degree in behavioral sciences, worked as a psychiatric RN for several years, and spent a few more years working for the American Red Cross where she still volunteers as an instructor. She credits her sense of humor to her former careers since comedy helped preserve whatever was left of her sanity. She is a multi-published, award-winning author of humorous erotic romances.

Represented by the Nancy Yost agency in New York, NY, she lives in beautiful New Hampshire with her true-life hero husband and a spoiled brat cat.

~~~

Where there's fire, there's Ash

www.ashlynchase.com
Check out my news, contests, videos, and reviews.

http://www.myspace.com/ashlynchase
Find me on MySpace and be my friend.

If you enjoyed this book, tell your friends, on Goodreads, Facebook, and Twitter.

And you can always chat with me online at my fan loop:

http://groups.yahoo.com/group/ashlynsnewbestfriends/

For more from Ashlyn Chase,
read on for an excerpt from

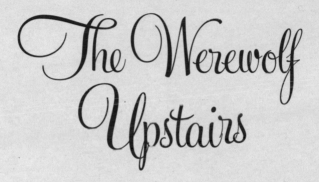

The Werewolf Upstairs

Coming soon from Sourcebooks Casablanca

After the arraignment Konrad asked Roz to join him for lunch. Fortunately, she had no more cases so they decided to grab takeout and enjoy a long walk home. The sunny sky held the promise of a warm, spring day.

"You were brilliant." Konrad hoped he hadn't blown his chances with his sexy attorney and neighbor.

"Aw, shucks. I'll bet you say that to all the public defenders."

His smiled faded and his gaze dropped to the sidewalk. "It really was my first and only arrest, but I know how you feel about the guys you defend. I guess you aren't interested in me now. I was hoping to ask you out."

She touched his arm and the spot tingled. "This is different. You were innocent."

If only… Konrad hated to deceive her, but there was no way he could explain his abilities without exposing what he was, and therefore, the existence of his kind. Not to mention that he needed time to discover if she could be his mate. He had the sneaking suspicion that the beautiful lawyer might just be the one—and he had to check out that theory. If he didn't, he could spend his whole life wondering.

She smiled up at him. "So, where do you want to eat lunch? Indoors or out?"

He contemplated her soft expression, and glanced up just in time to witness a child drop his mother's hand and dart out into traffic. The mother screamed and Konrad dropped their bag of take-out, rushing after him without a thought. He scooped up the little boy seconds before a car's brakes squealed.

The car hit Konrad, but as he staggered, he held the boy steady. The tot was untouched.

The mother cried out, "Oh, thank God!"

Even though Konrad limped to the sidewalk, it was mostly an act. The car's bumper was slightly dented, so he had to make it look good.

As he passed the boy to his relieved mother, he winced.

She hugged her son close and stared at Konrad. "Oh my goodness. Are you hurt?"

"I'll be fine. Probably just a bruise. Nothing broken."

The driver of the car rolled down his window and yelled, "Hey, lady. Keep your friggin' kid out of the street."

Konrad turned to him and said, "We're fine. Thanks for asking."

The driver flipped him the bird and sped off.

"If you hadn't been there…" Tears welled up in the mother's eyes and she bit her lower lip.

"I'm just glad I was able to help, ma'am."

He glanced at Roz for the first time since he'd bolted into the street. Her mouth hung open and her eyes were wide with awe.

"Are you sure you're okay?" Roz asked. "I mean, you took a pretty hard hit."

"Nah, I'm made of strong stuff. I drink lots of milk—rich in calcium."

The woman grappled for her purse. "Sir, let me give you a reward."

"Aw, heck no. I'm just glad I saw what was happening in time to stop it."

"I insist."

"Tell you what. Take the money and buy one of those child harnesses." He ruffled the boy's hair. "Some precocious children need to be protected from themselves."

She smiled and nodded. "Thank you, I will. I'm truly grateful." Then she squinted at the kid and said, "You're in the dog-house, young man. And just for that, I'm getting you a leash!"

"I can't believe you saved that child without getting killed."

"Yeah, I don't know what I was thinking. I guess I wasn't thinking at all— just reacting to the situation."

"You were so brave and so selfless." *And so amazing and so... hot!*

He smiled and placed a finger under her chin. Tipping her face up, he bent low, hovering just over her lips. "Can I have a kiss as my reward?"

"I'm sure the boy's mother would have kissed you if you'd asked." Roz was teasing, but also trying to keep her distance. After all, he had just been in trouble with the law.

"I didn't want to kiss *her*. I'm asking *you*."

Aw, I'm melting. Roz slipped her arms around his neck and closed her eyes. He held her in a surprisingly gentle embrace and closed the short gap between their lips.

The pressure was just right. Firm, but not bruising. He opened his mouth slightly and slanted his head, allowing her to deepen the kiss if she wanted to. She answered by slipping her tongue past his teeth, but something sharp pricked her.

She almost pulled away, but his big paw of a hand cradled her head and kept her mouth fused to his. He slipped his tongue past her lips and lapped at the sore spot. Suddenly, the pain faded and disappeared.

Roz let her body mold to his and felt petite in his arms. *Now, that's a first.*

The hot, drugging kiss continued, right there on the sidewalk heedless of passersby and traffic. The world fell away and soon the only thing she could name that existed outside herself was his arousal nudging her stomach.

She even wanted to incorporate the hard length inside her body and join with him completely. *Whoa, where did that thought come from?*

"It came from us, darling."

Roz snapped out of her trance. Pulling away, she mumbled, "Wha… What just happened?"

Konrad kissed her forehead and smiled. "I think it's called telepathy."

"You heard me too?"

"Yes, as if you were speaking inside my head."

Shocked, Roz lost the power to communicate—or breathe.

Konrad stroked her cheek with his thumb. "It's never happened to me before, but I've heard of it. Certain members of my family can do it with their m… Uh, people they're very close to."

She inhaled deeply and tried to steady herself. "Well, I've never heard of it happening to anyone, at all." Suddenly she remembered what he'd *heard* and heat rose to her cheeks. "To tell you the truth, I'm a little embarrassed you overheard what I was thinking. I'm not sure I want anyone listening to my warped mind."

Konrad wrapped an arm around her and gave a side squeeze. "Don't worry. I won't tell a soul how warped you are."

"Hey!"

He laughed. "I was just messing with you. I think you're beautiful. Inside and out."

She gazed at him as if mesmerized. No man had ever said she was beautiful, at least not convincingly. But his eyes were telling the truth. *He really thinks I'm beautiful!*

"Inside and out."

"Now cut that out. I just said I don't want you listening to me while I'm thinking."

"Then don't think so loud."

"Don't think so… what?"

"I doubt I hear all of your thoughts. Just the ones that come across clearly."

Roz crossed her arms and pouted. "Oh, that's just great. So, now I'll have to keep my mind a jumble in order to have any privacy?"

Konrad shrugged. "This is new to me, too. I guess we'll have to figure it out together. Let's go home." He kept his arm around her and guided her to walk beside him. She wanted to slip her arm around his waist too, but regardless of what just happened, it seemed too soon.

"Maybe I can talk to my brother about it. He might know if there's a shut off button."

"Has he experienced telepathy?"

"No, but he… Well, he's closer to the rest of the family than I am. He can probably ask them for me."

"Oh, so you've had a falling out with your family?"

"You could say that."

"I don't know what I'd do without my mother and brother." *My step-dad can go to hell, though.*

"What did your stepfather do?"

"Oh, damn. Did I think that out loud?"

He smiled. "Don't worry, I won't tell a soul. But I'd like to know so I don't do the same thing."

She snorted. "If you did, the circumstances would be totally different." *Like, mutually consensual.*

"Oh, no! You mean he…"

"Get the fuck out of my head, will you?"

Konrad stopped walking and leaned over to give her a warm, tender hug. Then he whispered in her ear. "I'm sorry that happened to you."

She gently pushed him away. "It wasn't when I was a kid or anything. I was in high school, and it only happened once. He came home from a party drunk. My mother went right to bed. He—he came into my room uninvited and tried to kiss me a little too amorously. He put his hand on my breast and I shoved him off."

"Crap. That must have been frightening."

"Yeah, not to mention disgusting."

"Did your mother ever find out?"

"Yeah, I told her, even though he told me not to. He said it was my word against his and he'd deny it. But I figured she deserved to know."

"That was brave of you. A lot of girls would have kept it bottled up inside and acted out in some other way. Did she protect you?"

"She booted his ass soon after I told her. Then we both went to counseling."

He squeezed her shoulder and continued walking. "Thank God for that. Some mothers don't believe their own daughters. I saw some of that as a teacher. That's when the kids act out to get the attention of someone—anyone who might help."

"Yeah, in that way I was fortunate."

"How old were you?"

"Seventeen. Too old to call anything that might have happened statutory rape, but too young to be a legal adult."

"Damn. If he'd pushed it, I hope you'd sue his ass off."

"That would have been difficult. My stepfather was a lawyer. He said he'd make me look like I was totally crazy if I tried to ruin his reputation." She looked up at him with a sad smile. "And what teenager hasn't acted totally crazy from time to time?"

Konrad shook his head. "Well, at least you got counseling to help you put it in perspective. Is your mother okay?"

"My mom is strong. She put us kids first. Like I said, she threw him out and threatened to take him for everything he owned if he contested the divorce."

"Did anything happen to your brother?"

"No, except he wanted to kill my step-father when he found out. He was always my protector."

"Well, now you have me."

Surprised, Roz stiffened momentarily, then offered him a weak smile. "Thanks, that's sweet of you, but we just met."

"So?"

Roz chuckled. "Seems like I've picked up another protector whether I like it or not."

"Oh, you'll like it, all right."

She halted and her eyes widened.

"Oh, no. I didn't mean that the way it sounded. Please don't worry. I'll never pressure you." A second later, the thought, *"I hope"* popped into his mind.

Roz took a couple of steps away from him. "You hope? What the hell does that mean?"

"I—I would never... It's just that I'm so attracted to you, it's like... I can't explain it. Just know that I'll never hurt you—or let anyone else hurt you, either." He shook his head vigorously. "Never, ever." He enveloped her in a tender hug. "I promise."

His mate. He'd found her! At last. Telepathic communication didn't just happen. He had only heard of it in mated couples. Even then, not every couple was lucky enough to experience it.

His canine accidentally scraped her tongue. Her blood must have triggered the telepathy. Now he was burning to find out if they were compatible in bed. But if he rushed her, he could scare her off. *Especially with her history*.

She interrupted his thoughts. "What's so special about my history?"

"Huh?"

"You were saying... or rather thinking, something about my history. Something special?"

"Oh. It was nothing." *Damn, this telepathy is going to be a pain in the ass.*

"Tell me about it."

"Shit. You heard that too?"

Roz giggled. "This is really weird. Kind of fun, but totally bizarro."

Konrad took a deep breath. "Let's go home and try not to think until we get there. Are you up for a jog?"

"Sure. If I get tired, I'll walk and meet you there."

"Or I can carry you."

Roz burst out laughing. "Yeah right. I may not weigh as much as a ton of frozen food, but I'm no lightweight."

"Sure you are." He turned his back to her and squatted slightly. "Hop on."

"What? Are you nuts? You want to give me a piggyback?"

"Why not? We're going to the same place and we want to get there quickly."

"I'll slow you to a crawl."

"Try me."

Roz folded her arms. "I'm not getting on your back."

"Why not?"

"Because I weigh too much." *And I don't want you to know how much too much.*

"Suit yourself." Konrad turned back toward her and scooped her up in his arms.

She shrieked.

As he strode off in the direction of their building, only a few more blocks away, she wriggled in his grasp. "Put me down!"

"If you don't stay still, I might drop you."

"Fuckin' caveman."

"Did you know that contrary to popular opinion, the

cavemen were neither slovenly nor dim-witted? That by their survival alone, regardless of having no manuals, no education, no knowledge of science or mathematics at all, they managed to live beyond puberty to raise the next generation. That points to intelligence."

"What are you, Mr. Wikipedia? Did you just Google 'cavemen'?"

"No, I'm trying to impress you. It's also agreed that language has been around for a million years or more. They developed language in order to communicate with each other. In order to do that, they must have been extremely intelligent."

"Yeah, yeah. You're a freakin' rocket scientist. Now put me down! I'm too old to be carried like a baby."

"I've got a better idea." He set her on her feet.

"Whew, finally. I—"

Konrad dipped down and came up with Roz draped over his shoulder.

She gasped.

"If you're going to accuse me of being a caveman, I might as well act like one."

Roz thumped him on his back. "Put me down this minute!"

"Just relax and enjoy the ride."

"I don't usually hear that until I make it to the bedroom."

Konrad laughed, but ignored her plea and strode off in the direction of their building as if she weighed no more than a sack of tennis balls. Then he added to her embarrassment by whistling.

"Oh, very nice. What if I have to fart while I'm up here?"

"Then fart. We're traveling downwind."

Roz giggled and bounced along with Konrad's long strides. *I give up.*

"Good."

"It's your hernia."

"You're not as heavy as you think you are. So many women have negative self-images. You think you have to be bony to be beautiful, when it's the opposite for most guys."

"Oh, really?"

"Well, I guess I can't speak for the entire male population, but most guys I know like a little meat on their women." He patted her ass.

A passing couple laughed.

"Oh, for Christ's sake. Do you have to embarrass me completely and totally?"

"If that's what it takes to convince you that you're ravishing…"

She sighed. *Ravage me when we get back to your place and I might believe you.*

Konrad slowed his march. "Did you mean for me to hear that?"

"Put me down and I'll tell you."

He quickly set her on her feet and grasped her shoulders to steady her.

She looked up into his serious face and took a risk. "Yeah, I meant it."

He straightened and his eyes widened. "I'll race you."

They grinned at each other, then took off running the final block to their building.

Available February 2011

50 Ways to Hex Your Lover

BY LINDA WISDOM

"A magical page-turner...had me bewitched from the start!"

—Yasmine Galenorn,
USA Today bestselling author of *Witchling*

JAZZ CAN'T DECIDE WHETHER TO SCORCH HIM WITH A FIREBALL OR JUMP INTO BED WITH HIM

Jasmine Tremaine is a witch who can't stay out of trouble. Nikolai Gregorivich is a vampire cop on the trail of a serial killer. Their sizzling love affair has been on-again, off-again for about 300 years—mostly off, lately.

But now Nick needs Jazz's help to steer clear of a maniacal killer with supernatural powers, while they try to finally figure out their own hearts.

978-1-4022-1085-3 • $6.99 U.S. / $8.99 CAN

Hex Appeal

BY LINDA WISDOM

"Kudos to Linda Wisdom for a series that's pure magic!"

—Vicki Lewis Thompson,
New York Times bestselling author of *Wild & Hexy*

JAZZ AND NICK'S DREAM ROMANCE HAS
TURNED INTO A NIGHTMARE...

FEISTY WITCH JASMINE TREMAINE AND DROP-DEAD GORGEOUS
vampire cop Nikolai Gregorivich have a hot thing going,
but it's tough to keep it together when nightmare visions
turn their passion into bickering.

With a little help from their friends, Nick and Jazz are in a
race against time to uncover whoever it is that's poisoning
their dreams, and their relationship...

978-1-4022-1400-4 • $6.99 U.S. / $7.99 CAN

Wicked by Any Other Name

BY LINDA WISDOM

"Do not miss this wickedly entertaining treat."

—Annette Blair,
Sex and the Psychic Witch

STASI ROMANOV USES A LITTLE WITCH MAGIC IN HER LINGERIE shop, running a brisk side business in love charms. A disgruntled customer threatening to sue over a failed spell brings wizard attorney Trevor Barnes to town—and witches and wizards make a volatile combination. The sparks fly, almost everyone's getting singed, and the whole town seems on the verge of a witch hunt.

Can the feisty witch and the gorgeous wizard overcome their objections and settle out of court—and in the bedroom?

978-1-4022-1773-9 • $6.99 U.S. / $7.99 CAN

Hex in High Heels

BY LINDA WISDOM

Can a Witch and a Were find happiness?

Feisty witch Blair Fitzpatrick has had a crush on hunky carpenter Jake Harrison forever—he's one hot shape-shifter. But Jake's nasty mother and brother are after him to return to his pack, and Blair is trying hard not to unleash the ultimate revenge spell. When Jake's enemies try to force him away from her, Blair is pushed over the edge. No one messes with her boyfriend-to-be, even if he does shed on the furniture!

Praise for Linda Wisdom's Hex series:

"Fan-fave Wisdom… continues to delight."
—*Romantic Times*

"Highly entertaining, sexy, and imaginative."
—*Star Crossed Romance*

"It's a five star, feel-good ride!" —*Crave More Romance*

"Something fresh and new."
—*Paranormal Romance Review*

978-1-4022-1895-8 • $6.99 U.S. / $8.99 CAN

IN OVER HER HEAD

by Judi Fennell

"Holy mackerel! *In Over Her Head* is a
fantastically fun romantic catch!"

—Michelle Rowen, author of *Bitten & Smitten*

○ ○ ○ ○ ○ HE LIVES UNDER THE SEA ○ ○ ○ ○ ○

Reel Tritone is the rebellious royal second son of the ruler
of a vast undersea kingdom. A Merman, born with legs
instead of a tail, he's always been fascinated by humans,
especially one young woman he once saw swimming near
his family's reef...

○ ○ ○ ○ ○ SHE'S TERRIFIED OF THE OCEAN ○ ○ ○ ○ ○

Ever since the day she swam out too far and heard voices
in the water, marina owner Erica Peck won't go swimming
for anything—until she's forced into the water by a shady
ex-boyfriend searching for stolen diamonds, and is nearly
eaten by a shark. Luckily Reel is nearby to save her, and
discovers she's the woman he's been searching for...

978-1-4022-2001-2 • $6.99 U.S. / $7.99 CAN